A blaze of possessiveness roared through him, the need to stake his claim, to mark her as his, now and forever.

He was aware of the fine tremors that shimmered through her, of the way his thigh fitted between hers and how the cradle of her hips rocked against him. The intoxicating scent and taste of her filled his senses.

He was aware of everything about her. Only her. The rest of the world receded.

He was so far gone that he didn't care about control, about leashing it, about the fact that someone might walk back into the office and discover him alone with her, kissing her. There was just Tiffany…and him.

And she was going to marry him.

Only him.

SAVED BY THE SHEIKH!

BY
TESSA RADLEY

Published in Great Britain 2011
by Mills & Boon, an imprint of Harlequin (UK) Limited,
Eton House, 18-24 Paradise Road, Richmond, Surrey TW9 1SR

ISBN: 978 0 263 88228 5

51-0611

Harlequin (UK) policy is to use papers that are natural, renewable and recyclable products and made from wood grown in sustainable forests. The logging and manufacturing processes conform to the legal environmental regulations of the country of origin.

Printed and bound in Spain
by Blackprint CPI, Barcelona

This is for the readers who wrote asking about
the fate of Shafir's brothers, Rafiq and Khalid.
Rafiq's story is for you. Enjoy!

Tessa Radley loves traveling, reading and watching
the world around her. As a teen Tessa wanted to be an
intrepid foreign correspondent. But after completing a
bachelor of arts degree and marrying her sweetheart, she
became fascinated by law and ended up studying further
and practicing as a lawyer in a city firm.

A six-month break traveling through Australia with her
family reawoke the yen to write. And life as a writer
suits her perfectly—traveling and reading count as
research, and as for analyzing the world...well, she can
think "what if?" all day long. When she's not reading,
traveling or thinking about writing, she's spending
time with her husband, her two sons or her zany and
wonderful friends. You can contact Tessa through her
website, www.tessaradley.com.

Dear Reader,

Welcome back to the desert kingdom of Dhahara. If you read *The Untamed Sheikh* you would've got to know Shafir and would've met his brothers, Rafiq and Khalid. Part of the challenge I faced in this book was finding a heroine to match Rafiq. Megan was so popular with readers that I knew this heroine would have to be pretty unique.

So, for *Saved by the Sheikh!* I started off by searching for a name no one I knew owned. I came up with Tiffany. Hints of *Breakfast at Tiffany's*. The glamour of Tiffany's, the jeweler. I adored the softness and vulnerability the name also seems to possess. Utterly feminine and exquisitely beautiful.

Despite never having met a Tiffany in my life, within months of starting to write the story, I'd met three Tiffanys. The first was an aspiring writer who won a breakfast at the RWA Conference in Washington, DC, with myself and author Abby Gaines. The second was Tiffany Clare—who by some coincidence I met a day or so later also in DC—and whose debut historical romance, *The Surrender of a Lady*, has recently been released. The third Tiffany has the most wonderful name of all: Tiffany Light. When I told her that her name, without question, belonged to a romance heroine, Tiffany told me that her middle initial is D...Tiffany D. Light. Naturally, I wished I'd thought that up myself!

It's moments like these that add so much fun and wonder to the world of being a writer. You never quite know what will happen next...

I hope you enjoy Tiffany and Rafiq's story. Right now I'm thinking about who I'm going to match Khalid up with... and that promises to be a whole lot of fun.

Happy reading!

Tessa Radley

One

A male hand beckoned through the swirling silvery wisps generated by a smoke machine.

Tiffany Smith squinted and located Renate leaning against the white marble bar flanked by two men. Relief kicked in. The Hong Kong club was crowded—and a lot busier than Tiffany had expected. The harsh, beating music and flashing strobe lights had disoriented her. And the spike of vulnerability she had experienced in the aftermath of having her bag snatched yesterday with her passport, credit card, traveler's checks and cash returned full blast.

Picking up two cocktail menus, Tiffany headed through the mist for the trio. The older man was vaguely familiar. But it was the younger of the two men who watched her approach, his dark eyes cool, assessing—even critical. Tiffany switched her attention to him. He wore a dark formal suit and had a distant manner. Taking in the high cheekbones and bladed nose that gave his face an arrogant cast, she lifted her chin to stare boldly back at him.

"I'm not sure what Rafiq wants but Sir Julian would like a gin and tonic," Renate said, smiling at the older man who must have been at least three inches shorter than she. "And I'll have a champagne cocktail—the Hot Sex version."

Sir Julian. Of course! That would make him Sir Julian Carling, owner of Carling Hotels. If this was the kind of clientele Le Club attracted, tips would be good.

"Sure I can't get you something a little more adventurous?" *Expensive,* Tiffany appended silently as she passed the men the cocktail menus with her sweetest smile.

Not for the first time she thanked her lucky stars for the chance meeting with Renate when she'd checked into the hostel yesterday after her return from the police station and the embassy. Last night's accommodation had used up her last twenty Hong Kong dollars.

This morning Renate had generously shared her breakfast cereal with Tiffany and offered to bring her along to Le Club tonight to make some quick cash as a hostess serving drinks.

It had been Renate who had showed her where the trays of "champagne cocktails" were kept. Lemonade. *Cheap* lemonade. For the hostesses. Geared at getting the well-heeled patrons to order and imbibe more of the elaborate, expensive cocktails with outrageously sexy names for which Le Club was apparently famed—as well as billing them for the hostesses' over-priced lemonade cocktails. Tiffany had silenced her scruples. Renate had done her a favor. Anyway, Sir Julian seemed untroubled at the prospect of footing the bill for Renate's bogus champagne cocktails.

It was none of her business, Tiffany told herself. She

would keep her mouth shut and do as ordered. She was only here for the tips. For that she would smile until her face hurt. She glanced at the younger man, about to give him a glittering grin but his expression deterred her. His eyes were hooded, revealing none of his thoughts. Even in the crush of the club he seemed to create a ring of space around him. A no-go area.

She dismissed the thought as fanciful and forced a smile. "What can I get you to drink?"

"I'll stick with the gin and tonic." Sir Julian gave her a smile and passed back the cocktail menu.

"A Coca-Cola. Cold, please. With ice—if there's any that hasn't melted yet." The man Renate had called Rafiq curved his lips upward, lighting up the harsh features and giving him a devastating charm that had Tiffany catching her breath in surprise.

He was gorgeous.

"Sh-sure, I'll be right back," she stuttered.

"We'll be in one of the back booths," said Renate.

Tiffany found them easily enough a few minutes later. She handed Renate and Sir Julian their drinks before turning to the man seated on the other side of the booth.

Rafiq, Renate had called him. It suited him. Foreign. Exotic. Quintessentially male. Wordlessly Tiffany passed him the soda, and the ice he'd requested rattled against the glass.

"Thank you." He inclined his head.

For one wild moment Tiffany got the impression that she was expected to genuflect.

Renate leaned forward, breaking her train of thought. "Here."

Tiffany took the cell phone Renate offered, and gazed at the other woman in puzzlement. With two hands Renate mimicked taking a photo, and realization dawned. Tiffany studied the phone's settings. Easy enough. By the time Tiffany glanced up, Renate had draped herself over Sir Julian, so Tiffany raised the phone and clicked off a couple of shots.

At the flash, Sir Julian came to life, waving his hands in front of his face. "No photos."

"Sorry." Tiffany colored and fumbled with the phone.

"Are they deleted?" Rafiq's voice was sharp.

"Yes, yes." Tiffany shoved the phone behind the wide leather belt that cinched in her waist, vowing to check that the dratted images were gone the next time she went to get a round of drinks.

"Good girl." Sir Julian gave her an approving smile, and Tiffany breathed a little easier. She wasn't about to get fired before she'd even been paid.

"Sit down, Tiff, next to Rafiq."

The younger man sat opposite—alone—that ring of space clearly demarcated. Pity about the grim reserve, otherwise he would certainly have fitted the tall, dark and handsome label.

"Um…I think I'll go see if anyone else wants a cocktail."

"Sit down, Tiffany." This time Renate's tone brooked no argument.

Tiffany threw a desperate look at the surrounding booths. Several of the hostesses Renate had introduced her to earlier sat talking to patrons, sipping sham champagne cocktails. No one looked like they needed assistance.

Giving in, Tiffany perched herself on the edge of the padded velvet beside Rafiq, and tried to convince herself that it was only the gloom back here in the booths that made him look so…disapproving. He had no reason to be looking down his nose at her.

"They should put brighter lights back here," Tiffany blurted out.

Rafiq raised a dark eyebrow. "Brighter lights? That would defeat the purpose."

Puzzled, Tiffany frowned at him. "What purpose?"

"To talk, of course." Renate's laugh was light and frothy. "No one talks when the lights are bright. It's too much like an interrogation room."

"I would've thought the music was too loud to talk." Tiffany fell silent. Now that she thought about it, it wasn't quite so loud back here.

Rafiq was studying her, and Tiffany moved restlessly under that intense scrutiny. "I'm going to get myself something to drink."

"Have a champagne cocktail—they're great." Renate raised her glass and downed it. "You can bring me another—and Sir Julian needs his gin and tonic topped up."

Rafiq's mouth kicked up at the side, giving him a sardonic, world-weary look.

He knew. Tiffany wasn't sure precisely *what* he knew. That the hostesses' drinks were fake? Or that the patrons would be billed full price for them? But something in his dark visage warned her to tread warily around him.

She edged out of the booth, away from those all-seeing eyes.

It was ten minutes before Tiffany could steel herself to return with a tray of drinks.

"What took so long?" Renate glanced up from where she was snuggled up against Sir Julian. "Jules is parched."

Jules?

Tiffany did a double take. In the time that she'd been gone Sir Julian Carling had become Jules? And Renate had become positively kittenish, curled up against the hotelier, all but purring. Tiffany slid back into the booth beside Rafiq and thanked the heavens for that wall of ice that surrounded him. No one would get close enough to cuddle this man.

"That surely can't be a champagne cocktail?" Rafiq commented.

She slid him a startled glance. Was he calling her on Le Club's shady ploy to overcharge patrons?

"It's water."

That expressive eyebrow lifted again. "So where's the Perrier bottle?"

"Water out of the tap." Although on second thought, perhaps it might've been more sensible to drink bottled water. "I'm thirsty."

"So you chose tap water?"

Was that disbelief in his voice? Tiffany swallowed, suddenly certain that this man was acutely aware of everything that happened around him.

"Why not champagne?"

She could hardly confess that she was reluctant to engage in the establishment's scam, so she replied evasively, "I don't drink champagne."

"You don't?" Rafiq sounded incredulous.

"I've never acquired the taste."

More accurately she'd lost the taste for the drink that her mother and father offered by the gallon in their society home. The headache it left her with came from the tension that invariably followed her parents' parties rather than the beverage itself.

An inexplicable wave of loneliness swamped her.

Those parties were a thing of the past....

Yesterday she'd tamped down the fury that had engulfed her after speaking to her mother, and called her father. To have him wire her some money—even though the thought of asking him for anything stuck in her throat—and to give him a roasting for what she'd learned from her mother.

This time he'd broken her mother's heart. He'd been tearing strips off that mutilated organ for years, but taking off with Imogen was different from the brief affairs. Imogen was no starlet with her eye on a bit part in a Taylor Smith film; Imogen had been her father's business manager for years.

Tiffany *liked* Imogen. She *trusted* Imogen. By running off with Imogen, her father had sunk to a new low in her estimation.

But Taylor Smith could not be found. No one knew where he—and Imogen—had gone. Holed up in a resort someplace, enjoying a faux honeymoon, no doubt. Tiffany had given up trying to reach her father.

"What else don't you like?" Rafiq's voice broke into her unpleasant thoughts. For the first time he was starting to look approachable—even amused.

What would he say if she responded that she didn't like arrogant men who thought they were God's gift to womankind?

The diamond-cutter gaze warned her against the reckless urge to put him down. Instead she gave him a fake smile and said in dulcet tones, "There's not much I don't like."

"I should have guessed." His mouth flattened, and without moving away, he managed to give the impression that he'd retreated onto another planet.

Had there been a subtle jibe in there somewhere that she'd missed? Tiffany took a sip of water and thought about what he might've construed from her careless words. *Not much that I don't like.* Perhaps she'd imagined the edge in his voice.

Across the booth Renate whispered something to Sir Julian, who laughed and pulled her onto his lap.

Conscious of the flush of embarrassment creeping over her cheeks, Tiffany slid a glance at Rafiq. He, too, was watching the antics of the other couple, his face tight.

What in heaven's name was Renate up to?

The rising heat resulting from the crush of bodies in Le Club and the sight of Renate wriggling all over Sir Julian compounded to make Tiffany feel…uncomfortable… unclean.

She downed the rest of the water. "I need the bathroom," she said in desperation.

In the relative safety of the bathroom, Tiffany opened the cold water tap. Cupping her hands, she allowed the cool water to pool between her palms. She bent her head and splashed her face. The door hissed open behind her.

"Don't." Renate's hand caught at hers. "You'll ruin your makeup."

"I'm hot." And starting to fear that she was way out of her depth.

"Now we'll have to do your face again." Renate sounded exasperated.

Tiffany held her hands up to ward Renate off. She didn't want another thick layer of foundation caked onto her skin. "It was too hot. My face doesn't matter. I'm not here to find a date," she said pointedly.

"But you need cash," Renate responded, her makeup bag already open on the vanity counter. "Jules says that Rafiq is a business acquaintance—he must have a fat wallet if he's associated with Jules."

"Fat wallet? You mean I should steal from him?"

Disbelief spiked in Tiffany. She turned to look at her newfound friend. Was Renate crazy? Tiffany was certain that Rafiq's retribution would be swift and relentless. She was feeling less and less comfortable about Renate's idea of easy money. "I could never do that."

Renate rolled her eyes. "Don't be dumb. I don't rip them off. You don't want to get arrested for theft. Especially not here."

"Certainly not here—or anywhere," Tiffany said with heartfelt fervor. As desperate as she was, the idea of a Hong Kong jail terrified her witless. "Yesterday's visit to the police station was more than enough."

She'd had her fill of bureaucracy after spending the entire day yesterday and most of today reporting the loss of her purse to the police, followed by hours queuing at the embassy, trying to secure a temporary passport… and a living allowance for the weekend. All hope of cash assistance from the embassy had been quashed once the official had realized who her father was. A father who was nowhere to be found.

On Monday a shiny new credit card would be couriered to her by her bank back home. And her temporary travel documents would be ready, too. For the first time since leaving home, Tiffany almost wished she had access to the allowance her father had cut off when she had chosen to do this trip with a friend against his wishes. What had started out as an exciting adventure was turning into a nightmare, costing much more than she'd ever dreamed.

But buying an air ticket home was Monday's worry. For now she only had to make it through the next two days.

Thank goodness for Renate.

Despite her sexual acrobatics in the booth, the other woman had saved Tiffany's skin by offering her this chance to earn some cash tonight. She owed her. "Renate, are you sure flirting with Sir Julian is a good idea? He's old enough to be your father."

"But he's rich."

Renate was fiddling in her purse, and Tiffany couldn't read her expression.

"That's what you want? A rich man? You think he'll marry you?" Concern made her say, "Oh, Renate, he's probably already married."

Renate drew out a lipstick tube and applied the glossy dark plum color then stood back to admire the dramatic effect against her pale skin and bleached-blond hair. "Of course he is."

"He is?" Shocked by Renate's nonchalance, Tiffany stared. "So why are you wasting your time on him?"

"He's a multimillionaire. Maybe even a billionaire. I recognized him the instant he arrived—he's been here before, but I've never gotten to—" Renate broke off and shot Tiffany a sidelong glance "—I never got to meet him. He's already promised to take me with him to the races later in the week."

Tiffany thought of the aching hurt she'd detected in her mother's voice yesterday when her mom had blurted out that Dad had taken off with Imogen.

"But what about his wife, Renate? How do you think she'll feel?"

Renate shrugged a careless shoulder. "She's probably too busy socializing with her country-club friends to notice. Tennis. Champagne breakfasts. Fancy fundraisers. Why should she care?"

Tiffany was prepared to stake her life on it that Sir Julian's wife did care. Speechlessly, she stared at Renate.

"The last girl he met here got a trip to Phuket and a wardrobe of designer dresses. I'd love that." She met Tiffany's appalled gaze in the mirror. "Don't knock it—maybe Rafiq is a millionaire, too. He might be worth cultivating."

Cultivating? An image of Rafiq's disdainful expression flashed before Tiffany's vision. He was so not her type. Too remote. Too arrogant. And way too full of his own importance. She didn't need a gazillionaire, much less one who had a wife tucked back in a desert somewhere.

All she wanted was someone normal. Ordinary. A man with whom she could be herself—no facades, no pretence. Just Tiffany. Someone who would learn to love her without drama and histrionics. Someone with a family that was real…not dysfunctional.

"Tiff, you need money." Renate flashed a sly look over her shoulder as she turned away to a soap dispenser set against the tiled wall. "What could be wrong with getting to know Rafiq a little better?"

Getting to know Rafiq a little better? Could Renate possibly mean that in the sense it had come across? Surely not.

"Here." Renate pressed something into her palm.

Tiffany glanced down—and despite the cloying heat, she turned cold. "What in heaven's name do I need a condom for?"

But she knew, even as Renate flipped back her short blond hair and laughed. "Tiffany, Tiffany. You can't be that innocent. Look at you. Big velvety eyes, peachy skin, long legs. You're gorgeous. And I'll bet Rafiq is very, very aware of it."

"I couldn't—"

Renate took both her hands, and brought her face up against Tiffany's. "Honey, listen to me. The quickest way to make some cash is to be as nice to Rafiq as he wants. You'll be well rewarded. He's a man—a rich one judging by that handmade thousand-dollar suit. He came here, to Le Club, tonight. He knows the score."

Horror surged through Tiffany. "What are you saying?"

"The men who come to Le Club are looking for a companion for the night. The whole night."

"Oh, God, no." She wrenched her hands free from Renate's hold and covered her face. The clues had been there lurking under what she'd seen as Renate's friendliness. *You can borrow my minidress, Tiff, it does great things for your legs. Your mouth is so sexy, a red lipstick will bring out the pout. Be nice, Tiff—you'll get more tips.* How had she missed them?

Stupid!

She'd been so grateful for what she'd seen as Renate's friendship...her help....

Tiffany dropped her hands away from her face.

Renate's features softened a trifle. "Tiff, the first time is the worst. It'll be easier next time."

"Next time?" She felt absolutely and utterly chilled. And infinitely wiser than she had been even an hour ago. Renate was no well-meaning friend; she'd misled Tiffany. Purposefully. A sense of betrayal spread through her.

"There won't be a next time." Tiffany had no intention of ever setting a foot back in this place.

Renate picked Tiffany's tiny beaded purse off the vanity slab and slid the condom inside. "Don't be so sure."

Tiffany snatched her purse up and looped the strap around her wrist. "I'm leaving."

"First shift ends at ten," Renate pointed out. "If you leave before that, you won't get paid for the hours you've worked. Work another shift and you'll earn even more."

Tiffany glanced at her watch. Nine-thirty. She had to last another thirty minutes. She needed that cash to pay for her bed at the hostel. But another shift was more than she could manage. She met Renate's gaze. "I'll wait it out."

"Think about what I said. It's no big deal after the first time—I promise." For a moment something suspiciously akin to vulnerability glimmered in Renate's eyes. "Everyone does it—there's a lot of demand for young foreign female tourists." Renate shrugged one shoulder. "Rafiq is good-looking. It won't be too bad. Would you rather be broke and desperate?"

"Yes!" Tiffany shivered. Rafiq's disdain suddenly made sense. He thought—

Her hand froze on the door handle.

God. Surely he didn't intend… No, he hadn't even exhibited any interest in her. She'd only served him a drink—there'd been no hint of anything more. "At least Rafiq isn't expecting to sleep with me."

"Of course he is." The look Renate gave her was full of superiority. "Although sleeping will have little to do with it—and he will undoubtedly pay well."

The chill that had been spreading through Tiffany froze into a solid block of ice. It took effort to release the door handle she was clutching. "I'd rather starve!"

"You won't starve—not if you do what he wants."

"No!" Tiffany clenched her fists, a steely determination filling her. "And I won't starve, either." She'd foolishly trusted Renate. But she intended to make the best of the situation. "I'm only a waitress tonight—and he still owes me a tip."

Right now that tip meant tomorrow's food, and when she walked out of there at ten o'clock with her shift money, it would be with a generous tip, too.

Rafiq found himself blocking out Julian Carling's overloud voice as he focused on the archway to the right side of the bar where Tiffany and Renate had reappeared.

Tiffany wasn't the kind of woman Rafiq would ever

have expected to meet at a place like Le Club. Her face had a deceptive freshness...an innocence...at odds with the scarlet lipstick and the frilly, short black dress. He snorted in derision. It only went to show the ingenue act was exactly that—an act.

Yet as she neared the booth, Rafiq could've have sworn he saw her gulp.

She handed him a tall iced soda and stared at him with wary eyes.

"Thank you." Rafiq's body grew tight. He wasn't accustomed to evoking that kind of look on a woman's face. Usually there was admiration, a yearning for the worldly goods he could bestow. And a healthy dose of desire, too.

But Tiffany wore none of the too-familiar expressions.

Instead her pupils had dilated and transformed her eyes to dark holes in a face where her skin had lost its lotus-petal luminescence.

Apprehension. That's what it was. A touch of fear. As though someone had told her he trafficked in human beings—or worse.

He switched his narrowed gaze to Renate. Had *she* told Tiffany something to result in that pinched expression?

While the statuesque blonde had instantly identified Sir Julian, who was something of a celebrity in Hong Kong, much to Rafiq's relief she had not recognized him. Rafiq had wryly concluded that royal sheikhs didn't have the same cachet as hoteliers. In fact, he'd been ready to call it a night as soon as he'd realized what kind of a place Le Club was. One celebratory drink with Julian out of politeness to seal the first stages of the proposal they'd put together for a hotel in his home country of Dhahara, and he'd intended to leave.

Then Tiffany had chosen water over fake champagne cocktails and he'd been intrigued enough to want to find out what kind of game she was playing.

Flicking his gaze back to her, he took in the stiff way she held herself. Only the tilt of her chin showed something of the woman he'd glimpsed before, the woman who had demanded more light in this tacky made-for-seduction booth.

Rafiq intended to find out what had disturbed her. Shifting a little farther into the booth to give her space to sit, he patted the seat beside him. She ignored the velvet upholstered expanse, and fixed him with the same dazed stare of a rabbit confronted by a hunting hawk.

His frown deepened.

She swallowed, visibly uneasy.

"Sit down," he growled. "Contrary to popular opinion, I don't bite."

Her gaze skated away from his—and she blanched. He turned his head to see what had caused such an extreme reaction.

Renate was stroking a finger over Julian's fleshy lips and the hotelier was nibbling lasciviously at the pad of her thumb. Even as they watched, Sir Julian took it into his mouth and sucked it suggestively.

Rafiq compressed his lips into a tight line. Only yesterday he'd been invited to Sir Julian's home for dinner. The hotel magnate had proudly introduced his wife of almost three decades as the love of his life…and produced a daughter with whom he'd tried to match Rafiq.

"Nor do I devour thumbs," he murmured to Tiffany. To his surprise, relief lightened her eyes. Surely a sucked thumb was tame for a place like Le Club?

For the first time he saw that her eyes were brown with gold streaks. Until now it had been her hair and peachy skin that had snagged his attention. Not that he'd been looking—he wasn't interested in a woman who earned her living the way Tiffany did.

Abruptly, he asked, "Why do you choose to work here?"

"Tonight is my first time. Renate brought me—she said it was a good place to make cash."

He withdrew imperceptibly at her confession. She'd come prepared to barter her body for cash? "You want money so desperately?" When she failed to respond, disappointment filtered through him like hot desert sand winnowing through his fingers, until nothing remained save emptiness. "You should leave," he said.

A flush crept along her cheekbones. She looked down at the table and started to draw patterns on the white linen tablecloth with her index finger.

Rafiq looked away.

Across from them Julian's hand had weaseled its way under the neckline of Renate's dress, and Rafiq could see the ridges under the stretchy electric blue fabric where the other man's fingers groped at her rounded breasts. Renate giggled.

This was what Tiffany was contemplating?

"Will it be worth it?" he asked her.

She didn't answer.

He glanced down at her. Her attention was riveted on the couple on the other side of the table. She looked distinctly queasy.

"You'd let a man paw you for money?" He sounded harsher than he'd intended. "In front of a roomful of strangers?"

"I think I need the bathroom again."

She looked as if she were about to throw up as she bolted from the booth. Good. His deliberate crudity had shaken her. She'd said tonight was her first night. Maybe he could still talk sense into her. Perhaps there was still a chance to lure her away from such a recklessly destructive course of action.

His mouth tight with distaste, Rafiq threw a hundred-dollar note down on the table and rose to his feet to follow her.

Two

Rafiq was leaning against the wall when Tiffany emerged from the bathroom, his body lean and supple in the dark, well-fitting suit. He straightened and came toward her like a panther, sleek and sinuous.

Tiffany fervently hoped she wasn't the prey he intended hunting. There were dark qualities to this man that she had no wish to explore further.

"I'm going to call you a cab."

"Now?" Panic jostled her. "I can't leave. My shift isn't over yet."

"I'll tell whoever is in charge around here that you're leaving with me. No one will argue."

She assessed him. The hard eyes, the hawk-like features, the lean, whipcord strength. The way he had of appearing to own all the space around him. Yes, he was right. No one would argue with him.

Except her. "I'm not going anywhere with you."

Something flared in those unfathomable eyes. "I wasn't intending to take you anywhere…only to call for a cab."

"I can't afford one," she said bluntly.

"I'll pay for your damned cab."

Tiffany started to protest, and then hesitated. Why shouldn't he pay for her fare? He'd never coughed up the service tip she needed. Though the disquieting discussion with Renate had made it clear that tips in this place required more service than just a little company over drinks. Renate was clearly going to end up in Sir Julian's bed tonight. For what? A visit to the races tomorrow…and a wad of cash?

Tiffany had no intention of following suit. She'd rather have her self-respect.

Yet she couldn't afford to be too proud. She needed every cent she could lay her hands on. For food and accommodation until Monday. If Rafiq gave her the fare for a cab, she could sneak out the back while he was organizing it and hurry to her lodgings on foot. It wouldn't be dishonest, she assured herself. She'd earned the tip he'd never paid.

"Thanks." The word almost choked her.

He was suddenly—unexpectedly—close. Too close. Tiffany edged away and suppressed the impulse to tell him to stick his money. Reality set in. The cab fare, together with the miserly rate for tonight's work, which she'd be able to collect in less than ten minutes, meant she'd be able to pay for her accommodation and buy food for the weekend.

Relief swept through her.

All her problems would be solved.

Until Monday…

Over the weekend, she'd keep trying her father. Surely he'd check his e-mail, his phone messages, sooner or later? Of course, it would mean listening to him tell her he'd been right from the outset, that she wasn't taking care of herself in the big, bad world. But at least he'd advance her the money to rebook her flights and she'd be able to get back to help her mom.

"I'd appreciate it," she said, suddenly subdued. Tiffany halted, waiting for him produce his wallet.

"Let's go."

His hand came down on the small of her back and the contact electrified her. It was the humidity in the club, not his touch that had caused the flash of heat, she told herself as she tried to marshal her suddenly chaotic thoughts.

Her money.

"Wait—"

Before she could finish objecting he'd propelled her past the bar, through the spectacular mirrored lobby and out into the oppressive heat of the night. Of course there was a cab waiting. For a men like Rafiq there always were.

"Hang on—"

Ignoring her, Rafiq opened the door and ushered her in and all of the sudden he was overwhelming in the confined space.

"Where to?" he asked.

He'd never intended to hand her cash. And she hadn't had the opportunity to collect her earnings, either.

"I didn't get my money," she wailed. Then it struck her that he shouldn't be sitting next to her with his thigh pressed against hers. "You said you weren't coming with me."

"I changed my mind."

His smile didn't reach his midnight-dark eyes. Then he closed the door, dousing the interior light. Tiffany didn't know whether to be relieved or disturbed by the sudden cloak of darkness. So she scooted across the seat, out of his reach, trying to ignore his sheer, overwhelming physical presence by focusing on everything she'd been cheated of. Food. Lodgings. Survival.

She could *survive* without food until Monday. It wouldn't kill her. When she went back to the embassy she wouldn't let pride stop her begging for a handout for a meal. But she needed a roof over her head.

"I'm not going to be able to get that money back." She hadn't worked out her shift. "I doubt they'll take me back tomorrow now." There were strict rules about telling the management when you were leaving—and with whom. Tiffany had thought it was for the hostess's protection.

"You don't want to work there—find somewhere else." Rafiq murmured something to the cabdriver and the vehicle started to move.

Tiffany didn't bother to explain that she didn't have a visa to work in Hong Kong, that she'd only turned up at Le Club for the night as a casual waitress. Worry tugged at her stomach. "I *need* the money for those hours I spent there tonight."

"A pittance," he said dismissively.

Anger splintered through her. "It might be a pittance to you but it's *my* pittance. I worked for that money."

"And for what do you so desperately need cash? An overloaded credit card after frequenting the boutique stores at Harbor City's Ocean Terminal?"

His drawling cynicism made her want to smack him. Instead she tried to ignore him and huddled down into the corner as far away from him as she could get in the backseat. He was *so* overbearing. So certain that he was right about everything. Assuming she was a shopaholic airhead. Making decisions for her about where she should work, about when she should go home.

God help any woman silly enough to marry him—he'd

be a dictator. Maybe he was already married. The thought caused a bolt of shock.

What did she care whether he was married?

That fierce, dark gaze clashed with hers. "I'm waiting."

Trying frantically to regroup, she said, "For what?"

"For you to tell me why you're so desperate for money."

Tiffany cringed at the idea of telling him. "It makes me sound stupid."

He arched an eyebrow. "More stupid than working at Le Club?"

She supposed he was right. So she hauled in a deep breath and said reluctantly, "I was mugged yesterday morning. My passport was stolen *and* my credit cards *and* my cash."

It was mortifying. How many times had she been told to keep one card and a copy of her itinerary and travel insurance separate from the rest? How she wished she had. It would have saved a lot of grief. And a host of I-told-you-you-wouldn't-survive-alones from her father, when she finally managed to locate him.

"All that I had left was twenty Hong Kong dollars that I had in my pocket and I used that for last night's accommodation."

"How convenient."

The mocking note in his voice made it clear Mr. Arrogant Know-all thought she was lying.

"You don't believe me."

The seat gave as he shrugged. "It's hardly an original story. Although I prefer it to a fabricated tale about an ailing grandfather or a brother with leukemia."

He thought she was angling for sympathy. She stared

across the backseat in disbelief. "Good grief, but you're cynical. I hope I never become like you."

In the flash of passing lights she glimpsed a flare of emotion in his eyes. Then it vanished as darkness closed around them again. "And I hope, for your sake, that you are not as naive as you pretend to be."

"I'm not naive," Tiffany said, annoyed by the nerve he'd unwittingly struck. He sounded exactly like her father.

"Then come up with a better story."

"It's true. Do you think I'd voluntarily make myself look like such an airhead?"

"The helpless, stranded tourist might work on some."

She glared at him under the cover of night.

His voice dropped to a rasp. "Perhaps I'm the fool. I find myself actually considering this silly tale—against my better judgment."

"Well, thanks." Her tone dripped affront.

Unexpectedly he laughed aloud. "My pleasure."

The sound was warm and full of joy. The cab pulled up at a well-lit intersection and the handsome features were flooded with light. Tiffany caught her breath at the sudden, startling charm that warmed his face, and somewhere deep in the pit of her stomach liquid heat melted. For a heady fragment of time she almost allowed herself smile, too, and laugh at the ridiculousness of her plight.

Then she came to her senses.

"It's not funny," she said with more than a hint of rebellion.

Rafiq moved his weight on the seat beside her. "No, I don't suppose it would be—if your story were true."

Rafiq's brooding gaze settled on the woman bundled up against the door. If she moved any farther away from him, she'd be in serious danger of falling out. Was she telling the truth? Or was it all an elaborate charade?

The lights changed and the vehicle pulled away from the intersection. "Don't you have anyone you can borrow money from?"

She turned her head and looked out into the night. "No."

Frowning now, Rafiq stared at the dark shape of her head and pale curve of her cheek that was all he could see from this perspective, highlighted every few seconds by flashes from passing neon signs.

"What about your friend Renate? Can't she help you out?"

She gave a strangled laugh. "Hardly a friend. I only met her today. She lodges at the hostel I'm staying at."

Aah. He started to see the light. "There's no one else?"

She shook her head. "Not someone I can ask for money."

Rafiq waited for a heartbeat. For two. Then three. But the expected plea never came.

"You're traveling by yourself." It was a statement. And it explained so much, Rafiq decided, the reluctant urge to believe her growing stronger by the minute.

Tiffany shifted, and he sensed her uneasy glance before she turned back to the window.

She'd be a fool to tell him if she was. Or perhaps this was part of an act designed to make him feel more sympathy for a young woman all alone and out of her depth.

Had he been hustled by an expert? To Rafiq's disquiet he wasn't certain. And he was not accustomed to being rendered uncertain, off-balance. Particularly not by a woman. A young, attractive woman.

He was far from being an impressionable youth.

Three times he'd been in love. Three times he'd been on the brink of proposing marriage. And each time, much to his father's fury, he'd pulled away. At the last moment Rafiq had discovered that the desire, the sparkle, had burnt out under the weight of family expectation.

Rafiq himself didn't understand how something that started with so much hope and promise could fizzle out so disappointingly as soon as his father started to talk marriage settlements.

"So how much money do you need?" He directed the question to the sliver of sculpted cheek that was all he could see of her face.

This should establish whether he was being hustled.

A modest request for only a few dollars to cover necessities and shelter until she could arrange for her bank to put her back in funds would make it easier to swallow her tale.

"Enough to cover my bed and food until Monday."

Rafiq released the breath that he hadn't even been aware of holding.

As head of the Royal Bank of Dhahara he was familiar with all kinds of fraud, from the simplest ploys that emptied the pockets of soft-hearted elders to complex Internet frauds. Tiffany would not be seeing him again, so this was her only opportunity to try stripping him of a substantial amount of money and she had not taken it. She was in genuine need. All she wanted—and she hadn't even directly asked him for it yet—was a small amount of cash to tide her over.

This was not a scam.

The first whisper of real concern for the situation in which she found herself sounded inside his head. He had a cousin who was as close to him as a sister. He'd hate for Zara to be in the position that Tiffany was in, with no one to turn to for help. Rafiq knew he would make sure Tiffany would be looked after. "Tell me more."

"Except…" Her voice trailed away.

Every muscle in his body contracted as he tensed, praying that his instincts had not played him false.

"Except…*what?*" he prompted.

She averted her face. Even in the dark, he caught the movement as her pale fingers fiddled with the hem of the short, flirty dress. "I'm not sure that I'm going to have enough available on my credit card to pay for the changes to my flight."

"How much?"

Here it was. Rafiq forced his gaze up from the distraction of those fingers. She'd just hit him with the big sum—a drop in the ocean to him if she'd but known it—and he couldn't even see her face to read her eyes as his hopes that she was the real deal faded into oblivion. The tidal wave of anger that shook him was unexpected.

It shouldn't have mattered that she was a beautiful little schemer.

But it did.

Rafiq told himself it was because he wasn't often wrong about people, that he'd considered himself too wily to be taken in by a pretty face. *That* was why he was angry.…

Because of his own foolishness.

Not because he'd hoped against all odds—

She turned her head toward him, and her gaze connected with his in the murky darkness of the backseat. He almost convinced himself that he sensed real desperation in her glistening eyes.

Anger overpowered him. Damn her. She was good. So good, she belonged in Hollywood.

How nearly had she hooked him with her air of innocence and lonely despair?

And so much smarter than Renate. He would never have fallen for the platinum blonde's sexual promise of a one-night stand...but this woman... By Allah, he'd nearly bought everything she'd sold him. With her wide waif's eyes, her hesitant smile...she'd suckered him. Like Scheherazade, she was a consummate teller of tales.

Rage licked at his gut like hot flames. He was wise to her now.

He would not be deceived again.

No one made a fool of him. *No one*. And he hadn't fallen into her trap—he'd been fortunate enough to realize the truth before it was too late. No, not fortunate, he admitted, shamed. He'd almost been duped. A slip of a female had drawn him so close to the claws of her honeyed trap, and proven that he was not as wise as he liked to believe. He could still be taken in by a pair of heavily lashed eyes.

Tiffany had been a little too confident. The mistake she'd made had lain in her eagerness to reel him in too quickly.

"Where are we?"

The cab had slowed. Rafiq glanced away from her profile to the imposing marble facade lit up by pale gold light. "At my hotel."

"I never agreed to come here." Her voice was breathy, suddenly hesitant. Earlier he might have considered it uncertainty—even apprehension; now he knew it was nothing more than pretence.

"You never gave me any address when I asked." He opened his door and hid his anger behind a slow smile as he consciously summoned every reserve of charm he possessed. "Come, you will tell me your problems and I will buy you a drink, and perhaps I can find a way to help you."

This was the final test.

If she'd been telling him the truth, she would refuse. But if she was only after the money, she would interpret that smile as weakness, and she would accept.

Rafiq couldn't figure why it was so important to give her a last chance when she'd already revealed her true colors.

She hesitated for a fleeting moment and gave him a tremulous smile designed to melt the hardest heart. Just as he was about to surrender his cynicism, she followed him out of the cab.

The taste inside his mouth was decidedly bitter as she joined him on the sidewalk. Rafiq hadn't realized that he'd still had any illusions left to lose.

Inside the hotel, he headed for the bank of elevators. "There's an open pool deck upstairs that offers views over the city," he said over his shoulder as she hesitated.

Once in the elevator, Rafiq activated it with the key card to his presidential suite.

He brooded while he watched the floors light up as the car shot upward. A sweetly seductive fragrance surrounded him—a mix of fresh green notes and heady gardenia—and to his disgust his body stirred.

Rafiq told himself he wasn't going to take her up on what she was so clearly here for—he only wanted to see how far she was prepared to go.

Yet the urge to teach Tiffany a lesson she would never forget pressed down on him even as the sweet, intoxicating scent of her filled his nostrils. When the elevator finally came to rest, he placed his hand on the small of her back and gently ushered her out.

Balmy night air embraced Tiffany as she stepped through frosted-glass sliding doors into the intimate darkness of the hotel's deserted pool deck.

Overhead the moon hung in the sky, a perfectly shaped crescent, while far below the harbor gleamed like black satin beyond lights that sparkled like sprinklings of fairy dust.

Tiffany made for a group of chairs beside a surprisingly small pool, a row of lamps reflecting off the smooth surface like half a dozen full moons. She sank into a luxuriously padded armchair, nerve-rackingly conscious of the man who stood with his back to her, hands on hips, staring over the city…thinking God knew what. Because he was back in that remote space that he allowed no one else to inhabit.

When he wheeled about and shrugged off his suit jacket, her pulse leaped uncontrollably. He dropped into the chair beside her, and suddenly the air became thick and cloying.

"What would you like to drink?" he asked as a waiter appeared, as if that slice of time when he'd become so inaccessible had never been.

Tiffany rather fancied she needed a clear head. But she also had no intention of showing him how much he intimidated her. Her chin inched higher. "Vodka with lots of ice and orange." She'd sip it. Make it last.

Casting a somewhat mocking smile at her, Rafiq ordered Perrier for himself. And Tiffany wished she'd thought of that herself.

By some magic, the waiter was back in seconds with the drinks, and then Rafiq dismissed him.

She shivered as the sudden silence, the silken heat of the night and the sheer imposing presence of the man beside her all closed in on her senses. They were alone. How had this happened? He'd offered to buy her a drink…to lend a sympathetic ear. She'd imagined a busy bar and a little kindness.

Not this.

He turned his head. The trickle of awareness grew to a torrent as she fell into the enigmatic depths of his dark eyes.

Tiffany let out a deep breath that she'd been unaware of holding, and told herself that Rafiq was only a man. *A man.* Her father was a well-known film director. She'd met some of the most sought-after men in the world; men who graced covers of glitzy magazines and were featured on lists of women's most secret fantasy lovers. So why on earth was this one intimidating her?

The only explanation that made any sense was that losing her passport, her money, had stripped away the comfort of her identity and put her at a disadvantage. No longer her parents' pampered princess, she was struggling to survive…and the unexpected reversal had disoriented her.

Of course, it wasn't *him.* It had nothing to do with him. Or with the tantalizing air of reserve that invited her to crash through it.

This was about *her.*

About her confusion. It was easy to see how he had become appealing, an unexpected pillar of strength in a world gone crazy.

The rationality of the conclusion comforted her and allowed her to smile up at him with hastily mustered composure, to say in a carefully modulated tone, "I'm sorry, I've been so tied up in talking about me. What brings you to Hong Kong?"

His reply was terse. "Business."

"With Sir Julian?"

A slight nod was the only response she got. And a renewed blast of that do-not-intrude-any-further reserve that he was so good at displaying. He might as well have worn a great, big sign with ten-foot-high red letters that read Danger: Keep Out.

"Hotel business?"

"Why do you think that?"

Tiffany took a sip of her drink. It was deliciously sweet and cool. "Because he's famous for his hotels—are you trying to develop a resort?"

"Do I look like a developer?"

She took in the angled cheekbones starkly highlighted by the lamplight; his white shirt with dark stripes that stood out in the darkness; his fingers clenching the glass that he held. Even though he should've appeared relaxed sitting there, he hummed with tension.

"I'm not sure what a developer is supposed to look like. People are individuals. Not one size fits all."

He inspected her silently until she shifted. "What do you do, Tiffany? What are you doing in Hong Kong?"

"Uh…" She had no intention of confessing that she didn't do very much at all. She'd completed a degree in English literature and French…and found she still wasn't sure what she wanted to do with her life. Nor did she have any intention of telling him about her abortive trip with her school friend, Sally. About how Sally had hooked up with a guy and how Tiffany had felt like a third wheel in their developing romance. She'd already revealed far too much; she certainly didn't want Rafiq to know how naive she'd been. So she smiled brightly at him, took a sip of her drink and said casually, "Just traveling here and there."

"Your family approve of this carefree existence?"

She prickled. "My family knows that I can look after myself."

That was debatable. Tiffany doubted her father would ever believe she was capable of taking care of herself. Yet she also knew she had to tread carefully. She didn't want Rafiq to know quite how isolated she was right now.

"I've been keeping in close touch with them."

"By cell phone."

It was a statement. She didn't deny it, didn't tell him that her cell phone had been in the stolen purse. Or that she didn't even know where her father was right now. Or about her mother's emotional devastation. Far safer to let him believe that she was only a text away from communicating with her family.

"Why don't they send you money for the fare that you need?"

"They can't afford to."

It was true. Sort of. Tiffany thought about her mother's tears when she'd called her yesterday to arrange exactly that. Linda Smith née Canning had been a B-grade actress before her marriage to Taylor Smith; she hadn't worked for nearly two decades. The terms of her prenuptial agreement settled a house in Auckland on her, a far from liquid asset. It would take time to sell, and Mom needed her father's consent to borrow against it. In the meantime there were groceries to buy, staff to pay, bills for the hired house in L.A....and, according to her mother, not much money in the joint account. Add a husband who'd made sure he couldn't be found, and Linda's panic and distress had been palpable.

So, no, her mom was not in a position to help right now. She needed a lawyer—and Tiffany intended to arrange the best lawyer she could find as soon as she got back home. The more expensive, the better, she vowed darkly. Her father would pay those bills in due course.

But Rafiq wouldn't be interested in any of that.

"How did we get back to talking about me?" she asked. "I'm not terribly interesting."

"That's a matter of opinion." His voice was smoother than velvet.

Tiffany leaned a little closer and caught the glimmer of starlight in his dark eyes. A frisson of half fear, half anticipation feathered down her spine. She drew sharply back.

She must be mad....

Sucking in a breath, she blurted out, "Sir Julian was born in New Zealand. He owns a historic home in Auckland that often appears in lifestyle magazines." The change of subject seemed sudden, but at least it got them back onto neutral territory. "His father was English."

Unexpectedly, Rafiq didn't take the bait to find out more about his business acquaintance. "So you're from New Zealand? I couldn't place your accent."

"Because of my father's job, some of my schooling took place in the States, so that would make it even harder to identify." Her parents had relocated her from an Auckland all-girl school while they'd tried to juggle family life with her father's filming schedule. It had been awkward. Eventually, Tiffany and her mother had returned to live in Auckland. But her mother had frequently flown to Los Angeles to act as hostess for the lavish parties he threw at the opulent Malibu mansion he'd rented—and to keep an eye on her father. Tiffany had been seventeen the first time she'd read about her father's affairs in a gossip magazine. Like the final piece in a puzzle, it had completed a picture she hadn't even known was missing an essential part.

"Your father was in the military?"

She didn't want to talk about Taylor Smith. "No—but he traveled a lot."

"Ah, like a salesman or something?"

"Something like that." She took another sip of her drink

and set it down on a round glass-topped table. "What about you? Where do you live?"

He considered her. "I'm from Dhahara—it's a desert kingdom, near Oman."

"How fascinating!"

"Ah, you find me fascinating...."

Tiffany stared at him.

Then she detected the wry mockery glinting in his eyes. "Not you!" She gave a gurgle of laughter and relaxed a little. "Where you live fascinates me."

"Now you break my heart."

"Are you flirting with me?" she asked suspiciously.

"If you must ask, then I must be losing my touch." He stretched out his long legs and loosened his tie.

The gesture brought her attention to his hands. In the reflected glow of the lamplight his fingers were lean and square-tipped, and dark against the white of his shirt. The gold of a signet ring winked in the light. His hand had stilled. Under his fingertips his heart would be beating like—

"You might not think I'm fascinating but most women think I'm charming," he murmured, his eyes half-closed, his mood indecipherable.

She reared back. Did he know what was happening to her? Why her pulse had gone crazy? "You? Charming?"

"Absolutely."

Tiffany swallowed. "Most women must be mad."

A glint entered his eyes. "You think so?"

Danger! Danger! She recklessly ignored the warning, too caught up in the surge of adrenalin that provoking him brought. "I know so."

"You don't believe I could be charming?" He smiled, his teeth startlingly white in the darkening night, and a bolt of metallic heat shot through Tiffany's belly.

"Never!" she said fiercely.

"Well then, I'll have to convince you otherwise."

He bent his head. Slowly, oh, far too slowly. Her heart started to pound. There was plenty of time for her to duck away, to smack his face as she'd earlier in the cab told herself he richly deserved. But she didn't. Instead she waited, holding her breath, watching his mouth—why hadn't she noticed how beautiful it was?—come closer and closer, until it finally settled on hers.

And then she sighed.

A soft whisper of sound.

He kissed with mastery. His lips pressed against hers, moving along the seam, playing...tantalizing, never demanding more than she was prepared to give. No other part of him touched her. After an age Tiffany let her lips part. He didn't take advantage. Instead he continued to taste her with playful kisses until she groaned in frustration.

He needed no further invitation. He plundered her mouth, hungrily seeking out secrets she hadn't known existed. Passion seized her. Quickly followed by a rush of hunger. His hand came up and cupped the back of her neck. The heat of his touch sent quivers along undiscovered nerve endings.

Tiffany swayed, eyes closed beneath the sensory onslaught.

At last, an eternity later, he lifted his head and gazed down at her with hooded eyes.

"So," he said with some satisfaction, his fingertips rubbing in soft circles against the sensitized nape of her neck, "you will agree that most women are right. You are charmed."

Tiffany reeled under the deluge of what could only be cool calculation.

"*I* think that you are the most arrogant and conceited *playboy*—" she spat that out "—I have ever met."

For an instant he stared at her, and she steeled herself for retaliation…of a sexual kind.

He threw his head back and laughed.

"Thank you," Rafiq said when he was finally through laughing, bowing his head with mock grace, his eyes still gleaming with hilarity. "I am honored."

And Tiffany wished with wild regret that she'd smacked his face until her hand stung while she'd had the chance. Through lips that still burned from his kiss, she said, "You don't charm me."

Three

His amusement instantly evaporated.

Rafiq suppressed the flare of annoyance and studied her dispassionately. Her hostility surprised him. He'd thought she'd leap at the opportunity to seduce him. Had she gauged he was not easily swayed? Intrigued by the idea, he assessed her. Was the taunt a ploy to capture his attention? Was it possible that she'd known exactly who he was? Researched him?

He shook off the sudden concern.

No, she might be street-smart. But she was a nobody—an insignificant foreign girl illegally working in a dubious club in the backstreets of Hong Kong. He dismissed his apprehension.

"Don't look at me like that, you arrogant jerk."

No one talked to him like that. Certainly not a woman like her. With a growl he grabbed her hand and yanked her toward him. She made a little squeaking sound as she landed in his lap. Rafiq softened his hold, stroking his fingers in long sweeps along her spine. Bending his head, he nuzzled the soft skin of her neck, murmuring sweet words. Her gasp quickly turned to a moan of delight. He marshaled every seductive trick he knew. She responded like a moonflower opening, overwhelming him with her sweet response.

Rafiq fought against the intoxicating pleasure her soft body unlocked. Told himself he was still in control. After all, he'd only teased her...flirted with her...*kissed* her to determine how far Tiffany was prepared to take this scam.

It was a test.

He told himself she'd failed. Dismally. Even as she'd kissed him like angel. He should've been thrilled he'd been proved right.

Instead he drowned in her unresisting softness.

When she shoved at his chest, he blinked rapidly in surprise and shook his head to clear it. "What?"

She scrambled to her feet, her breathing unsteady, her eyes blazing. "You misled me. I didn't come here for this. I'm not so desperate for a place to sleep."

Before she could spin away, he caught her arm.

"Tiffany, wait. You insult both of us. You might think I'm a jerk but I never assumed you came with me to find a bed for the night." Although perhaps the possibility should've occurred to him.

There was something about her that made him want to believe she wasn't like that. Maybe it was her wide brown eyes that gave her such an air of sincerity. Or the baby-soft skin beneath his fingertips...

He brushed the observation aside. She was a woman—of course her skin was soft. It made her no different from a million other women.

Time to get rid of her, before she had him believing the tales she'd spun. He dropped her arm and drew his wallet from the back of his pants, flipping it open to extract a five-hundred-dollar bill. To his surprise his fingers still shook from the aftershocks of the kiss. "Here, this is your tip for serving me drinks—that should help cover your accommodation for a couple of nights." If indeed, that story was true.

Bowing her head, Tiffany mumbled, "I can't take that."

"Why not?" By Allah, she drove him mad. What did she want from him? "I always intended to give you something to tide you over."

Rafiq tried to figure out her agenda. He still wasn't sure what she was after. She was such a curious mix of sophistication and spontaneity. On the one hand she'd almost convinced him her purse and passport had been stolen and all she wanted was a few dollars for a couple of nights' budget accommodation. Hah, he was even ready to give it to her. In the next breath she'd told him she couldn't afford the airfare home, leaving him certain that he was being manipulated by an expert.

He couldn't work out whether she was simply a victim or extremely smart.

But his conscience wouldn't allow him to leave her homeless in case she really had been the victim of petty crime. He thought of his cousin Zara, of his brother's wife, Megan. What if it had been one of the women of his family in such a predicament? He would hope that someone would come to their aid.

"Take it, please."

She stared down at the note in his hand. "It's too much. After that kiss it would feel...wrong," she mumbled, her hair blocking him from seeing her face.

He couldn't help noticing the catch in her voice.

"Okay." Growing impatient with himself, for being so aware of the woman, he opened the billfold again and extracted a twenty and a ten before shoving the other note back. "Take this then—it's not as good a tip as you deserve, but at least you won't suspect my motives."

She tilted her head back and stared at him for a long moment. "Thank you for understanding."

Tears glimmered in her eyes.

"Oh, don't cry," he said roughly.

"I can't help it." She sniffed and wiped her fingers across her eyes. "I'm sorry for calling you a jerk."

Rafiq found himself smiling. She enchanted him, this woman whom he couldn't get a fix on. One minute he had her down as the cleverest schemer he'd ever met, the next she appeared as sweetly innocent as his cousin Zara.

She leaned forward. The scent of gardenias surrounded him. She rested her palm against his chest, her hand warm through the fine cotton of his shirt. Rafiq's breath caught in his throat.

But the hunger he felt for Tiffany bore no resemblance to the sisterly love he showered on Zara.

By the time Tiffany rose on tiptoes and pressed soft lips against his cheek, he was rigid with reaction.

"Thank you, you've saved my life."

She smelled so sweet, the body brushing against him so feminine, that Rafiq couldn't stop his arms from encircling her. He drew her up against him. "Oh, Tiffany, what am I supposed to make of you?"

"I'm not very complicated at all—what you see is what you get," she muttered against his shirt front.

He felt her smile against his thundering heart, heard her breath quicken as his arms tightened convulsively around her…and was lost.

* * *

A long time seemed to pass before Rafiq lifted his lips from hers.

As Tiffany's fingers crept up his shirt and hooked into his loosened tie, Rafiq forgot that he'd started this driven by perverse curiosity and affronted male pride, to see if Tiffany would kiss him when she'd vowed that she wasn't affected by his brand of charm.

It had all changed.

His tightly leashed control was in shreds.

All he could think about was tasting her again…and again.

Her fingers froze. "What are we doing?" She sounded as befuddled as he felt. "Anyone could walk in on us through those sliding doors."

"No." He shook his head. "That's not true. This private pool and deck are part of my suite—my key card activated the entry doors onto the deck."

Her breath caught—an audible sound. "Your suite? You said we'd have a drink.… I would never have entered your suite."

She'd withdrawn. Her eyes had grown dark and distrustful. Rafiq gathered she was making unfavorable assumptions about his motives. He couldn't blame her. "The bar downstairs is noisy—and full of inebriated men at this time of night. We wouldn't have been able to hear ourselves think." Much less talk.

"Oh…"

Unable to help himself he stroked a finger along the curve of her jaw. Soft curls trailed over the back of his hand. "You are very beautiful, do you know that?"

"Not beautiful." She sounded distracted.

He stilled his fingers, and cupped the side of her face.

Tilting it up, he looked down into her wide eyes. "Beautiful."

She shook her head. "Not me. Pretty, maybe, at a stretch. But in this light you wouldn't even be able to tell."

No one could call her vain. "My eyes are not the only senses attuned to you. I don't need bright intrusive light to remember that your eyes are the haunting tawny-brown shade of the desert sands streaked with the burnished gold of the setting sun. I don't need light to feel." Gently he rubbed her bottom lip with the pad of his thumb. "Your mouth is the crushed red of the satiny petals in the rose gardens of Qasr Al-Ward." His fingers explored her cheeks. "Your skin is softer than an almond blossom. Your cheekbones are carefully sculpted by a masterful hand to ensure that as you grow older you will only grow more beautiful."

Tiffany felt herself color.

A beat of time elapsed. Tiffany tried to summon the anger that had scorched her only a moment before when she'd discovered he'd brought her to his suite, but it had vanished. His touch, the heat of his lean body, the force of his soft words had overwhelmed her. She couldn't think of a single thing to say. She'd never met anyone remotely like him. He was way out her league.

Finally she gave up trying to understand the emotion that flooded her. Linking her fingers behind his neck, she pulled his mouth back to hers, his hair thick and silken under her fingers. His thigh moved against her hip, making her aware of the hard, muscled strength of him. When the kiss ended, Tiffany discovered that her heart was pounding.

Tilting her head back, she looked up into his face. His eyes glowed, he'd warmed, he was a long way from being the remote, distant stranger. A heady sense of being on a precipice of discovery overtook her.

Before she could speak, Rafiq grasped her hand. "Come."

He led her through a pair of French doors into a darkened room. A flick of a switch and dim lighting washed the room, revealing a king-size bed in a sumptuously decorated room.

Tiffany hesitated for a microsecond as Rafiq shrugged off his shirt. Then he turned her in his arms and the moment of cool analysis was gone.

Her wide, elasticized belt gave.… She heard something fall, and dismissed it. The zip on the back of her borrowed dress rasped down. His hands closed over the shoulder straps and eased them down her arms along with the tiny, dainty bag looped around her wrist. She didn't have any time to feel exposed…or naked. Only relief that the tight dress was gone. Rafiq drew her against his bare torso, his skin smooth and warm against hers.

His fingers tangled in her hair, before moving in small circles down her back, setting flame to each inch of flesh he massaged.

Tiffany flung her head back. A moan escaped. Desire flared uncontrollably within her and her nipples peaked beneath the modest black bra she wore. She didn't even feel Rafiq loosen the back before the plain bra gave and he removed it, tossing it over the bed end. Then he was on his knees in front of her, easing her heels off, sliding the cotton briefs down her legs, his touch trailing fire down the insides of her thighs.

She started to shake.

The explosive hunger that consumed her was unfamiliar. Powerful. Incredible. A new experience. He buried his face in her belly. Goose bumps broke out over her skin as sensation shook her to her soul. Her hands clutched at his hair, the texture rough as she closed her fingers over the short strands.

"I'm going to pleasure you—but we're not going to make love," he murmured.

Relief, instantly followed by a crazy kind of disappointment spread through her. "Why won't we make love?"

Did he think he was too good for her?

"I'm not…equipped."

"Equipped?" Then it struck her what he meant. "Oh."

The next thought was that if he didn't carry condoms around with him, then he didn't do casual sex, either. It made her almost start to like the man who had her in such a sweat.

Perversely, it made her want him to make love to her.

Tiffany reached for the puddle of her dress on the floor and found her bag. Opening it she extracted the condom that Renate had stuck in. "I only have one."

"Better than nothing," he growled.

Then he had her on the bed and everything started to move very fast. She closed her eyes as his mouth teased her nipple, arousing sensations she'd never experienced. A wild, keening sound broke from her throat as his teeth teased her burgeoning flesh. His hands were everywhere.… He knew exactly what to do to reduce her to a state of quivering arousal. Her body turned fluid. It seemed to know exactly what he wanted…how to respond to his every move.

When he finally moved over her, her legs parted. Opening her eyes, she glimpsed the tense line of his jaw, the fullness of a bottom lip softened by passion. He shifted into the space between her legs, his body so male, so unfamiliar against her own. He moved his hips, and Tiffany tensed, fighting the instinct to resist.

The pressure. Her breath caught in the back of her throat. He wasn't going to fit. Staring at the mouth that had wreaked so much pleasure, she waited uncertainly. Suddenly her body gave, and the pressure eased. The shudders subsided. Her heart expanded as he sank forward. A glow of warmth swept her. Her hands fluttered along the indent of his spine as a powerful, primal emotion swept her.

Tiffany thought she was going to cry with joy, at the beauty of it all.

The warmth spiraled into a fierce, desperate heat as he moved within her. As the friction built, she could feel herself straining to reach a place she'd never been. Her body tightened, no longer hers, taken over by the passion that ripped through her.

"Relax," he whispered in her ear. "Let it happen."

She didn't know what he was talking about. Yet the warmth of his breath against her ear caused a fresh wave of shivers to race up and down her spine, spreading out along every inch of her skin.

This time she didn't fight the sensation. She allowed it to sweep her away. Pleasure soared.

He grew still. Then he moved, his body driving in quick thrusts into hers, his breath fast.

A cry of shock caught in her throat as her body convulsed. Waves of heat broke, rippling through her, a tide of inexorable sensation that left her limp.

Tiffany opened her eyes and blinked against bright sunlight.

Disorientation was quickly followed by a suffocating sense of dread. *What had she done?* Slowly, she turned her head against the plump oversized pillow.

The space beside her in the giant king-size bed was

empty. Rafiq was already awake…and out of the bed. With any luck he'd stay closeted in the bathroom until she could escape. Except she could hear no sound. Perhaps he'd gone to have breakfast…a swim…to work out. Anything.

Tiffany didn't care so long as she didn't have to confront him.

A movement drew her gaze to the floor-to-ceiling windows where the drapes had already been thrown back. Squinting against the gauze-filtered sunlight, Tiffany made out the dark shadow of a backlit figure.

Rafiq.

She shifted and he must've heard the movement, because he wheeled around and spoke. "You're awake."

Too late to squeeze her eyelids shut and fake sleep.

"Yes." She offered him a tremulous smile, and tried to read his expression, but bright light behind him frustrated her attempt.

"Good."

Was it? She wasn't so sure. He moved closer and came into focus. The passionate lover from last night's dark, delicious world had vanished. Replaced by the aloof man she'd met—was it only the evening before?

Tiffany shuddered.

"You're already dressed." Did she have to sound so plaintive?

He shrugged. "I have a busy day planned."

And it was time for her to make herself scarce.

He didn't need to speak the words out loud. It was painfully obvious.

But she had no intention of getting out of bed with him standing less than three feet away. She was naked under the sheet. And he was impeccably, immaculately dressed. She'd exposed more of herself than she'd ever intended, and she had no one but herself to blame. He would not see another inch of her body. A fresh flush of humiliation scorched her at the memory of what had passed between them last night.

Tiffany raised her chin and bravely met his granite gaze. "So why are you still here?"

"I've been waiting for you to awaken."

The harsh features that had been aflame with desire last night had reverted to keep-out coldness. Any hope that he'd wanted to tell her something momentous withered. Her stomach balled into a tight knot.

"Why?"

He reached into his jacket pocket.

His fist uncurled. A cell phone lay there—slim and silent.

Tiffany frowned, trying to make sense of the tension that vibrated from him. And what it had to do with her. "That's Renate's phone. I slipped it into my belt—"

"You took pictures last night."

Oh. Darn. She'd forgotten all about that. "I meant to delete—"

"Yes." His mouth curled. It was not a nice smile. "I'm sure you meant to. But you didn't. And you assured Sir Julian that you already had deleted the images."

She'd been scared of losing her job—now she'd been caught in a lie. She wriggled under the sheet, trying to think of how to explain. In the end she decided she'd probably be better off remaining silent, before she dug herself into a deeper hole. What a mess.

"Nothing to say?"

"Why do you care?"

"Oh, I care." He brandished the phone at her. "One of the photos is of me with Sir Julian—and enough of Renate to make sure the viewer knows exactly what kind of relationship she's contemplating with him."

"I didn't mean—"

"Of course, you didn't." He sneered. "You were very interested in talking about Sir Julian Carling last night, too."

"I was making conversation." Tiffany was utterly bewildered by the turn the conversation had taken. "So what?"

His eyes darkened. "So what? That's all you have to say for yourself?"

Tiffany drew the top sheet more securely around herself. What had possessed her to let this daunting stranger get so close last night?

"You are wise to be nervous."

"I'm not nervous," she lied. "I'm confused."

The silence swelled. Tiffany *was* growing decidedly nervous. Her gaze flitted toward the door. Even if she made it out the room, she wouldn't get very far without any clothes. And she doubted she'd have time to scoop up her dress and bag off the floor.

She turned her attention back to him and decided to brazen it out. "Why are you angry?"

His eyebrow shot up. "You expect me to believe you don't know? Come, come, it's enough now."

Tiffany decided it would probably be better to say nothing. It would only enrage him further. So she waited.

"There's a text message from your friend on her phone asking how your night went."

The expression of distaste on his face told her that he'd jumped to the conclusion that she'd discussed sleeping with him with Renate.

Damn Renate. "You're misunderstanding—"

He held up a hand. "I don't want to hear it. How much do you want?"

"What?"

"To forget that you ever saw me with Sir Julian."

Her mouth dropped open. He was delusional. Or paranoid. Or maybe just plain crazy. That was enough to make her say hastily, "Just delete the images—it's what I meant to do last night. I forgot…and then I forgot to give the phone back to Renate."

"How convenient."

Tiffany didn't like the way he said that.

"When you didn't respond, your friend's texts make it clear she's decided you must've stolen her phone." He smiled, but his eyes still smoldered like hot coals. "That you're planning to sell the images yourself."

"I wouldn't do that!"

He made a sound that sounded suspiciously like a snort. "Sell the images or steal her phone? Since when is there honor among thieves?"

What on earth was he getting at? She gave him a wary glance, and then said, "Just say what you mean."

"You and your friend intended to blackmail me and Sir Julian. Your friend has decided you've decided to proceed alone. I think she's right."

"Blackmail?"

He was definitely, certifiably crazy. Her eyes flickered toward the door again. Maybe, just maybe she could get out of here…and if she yanked the sheet along, she'd have cover.

"You're not going anywhere," he growled and sat down on the bed, pinning her under the sheet that she'd been planning to escape in, wrapped around her like a toga.

"I know." She gazed at him limpidly.

His eyes narrowed to slits. "That look won't work. I know you're no innocent."

If he only knew.

"Uh…" Tiffany's voice trailed away. No point telling him, he wouldn't believe her.

"So what were the two of you intending to do with the photos?"

"Nothing."

He shook his head. "You take me for a fool. Your friend was desperate to know whether you still had the phone and the photos. Someone was ready to buy them. You were in on the deal."

She wasn't going to argue with him. Not while he was looming over her, and she wasn't wearing a stitch under the scanty cover that the hotel's silk sheet provided. No way was she risking sparking the tension between them into something else…something infinitely more dangerous.

Panic filled her. "Get off me!"

He didn't budge. "Here's what's going to happen. I'm going to delete the images from the phone. Then I'm going to buy you the ticket that you were so desperate for last night. Then I never want to see or hear from you again. Do you understand?"

Tiffany nodded.

He sat back and she breathed again.

"I'm not going to give you the money you so badly want. I'm going to take you to the airport and pay whatever it takes to get that ticket changed—so I hope you really need a flight to Auckland."

"I do," she croaked.

He pushed himself away from her. "It will be waiting for you downstairs when you are ready to leave."

As he rose from the bed, her bravado returned. Her chin lifted. "I don't need you to take me to the airport—it won't help. My temporary travel documents will only be ready on Monday. I'll take a cab back to the hostel."

"I want you out of Hong Kong."

"I have no intention of staying a minute more than I have to. Nor will I cause you any grief. I promise."

He gave her one of those narrow-eyed glances that chilled her to the bone. "If I learn that you have—"

"I'm not going to do anything. I swear. And, believe me, I intend to pay you back," she said fervently. Tiffany had no intention of being beholden to this man.

He waved a dismissive hand. "Please. Don't lie."

"I *will* repay you. But I'll need your bank details."

"To further scam me?" The bark of laughter he gave sounded ugly. His eyes bored into hers. She didn't look away. The mood changed, becoming hot and oppressive. Something arced between them, an emotion so intense, so powerful that she lost the ability to think.

Without looking away, Rafiq reached into his pocket for his wallet. This time he extracted a small white card. "Here are my details. You can post me a check…but I don't want to see you again. Ever."

It stung.

Determined to hurt him, she flung the words back at him. "I have no intention of seeing you again." Then, for good measure, she added defiantly, "Ever."

She bit her lip hard to stop it trembling as he swung away, and she watched him head for the door with long, raking strides. When the door thudded shut behind him, she glanced down at the card she held.

Rafiq Al Dhahara. President, Royal Bank of Dhahara.

She should've known. He wasn't any old banker. He was the boss. The man who had showed her a glimpse of heaven would never be an ordinary man.

Four

Rafiq could not settle.

He'd been restless for weeks now. He told himself it was the fierce desert heat of Dhahara that kept him awake deep into the heart of the night. Not even the arctic air-conditioning circulating through the main boardroom of the Royal Bank of Dhahara soothed him.

"Stop pacing," Shafir said from behind him. "You called us in to talk about the new hotel you've financed, but now you wear holes in that kelim. Sit down and talk." He tapped his gold pen against the legal pad in front of him. "I'm in a hurry."

Swiveling on his heel, Rafiq put his hands on narrow hips, and scowled down at where his brother lounged in the black leather chair, his white robes cascading about him. "You can wait, Shafir."

"I might, but Megan won't. My wife is determined to spend every free minute we have at Qasr Al-Ward." Shafir flashed him the wicked grin of a man well satisfied by that state of affairs. "Come for the weekend. Celebrate that the contracts for the new Carling Hotel are in place. It'll give you a chance to shed that suit for a couple of days."

Shaking his head, Rafiq said, "Too much else to do. I'll resist the call of the desert." He envied his brother the bond he had to Qasr Al-Ward, the desert palace that had been in the family for centuries. Since his marriage to Megan, Shafir had made Qasr Al-Ward their home.

"Don't resist it too long—or you may not find your way back."

"Why don't you take our father?" Rafiq wasn't eager to engage in the kind of analysis that Shafir's sharp gaze suggested was about to begin. In an effort to distract his brother, he tipped his head to where King Selim was intent on getting his point across to his firstborn son. The words "duty" and "marriage" drifted across the expanse of the boardroom table. "That way Khalid might get some peace, too."

Shafir chuckled. "Looks like our father is determined not to give him a break."

"You realize your marriage has only increased the pressure on Khalid?"

Stabbing a finger at his brother's chest, Shafir chuckled. "And on you. Everyone expected you to marry first, Rafiq. Unlike Khalid, your bride isn't Father's choice. And unlike me, women don't view you as already wed to the desert. You spent years abroad—you've had plenty of opportunity to fall in love."

"It wasn't so straightforward." Rafiq realized that was true. "There were no expectations on you, Shafir. No pressure. You've always done exactly what you want."

His brother had spent much of his life growing up in the desert; he'd been allowed rough edges, whereas

Rafiq had been groomed for a corporate role. Educated at Eton, followed by degrees at Cambridge and Harvard. There had been pressure to put thought and care into his choice of partner—someone who could bear scrutiny on an international stage. A trophy wife. A *powerful* trophy wife.

How could he explain how a relationship that started off as something special could deteriorate into nothing more than duty?

"Take it." His father's rising voice broke into his thoughts.

Rafiq refocused across the table. His father was trying to press a piece of paper into Khalid's hand. "All three of these women are suitable. Yasmin is a wealthy young woman who knows what you need in a wife."

"No!" Khalid's jaw was like rock.

"She's pretty, too." Shafir smirked.

"I don't want pretty," his eldest brother argued.

Pretty. Rafiq shied away from the word. Tiffany had thought she was pretty. Not beautiful. Pretty. Rafiq had considered her beautiful.

"I want a woman who will match me," Khalid was saying. "I don't care what she looks like. I need a partner… not a pinup."

"Hey, my wife is a partner," Shafir objected. "In my eyes she's a pinup, too."

Newly—and happily—married, he'd become the king's ally in the quest to seek a suitable wife for his brothers. Although Rafiq suspected that Shafir was only trying to drive home how fortunate he'd been to find his Megan. If he could find a woman as unique, as in tune with him as Megan was with Shafir, he'd get married in a shot.…

Khalid bestowed a killing look on Shafir, who laughed and helped himself to a cup of the rich, fragrant coffee that the bank's newest secretary was busy pouring into small brass cups.

"Thank you, Miss Turner." To his father Khalid added, "I don't need a list. I will find my own wife."

Rafiq craned his neck, peering at the list. "Who else is on there?"

"Farrah? She's far too young—I don't want a child bride."

"Leila Mummhar."

Rafiq's suggestion had captured his father's attention.

"Pah." The King flung out his arms. "Don't *you* give him advice. I was certain you'd be married long before Shafir. Now look at you—no woman at your side since your beloved departed."

"Shenilla and I had...differences." It was the best way to describe the pushy interest that Shenilla's father had started to exert as soon as they'd considered him hooked. Shenilla was a qualified accountant, she was beautiful, her family was well respected in Dhahara. On paper it was the perfect match.

Yet he'd run....

"Differences?" His father growled. "What is a little difference? Your beloved mother and I had many differences while we were courting. We overcame them and—"

"But your marriage was expected," Rafiq interrupted. "It was arranged between your families from the time you were very young. You could not end such a relationship."

The king shook his head. "It made marriage no easier. But we worked at it. Happiness is something to strive for, my son, every day of your life. And you were so in love. Ay me, I was so certain that this time it would be right."

How could Rafiq confess that he'd been sure that Shenilla had been perfect for him, yet once their families had become involved as quickly as he'd fallen in love with her, he'd fallen out again? And it hadn't been the first time. Before that there had been Rosa and before her, Neela. He wasn't indiscriminate. His cautious courtships lasted for lengthy periods—that was expected after the care he put into the choice. But just when they got to the point where formalities like engagements became expected, when the pressure to set a wedding date was applied, the love dwindled, leaving only a restless need to escape the cloying trap the relationship had become.

"Khalid, you may object now but you know your duty." The king patted his firstborn son on the shoulder. "Choose any one of those women and you will be richly rewarded."

Rafiq eyed the list and thought of the requirements he'd set for women he considered in the past—after all he was a practical man, his wife would have to fit into his world. Wealthy. Beautiful. Well connected. "Yasmin comes from a powerful family."

Khalid shook his head fiercely. "No, it's not her family I'd be marrying. And I want more than power, wealth and looks in a bride. She must be able to keep me interested for many years, long after worldly goods are forgotten."

Interested? Rafiq's thoughts veered to the last woman who had occupied his bed.

Tiffany had kept him interested from the moment he'd met her. Yes, he'd told her she was beautiful. And he'd meant it. But she was nothing like the other beauties he'd dated. Her features reflected her every emotion, and the graceful way she moved had held him entranced. She certainly fulfilled none of the other criteria he looked for in a wife…she'd never be suitable.

It shamed him that in one short night with little effort she'd stripped him of the restraint and control he prided himself on. It had disturbed him deeply that a woman whom he didn't love, held no fondness for, a woman he suspected of being a con artist, a blackmailer, could hold such power over him.

She'd insisted she'd had no intention of bedding him; she'd been as deliciously tight as a virgin, yet she'd produced a condom at the critical moment. And she'd lied about deleting the photos she'd taken of him and Sir Julian. The more he thought about it, the more he decided he'd been played for a fool by an expert.

He'd given her his business card.

Fool!

He stared blindly at the list he held until Shafir stretched across the boardroom table and snagged it. His brother studied it…and hooted with laughter, pulling Rafiq out the trance that held him immobile. "I can't believe Leila is on here—she's more work than all the bandits that hide on the border of Marulla."

"It would make political sense—we would be able to watch her relations," the king growled.

"Father, we don't want the trouble that her uncles would bring." Rafiq shook his head as he referred to the spats that the two sheikhs were infamous for waging. "Pick someone with less baggage."

Khalid fixed his attention on Shafir. "Maybe I should do what you did…choose a woman with family on the other side of the world. That way I will have no problem with my inlaws."

Suppressing the urge to grin, Rafiq waited for his father to launch into a tirade about the sanctity of family. But his father wore an arrested expression. "Rafiq, did you not say that Sir Julian Carling has a daughter?"

"Yes." Rafiq thought of the woman he'd once met. "Elizabeth Carling."

Despite the dislike he'd taken to Sir Julian, there'd been nothing wrong with the daughter. Elizabeth had everything he usually looked for. Wealth, beauty, connections. Yet there'd been no spark. Not like what he'd experienced with Tiffany—if such a wild madness could be termed a spark. It had been more like a conflagration.

At last he nodded. "Yes, she would be a good choice for Khalid."

"Add her to the list," his father commanded Shafir. "Rafiq says her father is coming to Dhahara to inspect the site for the new Carling Hotel. Her father is a very wealthy man." King Selim gave his eldest son an arch look, and leaned back in his chair. "I will invite Lady Carling and his daughter, too."

Even as Khalid glared at him, the young secretary reappeared in the doorway, concern in her eyes. "The CEO of Pyramid Oil is here for his appointment. What shall I tell him?"

"That's right, run, before I kill you for adding to the pressure," his brother muttered, but Rafiq only laughed.

"Discussing your future took the heat off me, so thanks."

Khalid snorted in disgust.

Still grinning, Rafiq turned to the young secretary. "Miss Turner, give us five more minutes—by then I will be done."

Tiffany stepped out of the cab into the dry, arid midday heat of Dhahara. Hot wind redolent of spices and a tang of the desert swept around her. In front of her towered the Royal Bank of Dhahara. The butterflies that had been floating around in her stomach started to whip their wings in earnest.

Sure, she'd known from his gold-embossed card that

Rafiq would be an important man. President, Royal Bank of Dhahara. But not *this* important.

Yet coming here had been the right thing to do. She'd never doubted her path from the moment the doctor had confirmed her deepest fear. But being confronted with the material reality of where Rafiq worked, knowing that it would be only minutes before she saw him again, made her palms grow moist and her heart thump loudly in her chest.

She paid the driver and couldn't help being relieved that she'd had the foresight to check into a city hotel and stow her luggage in her room before coming here. Pulling a filmy scarf over her hair, she passed the bank's uniformed guard and headed for the glass sliding doors.

Inside, behind the sleek, circular black marble reception counter, stood a young, clean-shaven man in a dark suit and white headgear. Tiffany approached him, determined to brazen this out. "I have an appointment."

His brow creased as he scanned the computer screen in front of him, searching for an appointment she knew would not be listed for today…or any day. Finally he shook his head.

But Tiffany had not come this far to be deterred. She held her ground, refusing to turn away.

"Call Rafiq Al Dhahara." Her conjuring up the name she'd memorized from the business card caused him to do a double take. "Tell him Tiffany Smith is here to see him." She mustered up every bit of authority that she had. "He won't be pleased if he learns you sent me away without bothering to check."

That was stretching the truth, because Rafiq might well refuse to see her. Even if he did agree to speak to her, he would certainly not be pleased to find her here in Dhahara.

But the bank official wasn't to know that.

Tiffany waited, arms folded across a stomach that was still behaving in the most peculiar fashion, as it fluttered and tumbled over.

He picked up a telephone and spoke in Arabic. When he'd finished, his expression had changed. "The sheikh will see you."

The sheikh?

Oh, my. This time her stomach turned a full somersault. "Sheikh?" she spluttered. "I thought he was—" she searched a mind gone suddenly blank for the impressive title on his business card "—the president of the Royal Bank of Dhahara."

The bank official gave her a peculiar look. "The royal family owns the bank."

"What does that have to do with Rafiq?"

He blinked at her casual use of his name, and then replied, "The sheikh is part of the royal family."

Before she could faintly repeat "royal family," the elevator doors to the left of the marble reception counter slid open, and Rafiq himself stepped out.

His face was haughtier than she remembered, his eyes darker, his cheekbones more aristocratic. Sheikh? Royal family? He certainly looked every inch the part in a dark suit with a conservative white shirt that even in this sweltering heat appeared crisp and fresh. Yet his head was uncovered, and his hair gleamed like a black hawk's wing. After all the soul-searching it had taken to bring her here, now that she faced him she couldn't think of a word to say.

So she settled for the most inane.

"Hi."

"Tiffany."

The sphinxlike gaze revealed no surprise. He'd told

her he never wanted to see her again. *Ever.* Now she stood before him, shifting from one foot to the other. The displeasure she'd expected was absent. Typically, he showed no emotion at all. The wall of stony reserve was as high as ever.

He bowed his head. "Please, come with me."

If it hadn't been for one never-to-be-forgotten night in Hong Kong, she'd never have known that his reserve could be breached.

That night...

The memory of the catastrophic extremes, heaven and hell, pleasure and shame, still had the power to make her shudder.

Tiffany had been sure nothing would make her contact him again. Nothing. But she'd been so wrong. She pressed her hand to her belly.

Her baby...

He ushered her into the elevator. Unexpectedly, the elevator dropped instead of rising. Her stomach rolled wildly. Tiffany gritted her teeth. Seconds later the doors opened to reveal a well-lit parking level where a black Mercedes-Benz idled, waiting. Rafiq strode forward and opened the rear door.

She hesitated. "Where—?"

His dark gaze was hooded. "There is no privacy here."

He was ashamed of her.

Despite a tinge of apprehension Tiffany swallowed her protests and, straightening her spine, stepped past him and slid into the leather backseat.

She'd come to Dhahara because of her baby. Not for herself. Not for Rafiq. For their unborn child.

She couldn't afford to let fear dominate her.

For her daughter she had put aside her desire never

to encounter Rafiq again. For the baby's sake, she would keep her relationship with Rafiq cordial. Unemotional. Her daughter deserved the right to know her father. Nor could she allow herself to indulge in wild notions that he might kidnap her child, hide her away.

He was a businessman. He'd told her he'd been educated in England and the United States. He headed a large bank. Even it if was a position he'd gotten through nepotism, neither he—nor his royal family—could afford the kind of international outcry that would come from taking her baby from her. He was a single man—or at least she hoped he was—what would he do with a baby?

The silence was oppressive. Fifteen minutes later the Mercedes came to a smooth stop, and the rear doors opened. Rafiq's hand closed around her elbow—to escort her or ensure she didn't escape? Tiffany wasn't sure. As he hurried her up a flight of stairs, she caught a glimpse of two guards in red berets standing in front of stone pillars that flanked a vast wooden front door. Then the door swung inward and they were inside a vaulted entrance hall.

She gazed around, wide-eyed. Despite the mansions she'd seen, this dwelling took luxury to new heights. "Where are we?"

"This is my home."

A hasty glance revealed magnificent dark wooden floors covered in Persian rugs, original art hanging on deep blue walls. Refusing to be impressed, Tiffany focused her attention on Rafiq. "Is there somewhere we can talk?"

His lips quirked, and something devilish gleamed in his eyes. "Talk? Our best communication is done in other ways. I thought that must be why you are here."

Damn him for the reminder.

Tiffany compressed her lips. "I need to talk to you."

"Whenever we talk, it seems to cost me money." The humor had vanished, and he gave her a brooding look.

His words only underscored what she already knew: he thought her the worst kind of woman. What would he say when he discovered she was pregnant with his child? A frisson of alarm chilled her.

"I haven't come all this way for money, Rafiq."

"I'm very relieved to hear that."

He strode down a hall hung with richly woven tapestries that held the patina of age. Tiffany resisted the urge to slow and inspect them.

"But for the moment I will reserve judgment," he was saying. "I will be more convinced of that once I have heard what you have to say to me."

He didn't believe her. He thought this was about money.

"Hey, I sent you a check for what you gave me," she protested. She hadn't wanted to be in his debt.

"Sure you did."

"I sent it last week. Maybe it's still in the mail." She'd meant to send it earlier. Discovering she was pregnant had wiped all other thoughts out of her head. But now she was seriously starting to wish that she had called...not come all this way to give him the news about his impending fatherhood.

Yet it had seemed the right thing to do. She'd wanted to break the news in person, not over the phone separated by thousands of miles, unable to register the nuances of his expression. And certainly not by an e-mail that might go astray.

This was too important. Her child's whole life, her baby's relationship with her father, would be determined by the course of this conversation.

And she wasn't about to let Rafiq Al Dhahara cause

her to regret the decision she'd made to come here to tell him.

Pushing open a door, he gestured for her to precede him. Tiffany entered a book-lined room that was clearly a man's domain. *His* domain. Before her nerve could give out, she drew a deep breath and spun to face him.

"I'm pregnant," she announced.

Rafiq went very still, and his eyes narrowed to dark cracks that revealed nothing.

All at once the dangerous man she'd seen glimpses of in Hong Kong, the man she'd known lurked under the polite, charming veneer, surfaced.

"We used a condom," he said, softly.

She spread her hands helplessly. "It must've been faulty."

"Did you know it was faulty?"

"What's that supposed to mean?"

"Did you tamper with it?"

"How?" Outrage filled the question. "It was sealed!"

"Nothing a pinprick couldn't have taken care of."

"You're sick."

His mouth tightened. "Be careful how you talk to me."

Tiffany's front teeth worried at her bottom lip. His gaze flickered to her mouth, before returning to clash with hers. "How much do you want?"

"What?"

She stared at him, not sure she'd heard right. His eyes were fixed on her, his mouth tight. No sign of softness in the features that were so difficult to read. He'd pay money so that he'd never have to see his child again?

What kind of man did that?

Tiffany turned away, defeated. At least she would always carry the knowledge in her heart that she'd tried. And if her daughter one day wanted to know who her father was, she'd tell her. Rafiq might be a sheikh. He might be desert royalty. But he would be the loser...he'd have forfeited the chance to know his child.

But he'd been given the choice.

"I've been a fool."

Tiffany spun back and focused on him. He'd positioned himself behind an antique desk. One hand was raking through his hair. Straight and dark, it shone like silk under the overhead lights.

Unable to bear to look at him, she closed her eyes.

He'd been a fool? What did that make her?

"And I have absolutely no excuse. I even know how the scam works. Start with small amounts, get the idiot hooked and then, when he can't back out, increase the amount."

Her mouth fell open as she absorbed what he was saying. "You honestly think I'd travel *here* to blackmail you?" Her hand closed protectively over her belly. "That I'd blackmail the father of my child?"

From beyond the barrier of the desk, his glance fell to her still-flat stomach, and then lifted to meet her eyes. Black. Implacable. Furious. Tiffany felt the searing heat of his contempt. "Enough. Don't expect me to believe there is a child."

Rafiq thought—

She shook her head to clear it. "You really do think I came all this way to blackmail you."

He arched a brow. "Didn't you?"

"No!"

"Previous experience makes that impossible for me to believe."

What was the point of arguing that she hadn't wanted to blackmail him in the past, either? Tiffany placed her fingertips to her pounding temples. God, why had she allowed her conviction that she was doing the right thing to persuade her to come? He didn't care about the child. All he cared about was protecting himself.

There was nothing here for her daughter…nothing worth fighting for.

She started to back away.

"Where are you going?"

"To my hotel. I'm pregnant. It was a long flight. I'm tired. My feet ache. I need a shower and a sleep." She listed the reasons in a flat, dead tone.

He was around the desk before she could move and caught up to her with two long strides. Planting himself in front of her, he folded his arms across his chest. "You will stay here."

Tiffany shook her head. "I can't stay here." He was a man—an unmarried man. It would not be sanctioned. "Besides, my luggage is already at the hotel."

His jaw had set. "I am not letting you stay in the city alone. I want you where I can watch you. Give me the name of the hotel and I will have your luggage sent here."

"I'd be your prisoner."

"Not a prisoner," he corrected, "my guest."

"It's hardly appropriate for me to stay here, even I know—"

Holding up a hand, he stopped her mid-sentence. "My aunt Lily will come stay. The widow of my father's brother, and the perfect chaperone. Zara, her daughter, is away studying at present, and Aunt Lily is missing her. She's Australian, so you should get along well. But don't think you can wind her around your little finger. I will be there all the time you are together. Rest tonight, and I will escort you back to the airport myself tomorrow."

Taking in his hard face, Tiffany made herself straighten. She'd come all this way, and he didn't even believe she was pregnant. Right now she was too weary to argue further but she'd be damned if she'd let him see that. He'd only interpret it as weakness. Tomorrow she'd be ready to fight again.

At least she'd have a chance to meet a part of his family, his aunt. For her daughter's future relationship with her father, Tiffany knew she would do her best to get along with the woman.

Before he took her by the scruff of her neck and threw her out of his country.

Five

Tiffany hadn't been lying about being weary, Rafiq saw that evening. Seated across from him at the dinner table, alongside his aunt Lily, who was clearly bursting with curiosity about her presence in his home, Tiffany barely picked at her food.

There were shadows beneath her eyes. Pale purple hollows that gave her a heart-wrenching fragility that tugged at him—even though he refused to put a name to the emotion.

The array of dishes at her elbow remained untouched. The succulent pieces of skewered lamb. The breads baked with great care in his kitchens. The char-roasted vegetables on earthenware platters. Even her wineglass remained full. Something of the fine spread should have tempted her. But nothing had.

Finally, his aunt could clearly contain herself no longer. "My daughter is at university in Los Angeles. Did you meet Rafiq when he studied abroad?"

Rafiq answered before she could reply. "Tiffany and I are…business acquaintances. She's been traveling—and decided to visit." It didn't satisfy his aunt's curiosity but she wouldn't ask again.

"You look tired, dear."

"I am." Tiffany gave Lily a smile. "I can't wait to go to bed."

"After dinner I'll show you where the women's quarters are."

"Thank you."

The subdued note in her voice made Rafiq want to confront the turmoil that had been whirling around inside his head. He'd been rough on her earlier. Even his aunt could see that her travels had worn her out.

A trickle of shame seeped through Rafiq, then he forced it ruthlessly aside. What else was he supposed to have done? Accepted the lie that she was pregnant? Paid through the nose for the privilege of silencing her new blackmail attempt?

Never.

He'd taken the only course of action open to him: he'd brought her here, away from the bank, away from any possible contact with his father, brothers and staff to learn what she wanted.

Pregnant? Hah! He would not let her get away with such a ruse. Now she was confined to his home. And he would make sure she wasn't left alone with his aunt. He made a mental note to assign one of the maids to keep the women company. His aunt would never gossip in front of the servants.

Tomorrow she would leave. He'd escort her to the airport himself. He certainly wouldn't allow himself any regrets. Tiffany was not the stranded innocent she'd once almost managed to con him into believing she was. He'd already allowed her to squeeze him for money once.

By foolishly possessing her, taking her under a starlit sky, he'd made a fatal mistake. One that she would milk for the rest of her life—if he let her.

Rafiq had no intention of becoming trapped in the prison she'd created with her soft touches and sweet, drugging kisses.

He became aware that Tiffany was talking to his aunt. He tensed, and started to pay attention.

"You must miss your daughter," Tiffany was saying.

Lily nodded. "But I'll be joining her when the holidays come. She wanted a little time to find her feet."

"How lucky for her that you respect her need for independence."

"I still worry about her. She had a bad romantic experience a while back."

That was enough! He wasn't having this woman interrogating his family, discovering pains better left hidden.

"Wine?" Rafiq brusquely offered Tiffany.

She shook her head, "No, thanks." And focused on his aunt. "Do you have any other children?"

"No, only Zara."

"I'm an only child, too."

"Oh, what a pity Zara wasn't here for you to meet. You would've gotten along like a house on fire."

Rafiq narrowed his gaze. If Tiffany even thought she might threaten his family's well-being she would learn how very ruthless he could be.

"I would've liked that."

She sounded so sincere. His aunt was glowing with delight. Lily put a hand on his arm, "I'm sure your father and brothers would like to meet Tiffany."

"I'd like that but—"

His killing glare interrupted the woman who had caused all this trouble. "Tiffany will not be staying for very long," he said with a snap of his teeth.

Aunt Lily looked crestfallen. "What a pity."

Rafiq wished savagely that he'd been less respectful of Tiffany's modesty. He should've known better than to introduce her to any member of his family.

"She'll be leaving us tomorrow."

The bedchamber Lily and the little plump maid called Mina showed Tiffany into was rich and luxurious. Filmy gold drapes surrounded a high bed covered by white linen while beautiful handwoven rugs covered the intricately patterned wooden floors. On the opposite walls, shutters were flung back to reveal a view of a courtyard containing a pool surrounded by padded loungers. Water trickled over a tiered fountain on the far side of the pool, the soothing sound adding to the welcome.

It felt as if she'd been transported into another, far more exotic, world.

Alone, Tiffany stripped off her crumpled clothes and pulled on a nightie. She felt dazed and disoriented and just a little bit queasy. Jet lag was setting in with vengeance.

Through an open door, she caught a glimpse of an immense tub with leaping dolphins—dolphins!—for faucets before weariness sank like a cloud around her. She padded through to the large bathroom to brush her teeth before heading for the bedchamber and clambering between the soft sheets where sleep claimed her.

The next thing she knew she was being wakened by the loud sound of knocking. Seconds later the door crashed open.

Tiffany sat up, dragging the covers up to her chin, thoroughly startled at being yanked from deep sleep.

"What do you want?" she demanded of the man looming in the doorway.

"Neither of the maids could awaken you." Whatever had glittered in Rafiq's eyes when the door first opened had already subsided.

"I was tired," she said defensively. "I told you that last night."

"It's late." He glanced at his watch. "Eleven o'clock. I thought you might've run out—" He broke off.

Eleven o'clock was all she heard. "It can't be that late."

He strode closer, brandishing the square face of his Cartier timepiece in her direction. "Look."

The wrist beneath the leather strap was tanned, a mix of sinew and muscle. Oh, God, surely she wasn't being drawn back under his thrall?

"I believe you," she said hastily, her grip tightening on the bedcovers as she pulled them up to her chin so that no bare flesh was visible. Her stomach had started its now-familiar morning lurching routine.

"Will you please *go?*"

And then it was too late. Tiffany bolted from the bed and into the adjoining bathroom, where she was miserably and ignominiously sick.

When she finally raised her head, it was—horror of horrors—to find Rafiq beside her, holding out a white facecloth. She took it and wiped it over her face, appreciating the cool wetness.

"Thanks," she mumbled.

"You look terrible."

This time her "Thanks" held no gratitude.

"I don't like this. I'm going to call a doctor." He was already moving away with that sleek, predatory stride.

"Don't," Tiffany said.

He halted just short of the bathroom door.

"There's nothing wrong with me." She gave him a grim smile.

"Maybe it was something you ate." Two long paces had him at her side. "You may need an antibiotic."

"No antibiotic!" Nothing was going to harm her baby. "I promise you this is a perfectly normal part of being pregnant."

His hands closed around her shoulders. "Oh, don't try that tall tale again."

"It's the truth. I can't help that you're too dumb to see what's right in front of your nose." She poked a finger at his chest, but to her dismay he did not back away. Instead she became conscious of his muscled body beneath the crisply ironed business shirt. A body she'd touched all over the night they had been together...

She withdrew her finger as though it had been burned.

"I'm not dumb," he growled.

Right. "And I'm not pregnant," she countered.

"I *knew* you were faking it."

The triumph in his voice made her see red. "Oh, for heaven's sake!"

Tiffany broke out of his grasp and, slipping past him, headed for the bedroom. Grabbing her purse off the dressing table she upended it onto the bed and scrabbled through the displaced contents. Snatching up a black-and-white image in a small frame she spun around to wave it in front of his nose.

"Look at this."

"What is it?"

Couldn't he see? He had to be blind…as well as obtuse.

"A photo of your daughter."

"A photo of my daughter?" For once that air of composure had deserted him. "I don't have a daughter."

She pushed the picture into his hands. "It's an image from a scan. A scan of my baby—" *their baby* "—taken last week. See? There's her head, her hipbone, her arms. That's your daughter you're holding."

His expression changed. When he finally raised his head, his eyes were glazed with shock.

"You really *are* pregnant."

Six

"No, I'm only faking it. Remember?"

Rafiq glared at Tiffany, unamused by the flippant retort—and the sharp edge he detected beneath it. He tightened his grip on the photo, conscious of a sense that his world was shifting.

"So how do you know it's a girl? Can they tell?"

She stared down her nose at him in a way that made him want to kiss her, or throttle her. Then she said, "My intuition tells me she is."

Her intuition? The ridiculous reply brought him back to reality, and he shut down the string of questions that he'd been about to ask. Rafiq almost snorted in disgust at how readily he'd crumbled. She was softening him up—and worse, it was working.

"You don't think I'm going to fall for this?" He shoved the picture back at her. "This could be any man's baby."

Her fingers closed around the small framed image with

great care. She slid it into the bag and walked back to the dressing table where she set the bag down. Her back to him, she said, "Doctors will be able to estimate the time of conception close enough to that night—"

"They won't be able to pinpoint exactly. The baby could've been conceived anytime around then." He paused as she wheeled around to face him. "It doesn't mean it is *my* child." He sneered. "I hardly met you under the most pristine conditions."

The gold flecks in those velvet eyes grew dull. "I told you that it was my first night at Le Club."

"I don't know you at all." He shrugged. "Even if it was the truth, who knows what's behind it?"

Tiffany flushed, and the gold in her tawny eyes had brightened to an accusatory flame. She looked spirited, alive, and Rafiq fisted his hands at his sides to stop himself from reaching for her. Instead he said, "I want to have DNA tests done before I pay a dollar."

"Have I demanded even one dollar from you since I got here?" she asked, her eyes blazing with what he realized in surprise was rage. Glorious, incandescent rage that had him blinking in admiration.

"I'm sure you intend to demand far more than that."

"There's no trust in you, is there?"

"Not a great deal," he said honestly. "When you grow up as wealthy as I have there's always someone with a new angle. A new scam."

"Everyone wants something from you?"

He shrugged. "I'm used to it."

There was a perturbing perception in her gaze. As if she understood exactly how he felt. And sympathized. But she couldn't. He'd found her in the backstreets of Hong Kong—hardly the place for someone who could have any insight into his world.

Crossing to the bedroom door that he'd left wide open, he paused. "I'll arrange for the DNA tests to be done as soon as possible." That would give him the answer he wanted and put an end to this farce.

"But you were going to take me to the airport."

Rafiq's gaze narrowed. Tiffany looked surprisingly agitated. "You're not staying in Dhahara long. You'll be on the first plane out once I have confirmation that your child is not mine. You're not going to hold that threat over my head for the rest of my life."

Once a week Rafiq met his brother Khalid for breakfast in one of Dhahara's seven-star hotels. As the two men were heavily invested in the political and economic well-being of the desert kingdom, talk was usually lively. But Rafiq was too abstracted by the rapidly approaching appointment for his and Tiffany's DNA tests that he'd arranged after their argument yesterday.

Before he could temper it, he found himself asking, "Khalid, have you ever thought what might happen if you get a woman who is not on father's list pregnant?"

His brother's mouth fell open in surprise. He looked around and lowered his voice. "I take great care not to get a woman pregnant."

So did Rafiq. It hadn't helped. He'd been a fool. "But what if you did," he pressed, pushing his empty plate away. "What would you do?"

Khalid looked disconcerted. "I don't know. One thing is for sure, an abortion would be out of the question. I suppose it would depend on the situation. The woman in question would have to be suitable for me to consider marrying her."

Suitable. Just thinking of the night he'd met Tiffany

made Rafiq squirm. She couldn't have been more totally *un*suitable if he'd scoured the entire earth. "That is true."

And there lay his problem.

"Of course," continued his brother, then pausing as a white-garbed waiter filled their cups with black, fragrant coffee and waiting until he'd left, "there has never been an illegitimate heir in our family. That's something else to consider. I suppose even an unsuitable marriage would be better than that," mused Khalid. "Later I could always find a second, more suitable wife who would perform the state duties."

Rafiq had never considered marriage to Tiffany an option. As he sipped his coffee, another thought occurred to him. "If there's a marriage, then there's divorce, too."

Khalid frowned. "As a last resort. It's never popular for a ruler to divorce a consort."

But, even though his brother didn't know it, they weren't talking about Khalid. They were talking about *his* situation. And Rafiq was not heir to the throne. It wouldn't attract the same degree of censure.

Marriage to legitimize the child followed by divorce might work…*if* the child turned out to be his.

Rafiq set his cup down and flicked back a starched cuff to glance at his Cartier watch. Time to go. Tiffany would be waiting for him to collect her from his residence. "It's later than I thought. I have an appointment—I must go."

"If I divorced her, I'd make sure the child—if it was a boy—was well out of her control," said Khalid thoughtfully.

Arrested, Rafiq turned to gaze at his brother. *Of course.* "Thank you."

While Khalid shook his head in bemusement, Rafiq strode across the dining hall with a light heart. Sometimes the solution to a seemingly insurmountable problem was far simpler than a man dreamed.

The doctor's rooms were surprisingly modern. A glass desk paired with crisp-white walls hung with framed sketches of flowers gave the room a contemporary feel. Nothing like the heavy dark furniture Tiffany had expected. Even more astonishing was the fact that the doctor was female. Although on second thought, that shouldn't have surprised her. No doubt many Dhaharan men preferred their wives to be examined by a woman doctor.

Yet it was the doctor's words that had caused the tension that presently gripped Tiffany. Shaking her head until her hair whipped about her face, she turned to Rafiq and said defiantly, "I'm not agreeing to that."

Rafiq gave Dr. Farouk a charming smile. "Excuse us for a moment, please."

The doctor rose to her feet. "Of course, Your Highness. I'll be next door when you need me."

A few words and a smile from him, and the doctor simply obeyed? Vacating her own office? Tiffany was taken aback at the display of his power.

No wonder Rafiq believed he could get whatever he wanted.

"I'm not signing the consent for surgery." Tiffany gestured to the paper that lay on the desk.

Rafiq raked a hand through his hair, rumpling the sleek perfection. "I was prepared to undergo the indignity of a test—why can't you be more cooperative?"

"A swab taken from your inner cheek?" She snorted. "That's nothing. If it was just a simple DNA test, I wouldn't have a problem. But you heard the doctor. Getting the baby's DNA is not going to be that easy."

The doctor had laid the options out for them. Getting the baby's DNA would require a surgical procedure. Because Tiffany was only ten weeks pregnant, amniocentesis could not be performed. Instead, a thin needle, guided by ultrasound, would pass through her cervix to retrieve little fingers of tissue from the wall of the uterus beyond. Like her baby, the tissue, which the doctor had called chorionic villi, originated from the egg that Rafiq's sperm had fertilized.

"You're not going to change my mind," she warned him.

"Be reasonable—"

"Reasonable? You heard the doctor. The procedure holds risks to my baby."

He waved a hand. "Very slim percentages."

"Miscarriage is not a percentage I'm prepared to risk."

Rafiq's eyebrows lowered to form a thick line over his eyes, making him look fierce and formidable. "How else am I supposed to find out whether the baby is mine?"

She glared at him, determined not to let him know that her heart was knocking against her ribs. "You're prepared to risk this life growing within me, so that you can evade the responsibility of fatherhood?"

"That's not true—"

"Of course it's true." She averted her gaze. "You could easily wait until the baby is born, *then* have the necessary tests done. But no, that doesn't suit the great sheikh. So you want to risk my baby's life to get the answer you're expecting. Well, I'm not going to let that happen!"

"You're hardly in a position to dictate terms," he breathed from barely an inch away.

"I'm in the best position," she fired back. "I'm not signing that consent form."

"Then you'll lose any chance of a quick cash settlement."

"I don't need your monetary support. I just wanted you to know…" Her voice trailed away.

How to explain? Her childhood had been less than perfect, disrupted by her father's affairs. Rafiq might've been distant, but he'd struck her as honorable. She'd wanted her daughter to have a father. Resting her fingertips on her stomach, Tiffany said softly, "One day this baby will want to know who her father is—and I would never keep that from her."

"Nor would I. This is not an attempt to evade responsibility."

It appeared her accusation had irked him.

He leaned toward her. "Tiffany, understand this, as long as a child is mine, I will take care of it."

"It?" His use of the derogatory term revealed the disparity between them. "No baby of mine could ever be an 'it.' She's a person. Infinitely precious."

"That's why you have no choice but to take this test. So that I can give the child the best if it is mine." But he was looking less certain than he had only minutes ago.

"You could take my word," she snapped, but already Rafiq was shaking his head, his eyes beginning to glitter with what she recognized as annoyance. She held her ground. This was not an issue she was prepared to negotiate. "Then you have no choice but to wait until the baby is born."

Rafiq got to his feet and started to pace. "Neither of those are options I'm prepared to accept. I want hard evidence that your child is not mine—so I can escort you out of the country."

"I'm not risking a miscarriage. You can't force me to

undergo this procedure," she stated, and hoped like hell she was right. Nor could he make her stay.

Or could he? This was his domain, after all. When she'd come to Dhahara she hadn't known the extent of his power…that he was the king's son, a royal sheikh. And when she'd discovered that, she'd convinced herself that he wouldn't be interested in bringing up the child.

But now she was starting to get cold feet. His family made the laws in this country. Rafiq could do what he wanted to her—with her—and get away with it. Could he force her to have surgery against her will? Would he keep her in Dhahara if she wanted to leave?

Before her first flutterings of fear could develop into full-fledged panic, Rafiq had turned to face her. He stood still and erect.

Tiffany took in the magnificence of the man. The harsh hawk-like features. His dark suit that had to be handmade. The shine of his shoes. He could've stepped out of a magazine spread. Yet she didn't like what he was trying to persuade her to do.

"Look," she said, tempering her voice, "I told you my passport was stolen—you didn't believe me. Yet it was true."

"You blackmailed me."

"That's the interpretation you put on it." She pushed the fringe of her bangs out her eyes. "I bet you never thought you'd see the cash again. But I've paid you back in full. Now I'm pregnant—and you think that's a scam, too. Yet here we are in the doctor's office and it's true."

"How convenient."

She ignored his sarcasm and continued, "As much as you tell yourself I slept with the whole of Hong Kong, you must know that it's possible that you're the father of my child—"

Nothing she said appeared to be denting that shell. His eyes were still hard with suspicion. "We used a condom."

"And, of course, you'd like to put your faith in the percentages that say overwhelmingly that they're fail-safe?" She shook her head. "Because it suits you. Well, not this time. Something went wrong. Just like something could go wrong when the doctor takes the chorionic villi sample."

A frisson of unease slithered through her. She moved from one foot to the other under his stare. The fact that he was selfish enough to be prepared to jeopardize their daughter, a living being, had made her realize that maybe he wasn't the kind of father she wanted for her baby. How could she even contemplate occasionally leaving her daughter in his solo care?

The sooner she—and her unborn baby—left this country, the better for them both.

He didn't believe the baby was his, so he had no reason to stop her. The decision made, the tension that had been building within her started to ease.

"I'll leave Dhahara now. Today, on the first flight I can get. Once the baby is born, taking a sample from inside her cheek will be a breeze, compared to this invasive procedure. The solution is simple. Let's defer this discussion until then."

But instead of looking happy at the thought, he frowned. "Where would you go?"

His concern must stem for the prospect of the scandal he would face once it became known he'd fathered her unborn child. She knew all about gossip and scandal—it had been part of her world for too long. The best way to deal with it was to lie low.

"I can go to my parents' home in New Zealand." She

hesitated, contemplating telling him more about her parents, then decided it wasn't relevant, not now. She didn't even know where her father was. Thinking about her parents made her realize that soon there would be no home in Auckland. Her mother needed the money that the sale of the house would bring. "Although my mother will probably need to sell up the house in Auckland."

"Tiffany—"

She didn't need his pity. She rushed on. "There's a quiet seaside village I used to visit as a child." Her vision blurred at the memory of those carefree days. Everything had been so simple then. So happy. That was what she wanted for her child. "I'll go there."

He didn't look any happier. "I thought you wanted to meet my family. At least, that's what you had my aunt believing."

"I did. I mean, I do," Tiffany hastily amended her reply. "They're my daughter's family, too. But you've made it clear you can't wait to get rid of me. Why the sudden about-face?"

Tension quivered through him. "So why leave now? After coming all this way? What if it *is* my baby?"

Her daughter didn't deserve a father who would risk her very existence to evade paternity. No father would be better than that. She'd make up for her baby's lack of a father. She'd do everything in her power to be the best parent her daughter could have.

Rafiq was waiting for her response. She shrugged. "Do you care?"

Anger ignited in the back of his dark eyes, giving them a feral depth. "Yes. I care."

Sensing she'd miscalculated, she said quickly, "Well, after the baby is born, and once the tests have been done and your paternity confirmed, then you can decide whether you want a part in her life."

"You can bet your life on it I will."

Her instinct to flee wavered. Just as she'd decided he didn't want this baby, he ruined it by getting all passionate and showing her a glimpse of caring.

"My child will not be born illegitimate," he whispered. "There's never been an illegitimate heir born in my family." His carved features revealed no emotion. "That's why I need to know if the child is mine."

The unease deepened to panic. He didn't care about the baby at all. Only about legalities.

"It doesn't matter that the baby will be illegitimate. *She* will be loved." Tiffany gave *she* a not-so-subtle emphasis. "I'd never subject her to a marriage between parents who care nothing for each other." Her own parents had been wildly in love when they'd gotten married. Yet their marriage had become a battleground. Her father had been unable to resist other women, had helped himself to them like a child to candy.

When she married she would choose carefully. A nice, ordinary family man.

"It matters." His fist closed around her wrist.

Tiffany shuddered under the pressure of his fingers. "Well, this appointment is over. I'm not having this test done now, so this whole discussion is irrelevant until the baby is born."

In the meantime she was going to get her baby out of this country, out from under his control. She pulled her hand free of his and rose to her feet.

"Then I'm going to have to take your word that it's my baby." His features were stern as gazed up at her from where he sat, master of all he surveyed, in the doctor's office. "If you are lying to me, you will regret it."

"I'm not lying—"

He cut across her heated denial. "There's no option but for us to get married in the meantime."

"Get married?"

Tiffany was staring at him as if he'd taken leave of his senses.

Perhaps he had. Rafiq suppressed the urge to smile grimly at her wide-eyed shock. Did she not grasp the honor he'd offered her? But what choice did he have? He would use every advantage offered by his country's laws if the baby proved to be his own—he would marry her, divorce her and keep the baby as his own.

"I'm not marrying *you*."

She made it sound as if he were a particularly offensive variety of the male sex. As she pushed past him, he snagged her fingers between his, and growled, "Think of it as your lucky day. Lots of women want to marry me."

Tiffany opened her mouth, shut it and made a peculiar sound.

Rafiq leaned closer until her tantalizing fragrance enveloped him. "You wouldn't be thinking of claiming that you're so different from all those women, would you, Tiffany?"

The brief flash of awareness in her eyes turned quickly to something darker. He could see she remembered quite clearly what had happened the last time she'd vowed she was so different from the women who considered him charming. In fact, his determination to prove conclusively that she *did* find him charming was what had led to this present blackmail attempt of hers.

That realization alone should've leashed the reckless impulse to provoke her. But it didn't. Instead he remembered what she'd tasted like...the softness of her skin beneath his fingers…and every detail of what had followed on that hot, balmy night.

She was irresistible.

With a silent curse he realized he wanted to kiss her again. "Tiffany…"

He got to his feet and placed his hands on her shoulders, felt the shudder that quaked through her.

She didn't pull away. So he drew her closer. Breathed in the soft seductive scent of her. Filled his senses with her sweetness until he could wait no more.

Kissing Tiffany was like rediscovering a secret, shaded oasis filled with fragrant gardenias and leafy green trees. He hadn't even known that he'd missed her as intensely. Yet now he found himself drowning in her.

His eyes closed, he took his time to rediscover the softness of her mouth. When the kiss ended, the strength of the yearning to claim her mouth once again blindsided him. As he acted on the impulse, she shoved him away.

"Hey." He steadied her as the force of her shove caused her to stumble. "Steady."

She touched a mouth that, to his immense satisfaction, looked ripe and very well kissed.

"I don't want this!"

Rafiq quelled the impulse to prove her passionately wrong. Instead, he arranged his features into an expression of concern. "There's nothing wrong with enjoying kissing one's future spouse."

"No." She shook her head. "That's just it. We're not getting married."

He smiled to mask the impatience that surged. He wanted her. He would have her—once they were married. He'd sate himself then cut her loose. But she need not know that yet.

"Let's not play games, Tiffany. Marriage was the

ultimate prize you hoped to secure by coming here. You say it wasn't about blackmail or money. So that leaves only marriage." His lip curled. "Well, *you've* gotten all you could ever have wanted."

"I don't want to marry you!"

"You came here because you wanted to marry someone else?" Rafiq's mocking retort was met with silence. His gaze narrowed. A lightning-fast glance took in the slender fingers clenched into fists, her wary, defiant eyes.

There was someone else.

A blaze of possessiveness roared through him, the need to stake his claim, to mark her as his, now and forever. He yanked her up against him, tangled his hands in the tumbled waves of hair and captured her mouth roughly with his.

He was aware of the fine tremors that shimmered through her, of the way his thigh fitted between hers and how the cradle of her hips rocked against him. The intoxicating scent and taste of her filled his senses, and her tongue danced with his.

He was aware of everything about her. Only her. The rest of the world receded.

He was so far gone, that he didn't care about control, about leashing it, about the fact that Dr. Farouk might walk back into her office and discover him alone with her, kissing her. There was just Tiffany…and him.

And she was going to marry him.

Only him.

He broke the kiss and set her away from him with shaking hands. "There," he said, making his point. "You can't possibly share what we have with any other man."

"I don't."

Confused, he shook his head. Had he imagined the

expression on her face? No, it had been there. A look of yearning—and it hadn't been for him. He narrowed his gaze in a way that anyone who knew him well recognized. "Where is this fool who allows you to roam the bars of Hong Kong alone, untended? Who leaves you vulnerable to other men?"

"I haven't met him yet."

"What?" Rafiq felt like the world had tipped upside down. "We're arguing over a man who does not even exist?"

"Oh, he does exist." She wore a dreamy expression. "I know he does. Otherwise why was I put on earth? He's out there somewhere. I couldn't believe in love as much as I do, and have it not happen." A shadow passed over her face. "But I can promise you one thing—he's nothing like you. Suspicious. Distrustful. Emotionless."

"So what's he like then?" he scoffed.

Her eyes had gone soft and dewy. "He's ordinary. He's not famous. Or wealthy. He doesn't live in an obscenely ornate home, nor does he have movie-star looks—"

He bowed his head, and said with irony, "Thank you."

"I'm not referring to you," she said crushingly. "I'm trying to explain how ordinary he is. A white picket fence and two-point-four children kind of guy."

"Then what makes him so special?"

"He'll love me," she said simply. "And I'm the most important person in his whole world. In fact, I am his world. There's none of the pomp and circumstance that fills your existence."

The red tide that crashed over him couldn't possibly be jealousy. By Allah, the man did not even exist. Incredulous, he glared at her. Rafiq gazed into her clear, desert-and-sunshine eyes. His chest tightened.

Tiffany was speaking the absolute truth. She didn't want him. She wanted someone else…someone he could never be.

Seven

Tiffany might have won the skirmish about having a DNA test done, but the tension that filled the back of the chauffeur-driven limousine as they left the doctor's office warned her that there were still plenty of battles to come.

Rafiq broke the silence that stretched between them by leaning forward to issue instructions in Arabic through the intercom to the chauffeur.

"Let's walk," Rafiq said abruptly, as the Mercedes-Benz came to a stop and the back doors opened.

Tiffany followed him out and caught her breath at the sight of the park that sprawled in front of them, tall trees shading open green lawns and a forest of roses beyond. "Where is this?"

"These are the botanical gardens that lie between the hospital and the university. They were laid out by one of my ancestors. She loved gardens and roses."

"It's beautiful. So green. So unlike anything I ever expected to find in a desert."

"The unexpected surprise surpasses the expected."

"Is that a proverb?" she asked, and for a moment there was absolute accord, a sense of intimacy between them, as their eyes met and he gave her a slight smile.

"No, it's original. You can claim it if you wish."

The awful tension that had started in the doctor's rooms began to ease. She smiled back at him. "What a wonderfully romantic place."

"Don't hope to find your dream man here." Rafiq's face grew taut. "You may as well accept you're going to marry me."

Biting her lip, Tiffany walked swiftly away from him and considered her options. Marriage to Rafiq would make her parents' marriage look like a picnic at Disneyland by comparison. But the set of his jaw warned Tiffany to tread carefully. He might not believe the child was his, but he feared the slur of illegitimacy. Rafiq had decided to keep the scandal—and her—within his control.

She'd reached the rose gardens. She halted beside a bed of pale pink flowers. Rafiq stopped beside her. "Rafiq, be reasonable—"

"I'm being perfectly reasonable." He tipped his head back, and gave her a particularly arrogant look.

She gave a little laugh of disbelief. "You don't even believe I'm carrying your child." She touched her stomach. "Yet you're prepared to marry me. That's reasonable?"

"You didn't want to do the tests necessary to establish the baby's paternity, and I didn't force you. I'm prepared to take your word that it's my child and marry you, so that the real truth can be determined once the baby is born—as you suggested. How can you possibly accuse me of being unreasonable?"

He wore such a fake-patient expression that Tiffany ground her teeth. How had he managed to twist it all to make her the unreasonable party here?

To temper her rising agitation, Tiffany sucked in a steadying breath and tried to let the soft, warm wind that blew over the rose beds, releasing their sweet scent, soothe her frayed nerves. "All I wanted was to make sure that my daughter had a right to know who her father was. And to find out whether you would be prepared to acknowledge her—if she feels the need to seek you out one day. I had hoped we could visit. When she's older," she added hastily as his brows shot up, "she'll want to know who her father is."

He inclined his head. "Of course. I should've expected this. You came here to have me sign some sort of acknowledgment of paternity. A document that would enable you to claim maintenance, too."

"Coming here was never about money!" Tiffany almost stamped her foot. This was not about his ego. Or hers. It was about their daughter.

He spread his hands. "It no longer matters, Tiffany. Marry me, then as soon as the child is born we can test for paternity. If she is mine, I will support her. It is my duty."

Money. Duty. Those were the reasons a man like Rafiq married. It wasn't the kind of marriage she wanted for herself. Nor had she ever intended to marry a man of his wealth and position. She'd seen the strain a high-profile lifestyle had placed on her parents' marriage—a show-biz union—not a royal wedding, and her father didn't even have the kind of power this man did.

"Marriage between us would be a mistake," she argued desperately.

Rafiq was arrogant—even more arrogant than her

father. Tiffany shivered. Her father had trampled all over her mother's feelings with little respect. Given that the man before her had been treated like a proper prince since the moment he'd been born, she could expect even less from Rafiq.

If she were foolish enough to marry him…

"Why should it be a mistake?" His frown cleared. "We will work on it. All marriages take work."

Tiffany goggled at him, unable to believe what she was hearing. "You're prepared to put *work* into our marriage?" That was more than her father had ever done.

For a moment he hesitated, then he smiled, a charming smile that, despite all her reservations, caused tiny electric quivers to shoot through her. "Of course, I will work at it," he assured her.

So what if she reacted to his smile? She wanted the man. No problems there. Her body adored him. Just as well she wasn't ruled by her senses. "You'll really work at it?"

Rafiq's gaze bored into her. "You don't believe me, do you?"

She shrugged. "I'm sure you have great intentions."

"Why?"

"Why what?"

"Why can't you believe me?"

Okay, so maybe she'd been wrong. Her gaze slid away from his. Maybe marriage to him would work for their child. But it was a big decision to make—probably the biggest decision of her life. A group of students dressed in denim and some in traditional dress sauntered past them, chatting and laughing.

Tiffany drew a deep breath, weighing up whether to confide in Rafiq what a dreadful mess her parents' marriage had been, then dismissed the impulse. Why would Rafiq care?

When she turned her attention back to him, it was to find that he'd moved. He stood before her now, blocking her way, formidable and intimidating.

"I'm prepared to marry you, Tiffany. What have you got to lose?"

He said it as though she should be grateful for his largesse. It irked her that he thought she'd be such a pushover. "I'm not quite the nobody you think. My father is Taylor Smith."

He didn't react to the name. Finally he shook his head. "Should I know him?"

"In some circles he's very well-known. He's a film director."

"A film director." He raised an eyebrow. "What kind of film director?"

"He doesn't make skin flicks, in case that's what you're thinking." His films might be respectable, but her father's private life was a different story. The scandals that followed him would not meet the approval of someone as upstanding as Rafiq. "He's quite successful. He directed *Legacy*." Tiffany named a film that had taken the world by storm a couple of years ago. Recognition lit Rafiq's eyes.

"I watched that movie on the jet—it was about two years ago."

"That must've been when it first came out." His casual reference to flying by jet made Tiffany realize that while her father might travel by jet as part of his work, this man owned one. Help, his family probably owned a fleet of Lear jets!

"If your father is wealthy and successful, why were you working in Le Club?" he was asking.

Tiffany braced herself to hold his gaze. "After my purse was stolen, I called home. I discovered my father had left my mother for another woman the day before I met you in Hong Kong."

A host of unidentifiable emotions flickered over his face. "That would've been a shock."

"It was," she agreed, reaching blindly past him to touch a full, pink bloom, to give herself something to do. The velvet smoothness of the petals under her fingertips steadied her as she stroked them. "But there was nothing I could do. I could hardly add to my mother's stress at the time by telling her about the fix I was in—or asking her for money she didn't have. And my father was nowhere to be found. Nor could I have his business manager arrange it—because that was who he chose to run off with."

"So that's why—" He broke off.

"That's why what?" she prompted, glancing up at him.

The bitter chocolate of his eyes had turned black. "You had no one you could ask for money."

"I would've gotten out of there."

"By continuing to work at Le Club…by selling your body?" He looked suddenly, murderously angry.

"No, I would never do that!"

"Okay, I shouldn't have implied that you would. But now I understand why you are so reluctant to marry me."

"What do you mean?"

"You don't trust any man not to let you down."

Tiffany forced herself not to flinch. "That's ridiculous! You expected me to leap on your proposal? To marry you without thinking it through?" At his glowering expression, she said, "Oh, you did! I can see it on your face. Rafiq, how arrogant!"

Dark brows lowered over his eyes. "But when you think it through, you'll realize that it's the best option you have open to you." Rafiq reached forward and plucked one perfect, pale pink bloom then handed it to her. "Think of the child. This way the baby starts its life with both its parents."

Clutching the stem, Tiffany bent her head and inhaled the fragrance of the flower.

Yes. Rafiq was right. She had to think about her baby. Not about herself, what she wanted, but what would be best for her baby. She'd wanted to give her daughter the chance to have a meaningful relationship with her father, unbroken by the estrangement of living in separate countries she'd had with her father growing up.

Rafiq was offering that.

Raising her head, Tiffany said, "I need time to marshal my thoughts. Let me think about your proposal."

"I have a function tonight. I can afford to give you one night." He gave her a slow, incredibly sexy smile that caused her heart to roll over. "But be warned, I will demolish every one of your objections."

The Mercedes swept out of the forecourt of his home, returning Rafiq to the bank for the meetings that lay ahead for the rest of the day. Uncharacteristically, instead of pulling out his laptop and busying himself with the necessary preparation, he leaned back against the butter-soft leather headrest and stared out the window.

Tiffany came from a family that had wealth—and, possibly connections. It should've delighted him. It certainly made it easier to present her to his father as his prospective bride. The king would relish the red-carpet connection. Instead Rafiq felt as though someone had claimed a private treasure, one that he'd prided himself on discovering and appreciating when no one else did, and exposed it to the world.

Of course, the revelation meant that Tiffany didn't need

his resources, his wealth—as he'd mistakenly believed. She had no need to marry him, except for the baby's sake. She didn't even particularly want to marry him....

It was a startling realization. And it changed everything. Because he wanted her, had no intention of letting her go—at least not yet, and certainly not because of some fairy-tale notion of love that she desired.

They had so much more. She'd woken a fire, a depth of passion, that he'd never suspected existed within himself. He intended to stoke that fire, feed the flames and experience the full blast of the heat.

Tiffany *would* marry him.

The extent of his determination astonished him. What had happened to the part of him that withdrew when his paramours wanted a commitment and his father demanded a wedding date be set? Where had the voice of reason gone that anxiously warned him to take a step back before he got boxed in and caged for life?

Perhaps it was silent because this time he had an escape hatch. He stared unseeingly at the streetscape, not noticing the busy market as the Mercedes cruised past. Tiffany had even sensed it when she'd expressed her doubts about his promise to work on their marriage. The solution that had seemed so crystal clear after his discussion with Khalid was starting to become murky.

Because of this desire she roused in him.

Rafiq tried to tell himself this want wouldn't last. By the time the baby was born, the desire would be spent. Then he would do as he'd intended. *If* the DNA tests proved the baby was a member of their family, he would keep the baby—and divorce Tiffany. He'd have done his duty. The baby would be legitimate. In terms of the marriage contracts, he'd settle a fair sum of money on Tiffany.

He'd support his child. Make sure it—he, Rafiq

amended—went to the right schools, was given a fitting education and upbringing. The fact that Tiffany's father had wealth was an inconvenience, but Rafiq had no doubt he had the resources, the power, to win any legal battle her family chose to mount to seize the child. He would start by having Taylor Smith investigated to find out exactly what kind of financial resources the man had, and whether he possessed an Achilles' heel.

If the baby wasn't his…?

The Mercedes slowed to turn into the bank's underground car park. Still he hadn't started up his laptop, opened his calendar to view his coming appointments. The conundrum of Tiffany held his full attention. Rafiq didn't even want to think about how he would feel if it had all been an elaborate lie, if the baby wasn't his.

If she'd lied to him—he'd make Tiffany rue the day they'd ever met.

The night was long. Tiffany barely slept. Restlessness had taken hold of her.

Yes?

Or no?

What answer to give Rafiq?

Tiffany rolled into a ball, huddling her belly, and stared blindly into the darkness. If she refused to marry him and left Dhahara, while her daughter would have a mother, she'd grow up never knowing her father. Then what if Rafiq wanted nothing to do with her baby later…when she was older? At least if she married Rafiq now, he'd see the baby every day. A bond would form. How could it not?

Did she really have a choice?

With a sigh Tiffany flopped over onto her back. The man she'd met again in Dhahara was every bit as arrow-straight as the first time she'd met him. Suppressing her anxieties that she might lose her child, she'd come to Dhahara to establish contact with a banker…and discovered a sheikh. A royal prince.

Rafiq was a busy man. An important man. Tiffany already knew he traveled extensively. Would he take time out to spend with a family he'd never wanted? A baby daughter who was not the male heir he expected? Or would it be a reenactment of her own childhood with a father who was never home?

Through the window she could see only the brightest stars sprinkling the darkness. The moon was fuller than the sliver that had hung in the sky the night her baby had been conceived. If she married Rafiq, she would be the moon to his sun…barely meeting and separated by vast chasms of yawning space.

That realization made the decision so much easier. She did not want that kind of marriage. She would refuse his offer of marriage, and take her chances alone. One day she would tell her daughter who her father was. They didn't need Rafiq to be a family.

The decision that had been tormenting her made, Tiffany finally drifted off to sleep.

Tiffany's decision to turn down Rafiq's proposal was reinforced the next morning when she went down to breakfast and Lily hastily closed the newspaper she'd been leafing through—but not before Tiffany had caught a glimpse of Rafiq's handsome features spread over the page.

"May I?" She gave Lily a grim smile and reached for the paper.

Lily must've seen something in her face because she spread her hands helplessly. "You must realize, it's not my nephew's fault—women have been throwing themselves at him since he was a teenager."

So much for Rafiq's explanation to his aunt that they were business acquaintances. Lily had clearly read much more into their relationship.

Yet Lily's words brought no comfort. Tiffany stared at a series of photos of Rafiq at what was obviously a society event, a beautiful dark-haired woman clinging to his arm. This was why he hadn't been home for dinner last night. He'd generously given her time to make her decision, while he'd escorted another woman to a function.

Most women think I'm charming.

It appeared Rafiq had been right.

"She's beautiful," said Tiffany expressionlessly, her stomach tightening into a hard knot. *So this is how it begins.* It was her father all over again. There would always be women. The knowledge hurt more than she'd ever thought it could.

"It's the opening of the new wing of the hospital. Her family is well-known in Dhahara—and I'm sure Rafiq allowed himself to be photographed with her because of the large donation her family made to the new wing."

That possessive hand on his sleeve was a world away from polite. The tilt of the woman's head, her kohl-outlined eyes and society-goddess smile all announced her confidence in securing the man beside her to the world. Tiffany had never wanted a high-profile man who attracted women like bees to a honeypot. She had no intention of enduring what her mother had put up with.

Marriage to Rafiq was her idea of hell on earth.

She was going to say no—not only because her daughter deserved more than an absentee father, but also because she wasn't prepared to tolerate a string of photos with women that caused her to feel sick with doubt. Now she just had to communicate her decision to Rafiq. No doubt, he'd be glad to be rid of her. By tonight she'd be gone.

Turning her head away from Lily's concerned glance, Tiffany helped herself to apricots and dates and spooned over creamy yogurt and honey, sure that if she tried to eat anything more substantial she would gag—despite the beautiful display.

By the time Rafiq strode in minutes later, the offending newspaper had been folded and tucked away. Yet not even the flash of his white smile and his warm greeting could bring any softening to Tiffany's resolve. Her stomach started to churn, and nausea rose in the back of her throat.

Her spoon clattered into her bowl, and Tiffany pushed her chair back.

"Not so fast," Rafiq's tone made her pause. "Stay. We must talk."

Lily glanced at him. "I've got a few calls to make. I'll make them in your study if you don't mind, Rafiq."

Tiffany wanted to scuttle after Lily, anything to avoid the coming unpleasantness. Then she stiffened her spine. She'd sit across the table from Rafiq and give him her answer.

The sooner she got it over with, the better.

"I have one thing to ask of you," Rafiq said after his aunt had left them alone, his voice pure liquid. He'd pulled a chair up beside her, turning it so that he was so close that she could inhale the scent of lemon and soap.

Jolted out of her thoughts, Tiffany stared at him.

"We will create a tale of how we met. No one need ever know of our ignominious start. We will keep to the story that we are business acquaintances…who met during your time at university."

"You mean lie?"

He ignored her angry comment. "You did go to university, didn't you?"

He hadn't asked her that in Hong Kong. "I studied English literature and French. Our paths were unlikely to have crossed."

"You speak French?"

She nodded.

"Good," he said. "We will say that you assisted me with some translation."

He was sweeping her objections aside. Tiffany knew she had to make a stand, before he walked all over her. "I haven't said I'll marry you."

"Oh, we both know what your final answer will be. I only want to whitewash our meeting so that our families are not hurt by the scandalous nature of our first encounter."

Her father was far from an angel. And once Rafiq discovered Taylor Smith's affairs, he'd be trying to protect his family from the taint of her father's reputation. "Now that you know my family is wealthy, you're obviously no longer worried that I might blackmail you and Sir Julian," she said with a bite in her voice, the memory of the image of him and the beautiful woman still burning like salt in a raw wound.

He shook his head. And her heart leaped. Then he killed the hope. "The deal with Sir Julian has already been announced. It can no longer be jeopardized."

Already hurting with an emotion she didn't want to label for fear of admitting what she dared not confront, it stung that he hadn't admitted that he'd been wrong to doubt her.

"I'm not going to marry you," she said baldly.

There was a silence.

"I beg your pardon?" His voice turned ominously soft. To her relief he made no move to shift closer.

"I can't marry you."

As Taylor Smith's daughter, Tiffany was every bit as unsuitable as a blackmailing club hostess he'd met one night in Hong Kong. Her father might be a film director, but Tiffany had no doubt that his list of affairs had made him too scandalous for Rafiq's conservative family to tolerate.

He raised a brow. "You must marry me."

"The only reason for our marriage is to legitimize the daughter you're not even convinced is yours." It irked her to remind him of that, but right now she needed every argument she could muster.

"The DNA tests will tell the truth when the time comes." He reached out and took her hand. "But you're mistaken, Tiffany. The baby is far from the only reason I have for desiring to marry you," he argued, his eyes glowing with a light she was starting to recognize.

Oh, no!

Tiffany tried to free her hand, waving the other to ward him off. But when he trailed a finger down the side of her face, little quivers of delight followed in its wake. "Rafiq, that's not going to work," she said rather breathlessly.

"This always works for us."

Not today. Jealousy mushroomed into rage. "You haven't seen the photos in today's paper."

"What, a photo of me with the daughter of a man who donated to a cause I am a founding patron for?"

"It didn't look that innocent."

"Her hand was on my arm. I did not touch her. Pah, that's the paparazzi—always on the lookout for a scandal."

There was a ring of truth in his impatience.

But Tiffany had learned young that there was no whiff of smoke without a raging inferno someplace. A picture of her father with an adoring starlet in the gossip rags usually escalated into a passionate affair with the young actress in question not long after.

And Rafiq had admitted the first night they met that women found him charming. She had been warned.

Turning in her chair, Tiffany pulled the newspaper out from where she'd tucked it away on the seat beside her and unfolded it, spreading it out on the table, to glance at the image again.

She stared hard. Rafiq was facing into a camera, his expression carefully blank. No smile for the woman at his side. No glow of romance. Was Rafiq really different from her father? She wanted desperately to believe he was, but she had no intention of fooling herself that she could change such a man.

Perhaps the woman in the newspaper was indeed no more than a woman whose family he knew, a family who had donated a large sum to a good cause he sponsored.

She set the paper aside.

Rafiq was watching her. He hadn't even spared the paper a glance—he obviously didn't care what she believed. The ache in her chest that had begun when she'd first seen that picture intensified. It was an ache that was starting to concern her greatly.

"Have you ever been in love?" she asked suddenly.

"The kind of love that the poets wail about?" Rafiq grimaced. "Probably not. But the kind of love that makes me desire a woman? Then yes, several times—with a number of highly suitable women."

His candor caused a fresh stab of sharper pain.

Well, she'd asked, hadn't she? She could hardly complain when she didn't like the reply.

Shoring up optimism, she said, "But you never married any of them."

"I considered marrying one or two."

Tiffany blinked. "You did? So what stopped you?"

He shrugged, then glanced away, his lashes falling to mask his unfathomable eyes. His hair shone in the light of the morning sun that streamed through the high windows above and into the dining room. "The pressure of expectation. I only had to show a small amount of interest in a woman for my family, her family and the newspapers to start setting wedding dates."

His honesty startled her. She wished she'd never asked. "You felt trapped."

He met her gaze squarely. "Yes."

"Yet you have asked me to marry you—demanded that I marry you, in fact. After what you just told me, how do I know you're not going to back out at the last moment if you start to feel pressured?"

"I *have* to marry you," he pointed out. "You are with child—my child, you assure me." Then he smiled, his eyes crinkling, and her breath snagged in her throat. "And, at this stage, you have the advantage that your father hasn't produced marriage agreements for me to sign."

"And I'm supposed to be relieved by that?"

He laughed.

Tiffany didn't.

It was starting to occur to her that she had a much bigger problem on her hands than she'd ever dreamed. The man who'd asked her to marry him had been caught by the oldest trick in the book: pregnancy. And, worse, he was every bit as terrified of being trapped as she was of being cheated on.

"Do you expect a marriage of convenience?" he asked.

She did a double take. "You mean no sex?"

Rafiq was a passionate man. Their night together had proved that beyond a shadow of doubt. She wouldn't have picked him for a man who could survive the sexless wasteland that a marriage in name only would be. Unless he planned to go to other women…despite his marriage vows. The ache inside her intensified.

With a firm shake of her head, she said, "I don't know why I said that. It's irrelevant. I don't want the kind of marriage we'd have."

"Then we can have a different kind of marriage." His eyes grew lazy and he tugged the hand that he was holding, propelling her closer. Her chair scraped across the highly polished wooden floor. "With lots of sex."

"That's not what I meant—"

Before she could finish setting him right, his mouth closed over hers, full of ardor. Tiffany tasted coffee and desire. Deliciously tempting. She edged nearer. Closing her eyes, she sagged against him.

His body was hard against hers. He was aroused, she realized. She pulled away. "No!" Her voice was sharp. "I don't want that kind of marriage, either."

"You might think a marriage of convenience would work for the child's sake. You might think you want a romantic fairy tale." His eyes had darkened, coal-black, piercing. "But what I'm offering is the exactly the kind of marriage you want."

She wrenched herself out of his arms. "You don't know me. You have no idea what I want!"

His lips curved up, and his eyes smoldered. "Then why don't you tell me exactly what you want, and I will do everything in my power to give it to you."

Little frissons of excitement ran up and down her spine. It annoyed her that he could control her body's response so easily. "I've told you before—I don't want *you*. I want to marry a different kind of man altogether, someone—"

"Ordinary." The sexy smile vanished. "You're chasing

a chimera, Tiffany. Maybe you even believe it, but one day you will discover what I know already—that you have deceived yourself. You do not want anyone ordinary."

Tiffany pushed her chair back and rose to her feet. Forcing herself to laugh, the kind of light, careless laugh her mother gave when she pretended to dismiss her father's flirtations as inconsequential, she said, "So I suppose you're going to tell me exactly what kind of man I do want?"

"You want *me*."

Eight

As his stark words disappeared into a void of resounding silence, Rafiq knew at once he'd been far too forthright. Honeyed sentiments about love were what women wanted, not the honest, unvarnished truth.

Tiffany looked shaken. She opened her mouth, then closed it again. At last she found her voice. "Your arrogance knows no bounds."

Heat expanded inside his chest. "Have you forgotten where the conversation ended up last time you called me an arrogant jerk?" he asked softly, getting to his feet.

By the golden fire in her eyes he saw that she remembered. Perfectly.

"It won't end up in the same place this time."

He cocked an eyebrow, and gave her a slow smile as he advanced. "You are certain of that?"

"Absolutely!"

"I relish a challenge." And he watched the dismay dawn on her face with masculine satisfaction.

"Wait…" Tiffany backed up until the table was behind her. She held up her hands. "I didn't mean for you to interpret my statement that you were arrogant as a challenge to get me back into your bed—"

"You agree it will be too easy?" He kept coming, until her hands were flat against his chest. Could she feel the thud of his heart against her palms? He was intensely aware of the touch of her fingers through the silk of his shirt.

"Definitely not."

Despite his growing arousal, Rafiq was starting to enjoy himself. He suppressed a grin. "And that is a challenge for me to prove how easy it will be?"

She did a double take.

"No! I mean—" She paused, clearly fearful that he'd taken her denial as a fresh challenge.

"Hush." He placed a finger against her lips. "It's why I'm such a good negotiator."

This time he allowed himself a smug grin.

Her retort was cut off by the appearance of an aide at the door. "Your Highness, your office called. The first appointment for the day has arrived."

Rafiq glanced down at his watch. He had no intention of telling Tiffany that Sir Julian had arrived in Dhahara, not while he was trying to convince her to marry him. "He is early. My secretary is away. Please let Miss Turner, her assistant, know I will be in shortly."

After the aide had left, all teasing humor faded. Leaning forward he said, "Tiffany, what happened between you and me that night in Hong Kong—" Rafiq caught her hand in his "—should never have happened. It was dishonorable."

She stared levelly back at him. "I've got as much to lose

as you—I have no intention of telling the paparazzi about our night together…or the life we created."

Rafiq threaded his fingers through hers, aware of the quiver of her fingers. "I'm relieved to hear that." She opened her mouth to object. He continued quickly, "That night should never have happened. I don't know why—" He broke off and shook his head.

He still didn't understand what had happened to him that night. How he'd lost control so fast. Why it lingered in his mind…tempting him to repeat the experience, to the point where he couldn't wait to marry Tiffany and get her back into his bed.

Finally he said, "It doesn't change the fact that I will take responsibility for my actions."

She glanced up sharply. "Are you saying that you're prepared to believe that the baby is yours?"

Rafiq shook his head slowly. "I do not say that." *Yet.* "But I am prepared to concede that it is possible, and for that reason I am prepared to marry you."

"Even though it makes you feel trapped?"

He hesitated, then decided to let her believe it. He'd already told her he wanted her. She didn't need to know the full extent of the sexual power she held over him. He thought of her every waking moment. He'd never experienced anything like it. What harm would it do to let her think he was marrying her only out of duty? "We will discover the truth when the baby is born. Until then we will not talk of this again. It is about time you met my family, don't you think?" He smiled at her. "I will arrange for them to gather at Qasr Al-Ward, my brother's home—I think you will like it there."

Her eyes widened. "Wait—you can't drop a bombshell like that and leave."

"I'll answer your questions later."

Rafiq raised her hand and kissed the back. She gasped. It seemed as if he wasn't the only one affected by the sensual tie that bound them.

"If I don't leave now, I will be late for my appointment. I will send a car for you at five o'clock. Be ready. Tonight we will plan our wedding."

Rafiq had spoken the truth.

Tiffany lay in the marble bath with its dolphin faucets, soaking to relax her aching neck muscles, and admitted the truth to herself. She'd been fooling herself, she wanted him, only him. Only he had ever aroused an emotion that she could label possessiveness. Only Rafiq had ignited the heat within her that made her melt when he was near her.

She'd come to Dhahara to build a bridge to the future for her unborn daughter. She'd discovered a man she was no longer sure she would be able to walk away from.

So why didn't she throw caution to the wind and marry him? Because she still clung to part of her dream. She wanted more than a father for her child, and a lover for herself.

She wanted a man to marry her not because she was pregnant, not because she carried a royal heir, but because he loved her. But that dream was the biggest fairy tale of all.

The reality was that once Rafiq discovered how much the tabloids stalked her fickle father, it would outweigh the scandal of an illegitimate heir being born into the royal family. It was unlikely that he would need any second urging to drop her like a hot potato.

Sir Julian Carling had an agenda.

Rafiq sensed it as soon as the other man greeted him

as he stepped into the bank's wood-paneled boardroom.
As soon as the discussions about the new hotel were out
the way, Sir Julian pounced.

"My daughter, Elizabeth, was very taken with you,
Rafiq."

Rafiq could barely recall the debutante he'd met at Sir
Julian's home months ago. Across the wooden boardroom
table, he gave the older man a noncommittal smile and
put his slimline laptop back in its case. "I'm sure any man
would be flattered by her attention."

Sprawled in the leather-backed chair, Julian said, "She's
coming to Dhahara—the only reason she didn't come with
me now is a work commitment. She's very involved in the
Carling Hotel group, but she'd like to get to know you
better. Perhaps, once Elizabeth arrives, we can talk about
building a second hotel in one of the desert cities."

It was a bribe.

Rafiq had not managed to remain unwed for more than
three decades without developing an uncanny sixth sense
about matchmaking parents. But this time he got the feeling
that he was being craftily boxed in by a master operator.
Getting to his feet, he made it clear that the meeting was at
an end. "Julian, I must inform you that I'm getting married.
My bride and I will probably be away when your daughter
arrives."

"Married?" Sir Julian sat up and planted his elbows on
the boardroom table, displeasure written all over his florid
features. "When I spoke to your father only a few days ago,
he suggested I bring Elizabeth to spend time with you. He
said nothing about your marriage."

Because, at the time, his crafty father hadn't known.
Rafiq could have throttled the king. So much for taking
up his joking suggestion that Elizabeth Carling might suit
Khalid; his father had had another plan altogether.

"My bride and I will be married before the week is out."
Speaking with utmost confidence, Rafiq bent to pick up
his laptop case. He would give Tiffany—and the king—no
choice in the matter. She'd become a temptation he could
not withstand.

"I'll have to make sure I'm here to celebrate the
event."

"My fiancée wants a quiet, family wedding." As he
spoke, Rafiq wondered whether Tiffany would agree to a
marriage without her parents present to give their blessing.

Tiffany didn't know what she'd expected, but it certainly
wasn't the fortress of sun-bleached sandstone that rose out
the surrounding desert. She peered through the window of
the Mercedes-Benz to get a better look.

"Good heavens."

"Qasr Al-Ward," Rafiq announced as the black car came
to a stop in the graveled forecourt.

"Your brother and his wife live here?"

"Yes, my brother has made his home here—he spends as
much time as he can away from the city with his wife."

Only one wife?

But Tiffany bit back the sarcastic retort as the chauffeur
opened the door for her. The stifling heat of the late
afternoon closed around her. Alighting from the backseat,
she started to worry about the simple white dress she wore.

"I'm not dressed up enough."

"Don't worry. More often than not Shafir is covered in
desert sand. My brother won't even notice what you are
wearing." There was a gleam of humor in Rafiq's eyes.
"But if what you are wearing concerns you, I am sure
clothes can be found that will be more to your liking."

Shafir Al Dhahara wore flowing white robes with not

a speck of dust. But his wife was a surprise. Tiffany found herself enchanted by Megan—and it was clear that Shafir adored his wife.

"I have heard all about you," said a tall, dark man with liquid-gold eyes coming up to stand behind the couple at the top of the stone stairs that led to the vast front door. "Rafiq, aren't you going to introduce us?"

Well, Tiffany had heard nothing about him—she didn't even know who he was.

Rafiq waved a careless hand. "Tiffany, this is my brother, Khalid."

She smiled, and wondered how many more brothers Rafiq had.

As if Khalid had read her thoughts, he said, "There are three of us. I am the eldest and Shafir here is the middle son. Rafiq is the baby of the family."

Ha. Some baby!

Tiffany waited for Rafiq to object; instead he gave his brother a rough hug. "Father will be here later. He had a meeting with the council of elders. Now let us go inside."

The thought of meeting Rafiq's father, the king, was enough to give Tiffany the shakes. But before she could worry about it any further, Shafir's wife came up beside her.

"Would you like something to drink?" Megan asked. "It's going to be a hectic few hours."

A hectic few hours?

Despite her bemusement Tiffany requested a glass of soda.

"What did Megan mean by 'a hectic few hours'?" she asked, dropping back to speak to Rafiq.

He avoided her gaze.

She put a hand on his arm to stop him moving away. "Answer me."

"Ah, look at the lovebirds," chortled Shafir.

"Let Tiffany and Rafiq alone," Megan scolded her husband. "Rafiq, you can use your usual suite of rooms. Tiffany, for now, I've given you a chamber in the old harem—but don't let that freak you out."

Megan's statement did indeed freak her out. But not the bit about the harem. "A chamber?"

Did Megan mean a bedchamber? They weren't staying the night, were they? Rafiq had said nothing about that.

Megan nodded. "I'll send one of the maids to help you dress for the party."

Help her dress? Tiffany suddenly knew exactly how Alice must've felt when she blundered down the rabbit hole. "What party? I didn't think to bring a change of clothes with me."

"Your clothes—"

"Megan," her husband grasped her arm, "you talk too much."

Megan glanced around, a resigned expression on her face. "Have I put my foot in it again?"

Turning away from his family to confront a silent Rafiq, Tiffany demanded, "What is going on?"

Behind her she could hear Megan saying, "Dammit, I *have* put my foot in it. Why did none of you bother to tell me that she didn't know?"

Tiffany's sense of ire grew. "Don't know what?"

"Er—" Rafiq started to move past her. "Come through to the salon."

"Rafiq?" She grabbed at his sleeve. "Tell me."

"My family—every one—is here to celebrate our engagement this evening."

Tiffany's mouth fell open. *"Our engagement?"*

"You should've tried seduction, Rafiq." The male voice was followed by hoots of laughter.

Oh, dear God! "Do they know I'm pregnant?" she whispered, humiliation creeping over her in a sickly wave at the thought of their night together being the subject of ridicule.

A flare of color seared his cheekbones, but he didn't drop his gaze. "Ignore Shafir, he knows nothing. It's a joke—I once told him he should seduce Megan—he's simply trying to score points."

"Did he?" she asked in a low tone.

"By your expression, it looks like he did."

She shook her head impatiently. "Not now. Did he seduce Megan?"

"No, he decided to kidnap her instead."

"Kidnap her?" Tiffany's eyes stretched wide as they followed the rest of the party into a large room that overlooked lush gardens with tall palms and pools of water. *"Really?"*

He nodded. "He brought her here—and kept her under lock and key."

"You've got to be joking! Right?"

Rafiq shook his head. "No, I'm not. Ask Megan."

Megan's voice piped up, "What must Tiffany ask me?"

"Hush, wife," said Shafir, and everyone laughed.

"Did your husband kidnap you?" Tiffany stared at the other woman, sure that she was being mercilessly teased.

"Oh, yes. Except he wasn't my husband back then."

"And he kept you here until you agreed to marry him?"

Megan shook her head, and reached for Shafir's hand before casting him a loving glance. "He didn't force me to marry him—he was trying to stop me from marrying Zara's fiancé."

"Zara's fiancé?" Tiffany did a double take. "But Zara's Lily's daughter. Isn't she in L.A.?"

Shafir only laughed. "It's a long story."

"Sounds like one I should hear," Tiffany said darkly.

"Not before you marry me," objected Rafiq. "Although maybe I'll have to take a leaf out of Shafir's book and lock you up here."

She spun around. *"What?"*

Rafiq glanced at her annoyed face and then around at their attentive audience. "Excuse us, please."

He wrapped one arm around her shoulders, hooked the other behind her knees and swept her off her feet. He hoisted her high against his chest. Tiffany buried her face against his throat to drown out the whoops of laughter as he exited the room.

When they reached a sitting room where scimitars adorned a wall, he lowered her to her feet.

Tiffany couldn't restrain herself. "How could you do that? *In front of your family?* And how could you announce our engagement to them? I haven't even said I'll marry you."

His eyes were guarded. "Of course you will."

Tiffany threw her hands up. "But I haven't said 'yes.'"

He arched a brow in a gesture that had become endearingly familiar. "So say it."

After seeing how Shafir doted on Megan, Tiffany was wildly tempted to give in and let herself be dragged down the aisle. When she'd come to Dhahara to tell Rafiq about his baby, marriage was not what she'd expected. Yet she was unbearably tempted.

A pang pierced her.

"Don't look so desperate."

She lifted her head. "I'm not desperate."

"Only love makes you desperate." His mouth twisted. "And this match isn't about love."

He paused, and Tiffany wondered how he expected her to respond. When he remained silent, she said, "You will regret our marriage."

"What do you mean?"

This time there was no hesitation. It wasn't right to let him walk into a marriage without at least warning him. "The tabloids adore my father. He can always be relied on to deliver a story."

"Do you mean that he feeds them Hollywood leaks?"

"No, no. Nothing like that. He has affairs with actresses—much to my mother's grief." She clenched her hands at her sides. "Your family will not be happy."

"Tiffany." His hands closed over her shoulders. He pulled her up against his chest. He felt so unabashedly solid and male. "You need to understand that I am marrying you—not your father."

"He will cause you a lot of embarrassment."

Rafiq shrugged against her. "That is not your doing."

The last bastion of her line of defense crumbled. A warmth spread through her, and tears pricked at her eyes. Her hands crept up his shirt front and a fierce emotion shook her.

"Thank you," she whispered.

What did she have to lose? Pulling back a little, Tiffany met his melting gaze, and said, "Okay, I'll marry you."

Nine

The wedding contracts had been signed.

Once Tiffany had accepted his proposal, Rafiq had wasted no time in the week that followed to arrange their wedding.

He thought about their unborn child. His daughter perhaps…

How would he have felt if some stranger had gotten his daughter pregnant after a one-night stand? Rafiq realized he would've been furious!

With a little trepidation he'd approached inviting her parents, but Tiffany had decided against it. Her mother had a lot of adjusting to do, she'd explained, and right now she didn't feel like seeing her father.

Rafiq hadn't agreed, but he'd gone along with it. For Tiffany's peace of mind.

Now, oblivious of the knot of people clustered around, Rafiq waited beside the ancient well in the heart of Ain

Farrin, the village not far from Qasr Al-Ward where the spring, or *ain,* originated, and watched Tiffany come toward him through the grove of tamarisk trees.

His bride.

She wore a long, cream-colored silk dress embroidered with rich gold thread and topped with a gauzy silk wrap. A filmy veil covered her hair. Her hips swayed as she walked, a legacy of the high heels she wore.

Rafiq wasn't aware of his family, or the villagers who crowded around. He only had eyes for Tiffany.

Her eyes glittered beneath the draped veil. She stopped beside him in the dappled shade of an ancient olive tree, and he reached for her hands. Her fingers trembled as his fingers closed around hers.

His bride was nervous.

Tenderness flowed through Rafiq. An urge to protect her from anything that might harm her. He drew her toward him and turned to face the celebrant.

He closed his eyes as the holy words flowed over them. After placing a ring on her finger, he received one in return. They knelt, then circled the well in a train, while the village children tossed rose petals from the gardens of Qasr Al-Ward over them.

As he brushed the petals from her veil, he saw her eyes were dazed.

"Almost over," he mouthed, and his heart soared as he caught a glimpse of her smile through the spun-silk veil.

He would not let her down, he vowed. Nor would he ever abandon their daughter when she needed him most.

After the wedding festivities were over, they returned to Qasr Al-Ward. Rafiq had told Tiffany that Shafir and Megan had loaned them the ancient palace for a few days.

The knowledge that, with the exception, of a skeleton staff, they were totally alone, made her unaccountably edgy.

Rafiq was her husband.

They were married.

She was already expecting his daughter; this was not going to be the romantic honeymoon of newlyweds.

Yet as the sun sank over the distant horizon, leaving a glow of burnished gold over the desert sands, Tiffany followed Rafiq through corridors lit by torches set in wall sconces, and couldn't help being affected by the expectant air of exotic romance. It felt like a honeymoon. Blood pounded through her veins.

When he led her into a vast chamber lit by dozens of candles that illuminated a bed in the center, she balked.

"What about our marriage of convenience?"

That got his attention. He swiveled to face her. "It's not going to happen. I made that clear when I asked if you expected one. I know you, Tiffany, better than you think. I suspected you might have convinced yourself that was what you want."

"But you knew better."

The candlelight gave his skin a bronze cast. It threw warmth over the harsh features, and lit up the white pants and tunic he'd worn for their marriage. "I know what you want. You want me."

The bed behind him loomed large in the room. Tiffany could already feel that her breathing had quickened, that her body had softened. "You flatter yourself."

His mouth slanted. "Because I can never be the white knight of your dreams?"

The edge to his voice caused her to frown.

"Exactly."

"You're fooling yourself if you think you can exist

without passion. You were made to make love. I knew that the first night we were together."

Determined not to fall into his arms, she said, "I only slept with you out of gratitude."

His eyes began to glitter. "Did you?"

Her pulse accelerated and she crossed her fingers. "Yes."

"Thirty dollars worth of gratitude?"

She didn't like the way he made that sound. "Uh…"

"And this time you're sleeping with me because you're so grateful—" he stressed the word as he stalked toward her "—that I married you?"

"Of course not!"

She didn't back away as he came to a halt in front of her. "Then it must be because you know exactly how much pleasure is in store for you, hmm?"

Her stomach started to flutter. "No, Rafiq, no sex."

Not now. Not while he was in this mood, even though she knew she'd deliberately provoked him.

"It will be much more than sex." His voice deepened to a husky growl that turned knots in her stomach. "I will pleasure you, just you wait and see."

He planted his mouth on hers and her lips parted.

It didn't take long for him to elicit a response, even though Tiffany fought with herself to resist. To her utter frustration he raised his head just enough to put a space between them. "Are you suitably grateful for that?"

The high heels she wore meant her eyes were level with the sinful passion of his mouth.

"Just shut up," she said, flustered by the desire that bolted through her like a jab of electricity.

This time, when he took her in his arms, she went up on the tips of her toes, and met him halfway. All her objections had evaporated.

"You know I'll never forgive you for this, don't you?" she muttered when he lowered her to the soft satin covers.

He laughed as he slipped off her shoes. "I've been wanting to do that all day." Next he peeled off the veil and carefully eased the ivory and gold dress away from her shoulders.

He followed her down onto the bed. "You'll love every moment. That I will promise you."

When she woke the next morning it was to meet a pair of slumberous dark eyes. Embarrassment seared Tiffany. Her cheeks grew hot, her breasts, the heat spread.

Rafiq propped himself onto an elbow and started to smile as he gazed down at her. His eyes glowed. "You don't need to blush—we have done nothing to be ashamed of. We are married."

She gave an incoherent murmur.

He pushed the sheet away from her body. Tiffany snatched at the edge as it slipped away.

"Don't be shy." His hand stroked the soft flesh of her stomach. "I find it hard to believe there is a baby in here. You were so tight... You could've been a virgin."

Tiffany's flush deepened. "You're embarrassing me," she said.

"Why?" At her sharp inhalation, he said, "Let's have no pretense or secrets between us, Tiffany. I knew you were no virgin last night."

Her breath whooshed out in a frustrated sigh. "If there are to be no secrets, then you should know that the only other time we made...love—" she stumbled over the word "—I was a virgin."

Tiffany glanced up at him from beneath her eyelashes to see how he'd taken her revelation.

His face had gone curiously blank. After a moment's

pause, he said, "Ah, Tiffany, you need not worry. I did not expect to find an innocent that night we first met."

She fell silent, her lashes sweeping down against her cheeks.

"Do not sulk," he whispered, running a finger along the ridge of her nose. "I never wanted a virgin."

Her lashes lifted. She met his eyes, so close now, that a stab of desire spiked through her. "I'm not sulking! But I had hoped you'd gotten to know me better by now. That first night in Hong Kong, you thought I was scamming you—"

"I know—"

"I was in a desperate situation—"

"I know that—"

"I've repaid every cent you gave me. I've told you the truth about the baby—"

"Tiffany, Tiffany." He pulled her into his arms and rolled onto his back, tugging her over on top of his chest. "It doesn't matter whether you were a virgin or not." He lifted his head off the pillow and kissed her brow.

She opened her mouth to tell him that it did matter. That she needed him to trust her—as she'd trusted him by telling him about her parents, by confessing that her father would never be the ideal father-in-law. She needed a show of faith from him, too. And more than anything, she needed for him to believe that the baby was his. Just because she said so.

Not because of the incontrovertible results of a DNA test.

It hurt, this refusal to trust her. But he would learn that she hadn't lied to him—then he would be forced to apologize.

"Stop glowering at me." He ruffled her hair. "We will

make love. Then I will show you the desert that has always been so loved by my family."

Just as she had no doubt he intended, desire started to sing through her veins.

What did Rafiq love? Was it only sex? Would he ever love more than the attraction that burned so brightly, so wildly between them?

At that thought her heart thudded to a stop. Was this the reason she so desperately needed for him to trust her? Had she fallen in love with the husband she'd trapped into a marriage that he'd entered only from a sense of duty?

"Mom?" Tiffany pressed the telephone against her ear to overcome the hiss on the line. "How are you?"

"Holding together. I signed the final settlement papers yesterday—your father wasn't there."

Was that a wistful note she heard in her mother's voice? Tiffany fervently hoped not.

"Everything went smoothly," Linda Smith continued, "just as you said it would once we got a good lawyer."

"I'm glad." Tiffany gave a silent sigh of relief. Two months ago she'd found her mother a lawyer, and she'd gone with her to every appointment and provided moral support right up to the day before she'd left for Dhahara. With the settlement signed, at last her mother could start to put together the pieces of her life. "Have you thought any more about selling the house in Auckland and finding something cozier?"

Before Tiffany had left, her mother had still been adamant that she didn't want to move out of the house she'd shared with Taylor Smith—even though it was the best asset she owned. Tiffany had suspected her mother was clutching at straws, hoping her father would come to his senses and return.

How Linda could consider taking him back this time, when he'd physically moved out, Tiffany found hard to figure.

"No, I don't want to sell—and you'll need somewhere to stay when you come back from your holiday. Where was it you were going again?"

"Dhahara. Mom, there's something I need to tell you." Tiffany plunged on. "I'm not coming home for a while. I got married."

She held the handset away as her mother gasped, then squealed and reeled off a string of questions.

"I know it was sudden. But it was the right thing to do. His name is Rafiq…and the marriage was performed in a village near one of the family's homes. Three days ago."

This time her mother sounded more cautious than celebratory. "Three days ago? In that desert country?"

"Yes, Dhahara is a desert kingdom." Then, hoping it would reassure her mother, she added, "Rafiq is part of the royal family."

"Oh, honey, you will come visit?"

Tiffany's heart ached at the loneliness in her mom's voice. "Of course, we'll come see you. Rafiq travels a great deal—he's a banker. We'll visit soon. I'll talk to him, and let you know when."

"Tiffany…are you sure you're all right? It's such a long way away. I wish I could be there to help you."

"I'm fine. Honestly. You're better off selling the house than rushing across the world to see me."

Her mother sighed. "I don't want to move. And I feel I should be with you. I wish your father were here. He'd know what to do."

"I haven't told Dad about my marriage."

Tiffany heard her mother's intake of breath.

"But he's your father—he has a right to know."

"I will tell him, Mom." Eventually. "Right now I'm still too angry with him for walking out on you." And her father was equally stubborn—he hadn't contacted her since their stormy disagreement when he'd cut off her allowance, and told her that she'd be back soon enough with her tail between her legs.

"Tiffany, it's not your fight. With the counseling I started, I'm working on forgiving your father, and I'm starting to realize I may not have been the best wife."

"Oh, no, Mom—don't even think that! He had no reason to run around with other women. To walk out on you."

Silence hummed between them. At last her mother said, "But you need to let him know about your marriage. You're still his baby girl."

It had been a long time since she'd been his little girl. Tiffany gentled her tone. "When I'm ready—I'm not ready yet." More than anything in the world she needed time.

"Darling, are you sure you know what you're—"

"I'm expecting Rafiq's baby, Mom."

This time the silence was electric.

To break it, Tiffany said desperately, "I came to Dhahara to tell Rafiq about the baby. My little girl will need a mother *and* a father." Surely her mother, of all people, would understand that better than anyone in the world? "In time she'll need grandparents, too, so don't worry. I know I have to tell Dad the good news."

Just not now. Not while her own hurt at his countless betrayals would spill out.

"Oh, darling, you should've told me you were pregnant before you left."

Tiffany couldn't handle recriminations right now. "Mom, you had enough to cope with."

"I feel terrible. I didn't even guess—"

"You weren't supposed to."

There was a short pause as her mother absorbed that. Then she said, "I feel like I let you down."

"Nonsense," said Tiffany loyally.

"But—"

"Don't worry about me," Tiffany interrupted. "I'm fine, Mom. I needed to make this decision myself. No one else could make it for me. Not you. Not Dad. Only I can take responsibility for my actions. I went into this with my eyes wide open."

That wasn't strictly true. She'd gone in with some illusions. She hadn't expected their marriage to be so *physical*. She was terrified of losing her emerging sense of identity to the heady passion that only Rafiq had ever awoken in her.

And now he was her husband…

The man who shared her bed. Her body. His body. Every night.

At least she wasn't in love with him. Nor he with her. It was better that way. Falling for Rafiq would be insanely stupid. Tiffany was not about to let Rafiq break her heart— not even if she was pregnant with his baby.

But she couldn't share any of that with her mother. Instead she said, "Rafiq took me into the desert yesterday. Oh, Mom, it was so beautiful.… One day I will show you, too."

Then maybe her mother might understand.

Ten

Rafiq gazed down at his wife.

A heavy tide of satisfaction swept in the wake of the rush of desire. They'd made love…slept…then made love again as dawn streaked the horizon.

He should've been sated.

He wasn't.

It would be a long time before he could claim to have had enough of his wife. But he would wait for tonight before taking her again. The day was hers. He would let anticipation build through the long, hot hours. Take her to a souk to watch her touch the soft silks. For an outing in the desert to see the excited glow in her eyes. He'd take her anywhere she chose to go. It was refreshing to see his world—Dhahara—through her eyes. The want could wait.

Until tonight.

"What would you like to do today?" He walked two fingers along her arm.

She peeped at him from beneath her eyelashes in a way that caused his heart to hammer in his chest. "It's been a very busy week."

"Indeed it has been," he agreed huskily.

"Is it going to be as hot today as it was yesterday?"

"Hotter."

She pursed her lips, her expression thoughtful. Her lashes fluttered down against her cheeks. "Perhaps we could stay here."

"Perhaps we should."

A wanton warmth pooled in the pit of his belly. Rafiq could think of nothing more perfect than remaining exactly where they were—here in this bedchamber, the lacy white wooden shutters flung open to the whisper of the desert wind.

Tiffany was fitting surprisingly well into his life. His aunt Lily had taken a shine to her—probably because she was missing Zara. His brothers liked her. He was sure his father had enjoyed meeting her, too, although they had spoken only briefly the night of their engagement and at the wedding.

As for him…

He thought Tiffany was everything he'd ever wanted. Reaching out one hand, he pushed the curtain of silken hair off her face, then leaned down and pressed a kiss against her cheek. It was an impulsive gesture, done without plan. Yet she immediately turned her head and her lips clung to his in a kiss so gentle, so full of sweetness, that his chest grew tight.

He groaned softly.

He had intended to break the news of Tiffany's pregnancy to his family. To confess the real reason for their marriage. So that they knew that after the birth of the child the marriage could be dissolved. Yet somehow he'd kept putting it off. And now he couldn't very well announce she was pregnant—and in the same breath request them to keep his plan to divorce her secret from Tiffany.

In fact, Rafiq was starting to think that if the child turned out to be his, he might as well stay married to Tiffany....

Last night had only served to confirm that the nights alone would make it worth the sacrifice.

"I hadn't exactly meant to stay here—in bed—all day," she murmured breathlessly.

He reared over her and the tangled sheets fell away. "Why not?"

Tiffany glanced at his naked chest. When her gaze returned to his, her eyes glittered bright gold. "What will people say if we remain barricaded up in the bedchamber?"

He shrugged. Who cared? "That we just got married? That I can't keep my hands off my wife?"

He matched actions to the words and ran a hand along the delicate curves of her body. She shuddered and instantly his own desire rocketed.

"Rafiq!"

"What?" He bent forward to taste her again.

She fended him off with flat palms. "We shouldn't…"

"Why not?"

Her palms softened against his shoulders, toying with the sleek muscles of his arms, moving over his shoulders, drawing him close.

"You know," she breathed, "I can't think of a single good reason anymore."

"I am pleased." Rafiq's breath mingled with hers.

Then there were no more words, only touches so sensual, so arousing, that he forgot about everything except the woman in his arms.

The first week after their wedding passed in a whirl.

It was Thursday by the time they finally returned to Katar, the capital. That evening, Tiffany crossed the threshold of the dining salon in Rafiq's home and came to an abrupt halt.

She had not yet called her mother back—or discussed the possibility of a visit with Rafiq. Her poor mother must be going nuts.

"What is it?"

Rafiq moved from where he'd been standing beside the highly polished table. As he came toward her, Tiffany took in the black trousers and loose white shirt he wore. No dark suit. Yet the casual clothes only served to heighten his raw masculinity, and the top button left undone to reveal the smooth skin of his throat underlined it.

Tiffany jerked her attention away from that taunting bit of naked skin and back to his face. "Nothing. I just remembered something I've been meaning to do." She glanced around. "Where's Lily tonight?"

"We're married—there's no longer any need for my aunt to stay with us."

"Oh."

His aunt's presence had been comforting. Without her there was suddenly a whole new tension in the air.

Before she could bolt, Rafiq pulled the high-backed chair out for her.

"Thank you." Conscious of him behind her, Tiffany sat down. He smelled of sandalwood and soap and an exotic spice she didn't recognize. Focusing on the woven table mat in front of her, she gathered her thoughts as Rafiq settled into the seat opposite her. Finally she lifted her head.

Hamal, his chef, had entered and was lighting a dozen candles arranged in a heavy wrought-iron holder on the table. The golden glow of the flame washed over Rafiq's skin, the warmth softening the harsh, handsome features. Tiffany's stomach tightened and desire, never far away, licked at her belly.

As soon as Hamal retreated, Rafiq stretched out and took her hand. "Would you like to meet me for lunch tomorrow? A date? To make up for the lack of them before our wedding?"

She flushed with pleasure. When Rafiq was in this mood, he was downright easy to like. "That would be nice."

He relaxed slightly. "I've booked a table at the best Japanese restaurant in the city."

"Japanese?" she asked, surprised.

He nodded and Tiffany couldn't help noticing how the candlelight moved lovingly across his hair, bringing a bright sheen to the rich sable. As Hamal returned to place large, white plates on the place mats before them, Rafiq released her fingers. Unexpectedly, she found herself missing his touch.

"There's a fairly large Japanese community living in Dhahara—part of the booming motor industry. You'll enjoy the food."

"I look forward to it."

"There are some upcoming events I need to discuss with you."

So, not a date. A meeting. A little of the pleasure at his invitation went out of her. "What kind of events?"

Tilting his head to one side he said, "On Saturday

night there's a banquet in aid of the children's wing at the hospital."

No harm could come from attending that. Her wariness had been misplaced. Yet images from last week's newspaper floated through her mind. Pictures of Rafiq and an adoring, beautiful woman. Lily had said that had been at the opening of the hospital's new wing. This time *she* would be at Rafiq's side.

As his wife.

Something of her fierceness must've shown on her face, because Rafiq said, "I know. I know. I should've asked you before, but it slipped my mind." The smoldering look he gave her made it clear exactly what *had* been on his mind. "I'm the guest of honor, so we can't refuse."

Tiffany pushed away the memory of the other woman and took ruthless advantage of his admission of forgetfulness. "I need to ask you something, too."

"To take you shopping for clothes to wear?"

"No. More important."

The sensual warmth evaporated as his gaze jerked back to her face, intense and penetrating. "What is it?"

She wriggled, and crumpled the white linen napkin she'd just unfolded into a ball. "I spoke to my mother a few days ago."

"Your mother?" A crease appeared between his dark brows. "Did you tell her about the wedding?"

Tiffany nodded.

"And your father? Did you get in contact with him, too?"

This time she shook her head. "I'm not ready to talk with him yet." Then she added in a rush of honesty, "I didn't invite my mother to the wedding because I didn't want her to worry about me."

"You think marrying me would concern her?"

"It was easier to present her with a fait accompli." Tiffany helped herself to what looked like meatballs and spooned a mix of eggplant, tomato and okra on the side.

"That way she could do nothing about it."

"Exactly."

"So what's the problem?" he asked slowly.

"She's worried she's not going to see me as often as she'd like. I told her we'd go visit." From the corner of her eye she saw that Rafiq had started to eat, too. "And she's worried about why I married you. I told her I'm pregnant," she added in a rush.

Tiffany took a flatbread from a basket to give herself something to do. The mundane act of breaking the bread and first dipping the bits into olive oil then dredging them in *dukka,* a fragrant mixture of roasted nuts, toasted sesame and coriander seed, steadied her.

"You're not regretting our marriage already?" Rafiq's expression was somber.

Tiffany swallowed. Was he regretting the marriage? Did he feel trapped? "What makes you think that?"

"Good to know there is no cause for concern," he purred. "Though our lovemaking is so passionate that I would find that hard to believe…even though you keep me far away from your heart."

"I'd have to be a fool to let you into my heart. You're a prince of a wealthy desert kingdom. Eligible, rich, good-looking—"

"Thank you." He set down the knife and held up a hand. "I've heard enough. It is quite clear my attributes don't match up to your list."

Her mind went blank. "What list?"

His mouth kinked, but his dark brown eyes were uncomfortably grave. "For your white knight. Your ordinary prince. You want someone ordinary. A house with a white picket fence. Two-point-four children."

Oh, God. Had she told him all about that? "You remembered!"

He inclined his head. "Everything you've ever told me."

Help. "That's not a list. Not really."

At least, it wasn't the complete list. Above all else she wanted a man who loved her more than anything in the world. A man who would never stray and would be happy with her for all of his life. That man wasn't the distant, restless, easily charmed Rafiq ibn Selim Al Dhahara.

"It's just—"

"Just a way to make sure I know I don't qualify, hmm?" He lifted a brow inviting her to agree. "A way to keep me at a distance?"

Despite her sudden loss of appetite, Tiffany tore off a piece of bread and took a bite, chewed and swallowed.

At her sudden preoccupation, he smiled. But his flat eyes held no amusement; they were cool and watchful.

"It's not you..." Her voice trailed away.

"It's you. I know." He nodded. "But I find it interesting that you're prepared to admit you do not let any man close."

"I'm not admitting anything." Frustration filled Tiffany. "Look, it's nothing like that—you're misunderstanding me." But how to explain the fear that filled her? She didn't dare relax around him—it would be too easy to be charmed. Like all the other women he'd joked found him charming.

There, she'd admitted it. To herself. He charmed her. But she'd cut her tongue out before she let him in on the secret. "Surely you can understand that better than anyone in the world?"

"*I* can?"

She nodded. "You keep women at a distance, too."

He shook his head slowly. "Not to the same extent. I've had three very serious relationships. You were a virgin when we met."

"So you do believe me?" Tiffany couldn't believe her ears.

He shrugged. "You told me you're a virgin…I should give you the benefit of the doubt. It's not like you've made a habit of lying to me."

She wanted his unconditional trust.

He wasn't ready to give it.

Deflated, Tiffany backtracked to what they'd been discussing. "You might have had three serious relationships, but you didn't marry any of those women. Even though I'm prepared to stake money on it that they would've been more suitable for the position of your princess than I could ever be."

His hand closed over hers where it lay, clenched. "None of them matter now. You are my princess. And while you let me close in our marriage bed, there's always a distance between us. And I know why."

"My father has nothing to do with this!" she said quickly.

Didn't Rafiq realize he did exactly the same thing? As passionate as he was in bed, he was remote out of it. She was starting to hate the expressionless mask he wore to close the world—and her—out.

"I think your father has everything to do with it. I'm looking forward to meeting him."

"You're not likely to meet my father—we're not speaking." Determined to put a damper on his enthusiasm, she didn't notice his intense interest. "It's only my mother I intend to visit. She sounded lonely on the phone. And she's worried about our sudden marriage. When can we go?"

Two furrows creased his brow. "Should you be flying in your condition?"

"Pregnant women fly all the time."

"Not my wife."

His possessive growl caused her to blink.

Softening his tone, he added, "Why don't you invite your mother to come visit you here? My schedule is too full to travel right now—and later may be too close to the birth."

Not a no, but not a yes, either.

A twinge of apprehension shot through her. Was he refusing to let her leave? Did he intend to keep her hostage in Dhahara till the baby was born...or longer?

The more she considered that, the more apprehensive she grew.

"If you can't come, then I'll just have to go alone." She pushed her chair back. "Now I'm tired. I'm going to bed."

Alone, Rafiq retreated to the darkened courtyard at the heart of the house. During the day the back wall opened to a wide balcony that overlooked the desert on the edge of the city. But now the courtyard retained the warmth from the hot day in the paving around the pool.

Having shed his clothes, Rafiq sank into the silken water, and fought to clear his head. There was a sense of emptiness within him at Tiffany's departure. The night of pleasure he'd anticipated had been lost. Most frustratingly he couldn't identify how everything had gone so awry in such a short space of time. He'd forced himself not to follow her. She was pregnant. She needed rest. And he had no confidence in his ability to leave her alone.

This time he didn't think making love to her would have eased the tension that had flared between them.

Reaching the far end of the pool, he hoisted himself out and sat on the pool's edge.

Moonlight streaked the water's surface with silver stripes.

Rafiq swung his feet in circles and the silver light broke up as the water rippled, changing the pattern. Like Tiffany. Every time he thought he'd worked her out, Tiffany revealed another facet.

She was far more complex than he would ever have guessed that first night when he'd written her off as a woman after as much money as she could get in the shortest space of time—even if she had to use her body to get it.

He'd been wrong about that.

So wrong…

Feet still in the water, Rafiq propped his elbows on the stone behind him that was still warm from the day's heat and leaned back to stare into the arc of the desert night sky. With the moon so bright, only the most determined stars were visible. One star sparkled brighter than the rest in its group. His gaze homed in on it. It reminded him of his wife—the one who stood out, fascinating him.

In his heart he knew Tiffany had been an innocent—even though his brain was reluctant to accept it. Because that would mean that only he could be her baby's father—that his judgment of her had been criminally wrong.

He was rarely wrong.

And Rafiq was not yet ready to concede that he'd erred in his judgment. Certainly not aloud—as Tiffany had clearly wanted him to do earlier. When the sparkle had gone out of her eyes, he'd wished he had.

Sitting up, he reached for his towel.

Nor did he want to examine too closely why he was

reluctant to admit that he'd been wrong, why it shamed him to have judged her so harshly. He, Rafiq ibn Selim Al Dhahara, who had always been ruled by numbers and logic, had lost his head, and made a spectacular error.

And it all raised another interesting question...

One only Tiffany could answer. Rafiq paused in the act of toweling his hair. If she hadn't slept with him because of money, then why had she done it? Why had she let a stranger take something so precious?

She accused him of keeping women at a distance, of being the last man she'd ever wanted to marry. So why sleep with him when there'd been little hope of seeing him again?

She wanted an ordinary man, a house with a white picket fence, and a pigeon pair. That's what she'd harked back to every time—a fairy tale. He threw the towel to one side. They both knew he was as far from her ordinary prince as it was possible to get.

Water churned angrily as he pulled his legs out of the pool and rose to his full height.

The only answer that made any kind of convoluted sense gave him no comfort at all. Tiffany had gone for a man so far removed from everything she said she wanted because deep in her heart she had no intention of loving anyone. Ever. Not even the ordinary man he'd been so knotted up inside about.

She'd let him close only because he could never be her dream man.

He had to live with that. Or make her accept him as he was, royal prince, international banker, father of her child.

And most importantly, her husband.

Eleven

The Japanese restaurant Rafiq ushered Tiffany into the next day was decorated with deceptive simplicity. Low ceilings and white papered screens set in black lacquered frames gave the space intimacy, while gold-trimmed red wall banners and bamboo shoots in large ceramic pots emblazoned with gold pagodas added touches of luxury.

Rafiq was warmly welcomed by the elderly couple who owned the restaurant, whom he introduced to Tiffany as Mei and Taeko Nakamura.

To the Nakamuras he declared, "I have brought my wife to meet you."

Taeko bowed politely in her direction yet Tiffany suspected it was Mei's black-currant eyes that missed little.

"You said nothing of a wife when we saw you two weeks ago. I suppose this is the reason why you canceled your lunch last week. But shouldn't we at least have read about your wedding in the papers?"

"It will be announced in tomorrow's paper," Rafiq promised, grinning down at the little woman, not looking the least bit chastened.

That was more than Tiffany knew. She opened her mouth to interrupt him, but Mei was already saying, "So we know a secret." And her contemplative eyes settled on Tiffany's midline. Yet, much to Tiffany's relief, she didn't ask the obvious question and led them instead to a table in a corner secluded by screens.

What surprised Tiffany was the way Rafiq's austere features had lit up with pleasure at the sight of the elderly couple, making him appear quite different from the man who only ever presented an emotionless facade.

Nor did he need to order.

Taeko brought a platter of sashimi tuna and pink salmon, and it was quickly apparent that Rafiq was a frequent visitor, though Taeko produced a menu for Tiffany's inspection.

Mei dug out a cell phone and passed it to Rafiq to admire the latest photos of her granddaughter. He made appropriate noises and asked questions about the child whose name appeared to be Keiko, revealing an intimate familiarity with the family. Tiffany couldn't prevent a pang of sadness. If only he'd shown some of this easy joy when she'd shown him the scan images of their baby...

Instead he'd been horrified by the possibility that she might actually be pregnant with his child.

"The tuna is flown in daily," Rafiq told her as Taeko brought the beef teriyaki she'd ordered. "I never eat anything else here."

"I'll stick to beef—rather than raw fish," she said lightly, not wanting to make a point about her pregnancy.

"Delicious," she declared after the first mouthful of her meal.

As she tucked in, she couldn't help wondering whether Rafiq would one day show the same interest in their child as he'd shown for Keiko.

How would she feel about that interest? Rafiq appeared reluctant for her to leave the country to visit her mother. If he grew invested in their daughter, it was possible that he would take over the decision making for her child and leave her with no say.

It was something Tiffany had not considered in any depth before.

Foolish, perhaps.

Given his opinion about her in the past, she'd never anticipated that Rafiq would want to marry her. When he'd proposed, it had been so clear that his major preoccupation was waiting for the baby to be born so that he could wiggle off the hook of paternal responsibility. She'd never contemplated that he might actually want their daughter... or be eager for input into her upbringing.

Tiffany bit her lip.

She'd wanted her daughter to one day have the right to know her father. She'd been prepared to allow some kind of visitation schedule. But she'd never intended to put her daughter within Rafiq's total control.

Breathing deeply to control her rising panic, she tried to focus on what Mei was saying to Rafiq.

"How are Shafir and Megan? You have not brought them for a while."

"They spend every spare moment at Qasr Al-Ward." Rafiq rolled his eyes to the ceiling. "The price of love."

Relief seeped through Tiffany as she watched him joking with the Nakamuras.

Rafiq was no threat to her...or her daughter. He wasn't

a monster. He was only a man. A busy man, a banker of international repute. A desert prince. With a family who were loving.

Why would he want to take over the life of the daughter he'd disputed was his? Even when the tests proved he was the father, it was unlikely that he'd have the time—or the interest—to be a hands-on father.

As the reality of the situation sank in, she started to relax.

Taeko gave a sharp bark of laughter at something Rafiq said. He replied in Japanese, his eyes crinkling, and Mei swatted his arm with the white linen napkin she held.

Rafiq was laughing, his ebony eyes gleaming with mirth.

"You speak Japanese," Tiffany blurted out.

"He speaks German and a bit of Spanish, too." Mei gave her an odd look, and Tiffany felt herself coloring. What kind of wife lacked such basic knowledge about her husband?

She'd been so caught up in her own situation, her pregnancy, her parents' problems, their hasty marriage, she'd barely bothered to learn much about her new husband.

He smiled across the table at her, and her heart leaped at the understanding in his eyes. "What languages do you speak, Tiffany?"

"English and French."

Mei glanced at him in astonishment. "You don't know? Rafiq! What have you two been talking about?"

"Important things!" Rafiq's eyes held a wicked gleam, and Taeko roared with laughter.

Tiffany's flush deepened. Rafiq knew she spoke French. He'd covered up for her. She could've kissed him for making it clear that she wasn't the only one who had been neglectful.

"We will leave the two of you alone to learn more important things about each other." Mei took her husband by the arm and steered him away.

Once the incorrigible pair had departed, Tiffany asked, "How did you meet them?"

"They came to the bank one day needing a loan against the business." His eyes grew somber.

His expression sent a chill down Tiffany's spine. She waited, knowing there must be more to the story.

"Mei had grown so upset that security had to be called to calm her. I heard the commotion, and went to see what it was about. After all, I am ultimately responsible for the safety of everyone in the building."

"What was she upset about?"

"Their granddaughter needed a bone-marrow transplant. It was a procedure that was not available in Dhahara at the time. They needed to go to America. The business was already heavily in debt because of Keiko's medical bills."

"You helped them."

"I never said that."

He didn't need to. Tiffany studied him. "That was very generous of you."

"It wasn't only me—others helped, too. Children like Keiko are the reason I'm so involved in fundraising for the hospital." He glanced away from her intense gaze. "After lunch I am taking you shopping."

"Shopping?" The sudden transition to something so inconsequential confused her. "For Keiko?"

"No, for the press conference in the morning where our marriage will be formally announced and for tomorrow night's banquet. We agreed you needed clothes. You'll need something suitable to wear."

"Press conference?" The thought of the all-too-familiar paparazzi flashlights that dogged her parents' every step filled her with horror. "Can't we just release a statement?"

He shook his head. "This is part of my duty to the people of my country."

Just thinking about a press conference made her stomach sink. Thankfully, she hadn't been photographed for years—her parents had protected her from the relentless glare of Hollywood publicity. And living in Auckland had helped. Now that anonymity would prove a blessing. It was highly unlikely that the press would connect Tiffany, née Smith, wife of Sheikh Rafiq ibn Selim Al Dhahara, with Tiffany Smith, daughter of notorious film director Taylor Smith.

But Rafiq was newsworthy.

And Tiffany knew what would happen *if* her father glimpsed the photos. He would swoop, and try and take over running her life. She already had enough doubts about her own ability to run it, so she certainly didn't need her father wading into the fray.

Laying trembling fingers on his, she murmured, "Rafiq, what if the press report who my father is?"

He closed his free hand over the top of hers. "You need to reconcile with your father. Wait—" he said when she would've interrupted him. "Not for his sake but for your own peace of mind."

Tiffany stared at him rebelliously. "That's all very well, but what do we do if anyone asks today?"

He patted her hand. "Don't worry about it, I'll take care of everything. You worry about looking like a princess. Now let's go buy clothes."

Tiffany fought the urge to tell him she didn't need any clothes. Swiftly she reviewed the contents of her luggage. The long, slim gray skirt and white shirt she'd worn the day she'd arrived would not be glamorous enough for the media baying for photos of the royal sheikh's new bride. Her classic black trousers were not feminine enough and neither of the two maxi dresses she'd packed would be formal enough. And the white dress she'd worn the day she'd met his family was far too unsophisticated for the banquet in the evening—even if it had been created by a young designer whose dresses she loved. And the long dress with gold embroidery that Rafiq had produced for the wedding was far too elaborate for a morning press conference.

It galled her to admit Rafiq was one hundred percent right. None of the clothes she'd brought with her could be described as suitable.

Finally she said, "Okay, let's go shopping."

A discreet bronze wall plaque identified the high-end fashion house Rafiq took her to as Madame Fleur's. It would not have been out of place on Rodeo Drive. The interior of beech-and-chrome cabinetry with glass shelves and black marble floor tiles gave it a sophisticated edge. The black-and-silver labels on the meager range of garments on the racks held no prices. But the cut and quality of the clothes assured Tiffany the cost would be exorbitant.

Far more than she could afford to be indebted to Rafiq at present.

"Rafiq, I don't think—"

"Don't think. Madame and I will take care of everything, won't we?" From where he'd sunk onto a black velvet couch, Rafiq cast the charming smile that Tiffany was starting to recognize at the elegant middle-aged woman whose straight black skirt and black flounced shirt shrieked "French fashion." Predictably, Madame almost swooned and hurriedly agreed.

Tiffany's mouth tightened.

"I can choose my own clothes." It annoyed her that he thought she had no taste, no sense of style.

Swooping on a rack of satin and silks, she selected a dress that wasn't quite the shade of gold or honey or amber, but a mix of all three. At the sight of the cut, she hesitated. Only a woman with supreme self-confidence would wear a dress like this.

"I was thinking of something darker, more formal," Rafiq said, rising from his position on the couch. He picked a wooden hanger off a rack and held up a black satin dress with layered flounces from the hip down. "This is perfect."

"The black dress is beautiful, so elegant," Madame said after a rapid, assessing glance at Rafiq's face.

And very expensive.

Madame was determined to make a sale.

Tiffany suppressed a growl. Did everyone do exactly as he wanted?

"This one." Stubbornly Tiffany pointed to the dress she'd picked, her momentary hesitation forgotten.

"I don't think—" Rafiq paused. Passing the black dress into Madame's waiting arms, he smiled and came toward her with long, pantherish strides. Putting his hands on her shoulders he gazed down into her eyes, his own filled with velvety admiration. "You will look beautiful in whatever you wear. I want people to see you as I do—and black suits you."

"Okay, I'll try it first," she found herself saying. A hint of spine had her adding, "But I do prefer the other dress."

He brushed his lips against her forehead. "Thank you for trying on the black."

* * *

Rafiq knew he'd made the right choice. The dress Tiffany had chosen would be too garish. Black was sedate. Black befitted the wife of a prince of Dhahara.

When the curtains parted, she reappeared looking exactly as he'd expected. Elegant. Untouchable. *Suitable.*

"Excellent." He turned to Madame. "We'll take it."

Tiffany's expression grew rebellious. "Hang on. I don't often wear black."

He approached her and stroked her cheek. Lowering his voice so only she could hear, he murmured, "You were wearing black the night I met you."

She shuddered. "And what a mistake that was."

He couldn't deny that the cheap, shiny fabric of the too-tight dress with its short skirt and tight layers had been a little tacky. But she hadn't had the benefit of his—and Madame's—discerning taste. Although he had to admit that since that night Tiffany had worn surprisingly conservative clothes.

"That was Renate's dress—not mine." She spun away, and his fingers fell to his side. "Now I'll try the other dress."

Inside the dressing-room cubicle Tiffany found that she was trembling. Not with fear but frustration…and rising fury. She put her hands over her face. How could she have chickened out like that? Why hadn't she told Rafiq she wanted to select her own dress, something *she* liked? If he wanted to choose her clothes, he should wear them!

She gave a snort of angry laughter.

All her life she'd let people run her life—make choices and decisions for her. Her father. Her teachers. Imogen. Renate.

It wasn't happening anymore.

Her hands fell away from her face, and she stared at her image in the mirror with new eyes. She was pregnant. Soon she'd be a mother. She was in charge of her own life…and her daughter's. For a couple of minutes out there she'd wimped out when she'd agreed to try on the dress Rafiq had picked—and now he thought he'd won.

He almost had.

Yanking the zipper down, she slid the black dress over her hips and stepped out of it, then hung it on a padded wooden hanger.

The cubicle door opened and Madame swayed in, holding the dress that had caused all the trouble.

"Thank you." Tiffany gave the designer a demure smile as she took the dress. Her most charming smile—she could take a leaf out of Rafiq's book. She had no intention of allowing Rafiq to step in and take over—even if he was her husband. He might be rich. He might be a sheikh. He might be a royal prince. But she wasn't going to let him strip her of the independence and self-respect she'd managed to salvage in the past few months. If she did, she might as well go back home. And tell her father that he had won: she'd come home pregnant, penniless and needing someone else to take charge of her future.

This was no longer about a dress—whatever the darned color.

It was about her…her baby…and *their* future.

Rafiq had no faith in her taste. Based on Renate's dress, she couldn't really blame him. But none of the clothes he'd seen her in since had remotely resembled that awful outfit.

As the dress slithered over her head, Tiffany hoped wildly she had not miscalculated. Too late. She couldn't fold and let Rafiq choose what she was going to wear for the rest of their lives; she had to show him that unlike all the other women he knew, he couldn't simply get what he wanted from her with a charming smile or a fake caress.

Behind her Madame eased the zipper up. Tiffany heard her gasp.

"Très magnifique."

Tiffany spun around. The mirror showed a different woman to the black-clad one who had stood in front of it only minutes ago. This woman was young and vibrant…with a touch of vulnerability and an understated earthiness.

The dress was perfect.

It was her.

For one wild moment uncertainty engulfed her. Could she let Rafiq see her like this? The whole world? She hesitated. Then her spine firmed.

She wasn't ashamed of who she was.

Before she could have any further misgivings, she pushed the cubicle door open, and stepped proudly out, her head held high.

At the sight of her, Rafiq's first reaction was a blast of pure, primal possessive desire. Tiffany was his. All his. No man was going to wrest her from him. Ordinary or otherwise. His second thought was that the color could've been created especially for her. It was hard to see where skin ended and dress began—she'd struck lucky with her impulsive choice.

Instead of looking gaudy, the shade gave her skin a honey tone and turned her hair the burnished shade of bronze.

"What do you think?" Her eyes challenged his.

He gulped.

He didn't dare tell her what he was thinking.

That way lay…

Insanity.

Trying for cool, he said, "It suits you." But he ruined the effect by glancing down at the curves that the dress hugged. Rafiq started to sweat.

"Better than the black?" At the note in her voice his gaze jerked up.

She was taunting him.

No woman dared to taunt him.

Ever.

Even if she was his wife.

His eyes narrowed to slits. This time he took his time looking her over. When he finally reached her face, her lips were parted. He knew she'd be breathing in little gasps. Against his will, his body started to harden.

"Definitely better than the black." His voice came out in a hoarse croak. Without looking away he said to Madame, "We will take this dress."

Then he smiled slowly at Tiffany. No point wasting more time arguing over clothes, not when he was in such a hurry to get home and strip his wife of every item she was wearing.

So he said softly, "Now, which outfit did you have in mind for the press conference?"

Twelve

The front door of Rafiq's home clicked shut behind them.

"Come here, wife."

At Rafiq's growl, Tiffany glanced over her shoulder… and clashed with his hot gaze. He'd barely spoken in the Mercedes-Benz on the way home. And now he expected her to fall into his arms?

"Wait a moment—"

Before she could finish, he closed in on her. Despite her intention of resisting him, desire sparked into an inferno as his lips claimed hers. His hands gripped her shoulders. She swayed back until she came up against the coolness of the plastered wall. Rafiq's body was hard and solid against her curves, and his hands softened to caress the crest of her shoulders, then moved in tantalizing circles under the weight of her hair.

He kissed her until she could barely think.

To her astonishment Tiffany felt unaccountably safe

crushed against him. When he raised his head, it sank in that they were indulging in a passionate embrace, in broad daylight, in the lobby of his home with guards on the other side of the door and his staff in the house.

The impropriety of it made her flush. Pulling back from him, from the intensity of his touch, she yanked the neckline of her dress back into place. "Rafiq, what are you thinking? Your staff could walk in on us at any moment."

"I called and dismissed the house staff. And I secured the locks on the front door and set the security system when we came in." Smug satisfaction glowed good-humoredly in his eyes. "No one is going to interrupt us."

"You planned this!" she accused.

"No, it was a spontaneous reaction to the show you put on at Madame Fleur's store."

That damned dress was still causing trouble!

Before she could put the blame where it rightly belonged, he placed the tip of his index finger against her lips. "Enough talking, I want to kiss you."

Unable to resist a wicked temptation, Tiffany slid her tongue across the pad of his fingertip. He tasted of male and the tang of salt. She licked again. Slowly. Deliberately.

This time he took her mouth with a harsh groan.

The hunger rose more swiftly this time. His lips played with hers until Tiffany gave him a gentle nip. "Kiss me properly."

She hooked her hands behind his nape and pulled his mouth down square on hers. Her hunger silenced the wisecracks, she noted with satisfaction.

The next second the world spun around her. The floor tilted and the dark blue of the walls filled her vision. Tiffany clutched at the front of his shirt. "What are you doing?"

"Taking you somewhere where we can pursue this further." His lips hovered near her ear, the soft whisper of his breath sending delicious tremors though her. "Have you ever made love in a pool?"

"You know I haven't." Excitement quaked through her. "Have you?"

"Never."

"Then we'll have to teach each other how it's done."

They made it to the edge of the pool.

Rafiq deposited her on a lounging chair before straightening and wrenching off his tie. His shirt and trousers followed, landing in a heap on the mosaic tiles. In seconds he stood naked before her.

Breathing quickly, Tiffany eyed her husband with open admiration.

Muscled shoulders sloped to a lean waist, and his stomach was flat and taut. Her fingers itched to stroke the sleek skin.

He dropped down on his knees beside her, and he touched the length of her leg where the filmy maxi dress had fallen away with reverence. "Your skin is so soft," he whispered, "I can never have enough of you."

One day he would—it was how he was made, she knew. But that day wasn't here yet.

For now, he was all hers.

And she wasn't going to let him forget it.

He kissed the inside of her thighs, his fingers slipping under the lacy edge of her panties. Tiffany's breath caught as he slid the scraps of lace down her legs. She shifted restlessly. He was touching her again, making her sigh with delight, his fingers slick against her, arousing her to fever pitch.

She threw her head back and squeezed her eyes shut,

concentrating on the sensations that he aroused. The pleasure twisted higher...tighter.

"More," she moaned, her fingers reaching for him.

Her hand found his hardness, closed around him, felt him jerk.

Then he was on the lounger beside her, pulling her up against him, spoon-fashion, curled behind her. He drew her closer, hesitated, then surged inside her.

She gasped.

He started to move, slowly at first, then quicker. His mouth closed on her neck, nipping gently, causing her to shudder at the sensitive sensation. For a moment she hung suspended in space, a place between, where she was neither herself nor his, but something between. Then she shuddered and whirled into a world of pure pleasure.

When she'd finally come back to earth, she turned to face him, and hooked her arms around his neck. Staring deeply into his eyes, she whispered, "Oh, please say we can do that again?"

Yet the next morning nothing of the playful lover of the previous night remained.

Rafiq was all business.

Tiffany wore the apricot-colored suit she'd picked out that did amazing things for her skin. She knew she looked her best.

Rafiq had barely glanced at her. All he was intent on was lecturing her. If she hadn't known better, she might have thought he was nervous.

"Nothing will be said about how we met," he reminded her as the cavalcade that they were part of turned into the road in front of the palace, the king's main residence in Katar. "Do not get drawn into the work you were doing.

As far as the public is concerned we met through a mutual university friend."

When the doors of the limousine opened, she was ready for the popping clicks of the camera. Putting on her most gracious smile, she allowed Rafiq to help her out.

The press conference started innocuously enough—with Rafiq in total command.

The announcement of their marriage was made, causing a buzz of excitement. Rafiq indulged the journalists, fielding questions, posing with Tiffany for shots, until one journalist called to Rafiq to kiss her.

Her heart thudding, Tiffany turned, raising her face to his. One arm came around her shoulders, the other around her waist and then he paused, staring down at her.

A long moment passed, then all the clicks of cameras and flashing of lights faded. It was a taut moment, full of unspoken tension.

Tiffany waited, face uplifted for the kiss that never came.

Finally, amidst her confusion, he let her go, with a hoarse mutter in Arabic that she did not understand.

Then he took her by the hand and dragged her out of the auditorium, the gaggle of royal aides scurrying in their wake.

Tiffany hurried alongside Rafiq as he strode outside, his fingers tightly holding hers. One glance at his face revealed this was not a good time to ask what she desperately wanted to know.

What had gone wrong?

* * *

That mysterious moment this morning had wired Rafiq. Every time he looked at Tiffany, brushed her hand, a current of electricity blasted him.

Lust, he told himself as he strode the bank's hallways.

Triggered by that damned dress yesterday…and the cataclysmic passion that had followed.

He'd never intended to kiss Tiffany in front of the media this morning—his conservative father would never tolerate such a display. Yet by Allah he'd been tempted…

He'd almost done it.

It shocked him, how near he'd come to the edge.

Where was his control? His common sense?

His hunger, regardless of the cameras, had stunned him. Never before had his private emotions threatened to spill over into a public place.

Still brooding, he turned at the tap on his shoulder. He greeted his eldest brother.

"You are not with your wife," said Khalid.

"I left her in Aunt Lily's hands—gave her a chance to meet other women here tonight."

"Father wants to run a background check on her. He says we know nothing about her—he's worried you rushed into this marriage too impulsively."

"And Shafir didn't?"

"Ah, but that was different. Father was making sure Megan was being kept under surveillance, remember?"

Rafiq couldn't stop the jab of irritation. "It's a little late for that. I know everything I need to know about my wife. We announced our marriage to the world this morning. What does Father hope to achieve?"

Khalid gave him a wry grin. "Your happiness, probably.

I will tell him to forget the idea. He should be thankful that you are married—it's what he wanted after all."

"You will be next," warned Rafiq, his good humor restored.

Aunt Lily had introduced Tiffany to a circle of women as Rafiq's new wife, and Tiffany was aware of their curiosity. She'd warded off the more nosy questions with good grace, and cautiously answered the innocuous ones.

"Your dress…is it from Madame Fleur's?" asked one woman, openly admiring it.

Tiffany smiled demurely. Though a silk wrap was draped around her shoulders, she knew even without it the dress would be perfectly respectable. It was the cut and color that made it look so revealing, not the flesh it exposed. "Yes, it is."

"Not Rafiq's usual taste," said a beautiful woman who had joined the huddle. She was clad in a floor-length black sheath similar to the dress Rafiq had wanted Tiffany to wear tonight. "My name is Shenilla."

Tiffany smiled again. "Nice to meet you, Shenilla." Aware that everyone had fallen silent, she said, "Your dress is lovely."

Shenilla smoothed her hands over her hips, the movement oddly sinuous. "Rafiq chose it for me while we were still…together."

This time the lack of enthusiasm in the slanting eyes was overt.

Uh-oh. The woman in the newspaper photo. The daughter of the wealthy benefactor. And obviously one of Rafiq's former loves. "Oh."

Two of the group hurriedly excused themselves. Tiffany said something meaningless to the woman on the other side of Shenilla—then discovered it was Dr. Farouk, the doctor she and Rafiq had visited about DNA testing. A quick glance showed no sign of Rafiq.

Thrown to the lions—or in this case the lioness.

The image brought no amusement.

A waiter appeared and murmured something in the doctor's ear.

Dr. Farouk gave Tiffany an apologetic look. "Excuse me, duty calls—one of the older women is feeling breathless. I must check on her."

Left alone with Shenilla, Tiffany considered her next move.

She had to admit to a certain curiosity. This must surely be one of the women whom Rafiq had loved—then fallen out of love with. The woman was incredibly beautiful, with a regal elegance that made it obvious why Rafiq had picked her. Of course her father's wealth would've made her a good match, too. Tiffany was instantly conscious of the differences between them. This woman's hair was restrained in a smooth knot, her slanting eyes heavily outlined with kohl.

"Rafiq grows tired of all his women."

Tiffany started to object to being referred to as one of Rafiq's women, to point out she was his wife, but the sheen of moisture coating Shenilla's eyes stopped her.

"I was so certain I would be the one he married. Two years of my life I gave him, hoping every day that he would ask me to be his wife. Instead, not long before he went off to negotiate that hotel deal in Hong Kong, he invited me and my parents out to dinner and told us that our relationship was over." Shenilla swiped her fingertips under her bottom lashes. "I'm sorry, I must be embarrassing you."

Sympathy swept Tiffany, along with another sharp, piercing unidentified emotion. Rafiq had told her that it was the pressure from his family, from the woman and her family, that drove him to break off his relationships. Shenilla had just confirmed it.

"Not at all." She touched the other woman's arm. "You will find someone."

Shenilla sniffed, then nodded. "You are kind. I hope you will not suffer the same hurt, too."

Tiffany wanted to reassure her, tell her she'd been immunized against love a long time ago…but a painful tightness in the vicinity of her heart stopped her. Rafiq was nothing like her father.

"The only comfort I can offer you is that Rafiq is reputed to be faithful while the relationship lasts. A code with him. But there is always the knowledge that one day it will end." Shenilla gave a watery smile. "Although it must be different for you, as he loved you enough to marry you."

Before Tiffany could blurt out that he didn't love her, a hand settled on her waist.

"I see you have met Shenilla." There was a dangerous note in her husband's liquid voice.

Tiffany slid him a sideways glance, and caught the edge in his examination of his former lover.

"We're admiring each other's dresses." Then she remembered Rafiq had picked out the other woman's dress, and added hurriedly, "And comparing style notes. Shenilla was saying that black is one of her favorite colors."

Shenilla shot her a grateful look.

Rafiq pulled her closer to his side. Tiffany suppressed the fierce urge to move away. Couldn't he see the pain he was causing Shenilla? Was he so insensitive? No, he wasn't obtuse. He was doing it deliberately, warning the other woman that he would stand no threat to Tiffany.

She didn't know whether to hug him or scold him for his protectiveness. For the sake of Shenilla's pride, she decided to pretend she hadn't noticed, and continued chatting about the latest fall fashions, while Rafiq vibrated with tension beside her.

A mix of emotions rattled her. She wanted to shake him. She wanted to kiss him. What on earth was wrong with her?

He tilted his head sideways, and gave her a smile. Her heart rolled over.

Oh, no. Please. Anything but that.

Falling for Rafiq was the dumbest thing she could do. Already he'd been pressured by circumstance—and by a need to legitimize their child—to marry her. She'd unwittingly caught him in exactly the kind of trap that he'd avoided so assiduously all his life.

How could he feel anything but resentment toward her?

Thirteen

The intrusive ring of her cell phone woke Tiffany several mornings later.

Rolling over, she groped with one hand for the bedside table, and the ringing stopped.

With a groan she sat up. The first thing she realized was that the morning roller-coaster ride that her stomach had been on for weeks seemed to be over. The second was that the sound of running water meant Rafiq was in the shower in the adjoining bathroom. He hadn't yet gone to work. Checking the missed call, Tiffany recognized her mother's cell phone number. She hit Redial.

What could be wrong?

"Darling, where are you staying?" Her mother's voice sounded surprisingly clear.

Tiffany tried to collect her thoughts. "What do you mean?"

"We're here. In Dhahara."

"We?"

"Your father and I."

Tiffany stomach bottomed out, and she squeezed her eyes shut in horror.

"Where?"

"At the airport. We're about to catch a cab to come and see you."

No!

She heard the glass door click as Rafiq opened it. Any moment he'd be back in the bedroom. He knew she missed her mother; he'd said she needed to reconcile with her father. Had he arranged this?

"Mom—"

"There were photos of you all over the front page of the national newspaper that we were given in the airplane. But we couldn't understand a word of the story."

Darn it.

"Why is Dad with you?"

"Tiffany, I had to tell him about your marriage—I couldn't keep it from him. He's worried about you, darling. So we decided to come and see how you were."

Not worried so much as wanting to make sure she took his advice. Tiffany sighed.

"I wish you'd let me know you were going to tell him." She would've preferred to tell him herself.

"Your new husband is a hunk." Her mother sounded downright coy as she sidestepped Tiffany's comment. "You never mentioned that."

Straining her ears for sounds of the "hunk," Tiffany ignored the subtle rebuke. "Mom, why don't you go and book in at one of the city's hotels? I'll come see you in a couple of hours. Then maybe we can arrange to spend a couple of days together. Maybe we can go on an excursion into the desert."

"But we want to see you—"

The sound of footsteps made her say hurriedly, "I've got to go—I'll call you later."

Rafiq stood in the arch that separated the bedroom from the bathroom. "Who are you going to call later?" he asked, raising a dark eyebrow.

She hesitated. "My mom. Rafiq…"

He came swiftly across the room. "Problems?"

The concern in his eyes made her feel simply awful.

"Not really. Rafiq—" she bit her lip "—my mother is here, in Dhahara."

His expression brightened. "That's good. You wanted to visit your mother, now she can set her mind at rest."

She had to ask. "Did you call my mom and set this up?"

"No!" His brows jerked together. "I don't even have her contact details, come to think of it."

He had all the resources he needed to have found her if he'd wanted to. But she couldn't doubt him. She had to trust him at his word.

"Sorry." She chewed her lip again: "My father is here, too. I asked Mom why he came, and she says he's worried about me."

"Sounds like a father. Invite them to dinner." Rafiq walked into the closet. When he came out he was wearing trousers and shrugging on a business shirt. "They can stay here—there are plenty of bedchambers."

Oh, God. "You don't understand. My father always expects me to do what he wants."

He paused in the act of buttoning his shirt and raised that expressive eyebrow. "You're a married woman now."

"In his eyes I'll always be his little girl who can't run her own life."

"You're a grown woman. You're married, and soon you'll be having a baby. You'll be a parent yourself. He can only run your life if you let him."

"You're so right," she said in wonder. She'd never thought of herself in the context of being a mother in quite that way before—or how it affected her in relation to her father.

"You don't need to love him any less—he'll always be your father."

There was something so liberating in his words. She'd fought with her father so much over her freedom that they'd isolated each other. It didn't need to be that way. She would make her own choices, make it clear to her father this was her life, her choice, but that she would always love him.

If there was no battle, there could be no hostility. And her father had made his choices, too. He'd chosen Imogen over her mother. She needed to accept that. Her mother had already taken steps to deal with that reality. Now she had to do the same.

Maybe she could salvage something of their father-daughter relationship.

"Thank you, Rafiq." She raised her face to him and accepted his kiss.

"I must go, before you tempt me to collapse beside you and spend the day in bed."

"But, Rafiq—"

"Later." He picked up a dark suit jacket and slung it over his shoulder. As he reached the bedroom door he gave her a gentle smile. "Tell your parents I am looking forward to welcoming them to our home."

It was in that moment that Tiffany realized how much she truly loved him.

* * *

Several hours later Rafiq hurried toward the grand salon in his father's palace. He nodded to the aides. The double doors were flung open. Rafiq strode forward.

"Who was it you wanted to meet—"

The king was not alone. Rafiq stopped as he recognized the man seated in the brown leather armchair across from his father.

Sir Julian Carling rose to his feet and stretched out his hand. Rafiq shook it and raised an eyebrow in the king's direction.

"What is this about?"

His father looked wearier than Rafiq had ever seen.

"My son—" He broke off.

"What is it?"

But Rafiq had a sinking feeling that he knew. He gave the hotelier a narrow-eyed glare. Sir Julian looked away first.

"I have been concerned about this woman you have married."

"We have already discussed this, Father."

"I fear that I was too hasty—I should have pursued my first instinct and had her investigated."

"Father—"

The king held up a hand. "Stop. You will listen to what Sir Julian has told me. It is scandalous."

Blood roared in Rafiq's ears as he paced the length of the room. "I am not interested in what Sir Julian has to say about my wife."

The king shook his head sadly. "I fear she will not be your wife for much longer—you will have no choice but to divorce her."

Rafiq spun around. Sir Julian must have seen the rage

in his eyes because the millionaire almost overturned his chair in his haste to stand.

"Now look here, Rafiq—"

"Rafiq!" The lash of the king's tongue called him to order.

He drew a deep, shuddering breath.

"My son, you really do need to hear what Sir Julian is going to say."

"I know what he is going to say."

The king looked shocked. "You knew this woman is a prostitute?"

"That is a lie!"

This time Julian backed away five paces.

It was the king's turn to glance uncertainly at Sir Julian. "You are sure of these facts?"

"She has hoodwinked him," Sir Julian sputtered. "He found her in a flesh club in Hong Kong."

"What do you hope to get out of this?" Rafiq demanded, advancing on the hotelier.

"Your father has agreed that my daughter will make you a perfect wife. But Elizabeth will never agree to marrying a man who already has a wife. You will need to have your marriage annulled—fraud will be reason enough."

Rafiq's anger before was nothing to the rage that consumed him now.

"I do not want your daughter—I already have a wife. And no fraud has been committed that could merit annulling the marriage."

"She lied to you."

Rafiq shook his head. "Not so."

"But Elizabeth is coming to Dhahara to meet you."

"It is a waste of her time—and mine. Nor does it have anything to do with my wife."

"I invited her—" the King broke in "—Sir Julian and I have been talking."

Rafiq knew that tone of old. "What have you been negotiating?"

His father looked guilty. "You have always been a good, loyal son—"

"Oh, no!" Reminding him of his duty would not work this time. Rafiq shook his head.

"Your wife needs to be carefully chosen—"

"I know that—I've already done so."

"Ay, me. This is about sex."

Rafiq stared at his father. "It is not about sex—at least not in the way you mean. My wife is no Mata Hari, she hasn't the loose morals Julian suggests—" in fact the shoe was well and truly on the other foot "—but I admit I cannot keep my hands off her."

The admission freed something within him. Tiffany was important to him, more important than any woman he'd ever known. He wasn't letting her go. She was his.

"This concerns me. You are in the thrall of a woman who is manipulating you. I want you to divorce her before she causes a scandal we cannot fix." The king's face could've been carved from marble.

"Why? So I can marry Elizabeth Carling?"

King Selim's eyes grew shifty. "Sir Julian has offered to make a generous marriage settlement—"

"No! I am not divorcing Tiffany. Nor am I taking another wife. My wife was a virgin the first time I took her to my bed."

The astonishment on his father's face made Rafiq curl his hands into fists at his sides.

"The information I am revealing should be sacred to my wife and me, not dragged out in such a sordid situation."

"My son, if anything happens to me, to your brothers, you will sit on the throne."

The pressure was on. His father was pulling out the big guns. "And why should I marry a woman whose father has no idea of what it means to be faithful?" He didn't even spare Sir Julian a glance. "It was not I who broke marriage vows and slept with a backstreet whore that night in Hong Kong."

Sir Julian turned puce. "You can't talk to—"

"Oh, yes, I can," Rafiq cut in. "I don't want a wife who may have slept with a thousand men because of the example that has been set by her father." He could hear the pulse thudding in his head. "My heirs will be mine alone."

Then he realized what he had said. And the irony of it hit him full force. Tiffany never stopped worrying about the impact her father's notorious affairs would have on his family. He didn't care a fig for that. Yet, even more ironic was the fact that Tiffany was pregnant—and he'd disputed her baby's paternity. And now, in the heat of the accusations, he had defended her.

Because in his heart he knew she had been true. Everything about her was pure.

Her baby was his. He no longer required a DNA test to confirm the fact.

"My wife is pregnant."

A stunned silence followed his announcement. A flash of joy lit up his father's face. "Pregnant? My first grandchild! How I wish your mother was here." Shadows replaced the joy, and King Selim glanced surreptitiously at Sir Julian.

That look told Rafiq what he had feared—that the two of them had already gone far down the road of planning his wedding to Elizabeth Carling—and if Elizabeth hadn't objected to being the second wife, both men would no doubt have let Elizabeth occupy that place.

But Rafiq only wanted one wife, and he had chosen Tiffany.

Part of his choice had embraced a decision to believe in her—there was no reason not to. His place was not here arguing with Sir Julian. His first loyalty lay with his wife—she, and their unborn baby, were now his family.

Fourteen

Tiffany wished Rafiq would come home.

She'd put a call in to his office that her parents were already here. No doubt he would expect her to make the first move to reconcile with her father.

Yet, sitting on the balcony that overlooked a stretch of desert, her father was not making it any easier.

"If you'd stayed home, Tiffany, this mess would never have happened."

Tiffany suppressed the urge to roll her eyes and point out that he was the one who had walked out.

"Taylor, Tiffany is looking forward to having the baby." The stress around her mother's eyes as she ran interference caused Tiffany to wince.

At her father's look of disbelief she only said, "I am, actually."

"This is what you want?" Her father shook his head. "To

be stuck out here on the edge of the desert, where you don't even speak the language, with a man you barely know?"

"The desert is beautiful! Look at all the colors of the setting sun. I can learn the language—and I know enough about Rafiq to know that he's a decent man."

"Decent? What does that mean?"

Anger sparked. She remembered Rafiq's distaste that first night in Le Club when Sir Julian had pulled Renate onto his lap. She thought about how Shenilla had said he only ever dated one woman at a time. "That he would never betray me by running around with other women."

Her father's face changed.

"Oh, come look at this, Taylor, isn't it interesting?"

Her father allowed himself to be distracted by her mother's peacemaking attempts and Tiffany drew an unsteady breath as they both disappeared into the house. How could she have fallen back into this confrontational relationship with her father? Hadn't Rafiq told her he could only run her life if she let him? It was time to move on.

Suddenly she wished Rafiq was beside her. He understood her—better than anyone ever had.

A wave of gratitude swept her. She'd been fortunate to find a man who suited her perfectly—yet she was far from an ideal wife. Guilt ate at her. Given any choice, Rafiq would never have married her.

She was just as guilty of boxing him into a corner as all the women he'd so smartly evaded. And one day he was going to bitterly resent her for taking away his freedom.

"Looks like your husband will be able to keep you in a style that will be easy to get accustomed to. That's quite a display." Her father's return from where he'd been inspecting an illuminated manuscript in a glass case cut into her thoughts. "But I want to see that I can leave you in this man's care."

Tiffany refrained from telling her father that Rafiq had already saved her from more scrapes than her father ever had. That she loved him. That she wanted to stay by his side for every day of her life. That the last thing her husband needed was an overzealous parent—he'd had enough of those.

The sound of voices led Rafiq to where his wife and her visitors were sitting on the balcony overlooking the desert. He loved this spot in the evenings, when the heat subsided and the desert came to life. He paused on the threshold, drinking in the sight of Tiffany.

She was perched on one of the thickly padded chairs, the center point of the family group. If he hadn't known she was pregnant, the healthy glow of her skin and the sheen of her hair would've given it away. An older woman, who had to be Linda, with salt-and-pepper hair and a kindly face sat beside her, while a thin, bearded man full of nervous energy dominated the conversation.

Rafiq strode forward. All three of them looked up.

A shadow passed over Tiffany's face, then she leaped up. "Rafiq, you're here."

She clung to him, and there was a touch of desperation in the kiss she gave him.

"What's the matter?" he asked.

She shook her head, then let go of him.

Uneasy, he waited.

She introduced her parents with a bright smile, tension evident in every line of her body. Rafiq frowned, trying to fathom what was worrying her. At first he thought her parents might be causing her strain, but he couldn't see any evidence of that. Linda appeared to be doing her best to do everything to ease the situation, while Tiffany's father clearly thought of no one other than himself.

Tiffany caught his eye. "I'd like to talk to you, Rafiq."

Her somber expression caused a dart of concern.

After excusing himself from the company, he followed her down the stairs, along the walkway lined with palms, and onto the edge of the desert beyond. "What's wrong? Are you in pain? Is it the baby?"

The helplessness that he experienced was a first. Rafiq discovered he didn't like it at all.

She shook her head. "It's nothing like that."

But she kept knotting and unknotting her fingers. The gesture didn't reassure Rafiq. "Then what is it?" he demanded. "What's the matter?"

"I've trapped you into this marriage."

His heart stood still. "What?"

"You would never have married me if I hadn't been pregnant. It's just like all those other women who tried to corner you into marriage—except this time there was a baby. You couldn't get out of it. One day you're going to resent me—even the child."

An air of dejection surrounded her.

"That's not just any child. That's my daughter you're talking about."

Tiffany hesitated, then blurted out, "You said 'my daughter.' Do you mean that? Do you believe it? Or are you just saying it to make me feel better?"

"Oh, I mean it."

"And what about being trapped?"

"I'm not trapped."

Tiffany started to shake. "I thought…" She broke off.

"What did you think?"

"I thought that you were going to hate me. That you'd one day feel that I'd tricked you."

"Oh, Tiffany. I was always going to marry you."

"To legitimize the baby—out of duty."

"Because I wanted you. Because I couldn't keep my hands off you." He stepped up beside her and wrapped his arms around her, then rested his chin on her shoulder. "I don't care what your father does in his life, I want you. And nothing, not your father, not my father, is going to keep me from having you."

From her silence he knew that she required some mental adjustment.

So he added for good measure, "If you look behind us, you'll see that your father has just taken your mother's hand. His behavior is her problem—unless they decide to get divorced."

"Do you think she'd take him back? He's a serial adulterer.... He needs to grow up."

"So I've gathered."

"Did I tell you that?"

"You didn't need to." He stroked her hair. "But don't make the mistake of confusing me with your father."

"Oh, I won't," she assured him. "You're nothing like him. My mother is in for a lot more heartache if she takes him back."

"He may have missed her. He may want to change his ways. But don't think his behavior is your responsibility."

"I thought you would think—"

"You think entirely too much!"

She didn't smile. "So who my father is won't make you think any less of me?"

He shook his head. "Just like who your father is won't make me think any more of you, either." Then he started to laugh. "I'm not being totally consistent."

"What do you mean?"

"I told Julian that I had no intention of ever marrying

his daughter because I couldn't be sure she hadn't slept around as much as he has."

She pulled out of his arms, and swiveled to face him. The waning sunlight turned the tips of her lashes to gold. "Julian? You mean Sir Julian Carling?"

He nodded.

"But you can't marry her, you're married to me."

"You noticed," he said smugly.

"Of course I noticed!"

"Good."

He leaned forward and kissed her. He took his time, and did it thoroughly, not caring that her parents might be watching.

When he'd finished, she returned to the subject like a dog with a bone. "Why was Sir Julian talking to you about marrying his daughter?"

"He wasn't talking to me about it. He was discussing it with my father," he said then laughed as she placed her hands on her hips and glared at him. "They had decided I should divorce you and marry Elizabeth Carling."

"Divorce me?" Tiffany's bravado disappeared like a deflated balloon. She looked stunned, then apprehensive.

"Don't worry. I told them that I had no intention of divorcing you—that you were pregnant with my baby. And, yes, I believe that. Just as I believe that you were a virgin that first night we made love." He also knew that this woman would never bore him. She was his forever. "Now it's my turn to make a confession."

"What is it?"

He handed her a piece of paper. "I never did intend to stay married to you after we had the tests done."

"You intended to cut and run if the baby wasn't yours?"

He nodded. "And if it was mine I intended to keep the baby here, divorce you and send you home."

"What an utterly diabolical plot!"

"I know." He pointed to the paper she held. "That contract you're holding will ensure that you will feel safe, that I will never do something like that. You only need to sign it."

She glanced at it, then flung her arms around him. "You know I told myself I was looking for someone ordinary."

"The man that you're looking for is going to be very hard to find."

"No." She released him and shook her head. "I've decided he isn't what I want. I want someone special. Someone like you. No one ordinary would ever have confessed what you did—or given me that kind of assurance in writing. I love you. That's very hard for me to say. I'm beginning to think I never intended to love anyone. But I love you because you are incredibly special."

His heart stopped at her confession. "I love you, too. You are the most important person in my whole world. You fill my world," he whispered, drawing her back into his arms. "There is only you. There will only ever be you."

* * * * *

"I'm not sleeping with you tonight, Tony."

"Wrong," he said, pointing a finger at her. *"I'm* not sleeping with *you,* but I'm your husband whether you like it or not."

"What does that mean?" she asked.

"It means that I don't plan to tiptoe around you anymore, Rena."

He left her on the terrace and strode over to the wet bar, pouring himself three fingers of Scotch. He hated that Rena had it right this time. He *had* married her out of obligation and a sense of duty. But he hadn't expected her resentment to irk him so much.

Hell, he'd never had to beg a woman for sex in his life. And he wasn't about to start now.

MILLION-DOLLAR MARRIAGE MERGER

BY
CHARLENE SANDS

All the characters in this book have no existence outside the imagination of
the author, and have no relation whatsoever to anyone bearing the same name
or names. They are not even distantly inspired by any individual known or
unknown to the author, and all the incidents are pure invention.

Published in Great Britain 2011
by Mills & Boon, an imprint of Harlequin (UK) Limited,
Eton House, 18-24 Paradise Road, Richmond, Surrey TW9 1SR

© Charlene Swink 2010

ISBN: 978 0 263 88228 5

51-0611

Harlequin (UK) policy is to use papers that are natural, renewable and
recyclable products and made from wood grown in sustainable forests. The
logging and manufacturing processes conform to the legal environmental
regulations of the country of origin.

Printed and bound in Spain
by Blackprint CPI, Barcelona

Free book!
Plus, receive a FREE mystery gift

- -

If you have enjoyed reading this Desire romance story, then why not take advantage of this **FREE** book offer and we'll send you another title from this series absolutely **FREE!**

Accepting your **FREE** book and **FREE** mystery gift places you under no obligation to buy anything.

As a member of the Mills & Boon Book Club™ you'll receive your favourite Series books up to 2 months ahead of the shops, plus all these exclusive benefits:

- FREE home delivery
- Exclusive offers and our monthly newsletter
- Membership to our special rewards programme

We hope that after receiving your free book you'll want to remain a member. But the choice is yours. So why not give us a go. You'll be glad you did!

Visit www.millsandboon.co.uk for the latest news and offers.

Mrs/Miss/Ms/Mr .... Initials ....

BLOCK CAPITALS PLEASE

Surname ....

Address ....

....

....

.... Postcode ....

Email ....

D1FIA

NO STAMP NEEDED!

FREE BOOK OFFER
FREEPOST NAT 10298
RICHMOND
TW9 1BR

NO STAMP
NECESSARY
IF POSTED IN
THE U.K. OR N.I.

To my husband, Don,
the man I've been sharing chardonnay with
for all our years. A really good man,
like a fine wine, only gets better with age.

Charlene Sands resides in Southern California with her husband, school sweetheart and best friend, Don. Proudly they boast that their children, Jason and Nikki, have earned their college degrees. The "empty nesters" now enjoy spending time together on Pacific beaches, playing tennis and going to movies, when they are not busy at work, of course!

A proud member of Romance Writers of America, Charlene has written more than 25 romance novels and is the recipient of the 2006 National Readers' Choice Award, the 2007 Cataromance Reviewer's Choice Award and the Booksellers Best Award in 2008 and 2009.

Dear Reader,

Who doesn't find a champion sexy? And former race car driver Tony Carlino is that and a whole lot more. He's the man Rena Fairfield Montgomery hates with every breath she takes, but he's also the man she'd once loved. When Tony comes home to Napa to meet the terms of his father's will and run Carlino Wines, a deathbed vow to his best friend brings Tony back into Rena's life. She's a challenge he means to win, no matter the cost.

Set against the backdrop of Napa Valley where the air is flavored with the sweet pungent scent of ripening grapes and earth deep and rich with hearty vines, the first story in my *Napa Valley Vows* trilogy is about forgiveness and second chances and two young hearts who find their way back to each other years later with a vow that cannot be broken.

So sit back, get comfortable and have a fine glass of hearty California merlot.

Let's toast to loves lost and found again in Napa Valley!

Charlene

One

From the time Tony Carlino was six years old, he'd been infatuated with cars, speed and danger. Back then, the hills of Napa that create award-winning merlot and pinot had been his playing field. Racing his dinged up scooter down the embankment, he'd hit the dirt falling headfirst into a patch of fescue grass a hundred times over. But Tony never gave up when he wanted something. He hadn't been satisfied until he'd mastered that hill with his scooter, his bicycle and finally his motorcycle. He'd graduated to stock car racing and had become a champion.

Newly retired from racing, his present fascination had nothing to do with cars and speed and everything to do with a different kind of danger.

Rena Fairfield Montgomery.

He glimpsed the blue-eyed widow from across the gravesite where dozens were gathered. Valley winds blew strands of raven hair from her face, revealing her heartbroken expression and ruffling her solemn black dress.

She hated him.

With good reason.

Soon he'd walk into a land mine of emotion and nothing posed more danger to Tony than that. Especially when it came to Rena and all she represented.

Tony glanced beyond the gravesite to those hills and Carlino land, an abundance of crimson hues reflecting off foil covering the vines, keeping grape-eating birds from destroying the crop. The land he once resented, the vines that had fed his family for generations was his responsibility now. His father had passed on just months ago, leaving the Carlino brothers in charge of the huge empire.

Once again, Tony glanced at Rena and a face devoid of emotion, her tears spent. She walked up to the bronze coffin, staring blankly, as if to say she couldn't believe this. She couldn't believe that her beloved husband, David, was gone.

Tony winced. He held back tears of his own. David had been his best friend since those scooter days. He'd been there for Tony through thick and thin. They'd kept their friendship ongoing, despite a bitter family rivalry.

Despite the fact that Rena had loved Tony first.

Rena held back a sob and bravely reached out to the blanket of fresh flowers draped along the coffin. She pulled her hand back just as her fingertip touched a rose petal. At that moment, she glanced at Tony, her sad eyes so round and blue that a piece of him unraveled.

He knew her secret.

But Tony didn't give that away. He stared at her, and for that one small moment, sympathy and the pain of losing David temporarily bonded them.

She blinked then turned around, stepping away from the gravesite, her legs weak as all eyes watched the beautiful grieving widow say her final farewell to her husband.

Nick and Joe, Tony's younger brothers, stood by his side. Joe draped an arm around him. "We're all going to miss him."

"He was as good as they come," Nick added.

Tony nodded and stared at the car as Rena drove away from the cemetery.

"Rena's all alone now," Joe said, once Nick bid them farewell. "It'll be even more of a struggle for her to keep Purple Fields going."

Tony drew a deep breath, contemplating his next move. They'd been rivals in business for years, but her winery had been failing and was barely holding on. "She won't have to."

Joe stiffened. "Why, are you planning on buying her out? She won't sell, bro. You know she's stubborn. She's had offers before."

"Not like this one, Joe."

Joe turned his head to look him in the eye. "What, you're making her an offer she can't refuse?"

"Something like that. I'm going to marry her."

* * *

Rena got into her car alone, refusing her friends' and neighbors' well-meaning gestures to drive her home, to sit with her, to memorialize David Montgomery. She never understood why people gathered after a funeral, had food catered in and specialty wines flowing. They filled their plates, chattered and laughed and most times forgot the real reason they had come. She couldn't do that to David. No, he was too young to die. Too vital. He'd been a good man, an excellent and loving husband. She couldn't celebrate his life; he'd had so much more to live. So she spoke the words with sincerity to the guests at the funeral site, "I hope you understand that I need to be alone right now," and had driven off.

She rode the lanes and narrow streets of the valley as numbness settled over her. She knew this land so well, had traveled every road, had grown up in Napa and had married here.

She wept silently. Tears that she thought were all dried up spilled down her cheeks. She found herself slowing her old Camry as she passed the Carlino estate, the vibrant vineyards sweeping across acres and acres.

She knew why she'd come here. Why she parked the car just outside the estate gates. She blamed Tony Carlino for David's death. She wanted to scream it from the hilltops and shout out the unfairness of it all.

A flashy silver sports car pulled up behind her, and she knew she'd made a mistake coming here. From the rearview mirror, she watched him step out of the car, his long legs making quick strides to the driver's side of her car.

"Oh, no." She grasped the steering wheel and rested her forehead there. Biting her lip, she took back her wish to scream out injustices. She didn't have the energy. Not here. Not now.

"Rena?"

The deep rich timbre of Tony's voice came through the window of the car. He'd been her friend once. He'd been her world after that. But now all she saw was a drop-dead handsome stranger who should have never come back to the valley. "I'm fine, Tony," she said, lifting her head from the steering wheel.

"You're not fine."

"I just buried my husband." She peered straight ahead, refusing to look at him.

Tony opened the car door, and she glimpsed his hand reaching out to her. "Talk to me."

"No...I can't," she said with a shake of her head.

"Then let's take a walk."

When she continued to stare at his hand, he added, "You came here for a reason."

She closed her eyes holding back everything in her heart, but her mind wouldn't let go of how David died. Spurred by renewed anger, she ignored Tony's outstretched hand and bounded out of the car. She strode past him and walked along the narrow road lush with greenery. From atop the hill, the valley spread out before her, abundant with vines and homes, both big and small, a hollow of land where many families worked side by side to ensure a healthy crop.

She had promised David she'd hold on to Purple Fields, an odd request from his deathbed, yet one she couldn't refuse. She loved Purple Fields. It had been her parent's legacy, and now it was her home, her sanity and her refuge.

She marched purposely ahead of Tony, which was an accomplishment in itself, since he'd always been quick on his feet. His footsteps slowed. Then he let go an exasperated sigh. "Damn it, Rena. David was my friend. I loved him, too."

Rena halted. Jamming her eyes closed momentarily, she whirled around. "You *loved* him? How can you say that? He's gone because of you!" Rena's anger flowed like the rush of a river. "You should never have come home. David was happy until you showed up."

Lips pursed, Tony jutted his jaw out. Oh, how she remembered that stubborn look. "I'm not responsible for his death, Rena."

"He wouldn't have gotten behind the wheel of that race car if you hadn't come home. When you showed up, that's all David talked about. Don't you see? You represented everything David wanted. You ran away from the vineyards. You raced. You won. You became a champion."

Tony shook his head. "It was a freakish accident. That's all, Rena."

"Your return here brought it all back to him," she said solemnly.

"My father died two months ago. I came home to run the company."

Rena glared at him. "Your father," she muttered. Santo Carlino had been a harsh, domineering man who'd wanted to build his empire no matter the cost. He'd tried to buy out every small winery in the area. And when the owners refused, he'd managed to ruin their business somehow. Purple Fields had seen the brunt of the Carlino wrath for years. Yet her parents had fought him tooth and nail, keeping their small patch of life out of Carlino hands. "I'll not speak ill of the dead, but..."

"I know you despised him," Tony stated.

Rena stuck to her promise and held her tongue about Santo Carlino, but she couldn't help how she felt and made no apologies for those feelings. "Go away, Tony."

Tony's lips curved up, a sinful, sexy curl of the mouth that at one time had knocked her senseless. "This is my land."

She slumped her shoulders. "Right."

Rena inhaled sharply, mentally chastising herself for driving up here—a bonehead move, as David would say. She was even more remorseful that she'd taken this short walk with Tony.

With hasty steps she brushed by him, but his reach was long and painfully tender when he caught her arm. "Let me help."

A lump formed in her throat. He didn't know what he was asking. She'd never accept his help. She glanced into dark, piercing, *patient* eyes. That was something for the record books—a patient Tony Carlino. He hadn't become a national stock car champion from his ability to wait.

She shook her head briskly. "Please don't touch me."

Tony glanced at his hand lying gently on her arm,

then stroked the length of it, sliding his hand freely up and down. "I mean it, Rena. You need me."

"No, I'll never need you." She jerked her arm free. "You just want to ease your guilty conscience."

Tony's eyes grew hard and sharp.

Good.

She didn't need his help or his pity. She'd done without him for twelve years and didn't need anything he had to offer. All she wanted was to curl up in her bed and dream about the day when she'd hold her precious baby in her arms.

Tony rubbed his aching shoulder and stretched out his legs, closing the Carlino books for the day. His racing injuries had a way of coming back to haunt him whenever he sat at his father's desk. Maybe it was because Santo never wanted him to leave Napa. He'd chosen racing over the family business and had left it all behind twelve years ago.

He'd wanted more than grapes and vines and worrying about the weather, crops and competition. Of course, Santo Carlino hadn't taken it lightly. He'd cursed and complained and refused to speak to Tony when he'd left.

Tony pursued his dream despite his father's tirades. Being the oldest of three sons Tony was expected to take over the business one day with his brothers by his side. But as it turned out none of the three sons had stayed home to run the Carlino empire.

Now with Santo gone, Tony had no choice but to return. His father's last will and testament made sure that each of his sons spent some time together running the company. He'd stipulated that in order for any of them to claim their inheritance, the land, the company, the Carlino empire, one of them had to agree to become the new CEO within six months.

It was just another way for his father to manipulate them. But Tony hadn't come back to Napa for the money. He had plenty of his own. He'd come back to lay his father to rest and to let his weary body recover from injuries garnered in a wreck at Bristol Raceway just months before.

He'd called his younger brothers home. Joe, the real brain in the family, had been living in New York, trying to develop the latest software phenomenon. And Nick, the youngest, had been creating havoc in Europe, earning a reputation as a gambler and ladies' man.

Tony smiled at that. Little Nick had a wild streak that could lay shame to a young and virile Santo Carlino in his bachelor days. But if one thing could be said about his old man, it was that he was a loving and faithful husband. Tony's mother, Josephina, had tempered him with love and adoration. Many thought her a saint for putting up with Santo, but only the family knew that Santo would have died for her.

"So when's the wedding?" Joe entered the office at Carlino Wines with his hands on his hips, his studious dark brown eyes visible behind a pair of glasses.

When Tony glanced at him in question, Joe continued, "You told me you were getting married."

Tony shoved the ledger books away and leaned back in his chair. "You need a willing bride for a wedding."

"Wanna tell me why you chose Rena? Is it Purple Fields you're after? Or something else?"

A sigh emerged from deep in Tony's chest. He rubbed tension from his forehead. "Maybe I want it all."

"*Want* or need?"

Tony narrowed his eyes and gave his brother a look.

Joe shrugged in an offhanded way. "You've never spoken of marriage before. And the last thing I thought I'd hear at David's funeral was that you intended to marry his widow. Even if it is Rena. We all know she's not exactly your biggest fan."

Tony scoffed. How well he knew. "Hardly that."

"So, what is it? Do you love her?"

Tony's face crinkled up, despite his efforts to keep a blank expression. The truth was he had loved Rena when they'd been younger but he'd loved racing more. He wound up breaking her heart by leaving her behind to pursue his dreams.

Now he had a chance to make it up to her and honor the pledge he'd made David. At the time he'd made that vow it was a no-brainer. David was on his last breaths, and he'd implored Tony to take care of Rena and the child he'd suspected she carried. Tony hadn't flinched when he'd made that promise.

Did Tony want to marry Rena and raise a child that wasn't his? He simply didn't know. But it was what he planned to do.

"No, I don't love her." He stood and looked his brother straight in the eyes, lowering his voice. "This goes no further."

Joe nodded.

"I made David a promise to take care of Rena, the winery and…and their unborn child."

Joe pressed a finger to the bridge of his glasses, securing them in place. He contemplated a moment staring back at Tony then gave an understanding nod. "Got it. Rena knows nothing about this I suppose."

"Nothing."

"Are you seeing her?"

Tony winced, thinking back on the excuses she'd given him. "I've tried several times since the funeral."

"Not cooperating is she?"

"No."

"Can't imagine why she doesn't want to start up right where you left off twelve years ago," Joe said, mockingly. "She picked up the pieces after you left her. It was a hard fall, Tony. I remember hearing all about it. When she fell for David, everyone thought it was the right move. They were happy for her. Sorry, but your name was mud around here for a long time. Then you started winning races and people forgot about the pain you caused Rena. Except Rena. She never forgot. She really loved David, and now he's gone. You can't blame her for hard feelings. She's had it rough."

"I don't blame her. But I will honor my promise to David."

Joe grinned. "I respect your determination, Tony. How are you going to charm a woman who clearly…"

"Hates me?" Tony huffed out a breath. Unfortunately, what he had in mind didn't require a multitude of charm.

Just blackmail. He would give Rena what she wanted most in life. "I have a plan."

Joe shook his head. "You always do."

"It's time I set that plan in action."

Two

Rena looked in her closet as tears streamed down her face. It had been three weeks since the funeral, and David's clothes—his shirts and pants, his jackets and sweatshirts—still hung just beside hers. She reached out to touch his favorite blue plaid shirt. Her fingers lingered a bit and an image appeared of sitting by a cozy fire cuddling up next to David and laying her head on the soft flannel, his arm wrapped around her shoulder. She smiled at the memory, even through her tears. "What now, David?" she asked in the solitude of her bedroom.

She was a thirty-one-year-old widow. She never would have believed it. Not when just weeks ago she'd planned on telling David her joyous news...that they were to become parents. She'd had it all planned. She'd silk-screened T-shirts that said, "I'm the Daddy" and another that said, "I'm the Mommy" and the third tiny T-shirt said, "And I'm the Boss." She'd planned on giving David the set of them over his favorite dinner.

She hadn't gone to the doctor yet, relying solely on the pregnancy test she'd taken. She'd wanted David by her side when they heard the news officially. Now she'd be going to all of her appointments alone, facing an unknown future.

The only bright spot in all this sadness was the child she carried. She loved her baby with all of her heart and vowed to protect it, doing whatever it took to make a good life for him or her.

Rena closed the closet door unable to remove and discard David's clothes as she'd planned. "I'm not ready to let go," she whispered. She needed David's things around her, to feel his presence and warmth surround her. It gave her a sense of peace, odd as that might seem.

"Do you want me to help you with David's things, Rena?" Solena Melendez's voice broke into her thoughts. Rena turned to find her friend at the bedroom threshold, a concerned look on her face.

Rena smiled sadly. Since David's death, Solena made a point to check up on Rena every morning.

"Solena, no. But thank you." Solena and Raymond Melendez worked at Purple Fields—Solena in the wine-tasting room, Raymond overseeing the vineyards. They'd been loyal employees since Rena and David took over the winery after her parents' deaths.

"It will take time, Rena."

Rena understood that. She'd lost both of her parents. She knew the process of grieving. "I know."

"And when it's time, I will help you."

She smiled and wiped away her tears. "I appreciate that." She reached for Solena, and they embraced. Their relationship had grown over the years, and now Rena thought of Solena and Raymond as more than employees—they were dear friends. Friends whose salaries she may not be able to pay if she didn't get this bank loan.

"We have orders today," Solena said, breaking their embrace. "I'll make sure they go out on time."

"Orders are good," Rena acknowledged with a nod of her head. Thankfully, Solena reminded her daily that she had a winery to run. Purple Fields was small but well-respected, and they'd been holding their own until a slowing economy and bigger wineries started shoving them out. Smaller vintners weren't able to compete and sustain the same degree of losses as the more established ones.

"I have an appointment at the bank today." Though Rena held out little hope, she had to try. She needed a loan to make her payroll this month and next. She was due a small amount from David's life insurance policy, and that money would pay for her doctor bills and whatever was left over would go in trust for her child's future. No one knew about the child she carried as yet, and she'd planned to keep it that way for the time being. She'd not told a soul. Not even Solena.

"I will pray for good news," Solena said.

"So will I," Rena said.

Rena lingered a bit after Solena left her room, putting a little makeup on a face that had seen too many tears. With dark circles beneath her eyes, no amount of makeup could hide her despair. Her grief would be evident, yet she had enough pride to want to appear in control of her emotions when she met Mr. Zelinski at the bank. Bankers were wary of desperation. Rena understood that and prepared herself with facts and figures she hoped would prove that Purple Fields was holding its own and worth the risk of a loan.

Rena walked down the stone hallway and made it to the living room when a knock sounded at her door. "Who could that be?" she muttered, taking up her purse and the file folder for her bank appointment and tucking it under her arm.

She opened the door to Tony Carlino. More than surprised, Rena blinked. "Tony? What are you doing here?"

He cast her a grim smile. "You wouldn't return my phone calls."

"There's a reason for that. I don't care to talk to you."

"Maybe not," Tony said. "But I have to talk to you."

Rena took in a steady breath and calmed her nerves. Just the sight of Tony brought bad memories. She'd gotten over him once and had moved on with her life. She certainly didn't want anything to do with him now. "What could you possibly have to say to me?"

Tony glanced inside her home. He'd been here before many years ago, but she certainly didn't want to invite him in. She'd never minded that she'd come from humble beginnings and that her family home was cozy and rustic, where the Carlino mansion had four wings of stately elegance, two dozen rooms, Italian marble and ancestral artwork that went back a few generations.

"What I have to say can't be said on your doorstep, Rena."

Rena glanced at her watch. "I'm on my way out. I don't have time to talk to you."

"Then have dinner with me tonight."

"Dinner?" Rena had to focus hard not to wrinkle her face. "No, I won't have dinner with you."

Tony let go an exasperated sigh. "I don't remember you being so difficult."

She hadn't been when she'd first met Tony at the age of sixteen. She'd taken one look at him and had fallen in love. They'd been friends first, Rena keeping her secret that she'd fallen hard for a Carlino. Tony had a smile that lit up her heart, and when they laughed together, Rena thought she'd died and gone to heaven. It had been painful holding in her feelings, not letting on that she loved him. It didn't help matters that Santo Carlino was trying to run her parents out of business.

"You don't know me anymore, Tony." Rena lifted her chin. "If this is about easing your conscience about David, you're wasting your time."

Tony's face tightened. His dark eyes grew cold. He stared at her for a moment, then as if gathering all his patience, he took a deep breath. "I haven't got a guilty conscience, Rena. But what I have to say *is* about David."

Rena glanced at her watch again. It wouldn't do to be late for her appointment, yet he'd caught her curiosity. "What about David?"

"Have dinner with me and I'll tell you."

Pressed for time and jittery about her bank appointment, Rena relented. "Fine, I'll have dinner with you."

"I'll pick you up at eight."

"Okay, now at the risk of being rude, I really have to leave."

With a quick nod of agreement, Tony left and Rena breathed a sigh of relief. She wouldn't think about seeing him later and breaking bread with him. She'd seen the determined look on his face and knew he wouldn't take no for an answer. Frankly, she didn't have time to argue. The bank appointment was all she could focus on. "One hurdle at a time." She mumbled David's favorite words of encouragement every time they'd faced a challenge.

She had more important things to worry about than having dinner with Tony Carlino.

Tony drove out of the Purple Fields gates and turned right driving along the roads that would lead him to the Carlino estate. Vineyards on both sides of the highway spread across the valley rising up hills and down slopes, covering the land in a blanket of green.

He'd only been home about three months, and he still felt disoriented, unsure of his place here in Napa. He'd come home because his father had been ill. And now, as the oldest son, he had to assume responsibility for the business working alongside his two brothers. His father had expected as much from him.

The timing had been right for his return. He'd made his mark on NASCAR and had enjoyed every minute of his career until a crash and injury took him off the racing circuit. Perhaps it had been an omen to quit, but it wasn't until his father's passing that Tony realized he'd had no choice but to leave the racing world behind.

Somewhat.

He still had endorsement deals with various companies, and that could be an advantage to Carlino Wines. The Carlino name meant success, and people identified with that. Yet Tony's life had changed so drastically in such a short span of time, and now he planned on taking on a new responsibility with a wife and child.

Was he ready for that?

He questioned that reality now. His vow to David never far from his mind, Tony admitted, if only to himself, that Rena had been right about one thing. If he hadn't come home and rekindled their friendship, David would still be alive today.

Tony approached the Carlino estate and pressed the remote that opened the wide iron gates. He parked the car in front of the garage house and exited. He met up with Joe in the driveway, his brother ever the optimist wearing a smile and horn-rimmed glasses, slapped him on the back. "You look like you've seen a ghost."

He had, in a way. Visions of David's tragic death played in his head ever since he'd driven away from Purple Fields.

It had been a glorious afternoon in Napa, the temperatures in the low seventies with fresh sunshine warm in the air—a day that made you glad to be alive. Tony remembered thinking that, right before he witnessed David's crash.

Before he knew it, he was riding beside David in the ambulance.

"I think she's pregnant," David whispered, *struggling to get the words out.*

"Shh. Hang on, David. Please. Save your strength."

Tony's plea didn't register with David. He continued, his voice so low that Tony had to bend over to hear him.

"She won't drink," he'd confessed, *and Tony immediately understood. Vintners drank wine like others drank water.*

David's coherent pleas gave Tony hope, though he appeared so weak. So fragile.

"Tony," he'd implored.

"I'm here." He knew whatever David had to say must be important.

"Don't leave her alone. She deserves a good life. Promise me you'll take care of her. And our baby."

"I promise, David. I'll take care of Rena," Tony whispered, looking deep into David's fading eyes.

"Marry her," David said, grasping Tony's hand. *"Promise me that, too."*

And Tony hadn't hesitated. He squeezed David's hand. "I'll marry her."

David gave the slightest tip of a nod and closed his eyes. "Tell her I love her."

"Hang on, David. She's coming. You can tell her yourself."

Frantic, Rena rushed up to David the minute they'd reached the hospital. They'd had time together, spoke their last words and Tony hung back giving them privacy. When David let go, Rena cried out. Her deafening sobs for David shook Tony and reached deep into his soul. He'd never seen a woman fall apart like that.

Tony shifted back to the present and looked at his brother with a shake of his head. "I saw Rena today."

Joe wrinkled his nose and gave an understanding nod. "Which explains the haunted look in your eyes. Thinking of David, too?" he asked with genuine concern.

"Yeah, he's never far from my mind. I'm the race car driver. I'm the one taking risks, yet he was the one to die in a crash."

"People die every day in car accidents." Then Joe caught himself. He didn't have a cruel bone in his body. "Sorry, I didn't mean to sound callous, but you didn't encourage him to get behind the wheel. And it *was* an accident."

"I wish Rena felt that way. It would make what I have to do a whole lot easier."

"So, it didn't go well today?"

Tony shrugged. "She blew me off, but not before I made a dinner date with her."

"That's a start. It should get easier now."

Tony scratched his chin, the stubble grating his fingers. "Doubtful. Rena is as proud as she is stubborn."

"I hear you, Tony. I've learned my lesson with the opposite sex. No more relationships for me."

Tony looked his brother in the eye. "Sheila really did a number on you, didn't she?"

Joe lifted his shoulders in a nonchalant shrug. "I'm over it."

Tony believed him, noting the firm set of his jaw and his cool air of confidence, despite his casual shrug. Joe's gorgeous New York assistant had played him, using her charms to snare him into an engagement. But the minute a wealthier man had shown interest in her, she'd dumped Joe for greener pastures and married a man who was twice her age. Joe had been burned, and he wasn't going near the fire any time soon.

"I'm on my way to the downtown office," he said, changing the subject. "Good luck with Rena tonight."

"Thanks. And Joe, keep this quiet." It wouldn't do for news to get out that Tony was dating his friend's new widow.

"I've got your back, bro."

Rena parked her car outside her home, her hands frozen on the steering wheel as she looked with numbing silence at the house in desperate need of paint and a roof that had seen better days. Her garden had been neglected lately, the grounds and outer buildings weren't what they once were. But the vineyards beyond, whose budding grapes were the mainstay of her legacy, had the best terroir in the vicinity. Their merlot and cabernet wines won awards from the combination of good weather, soil and minerals. The vineyards had never let her down. "All I have left are those vines," she mumbled, her voice shaky. "What am I going to do?"

The news from Mr. Zelinski wasn't good. She hadn't known the lengths David had gone to in order to keep them in business until she'd pressed the banker to be brutally honest. She saw regret in his eyes and sympathy cross his features and knew of his reluctance to tell her the ultimate truth. Both the Fairfield and Montgomery families were part of the tightly knit Napa community and had been personal friends of the banker. She assumed it was out of respect for her mourning that he hadn't been knocking at her door demanding his money.

The grim news she received shook what little hope she had left. Not only couldn't she qualify for a loan but David had taken out a home equity line of credit to keep them going these past few months. Until that loan was repaid and her credit restored, she couldn't even think about asking for additional help from the bank.

She owed more money than she originally thought.

Tears welled in her eyes as the hopelessness of her situation enveloped her. From across the driveway, out among the vines she spotted Raymond checking the leaves, making sure the grapes were healthy.

A sob escaped. She knew what she had to do, and it hurt to even think it. She couldn't pay Solena and Raymond. She'd barely scraped up enough money to give them their last month's salary. She'd let her other employees go, but hoped she could keep her friends on. Now, it was clear she had to let them go as well.

Her heart breaking, Rena bounded out of the car and ran up the steps to her house, tears spilling down her cheeks. She couldn't face losing them, not after losing David so abruptly. Everything around her was changing too fast.

Yet she couldn't expect Solena and Raymond to stay. She knew they'd have no trouble finding employment at another vineyard. Both were efficient, dedicated and knew as much about winemaking as she did. Selfishly, she wanted to keep them close, to have them work the land and be here when she needed them. Rena had sad facts to face, and she didn't know if she was up to the challenge.

Slamming the door shut, she strode to her bedroom, wiping at tears that continued to fall. She tossed her files and purse aside, kicking off her shoes as she flopped down on her bed. She lay looking up at the ceiling, searching her mind for a way to keep her business afloat. What avenues had she missed? Who could she turn to for help? Finally, after a half hour of torturous thought, she came up with the only solution that made sense. She had no other option.

She had to sell Purple Fields.

Three

Tony debated whether to bring Rena flowers, remembering that she'd always loved the tulips that grew in the Carlino garden. "I like the purple ones best," she'd said when they were teens. "They're bright and happy, just waiting to put a smile on someone's face."

But he knew giving Rena her favorite flowers wouldn't put a smile on her face now. Nothing he could do—aside from vanishing off the face of the earth—would do that. He'd opted to knock on her door empty-handed, hoping that she hadn't changed her mind about tonight.

He'd sort of bulldozed her into this dinner date. What other choice did he have? He'd waited a respectable amount of time to approach her, allowing her time to heal from the shock of losing her husband. Yet, with a baby on the way and a failing business, Rena was in trouble. Tony didn't think he could wait much longer.

He'd promised David.

He drove his Porsche through the Purple Fields gates for the second time today and parked in front of the gifts shop-wine-tasting room adjacent to the main house. The quaint shop attracted tourists during the late spring and summer months when the weather was mild and the scent of grapes flavored the air. Rena had worked there during high school, serving sandwiches and cheese and crackers to their customers.

Tony ran a hand down his face, bracing himself for Rena's wrath. She wouldn't agree to his terms lightly, if at all. He got out of the car and walked the distance to the house. Using the metal knocker on the door, he gave three firm raps and waited. When she didn't come, he knocked again, louder.

"Rena," he called out.

He gazed over the grounds as the last remnants of evening light faded. Focusing intently, he glanced around at the other buildings and through the vineyards. There was no sign of her. Tony tried the doorknob, and to his surprise it opened.

She'd left the door unlocked.

He felt a surging sense of alarm. Rena lived alone now. It wasn't like her not to be cautious. Without hesitation, he walked inside the house. The entry that led to the living room was dark. As he took a few steps inside, it seemed the entire house was dark. "Rena?"

He made his way down the long hall and opened one door, peering inside to an empty room. He checked another room without success. When he got to the end of the hallway, he found the last door open. A small amount of moonlight illuminated the middle of the room where Rena slept on her bed.

Tony winced, seeing her sleeping soundly, her chest lifting and falling peacefully, her raven hair spread across the pillow. A few strands curled around her face and contrasted against her creamy complexion. She wore the same austere dress he'd seen her in earlier today, but it couldn't conceal the feminine slope of her breasts or the luscious curve of her hips.

Tony had loved her once. He'd taken her virginity when she was eighteen. When she'd cried, overwhelmed by emotion, he'd clung to her and assured her of his love. Rena had given herself to him one hundred percent and though he'd tried to give her everything she needed from him, he couldn't. He had another great passion—racing. It was in his blood. From the time he was a small boy, Tony needed to feel the wind at his back. He loved speed and thrilled at the danger of being wild and free. Later, he'd learned to harness his passion. He'd learned that precision and accuracy as well as spirit made you a winner.

He'd achieved his goals without much struggle. He'd been born to race. But he'd also disappointed his father by not working alongside him as was expected by the eldest son, and he'd hurt the girl he'd admired and loved most in the world.

Memories flashed again, of making love to Rena and how incredibly poignant and pure it'd been. But Tony's mission here wasn't to rehash the past but to move on to the future. Rena was David's widow now, and the strain of his death was evident on her beautiful face, even in sleep.

His first inclination was to quietly leave, locking the door behind him, but he found he couldn't move, couldn't lift his eyes away from her sad desolate face. So he stood at the threshold of her bedroom, watching her.

It wasn't long before she stirred, her movements lazy as she stretched out on the bed. Tony's gaze moved to the point where her dress hiked up, exposing long beautiful legs and the hint of exquisite thighs.

His body quickened, and he ground his teeth fighting off lusty sexual thoughts. Yet, quick snippets of memory emerged of hot delicious nights making love to her all those years ago.

Rena opened her eyes and gasped when she spotted his figure in the doorway. Immediate fear and vulnerability entered her eyes. She sat straight up, and when she recognized him, anger replaced her fear. "What are you doing here?"

"We had a date."

"A date?" To her credit, she did appear hazily confused. Then the anger resurfaced. "How'd you get in?"

"The door was unlocked. Not a good habit, Rena. Anyone could have gotten into your house."

"Anyone *did*."

Tony chose to ignore the swipe.

Rena swung her legs around and set her bare feet on the floor. She rubbed her forehead with both hands and shook her head. "I guess I fell asleep. What time is it?"

"Eight-fifteen."

She looked up at him. "Were you standing there all that time?"

"No," he lied. "I just got here. I was fashionably late."

She closed her eyes briefly. "I don't know what happened. I felt exhausted and fell into a deep sleep."

The baby, Tony thought. He'd had many a racing buddy speak about their wife's exhaustion during their early pregnancy. "Maybe it's all catching up with you. You've been through a lot this past month."

"You don't know what I've been through." She was being deliberately argumentative, and Tony didn't take the bait.

"How long before you can be ready?"

Her brows furrowed. "Ready?"

"For dinner."

"Oh, I don't think so. Not tonight. I'm not—" she began to put her hand to her flat stomach, then caught herself "—feeling well."

"You'll feel better once you eat. How long since you've eaten?"

"I don't know…. I had a salad for lunch around noon."

"You need to keep up your strength, Rena."

She opened her mouth to respond, then clamped it shut.

"I'll wait for you in the living room."

Tony turned and walked away, not really giving her

a choice in the matter. There were many more things he'd have to force upon her before the evening was through.

Rena got up from her bed, moving slowly as she replayed the events of the day in her mind. First, Tony had visited her this afternoon, a fact that still irked her. Yet he had something to say and he wouldn't leave until he got it off his chest. That's how Carlinos operated; they did what they darn well wanted, no matter how it affected other people. Bitter memories surfaced of her father standing up to Santo Carlino, but Rena shoved them out of her mind for the moment. She couldn't go there now.

Next came thoughts of her conversation with Mr. Zelinski at the bank. He'd been kind to her, confessing his hands were tied. She wouldn't be getting the loan she desperately needed. She wouldn't be able to pay her employees. Purple Fields was doomed.

Her head began to pound. She felt faint. Though her appetite had been destroyed today, she admitted that she really should eat something. For the baby's sake, if nothing else. She couldn't afford to sink into depression. It wouldn't be good for the unborn child she carried.

As quick as her body allowed, she got ready, cringing at her reflection in the mirror. Her face was drawn, her hair wild, her clothes rumpled. She washed her face, applied a light tint of blush to her cheeks, some lipstick to her lips and brushed her hair back into a clip at the base of her neck—just to appear human again. She changed her clothes, throwing on a black pair of pants and a soft knit beige sweater that ruffled into a vee and looked stylish though comfortable. She slipped her feet into dark shoes and walked out of the room. Whatever Tony had in mind, she certainly wasn't going to dress up for him.

Tony closed the magazine he was reading and rose from the sofa when she strode in. She squirmed under his direct scrutiny. "You look better."

She didn't comment yet noted genuine concern in his eyes. Why?

He strode to the door and opened it. "Shall we go?"

"Where are you taking me?"

Tony's expression flattened. He'd caught her meaning. "I've made arrangements, Rena. No one will see you with me."

If she weren't so upset about *everything,* her face might have flamed from his acknowledgment. She lifted her chin. "How's that possible?"

"We own half of Alberto's. It's closed to the public tonight."

"You mean you had it closed for my benefit?"

"You haven't had any use for me since I returned. I didn't think you'd like answering questions about being out with me tonight if anyone saw us."

Rena had almost forgotten that the Carlinos had their hands in other enterprises. They owned a few restaurants as well as the winery. They also owned stores in outlying areas that sold a line of products related to wine.

"This isn't a date, Tony. Just so we're clear."

Tony nodded. "Very clear."

Rena strode past him and waited for him to exit her house before she locked the front door. She moved quickly, and once he beeped his car alarm, she didn't wait for him to open the car door. She climbed into his Porsche and adjusted the seat belt.

"Ready?" he asked unnecessarily. Once they made eye contact, he roared the engine to life. "It's a nice night. Mind if I put the top down?"

"No, I could use a good dose of fresh air."

It's how Tony liked to drive, with the top down, the air hitting his face, mastering the car and the road beneath.

He hit a button, and mechanically the car transformed. He drove the road to Napa surprisingly slowly, as if they were out for a Sunday drive. Every so often, he glanced her way. She couldn't deny his courtesy.

Or the fact that she thought him the most devastatingly handsome man she'd ever met. She'd thought so since they'd first met the day he entered public school at the age of sixteen. Up until that point, the Carlinos had gone to an elite private school. But Tony hated the regimented lifestyle, the solitude and discipline of being in an academy. Finally, his father had relented, granting his sons the right to go through the public school system.

Tony had made a lasting impression on her, and they'd started out as friends. But the friendship had grown as they'd gotten closer, and Rena had become Tony's steady girlfriend two years later.

Despite his obvious wealth and place in Napa society.

Despite the fact that Santo Carlino and her father had become bitter enemies.

Despite the fact that Rena never *truly* believed she could have a lasting relationship with Tony.

"Care for some music?" he asked, reaching for the CD player button.

"If you don't mind, I'd like to be quiet."

She didn't want to rekindle memories of driving in Tony's car with the top down and the music blasting. Of laughing and telling silly jokes, enjoying each other's company.

"Okay," he said amiably.

They drove in silence, Tony respecting her wishes. Shortly, he pulled into Alberto's back parking lot. "I usually don't resort to back alley entrance ways," he said, with no hint of irritation. "Are you hungry?"

"Yes, actually quite hungry."

"Good, the food is waiting for us."

Before she managed to undo her seat belt, Tony was there, opening the car door for her. He reached his hand inside, and rather than appearing incredibly stubborn in his eyes, she slid her hand in his while he helped her out. The Porsche sat so low to the ground she would have fumbled like an idiot anyway, trying to come up smoothly to a standing position.

Sensations ripped through her instantly. The contact, the intimate way his large hand enveloped her smaller one, trampled any false feeling of ease she'd imagined. She fought the urge to whip her hand away. Instead, she came out of the car and stood fully erect before slipping her hand out of his. Composing herself, she thanked him quietly and followed him inside the restaurant.

"This way," he said and gestured to a corner booth lit by candlelight. True to his word, the entire restaurant was empty but for them. She sat down at one end of the circular booth, while he sat at the other.

The few times Rena had come here, she'd always felt as though she'd wandered in from the streets in Tuscany with its old world furnishings and stone fountains. Alberto's was one of finest restaurants in the county, serving gourmet fare and the best wines from Napa.

"I had the chef prepare a variety of food. I wasn't sure what you liked."

"You forgot that I loved pepperoni pizza?"

Tony's mouth twisted. "No one could inhale pizza like you, Rena. But I doubt it's on the menu tonight. Let's go into the kitchen and see what the chef conjured up for us."

Tony bounded up from the booth and waited. She rose and walked beside him until they reached the state-of-the-art kitchen. They found covered dishes on the immaculate steel counter along with fresh breads, salads and a variety of desserts sitting in the glass re-frigerator.

Tony lifted one cover and announced. "Veal scaloppine, still hot."

Rena looked on with interest.

Tony lifted another cover. "Linguine arrabiatta, black tiger shrimps with bacon and garlic."

Steam rose up, and she leaned in closer. "Hmm, smells good."

He lifted two more covers displaying filetto di bue, an oven roasted filet mignon, which smelled heavenly but was too heavy for Rena's tastes, and ravioli di zucca, which Tony explained was spinach ravioli with butternut and Amaretto filling. Since entering the aromatic kitchen, Rena's appetite had returned wholeheartedly.

"The ravioli looks good," she said. "And that salad." She pointed to a salad with baby greens, avocado, tangerines and candied walnuts.

"Great," Tony said lifting the covered dish of her choice. And one for him. "If you could grab that salad, we'll eat. Soon as I find us a bottle of wine."

"Oh, no wine for me," she announced. Tony glanced at her with a raised brow but didn't question her. "I'll have water."

"Your poison," he said with a smile. He set the dishes down on the table and took off again, bringing back a bottle of Carlino Cabernet and a pitcher of water.

They settled in for the meal in silence, Rena polishing off the delicious salad within minutes and Tony sipping his wine, eyeing her every move. "Quit looking at me."

"You're the best looking thing in this place."

She squeezed her eyes shut. "Don't, Tony."

He shrugged it off. "Just stating the obvious."

When he turned on the charm, he had enough for the entire Napa Valley and then some. "Do you mind telling me what's so important that you couldn't tell me earlier this afternoon?"

"After dinner, Rena."

With her water glass to her lips, she asked, "Why?"

"I want you to eat your meal."

She gathered her brows and shook her head. "Because…what you have to say might destroy my appetite?"

Tony inhaled sharply then blew out the breath. "Because you're hungry and exhausted, that's why."

"Why the sudden concern about my well-being?"

Tony softened his tone. "I've always cared about you, Rena."

"No, Tony. We're not going there. *Ever,*" she emphasized. She wouldn't go down that mental path. She and Tony had way too much history, and she thought she'd never heal from the wounds he'd inflicted.

"Can't you just forget for a few minutes who I am and who you are? Can't we break bread together quietly and enjoy a good meal?"

Rena relented but still questioned Tony's mysterious behavior. "Fine. I'll eat before the ravioli gets cold."

"That's a girl."

She shot him a look.

He raised his hands up in surrender. "Sorry." Then he dug into his filet mignon with gusto and sipped wine until he'd drained two goblets.

After finishing their entrées, Tony cleared the dishes himself, refusing Rena's help. He needed time to collect his thoughts and figure out how he was going to propose marriage to his best friend's new widow and not come off sounding callous and cruel. There was only one route to take and that was to tell her the truth.

Hell, he hadn't ever really thought about marriage to anyone *but* Rena Fairfield. As teenagers, they'd spent many a night daydreaming of the time when they'd marry. But then Rena's mother became ill, and Tony had been given a real opportunity to pursue his dream of racing stock cars. Leaving Rena behind to care for her ailing mother and help her father run Purple Fields had been the only black spot in an otherwise shining accomplishment. Begging her to join him served no purpose. She couldn't leave. She had family obligations. She loved making wine. She loved Purple Fields. She was born to live in Napa, where Tony had been born to race.

He'd hurt her. No, he'd nearly destroyed her.

Each time he'd called her from the racing circuit, she'd become more and more distant. Until one day, she asked him not to call anymore. Two years later, she'd married David. He hadn't been invited to the wedding.

Tony covered a tray with tiramisu, spumoni ice cream and chocolate-coated cannolis. He returned to Rena and answered her skepticism as she watched him place the food on the table. "What? Regardless of what you think, I wasn't born with a silver spoon. We had to do chores at the house. My father was a stickler for pulling your own weight."

"I would think you're one who is used to being served."

"I am. I won't deny it. Life is good now. I'm wealthy and can afford—"

"Shutting down a restaurant for the night to have a private dinner?"

"Yeah, among other things."

"I guess I should feel honored that you served me dinner. You must have a good reason."

"I do." He glanced at the desserts on the table and moved a dish of spumoni her way. "You love ice cream. Dig in."

Rena didn't hesitate. She picked up a spoon and dove into the creamy Italian fare.

Tony dipped into it as well, butting spoons with her. They made eye contact, and Rena turned away quickly. How often had they shared ice cream in the past?

After three spoonfuls of spumoni, Rena pushed the dish away. "Okay, Tony. I've had dinner with you. No one is around. So are you going to tell me why you needed to speak to me?"

"I know you hate me, Rena."

She steered her gaze toward the fountain in the middle of the dining area. "Hate is a strong word."

"So, you don't hate me?" he asked, with a measure of hope.

She looked into his eyes again. "I didn't say that."

Tony didn't flinch. He'd prepared himself for this. "What did David say to you before he died?"

She straightened in her seat, her agitated body language not to be missed. "That's none of your business."

"Fair enough. But I need to tell you what he asked

of me, Rena. I need you to hear his last words to me as I rode beside him in the ambulance."

Tears welled in her eyes. Tony was a sucker for Rena's tears. He never could stand to see her cry.

For a moment, fear entered her eyes as if hearing David's words would cause her too much pain. But then, courageously, she nodded, opening her eyes wide. "Okay. Yes, I do want to hear what he said."

Tony spoke quietly, keeping his voice from cracking. "He told me he loved you." Rena inhaled a quick breath, and those tears threatened again. "And that you deserved a good life."

"He was the kindest man," she whispered.

"His last thoughts were only of you."

A single tear fell from her eyes. "Thank you, Tony. I needed to hear that."

"I'm not through, Rena. There's more."

She sat back in her seat and leaned heavily against the back of the booth, bracing herself. "Okay."

"He asked me to to watch out for you. Protect you. And I intend to do just that. Rena, I intend to marry you."

Four

Tony might as well have said he was going to fly to the moon on a broomstick; his declaration was just as ridiculous. Still, Rena couldn't contain her shock. Her mouth dropped open. She couldn't find the words.

Her heart broke thinking that David's very last thoughts and concerns hadn't been for himself but for her. But at the same time, if what Tony had said was true, then a wave of anger built at her departed husband as well. How could he even suggest such a thing? Asking Tony to take care of her? To protect her? He was the last man on earth she trusted, and David knew that.

Didn't he?

"You can't be serious," she finally got out once a tumultuous array of emotions swept through her system.

"I'm dead serious, Rena." He pinned her with a sharp unrelenting look.

"It's ridiculous."

"Maybe. But it's David's last wishes."

"You're saying he asked you to marry me?" Rena kept a tight reign on her rising blood pressure.

Tony nodded. "I promised him, Rena."

"No, no, no, no, no, no." She shook her head so hard that her hair slipped out of its clip.

Tony held steady peering into her eyes. "Tell me what he said to you. His last words."

"He said," she began, her voice shaky, her expression crestfallen. "He said he loved me. And that he wanted me to keep Purple Fields." She looked down for a moment to compose herself. "He knew how much it meant to me."

"And you promised him?"

"I did. But I—" Flashes of her conversation with Mr. Zelinski earlier today came flooding back. There was no hope of saving the winery. As much as it hurt her, she'd resolved that she had no other option but to sell Purple Fields. Not only would her family's legacy be lost but so would her livelihood. Yet she needed to provide for her baby. That's all that mattered now, and selling out meant that she'd have enough cash for a year or two if she were very careful. "I can't keep it. I've already decided...to sell."

Tony sat back in his seat, watching as Rena tried to compose herself. So many thoughts entered her mind all at once that her head began to ache. She put her head down and rubbed her temples, to alleviate the pain and to avoid Tony's scrutiny.

"You don't want to sell Purple Fields," he said softly.

"No, of course not."

"You know what it would mean to Purple Fields if we marry? You'd have no more worry…I'd make sure of it."

She kept her head down. She didn't want to admit that marrying Tony would solve her immediate problems and she'd be able to keep her promise to David. But she also knew that her emotions would rule it out this time. She couldn't marry Tony Carlino.

He'd abandoned her when she'd needed him most.

He'd hurt her so deeply that it took a decent man like David to heal her and make her trust again. She had no faith in Tony, and marriage to anyone, much less him, was out of the question. Her wounds were still too raw and fresh.

Tony reached over and caressed her hand with his. Again, an instant current ran between them. "Think about it, Rena. Think about the promises we both made to David."

Twenty minutes later, as Tony drove her home, she still couldn't think of anything else. She wanted to save Purple Fields, to see it thrive and be successful again, but the cost was too great.

Tony walked her to the door. She slipped the key into the lock and turned to face him. "Good night, Tony."

Tony's dark eyes gleamed for a moment. He glanced at

her mouth, his gaze lingering there. Her heart pounded, and for an instant, she was that young smitten girl who banked on his every word. He leaned his body closer, his eyes on hers, and she remembered the chemistry between them, the joy of loving him and having him love her. Images that she'd thought had been destroyed came back in a flash. He slanted his head and she waited. But his kiss bypassed her lips and brushed her cheek. He grabbed the doorknob and shoved open her door. "I'll come by to see you tomorrow, Rena."

Rena stepped inside and leaned heavily on her door, her fingers tracing the cheek he'd just kissed. She squeezed her eyes shut and prayed for a way out of her dilemma.

A way that didn't include marrying Tony Carlino.

The next day, Tony knocked on Rena's door at noon. When she didn't answer the knock, he walked toward the gift shop and peeked inside the window. Solena Melendez waved to him, and he walked inside the store. "Good afternoon."

"Hello, Solena." Tony had met her at David's funeral for the first time. He'd learned enough to know that Solena and Rena were good friends, Solena being just a few years older. She lived in a residential area of Napa with her husband, Raymond, and they worked for Purple Fields since Rena and David took over from her parents. A quick glance around told him that though Solena kept the quaint gift shop immaculate, the shelves were only scantily stocked with items for sale. "I'm looking for Rena. Do you know where she is?"

"I'm right here." Rena came out of the back room, her arms loaded down with a few cases of wine.

Tony had an instant inclination to lift those heavy boxes from her arms but restrained himself. Rena was a proud woman.

She set the boxes down on the front counter. "I'll help you with these bottles in a minute." She smiled warmly at Solena and turned to Tony, her face transforming from warm to cold in a flash. "Follow me," she said and walked outside the shop and down the steps.

The air was fresh and clear, the sky above as blue as Rena's eyes. She walked past her house to the vineyards, and once they were out of earshot she turned to him. "Do you plan on showing up here whenever you want?"

Tony grinned. "Are you mad because I didn't call to make an appointment?"

"No. Yes." Her brows furrowed. "I'm busy, Tony. I don't welcome drop-by company unless they are paying customers."

"You're working with a skeleton crew. And working too hard."

Rena rolled her eyes. "I've been doing this work since I learned to walk, practically. Yes, I work hard, but I don't mind. Why are you here?"

"I told you I'd come by today."

"Checking up on me?"

"If you want to look at it that way."

Rena's face twisted in disgust. "I can take care of myself. I hate that David made you promise to watch out for me."

"I know you do. But a promise is a promise."

"And you don't break your promises, do you? Except to young girls you've pledged your heart to. Then you have no problem."

Rena turned away from him, but he couldn't let her get away with that. He reached out and grabbed her wrist, turning her around to face him. "I loved you, Rena. Make no mistake about that. I've apologized for hurting you a hundred times. But I couldn't stay here then, and you know it. And you couldn't leave with me, and you know that, too. We weren't destined to be together back then."

She yanked her arm free and hoisted her pretty chin. "We're not destined to be together ever, so why don't you go away."

"I'm not going anywhere. Not until I make myself clear. I'm offering you a business proposition, not a real marriage proposal. If you let go of some of your anger and pride, you'd see that. I'm offering you a way to save Purple Fields."

She remained silent.

"How long before you have to let Solena and her husband go? How long before you'll have to close the winery? You don't want to sell. Purple Fields is a big part of you. You love what you do."

"Don't," she said, her eyes filling with moisture. "Don't, Tony."

"Don't what? Speak the truth? You know damn well marrying me is the best thing all the way around."

"David's been gone only a short time. And…and, I don't love you." She pierced him with a direct look.

"I don't love you either," he said, softly so as not to

hurt her anymore. "But, in all these years, I've never wanted to marry another woman. I've never even come close."

He put his arms around her waist and pulled her toward him. Without pause, he brushed his lips to hers softly at first. When she didn't pull away, he deepened the kiss, relishing the exquisite softness of her lips, enjoying the woman that Rena had become. Soft, lush and incredibly beautiful.

When he broke off the kiss, he gazed into Rena's stunned blue eyes. "We may not have love anymore, but we have history and friendship."

She tilted her head stubbornly. "I'm not your friend."

"David wants this for both of us."

"No!" Rena pulled away at the mention of David's name. Confusion filled her expression, and she wiped her mouth with the back of her hand, as if wiping away all that they'd once meant to each other. "I can't marry you—no matter what you promised David. I still blame you for his death and, and…"

"And what, Rena? That kiss just proved we still have something between us. You can save your winery and honor David's last wish."

"You don't understand." Then Rena's eyes reflected dawning knowledge, as if a light had been turned on inside her head. She covered her flat stomach with her hand. "Your family prides itself on bloodlines. It's instilled in your Italian heritage. Everything has to be perfect. Everything has to be pure from the wine you make to the babies you bring into this world. Well, I'm pregnant, Tony. With David's baby. You'd be raising David's child as your own."

Tony didn't flinch. He didn't turn away. He didn't move so much as a muscle in surprise. That was his mistake. Rena expected shock. She expected him to change his mind, to withdraw his marriage proposal. It irked him that she thought so little of him.

Rena backed away, gasping at his nonresponse. Her mouth dropped open, and when she spoke, her voice broke with accusation. "You know. How? *How* do you know, Tony?" She pressed him for an answer.

"I didn't know for sure, until now."

Rena narrowed her eyes. "Tell me."

Tony sighed. "It was David. He suspected it."

Rena backed away, her hands clutching at her hair. Her shoulders slumped, color drained from her face. It was as if she relived his death all over again. She looked down at a patch of shriveled grape leaves on the ground. "He knew about our baby."

"I'm sorry, Rena."

Her eyes watered. "David won't ever meet his child."

"No, but he wanted to protect him and…you. I'm capable of doing that for you, Rena."

"But I don't want to marry you," she said softly.

Tony heard the resignation in her tone. She was considering her options. "I know."

She peered into his eyes. "How would it look? I'm barely a widow—and now I'm marrying my husband's friend."

Tony made this decision to protect Rena days ago. "No one has to know. We'll keep it secret."

"Secret?" She looked at him, puzzled.

"For a time, anyway."

She closed her eyes, contemplating. She battled with the idea of marrying him. Her facial expressions reflected her thoughts as they twisted to and fro.

He pressed his point. "Your winery needs help fast," he said quietly, and then added, "but more important, your child needs a father."

"Maybe that's true." Rena's eyes flooded with tears now, her voice filled with surrender. "But I don't need you, Tony. I'll never need you again."

That was the closest she'd come to a yes.

Tony made mental plans for their wedding day.

Rena cried herself to sleep for two nights, realizing the futility in denying the inevitable. She was cornered and had nowhere to run. She'd been waging mental wars inside her head since Tony's proposal for a secret marriage. She couldn't come up with any other viable solution to her dilemma. She was so heavily in debt she doubted she'd find anyone willing to take on such a big risk.

But how could she marry Tony?

How could she allow him to be a father to David's child?

It all seemed so unfair.

Rena stepped outside her house and squinted into the morning sunlight rising just above the hills. Golden hues cast beautiful color over the valley. This was her favorite time of day. When David was alive, she'd often wake early and come outside to tend her garden and open her mind to all possibilities. David would sit on the veranda to drink coffee and watch her. They would talk endlessly about little things and his presence would lend her peace and comfort.

But since his death, Rena had sorely neglected her garden. Today, she hoped she'd find solace working the soil and nurturing the lilies and roses. She needed this time to come to grips with what she had to do.

She put on her gardening gloves and took to the soil, yanking out pesky weeds, and with each firm tug, thoughts of what David asked from her in his death plagued her mind. He hadn't given her what she needed most—time to grieve. Time to try to figure out a way to save Purple Fields on her own. Instead, he'd hidden the facts from her and shielded her from bad news. David had always been a man she could count on, but he hadn't realized the toll his dying request would take on her.

She tugged at a stubborn weed, bracing her feet and pulling with all of her might. Emotions roiled in the pit of her stomach. Feelings she'd held in for a long time finally came forth as she felt the weed break with the ground. "I'm so mad at you, David, I could spit."

The weed released, easing from the soil slowly and Rena held it in her hands, staring at the roots that had once been secured in the earth. "You died and left me with this mess."

And when she thought tears would fall again, instead simmering anger rose up with full force. She was angry, truly angry with David. She was angry with herself.

But most of all, she was angry with Tony Carlino. Her anger knew no rationality at the moment. And for the first time since David's death, Rena felt strong in that anger. She felt powerful. She refused to let guilt or fear wash away her innermost feelings. David had let her down. Tony had blackmailed her.

But she didn't have to take it without a fight. She didn't have to lose control of everything she loved, just because fate had stepped in and knocked her down. New strength born of distress and determination lifted her. She still had a say in what happened in her life. Her primary obligation was to protect her unborn child and secure his future legacy.

Rena whipped off her gloves and stood up, arching her back and straightening out as a plan formed in her mind. With new resolve, she headed back into the house. She had a call to make. She needed expert legal advice and knew that Mark Winters, David's longtime friend, would help her.

She may be down temporarily, but she wasn't out.

For the first time in a long time, Rena felt as though she had some control about her destiny.

And it felt darn good.

Tony glanced at his watch, his patience wearing thin as he sat in a booth by the window at the Cab Café. Rena was ten minutes late. Had she backed out of this meeting at the last moment?

This morning, he'd been happy to hear Rena's voice on the phone. She'd called early, just as he was leaving for work and she'd sounded adamant that he meet with her today. She wouldn't give him a hint as to what the meeting was about, but since he'd proposed to her last week, he figured she'd come to realize that marrying him was inevitable. Not one to ever look a gift horse in the mouth, he'd cleared his schedule and shown up here five minutes early.

The boisterous teenage hangout held a good deal of memories for them both, and he wondered why she'd picked this particular place. At one time the Cabernet Café was a wine-tasting room but when that failed, the owner had changed the café's focus and now it thrived as a burger-and-fries joint.

A waitress wearing an apron designed with a cluster of purple grapes approached and Tony ordered coffee to pass the time. He decided to wait until he'd finished his first cup before calling Rena to see what the delay was.

Less than five minutes later, just as he was pulling out his cell phone, Rena stepped into the café. He rose from his seat and she spotted him. He gave her a little wave, which she ignored.

As she approached, Tony noticed she had shadows under eyes that were haunted and sad, but even that couldn't mask her genuine beauty. Her hair was pulled back from her face in a ponytail and she wore jeans and a blue sweater that brought out the sparkling hue of her eyes. Her purse sat on her shoulder but she also carried a manila folder in one hand. He waited until she reached the table and sat across from him before he took his seat.

"I was just about to call you. Thought you might have changed your mind."

She glanced at him and shook her head. "No, I'm sorry I'm late. I had an appointment this morning that ran a little long."

"What kind of appointment?" he asked, wondering what was so important to keep him waiting.

She glanced out the window, hesitating, and then turned back to him. "I had my first checkup today for the baby."

Tony leaned back against the vinyl booth and stared at her. "How did it go? Is everything okay?"

Rena couldn't seem to keep her joy from showing. She granted him a smile and her voice lifted when she spoke. "Yes, the baby is healthy. I'm due in October."

"That's good news, Rena." But the news also brought home the reality of what he was about to do. He would take responsibility for a child he didn't father. He would marry a woman who didn't love him. All of it hit him hard between the eyes. This was really happening.

He'd loved David as a friend, but he also knew that if it had been any woman other than Rena, he wouldn't have agreed to David's request. He wouldn't be doing this for a stranger. Though Rena would deny it, they had a connection. Their lives had been entwined for years. Marrying her wasn't as much a hardship for him as it was for her. "What else did the doctor say?"

She breathed out quietly. "He told me to try to stay calm. Not to let stress get me down."

"That's good advice, Rena. You've had a lot to deal with lately and you should try to relax for—"

"I don't need a lecture, Tony."

Her abrupt behavior had him gritting his teeth. Pregnant women were temperamental at times, at least that's what he'd heard from his married friends, but it was more than that with Rena. His proposal to her was nothing more than sugarcoated blackmail. Hell, he hated to add to her stress. But he owed David this and he had to see it through.

She looked at him and inhaled a deep breath. "I'm sorry. This isn't easy for me. Believe me, I have the baby's well-being in mind every second of the day. That's why it's been such a tug of war."

Tony had thicker skin than to be offended, but most women wouldn't consider a proposal from him a terrible thing.

The waitress walked up to the table again. "Hi, what can I get for you?"

Rena faced her without opening the menu. "I should have the California café salad."

"One California café salad, got it. And for you sir?"

"But," Rena interrupted and the waitress turned back to her, "I'm craving a chili cheeseburger with extra pickles."

The waitress grinned. "That's our specialty. Got it. And I'll make sure you get those pickles."

"Thank you. I'll have a lemonade too."

Tony ordered the same thing, and after the waitress left, he glanced at Rena. "You're having cravings? I wondered why you wanted to meet me here."

She lifted a shoulder and shrugged. "It's been a long

time and this morning when I got up, I couldn't stop thinking about having a chili cheeseburger."

"We sure ate our share of them when we were kids. We used to close down this place, remember?"

"Yeah, I do."

And for a moment, Rena's face softened. Tony remembered what it was like being with her back then. The fun times they'd had together. They'd been so close and so much in love.

Rena stared at the manila folder she'd set down on the table and her expression changed.

"What's going on?" Tony asked, glancing at the folder. "What's in there?"

"It's something I want from you."

Surprised, Tony looked at her, arching a brow. "Okay, so why don't you tell me?"

She slid the folder toward him. "It's a prenuptial agreement." Her eyes met his directly.

Tony hid his surprise well. He didn't react, though a dozen thoughts popped into his head all at once. He decided to hear her out and not jump to conclusions.

"If I marry you, I want Purple Fields to remain in my name. I want full ownership of the winery and vineyard. I want to have the final say in every decision having to do with it. My child will own Purple Fields one day, no questions asked. Have your attorney look it over. It's legal and there shouldn't be any problem."

Tony sighed heavily. "Rena, you do see the irony in this, don't you?"

Rena searched his eyes. "How so?"

"First of all, I don't want Purple Fields. Marrying me

has nothing to do with me getting my hands on your winery. The fact is, I'm worth tens of millions, Rena. Everything I own will be yours. I'm not asking for a prenuptial agreement from you."

"If you want one, I'd sign it."

"I don't want one, damn it! I'm not entering into this marriage lightly. If we marry, it'll be for keeps. We'll have a child and we'll be a family. Do you understand what I'm saying?"

"Yes, of course. But you've made promises to me before that you've broken, and now I have no choice in the matter. I want some control. You should understand that, being a Carlino."

Tony's lips tightened. He didn't want an argument, so he chose his words carefully. "This time it's different. This time, I'm not going to break any promises I make to you."

"I'd sleep better at night if I believed you."

Tony let go a curse.

Rena continued to explain. "I'm only protecting what's mine. Can you blame me? It's all I have left and I don't want to lose it."

Angry now, Tony didn't bother reading the agreement first. "Fine. I'll sign it."

He reached into his pocket and pulled out a pen. Then he slid the papers out and gave them only a cursory glance before signing his name at the bottom.

"Don't you want your attorney to look it over?" Rena asked, her expression incredulous, watching him slide the papers back into the folder.

He shook his head. "I know you well enough to

know there's nothing in this agreement that I'd find questionable. I *trust* you."

Rena sat back against the booth, her chin bravely raised. "I won't let you make me feel guilty about this."

"I'm not trying to make you feel guilty," Tony remarked gruffly. Then when he saw Rena holding back tears, he softened his tone. "I signed the papers. You're getting what you want—at least as far as Purple Fields is concerned. I never intended on taking that away from you." Then he braced his arms on the table and leaned in. Their gazes locked. "We have to make this work, Rena. If for nothing else but that child you're carrying."

Rena closed her eyes briefly. Her silence irritated him, as if she were trying to believe and trust in him. He wasn't like his ruthless father, but would Rena ever acknowledge that? "I know," she said finally.

Tony settled back in his seat. What was done, was done. He didn't want to rehash the past. It was time to look toward the future.

And live in the present.

Tony changed the subject as soon as the food was delivered. He wanted Rena to enjoy the meal she'd craved. Lord knew she needed to build her strength. She also needed some calm in her life and wondered if he could ever provide her that.

Without Rena actually saying so, the existence of the prenuptial agreement he'd just signed was an acceptance to his proposal.

Tony resigned himself to the fact that soon he'd be a husband to a pregnant and reluctant bride.

* * *

One week later, Rena stood beside Solena, Tony beside his brother Joe as they spoke vows before a Catholic priest in a little church just outside of San Francisco. Rena's mind spun during the entire mass thinking this was some kind of a bad joke. She couldn't believe she was actually marrying Tony Carlino, the boy she'd once loved beyond reason. The boy she'd dreamed of marrying with every breath that she'd taken. Now that dream seemed more like a nightmare.

As the priest blessed their union, Rena reminded herself of the reasons she'd made this decision.

Marrying Tony meant saving her winery from ruin.

It meant that she could honor David's last wishes.

It meant that her baby would never want for anything, much less a roof over his head or a meal on his plate.

They were good solid reasons. No sacrifice was too great for her child.

Father Charles finished the ceremony. "You may kiss the bride."

She hardly felt like a bride. She wore a pale yellow dress suit. Tony had provided her with a small calla lily bouquet and had placed a simple platinum band on her finger during the service. Out of reverence to David, he hadn't given her a diamond—she'd only just last week removed her wedding ring from her finger and tucked it away safely in her jewelry case. It had been excruciatingly hard letting go.

Tony's lips brushed hers softly. He smiled when he looked into her eyes. She granted him a small smile in return.

Joe and Solena congratulated them, their mood solemn. If Father Charles noticed the austere atmosphere at the altar, he didn't mention it. In fact, he pumped Tony's hand hard and embraced Rena.

Raymond approached with a handshake to Tony and a hug for her. Nick approached her with arms open and a big smile. "Welcome to the family. I've always wanted a sister. But I'll let you in on a little secret. I had a big crush on you in high school."

Rena chuckled and flowed into his arms. "No, you didn't."

"I did. But you were my big brother's girl." They broke their embrace and Nick stepped away, turning to Tony and slapping him on the back. "He's a lucky man. Be good to her or I might steal her away."

Tony glanced at her. "I'd like to see you try."

Rena bit her lip, holding back a smile. She'd seen the Carlino boys' teasing banter, and at times she had been a part of it. If anyone could make her laugh, it was Nick. He'd always been too clever for his own good. All the Carlino boys had their own brand of charm and she'd learned early on that each in his own way was a lady-killer.

The six of them dined in an out-of-the-way restaurant on the outskirts of San Francisco, and everyone sipped champagne when Nick proposed a toast. Rena pretended to sip hers, letting the bubbly liquid touch her mouth before she set her glass down. She was among her closest friends here, and though she'd explained to Solena and Raymond her reasons for this sudden secret marriage to Tony, she hadn't confessed about the baby yet. She needed time to come to grips with all that had changed in her life.

When the dinner was over, Rena walked outside with Solena, bidding her farewell. "I hope I'm not making a mistake."

Solena took her hand and squeezed gently. "Remember, David wanted this for you." She glanced at Tony who stood beside Raymond and his brothers. "Give him a chance," she whispered. "You loved him once."

"It's different now, Solena. There's so much hurt between us."

"I know. But if you find forgiveness, your heart will open."

Rena doubted it. She didn't know if she was capable of forgiving Tony. He'd destroyed her life not once but twice. Was she supposed to forget all that? Emotions jumbled up inside her, and she fought to control them. "I can't believe I married him."

Solena reached out to hug her tight. "It will work out as it's meant to. Be patient. And remember, I am always here if you need me."

Rena faced her and gratitude filled her heart. "I know you are." She reminded herself that if she hadn't married Tony, she wouldn't be able to employ her dear friends, and that was enough consolation for now.

Tony approached and put a hand to her back. "Are you ready to leave?"

She nodded to him and bid farewell to her friend, squeezing her hand tight. "I'll see you tomorrow, Solena."

"Yes." Solena glanced at Tony. "Congratulations."

"Thank you."

Once Raymond and Solena left, Tony took Rena's hand and guided her to his car. "You're not going to your own execution, you know."

"Did I say anything?" she quipped, slipping her hand away.

"Not in words."

She shrugged. "It's all so strange."

But before Tony could respond to that, Joe and Nick walked up. Nick smiled. "You did it, you two. *Finally.*"

Joe cleared his throat. "Let's leave them alone, Nick."

"Just wishing them well," he said. "I guess we'll see you at the house later."

Tony shook his head. "I'm not going back to the house tonight."

"You're not?" Rena's nerves jumped. She hadn't discussed with him what they'd do after they married. She'd only assumed that since the marriage was secret, he'd stay at his house and she'd stay at hers.

"No." He turned to her. "I've booked a suite at the Ritz-Carlton in San Francisco."

Joe grabbed Nick's shoulder and gave a little shove. "Let's go."

"I guess I'm going," Nick said with a cocky smile. "Congrats again, Rena. Big brother."

Rena watched them both get in the car and leave. She turned to Tony, dumbfounded. "Why did you get us a room at a hotel?"

"It's our wedding night."

She closed her eyes, praying for strength. "Surely, you don't expect—"

"You're my wife now, Rena. Did you expect me to remain celibate the rest of my life?"

Five

Rena sat stonily silent in the car all the way to the hotel, her expression grim and her pretty mouth deep in a frown. She said nothing as he checked in or on the ride in the elevator to the Presidential Suite.

A private servant opened the door and showed them inside. In awe, Rena gasped when she entered the suite.

Rich furnishings, stately artwork and a Steinway grand piano filled the living room. Tony put a hand to her back and guided her inside. The servant showed them around the suite, walking them through French doors to the master bedroom with an amazing view of San Francisco Bay, the master bathroom highlighted by a sunken whirlpool bath filled with scented flower petals, a second bedroom and an elegant dining room with seating for eight.

Once back in the living room, Tony dismissed him. "We won't need your services for the rest of the evening."

"Yes, sir," he said, and once he left the suite, Tony opened the French doors to the terrace.

"It's massive," Rena said, stepping outside and taking a deep breath of air. The sun began a slow descent on the horizon. "You could fit two of my gift shops in the terrace alone." Then she turned to him. "Why did you do this?"

"You deserve it, Rena."

Before she could respond, he turned her shoulders and pointed out toward the ocean. "Look, there's Alcatraz."

Rena focused on the island that had once been a notorious prison. "The view is amazing. All of this is amazing."

Tony kept his hands on her shoulders for a few seconds, caressing her lightly. The air fresh and clear, he breathed in and caught the subtle scent of her exotic perfume. She'd put her hair up for the wedding ceremony, giving him access to her throat. He took in another breath before he felt her stiffen. He backed away, giving her space and time to adjust to the situation and pulled out a white iron patio chair. "Sit down and enjoy the fresh air."

She did and he sat facing her. "I'm not the big bad wolf, Rena. I know this is difficult for you."

"Difficult doesn't begin to describe it. I never thought

I'd see this day." Her eyes appeared strained. Her body slumped with fatigue.

"What day?" he asked.

"The day that I'd be your wife."

"I'm not the villain here. I'm trying to do right by you and David. I'm going to save your business, take care of you and raise…our child."

Rena flinched, and regret filled her eyes. "You're trying to ease your conscience and fulfill an obligation."

Tony shook his head. "You won't cut me any slack, will you?"

"I'm sorry I'm not the doting wife you'd imagined. I can't be…this is all so unfair."

"I wish to hell David was alive, too. He was my best friend, damn it." Tony rose and paced the terrace. He hadn't planned on any of this. But he was trying to make the best out of a bad situation. He'd been patient with Rena, though she still blamed him for David's death. He'd tried to please her. He'd tried being the nice guy, yet she wanted no part of it.

Okay, the gloves were coming off.

"You're exhausted. Why don't you take a bath? It's waiting for you. Then get into bed."

Rena hoisted her chin. "I'm not sleeping with you tonight, Tony."

"Wrong," he said pointing a finger at her. "*I'm* not sleeping with *you*, but I'm your husband whether you like it or not."

"What does that mean?" She asked with real fear in her voice.

Tony was too annoyed with her to care. "It means that I don't plan to tiptoe around you anymore, Rena."

He left her on the terrace and strode over to the wet bar, pouring himself three fingers of scotch. He hated that Rena had it right this time. He *had* married her out of obligation and a sense of duty to David. But he hadn't expected her resentment to irk him so much.

Hell, he'd never had to beg a woman for sex in his life. And he wasn't about to start now.

Rena had never stayed in a hotel as extravagant as this one and decided to take advantage of her surroundings. True to Tony's word, the bathtub was steaming and waiting for her. Her body craved the warmth and tranquility a nice hot soak in a tub would provide. She closed the bathroom door and lit the candles that were strategically placed around the tub, sink and dressing area. The Ritz-Carlton knew how to pamper and she wasn't going to deny herself this pleasure. She kicked off her shoes, then stripped out of her clothes folding them neatly and setting them on the marble counter. She turned on the large LCD screen on the wall, finding a music station that played soulful jazz. All lights were turned down but for the flashing abstract images on the flat screen and the candles that burned with a vanilla scent.

Naked and relishing her impending bath, Rena stuck her toe in the water. "Perfect," she hummed, sinking the rest of her body into the exquisite warmth. For the first time in days, she relaxed.

She closed her eyes and obliterated all negative

thoughts. Instead, she thought of the baby growing inside her. She wondered if it was a boy or a girl. She hoped it would have David's kindness and intelligence and maybe her blue eyes. She hoped for so many things, but mostly she hoped her child would be happy.

A smile surfaced on her face as she pictured a sandy blond-haired little boy or a raven-haired little girl. Or perhaps a boy would have her coloring and a girl would have her father's. Either way, Rena would love that child beyond belief.

The door to the bathroom opened and Tony strode in. She gasped and sunk farther down into the tub. "What are you doing in here?"

Tony unbuttoned his shirt and dropped it onto the floor. He looked her over, his gaze following the valley between her breasts. "I'm taking a shower."

Her heart rate sped. "In here?"

"This is the master bathroom, right?"

Rena narrowed in on him. "How much have you had to drink?"

He cocked her a smile and shook his head. "Not enough, honey."

His shoes were off in a flash, and when he reached for his belt, she closed her eyes. She heard him stepping out of his clothes, open the glass shower door, then close it. The shower rained to life, and steam heated the room.

Rena opened her eyes slowly. Tony was deep into his shower, soaping himself up. She took a swallow and watched, unable to tear her gaze away. At one time, Tony Carlino was everything she wanted in life. Those old feelings surfaced, and she tried to shove them away, but it was darn hard to do. Not when he was built like a Greek god, stunningly masculine and boldly beautiful. He moved with grace and confidence, comfortable in his own skin. And so she watched him lather his body, wash his hair and let the water pelt down in streams over his broad shoulders, down the curve of his spine and into the steam that hid the rest of him from view. He turned abruptly and caught her staring. His brows elevated into his forehead, and the corners of his mouth lifted ever so slightly.

Rena turned away then, afraid that if he read her expression, he'd know what she was thinking. He'd know that some feelings can't be destroyed. Some feelings just simply…stay, no matter how hard you try to abolish them. They hide under the anger and pain, waiting.

When the shower spigot turned and the water shut off, Rena tensed. She didn't know what Tony expected. His comment about not tiptoeing around her had her perplexed. The shower door opened, and Tony stepped out, naked. Rena refused to let him intimidate her. She didn't look straight at him, but she didn't look away either. Instead she focused on a point beyond his head.

After wiping down his body, he wrapped the towel around his waist and glanced at her. "You should get out. You're getting cold."

His gaze lingered on her chest. No longer covered with flower petals and bubbles, her nipples were now visible beneath the water. She covered up and nodded. "I will, as soon as you're through in here."

Tony scrubbed the stubble on his face, contemplating.

"I guess I'll shave tomorrow. You can get out now." He reached over and handed her a plush chocolate-colored towel.

She grabbed it and hoisted it to her chin. "Well?"

"I'll be sleeping in the second bedroom. Get some rest, Rena." He bent over and kissed her on the cheek then cast her a rather odd look.

"What?" she asked, curious.

"When we were together, neither one of us would have imagined our wedding night to be anything like us."

She sighed. "No, not back then."

He nodded and left the room, leaving her with poignant and erotic memories of making love to him years ago when they'd been hot and wild for each other.

Rena slept heavily, her body needing the rest. When she woke, she snuggled into the pillow recalling her dream. She'd been out in the vineyards, the grapes ripe and ready to be picked, the air flavored with their pungently sweet aroma. She turned and David was beside her, his smile wide as he looked at the vines, then at her. "We'll have a good year." But then, David's face became Tony's. Somehow, within the eerie images of her mind, it had always been Tony out in the vineyard with her.

Disoriented, she popped her eyes open and gazed out the window as the San Francisco Bay came into view. She clung to cotton one-thousand-thread-count sheets and sat up in bed, looking around the master suite of the

Ritz-Carlton Hotel. It all came back to her now. David was dead, and she'd married Tony Carlino yesterday.

"Oh, God," she whispered.

"I see you're up." Tony stepped out of the bathroom, his face covered with shaving cream, his chest bare, wearing just a pair of black slacks.

Rena blinked, trying not to stare at his tanned, broad chest or the way he casually strode into the bedroom as if they'd been married for twenty years. "Did you sleep well?"

"Like a bab— Um, very well."

"You look rested," he said, then turned around and entered the bathroom again. She craned her neck to find him stroking a razor over his face. "Breakfast is ready if you're hungry," he called out.

She was famished. She'd discovered the first trimester meant eating for two. Finally, her appetite kicked in full force and that was good for the baby. Her child needed the nourishment and so did she. She'd been so terribly strained lately, with David's death, the failure of Purple Fields and her financial situation, that she'd lost her appetite. She'd had to force herself to eat. It was so much easier when she actually *felt* like eating.

"I'll get out of here in a sec," Tony said. "Give you time to dress. I'll wait for you in the dining room."

"Okay," she found herself saying.

Rena entered the bathroom shortly after Tony finished his shave. She splashed water on her face and combed her hair. While she'd often stay in her bathrobe during her morning breakfast routine, she found that too intimate to do with Tony. She dressed in a pair of slacks and a thin knit sweater that Solena had picked out of her wardrobe when Tony had secretly asked her friend to pack a bag for their stay here at the hotel.

Rena suspected Tony hadn't mentioned their wedding night at the Ritz to her, knowing she'd refuse. But yesterday after the wedding dinner, he'd just sprung it on her, catching her off guard. Just one more reason she didn't trust him. While others might see it as a romantic gesture, Rena felt as though she'd been deceived.

She entered the dining room and found Tony relaxing at the head of the table, reading the newspaper and sipping coffee.

He stood when she entered the room. "Morning again."

She managed a small smile then glanced at the antique sideboard filled with platters of food. "Where did all this come from?"

Tony shrugged. "It's the Presidential Suite."

"And that makes food magically appear?"

He laughed. "Yeah, I guess so."

"You might be used to being treated like this, but this is…overwhelming to me."

Tony walked over to stand before her. He searched her eyes. "I don't live like this, Rena. But it's a special occasion. I thought you deserved a little pampering." He stroked her cheek, his finger sliding along her jaw line tenderly. It had been so long since she'd been touched like this. So long since she'd had any real tenderness. She was nine weeks pregnant, and though she'd tried to be strong when David died, there were times when she just needed some gentle contact.

She looked into Tony's dark beautiful eyes, then lowered her gaze to his mouth. It was all the encouragement he needed. He took her carefully in his arms and bent his head, bringing their lips together in a soft kiss.

Rena relished his lips on hers, the gentle way he held her, the warmth and comfort he lent. It wasn't a sensual kiss but one of understanding and patience.

He surprised her with his compassion, and that made her wary. She couldn't put her faith in Tony—he'd destroyed that years ago. If she'd had any other way out of her dilemma she wouldn't have married him, despite gentle kisses and kind overtures.

"Rena, don't back off," he said.

"I have to. You offered me a business proposal. Your own words were, 'this isn't a real marriage.' And now, now…you're expecting me to fall into the role as your wife." She shook her head, and her emotions spilled out. "Don't you understand? At one time, I would have trusted you with my life, but now there's not much you could say or do to make me trust you. My heart is empty where you're concerned. I was forced to marry you… otherwise I wouldn't be here. I'm protecting myself, and my baby."

"That's what *I* intend to do, Rena. Protect you and the baby."

"No, you're going to help build my company back up. Period. I can't let you get too close to my child. I can't let you hurt my baby, the way you hurt me."

"How could I ever hurt your child?"

"The same way you hurt me. By walking out. By

leaving. By finding something more exciting than being a husband and father. While I've recovered from you leaving, it would be devastating to a child to be abandoned that way. My son or daughter may never get over it."

Anger flashed in his eyes. His jaw tightened, and his body went rigid. "I don't intend on abandoning either of you."

"What if you get the racing bug again? What if you're called back? It's in your blood, Tony. You love racing."

"That part of my life is over. I did what I set out to do. I'm not going back, ever."

Rena shook her head, refusing to believe him.

"You have my promise on that," he said. Then he spoke more firmly. "Did you hear me, Rena? I'll never leave you or the baby. It's a promise."

Tony stared at her for a long moment, and when she thought he was so angry he'd walk out of the room, he handed her a plate. "Eat up," he said. "We're going to have some fun today."

Rena glanced at him. "We are?"

"Yeah, even if it kills me."

Rena chuckled, despite the tension in the room just seconds earlier. She had to hand it to Tony for lightening the mood. "That's not my intention."

"Can I bank on that?"

She shrugged as she filled up her plate. "Sure," she offered. "You can bank on that."

They exited the hotel, and because it was a glorious day, they decided to walk the crowded streets. A few times, Rena and Tony got separated in the onslaught of foot traffic, so he grabbed her hand and they strolled along that way, browsing through shops. When Rena took a lingering look at a ruby necklace, her birthstone with a setting that was beautifully unusual, Tony dragged her into the store and purchased it for her. "You don't have to do this," she said.

"Consider it a wedding gift, since I didn't get you a diamond ring."

"I know, but I don't need this. What I need is for my vineyard to thrive and be solvent again."

"That'll happen too, Rena. You don't have to give up one to get the other."

Rena sighed inwardly. She'd been doing that most of her life, sacrificing her own needs and wants in order to assure Purple Fields' survival. It had been years since she'd known what it was like to simply have something she wanted without guilt.

Next they took the trolley to Fisherman's Wharf and ate clam chowder in sourdough bread bowls, then stopped at an ice cream parlor and ate sundaes until Rena thought her belly would expand out of her pants. "Oh, I'm so full."

"Me, too," Tony said, looking at her empty dish. "I guess you never get over loving hot fudge over strawberry ice cream."

"With nuts on top."

"Hmm and whipped cream. Remember the whipped cream fight we had?" Tony asked.

Rena remembered how they'd each taken out a can of Reddi-wip from Tony's refrigerator. No one was home and they'd just finished eating sundaes. "Yeah and you cheated!"

"I did not. I fight fair. I couldn't help it that your nozzle got stuck."

"You took advantage then and squirted me until I was covered with it. That stuff even got in my hair."

"You were sweet from head to toe," Tony said with a nostalgic smile.

The memory popped into her head of Tony kissing it off her until kissing wasn't enough. He'd taken her to his bedroom then, stripped her down and licked every bit of the whipped cream off. They'd made love in the shower, deciding that strawberry sundaes were their favorite dessert.

"I never have whipped cream without thinking of you," Tony said, his eyes fixed on hers.

Her cheeks heated and she inhaled sharply. "That was a long time ago." What she didn't add is that the same held true for her.

"But a good memory."

"I don't think about the past anymore," she fibbed.

He watched her intently. "Maybe you should. We had something special."

"'Had' being the key word." She refused to let Tony get to her.

Tony leaned over and kissed her on the lips. "Let's go," he said abruptly, taking her hand again. They rode the trolley back and checked out of the hotel. Rena took one last look around, feeling oddly sentimental. She blamed it on her fickle hormones.

When Rena thought they'd head back to Napa, Tony

drove her to a four-story shopping mall and parked the car. "What are we doing here?"

He grinned. "We're getting baby things."

"Baby things?"

"I promised you a fun day, and I figured a new mother-to-be would enjoy picking out furniture and clothes and whatever else the baby might need."

"Really?" Tempted by such an elaborate offer, Rena's heart raced with excitement. Offhand, she could think of dozens of items she'd need for the baby's arrival, and quite frankly, she didn't know how she'd manage to pay for all of it. Other than shopping at thrift stores, she was truly at a loss.

"I haven't a clue what a baby needs," Tony said, getting out of the car and opening the door for her.

"I'm on new ground here, too." She took his outstretched hand. "We'd always talked about having children, but—" Rena stopped and slipped her hand from his, her heart in her throat. How could she do this? How could she look at cribs and bassinets and baby swings when this was a dream she and David shared together? They'd always wanted a family. The time had never been right. She refused to think of the life growing inside her as an accident, but they hadn't really planned on this baby.

Rena ached inside thinking that David would never know his child. He'd never change a diaper, kiss its face or watch it take its first step. He'd never go to a ballet recital or little league game. He'd never know the joy of seeing his child develop into a smart-alecky teen or fall in love one day. David would have been there for his child. He'd have seen his son or daughter through the good times and the bad, because David was loyal and devoted. He would have made a wonderful father.

Rena's legs went weak suddenly. Her body trembled, and she knew she couldn't do this. She glanced at Tony, her voice a quiet plea. "I'm sorry. I don't think I'm ready for this."

Tony drew in a breath. "Right." He closed his eyes briefly, and Rena noted genuine pain there. "Okay, we'll do this another time. When you're ready."

She sighed with relief. "It's not that I don't appreciate—"

"I get it, Rena. I'm not the baby's father. Enough said."

Tony got back into his car and revved the engine, waiting for her to climb inside. She bit her lip and held back tears as she sank into the car. They drove to Napa in silence, Rena glancing at Tony's stony expression every once in a while.

She knew in her head that David was gone. He was her past, while this angry man sitting beside her was her future.

The irony struck her anew.

How many times had she hoped to be Tony Carlino's wife? Only to find now she should have been more careful what she'd wished for.

Six

Tony drove to Napa, a debate going on in his head. On one hand, he knew Rena still grieved, but on the other hand, he'd taken responsibility for her. She was his wife now. He couldn't let her dictate the terms of their relationship, not if he planned to really honor David's dying wish. So he drove past Purple Fields and down the highway leading to his home.

"Where are we going?" she asked.

"To my house."

Rena slanted him a dubious look. "Why?"

"Just stopping by to pick up some of my clothes to bring to Purple Fields."

Rena blinked before realizing his intent. "This was supposed to be a secret marriage, Tony. We can't live together."

Tony expected this argument. He pulled to the side of the road and stopped the car. Immediately, Rena's shoulders stiffened. She sat up straighter in the seat and faced him. Before he spoke, he searched her face for a long moment, reining in his anger. "Rena, we're not announcing to the public we're married. But I can't possibly work with you at Purple Fields and—"

"Watch out for me," she finished for him with a twist of her full lips.

She tried his patience, but Tony held firm. He'd made up his mind about this and decided it was best for both of them. "We'll be discreet. Purple Fields isn't exactly bustling with crowds."

"Thanks for the reminder."

"Rena, listen. All I'm saying is that you don't have a big staff that will spread gossip through the county. The place isn't on the main highway. In fact, you're in a remote location."

Rena's voice held quiet concern, and she refused to look at him. "I didn't think we'd live together."

Tony reached over to gently turn her chin his way. She lifted those incredible eyes to him. "You're my wife. I'm your husband. We *are* married. We'll keep the secret for a while, but make no mistake that I intend for us to live as man and wife. Now, if you'd rather move into the Carlino estate with me, we can—"

"No!" She shook her head. "No, Tony. That makes no sense. I need to be at Purple Fields."

Tony wasn't fooled. Rena's hatred for his father was evident in her blatant refusal. After Tony had moved away, Santo Carlino had tried to ruin all the local vintners in the area, and Rudy Fairfield hadn't been the exception. Once Tony was gone, his father had ignored Tony's protests to leave Purple Fields alone. The Fairfields had suffered, but they'd never fully succumbed to his father's ruthless business tactics.

Rena hadn't stepped foot in his house since. It seemed his new wife hated *everything* Carlino.

"Well then, it's settled. I'll move into your house."

Rena swallowed and gave him a reluctant nod.

He bounded out of the car and opened her door. She looked up and announced, "I'll wait for you out here. It's a nice day. I need the...fresh air."

Tony didn't push her. He helped her out, making a mental note that his Porsche wasn't a family car or comfortable for his pregnant wife. "I'll be a few minutes."

She nodded and stretched out, raising her arms, shaking out the kinks, confirming that he'd been right about the car.

Tony bounded up the steps and entered the arched wrought iron doors decorated with delicate metal vines that led to a breezeway. The house, set more like an Italian villa atop the hill, had four wings that met in the center by a large expansive living room and dining area overlooking the vineyards. Tony liked his privacy, and each of the Carlino men had lived in separate sections of the house once they'd grown up.

"Hey, I thought I heard you come in. How are the newlyweds?" Joe asked, approaching him as he began his ascent up the stairs.

Tony sighed. "Fine."

"That bad? I take it the wedding night didn't go so smoothly."

Tony knew Joe meant well. He wasn't prying; he was simply concerned. "She's still grieving."

"Understandable. Where is she?"

"Outside. She won't come in. But I plan to rectify that soon. She's not thrilled that I'm moving in with her."

"I wasn't sure of your plans. I guess it makes sense for you to live there for a while."

"I'll divide my time between here and there, Joe, but I'd appreciate it if you and Nick could hold down the fort for a few days without me."

"Sure, no problem."

"Thanks. You know," he began with a slant of his head, "if you'd have told me six months ago I'd be married to Rena and raising a baby, I wouldn't have believed it."

"Am I hearing a little bit of awe in your voice?"

"Yeah, well, maybe I'm adjusting to the situation a little better than my wife is."

"She'll come around. In fact, I think I'll step outside and say hello to my new sister-in-law. Maybe put in a few good words for you."

"I can use all the help I can get. Rena thinks she married the devil." He chuckled as he took the steps up to his bedroom. He'd been called even worse by some of the women he'd dated in the past.

And it had all been true.

"Tony?" Rena questioned him immediately when she realized where they were going. Tony hadn't taken her directly back to Purple Fields after he'd picked up his clothes from his estate. Instead, he'd driven to the cemetery where David was buried.

"Are you okay with this?" he asked.

Rena squeezed her eyes shut. Right after David died, she'd made daily trips to the cemetery to lay wildflowers by his grave. She'd come and sit on the grass just to feel close to him again. But after she'd learned about the promise he'd asked of Tony, she'd gotten so angry with him for his manipulation that she hadn't come back since. Now she realized the folly in that. David had tried to protect her. Even in death, he'd tried to take care of her. Guilt assailed her for being so shortsighted and selfish. She should have come more often. She should have honored the man who'd loved her. "Yes, I'm okay with this."

Once out of the car, Tony met her on the lawn and put out his hand. She glanced down at it and then into his reassuring eyes. "We'll do this together."

She slipped her hand into his, and silently they walked to the center of the Gracious Hill section of the cemetery. A new bronze headstone with David's name and birth date embossed in gold stared up at them. Rena sank to her knees and said a prayer. She sat there for a minute, looking down, running her fingers over the headstone, touching David's nameplate with infinite care.

Tony helped her up, and taking her hand, he spoke with reverence as his gaze drifted down toward the grave. "She's safe, David," he whispered. "We're married now. I'll take good care of her."

Overwhelmed with emotion, Rena let out a sob. Tears she couldn't hold back, spilled down her cheeks. The reality of the last few weeks came crashing down on her.

"It's okay, honey," Tony said softly. He turned his body and encompassed her in his arms, cradling her as she cried into his chest. She sobbed deeply, the pain emanating from deep within. Guilt and sadness washed over her.

Tony tightened his hold on her. "Let it out, Rena."

Cocooned in Tony's strength and warmth, she cried and cried until she finally managed to control her emotions. She sniffed and gulped in oxygen and stopped crying after several minutes, yet she couldn't let go of Tony. Wrapped up in his arms, she was grateful for the comfort, the gentle assuring words, the soft kisses to her forehead. She gave herself up to Tony allowing him to be strong for her. She needed this. She needed for once to let someone else take the brunt of her heartache.

"He's okay with this, Rena," Tony whispered. "It's what David wanted."

She knew that to be true. But she also realized she had just married a man who had hurt and betrayed her once—a man whom she blamed for her husband's death, a man who'd felt obligated to marry her. How could she find comfort in that?

"I was mad at David for asking this of you. Of me," she whispered painfully. "I haven't come here in weeks."

Tony stroked her back again and again, keeping her head pressed to his chest. "Don't beat yourself up, Rena.

You're a strong woman, but you have a right to all your feelings."

"Even the ones that scream I shouldn't have married you?"

Tony looked down into her eyes. "Yeah, even those."

"I don't intend on cutting you any slack," she said quietly.

"Planning on making my life miserable?"

"Not deliberately, Tony. But yes. You may want to move out before the week is over."

"Doubtful. I'm not going anywhere."

Then he leaned down and kissed her softly, exquisitely on her lips, and for the first time, Rena came close to believing him.

With arms folded, Rena watched Tony set his bags on the floor beside her bed. He faced her, his gaze direct and piercing. "I told you, I won't tiptoe around you any-more. We're going to live as man and wife."

Rena drew in a breath. Exhausted, she had no more tears to shed. She'd used up her quota and then some at the cemetery. Though her insides quaked and her head ached, she knew she had no choice but to accept Tony in her home and in her bed. He had pride. He was virile and strong and extremely sexy. She suspected women had thrown themselves at him all the time. He was a race car champion, an appealing bachelor who was definitely easy on the eyes. He'd probably had women in every town he traveled.

Though he'd been patient and kind to her the past few

days she knew she'd pushed him pretty far. And soon, he'd start pushing back.

He must have noted her fear, because his jaw clenched and he swore. "For God's sake, Rena. I'm not about to force myself on you. But we will sleep in the same bed."

Rena glanced at the bed, then up at him. "I understand."

"Ah, hell." He rolled his eyes at her robotic answer. "You'd think we'd never had sex before. Mind-blowing, earthmoving, do-it-until-we-can't-breathe-anymore sex."

Rena nearly tripped over her own feet backing up, his statement stunning her. Her face heated, and her body shook a little. Speechless, she lowered her lashes, fighting off memories of their lovemaking. He'd been blunt but accurate in his description. "That's when…" she began, almost unable to get the words out. "When we were in love."

"Right." Tony tossed his overnight bag on the bed. He pulled out aftershave lotion, deodorant, razors and a hairbrush. "You have a place I can put these?"

She pointed to the master bathroom. "It's small, but you should find some room on the counter."

She'd taken David's things out of the bedroom, unwilling to have that daily reminder of his absence. But she'd yet to remove his clothes from the closet. She'd be forced to now. Tony would need the room, and unlike his home with massive walk-in closet space, her closets were barely big enough for two people.

She held out hope that he'd get disgusted with her

small three-bedroom house and move back to the estate where he'd be ensconced in luxury.

Rena opened her closet and began gathering up David's clothes to make room for Tony's. Before she knew it, Tony stood beside her and placed a stopping hand on hers. "You don't have to do it now. You're exhausted."

"It needs doing. I just never could fa—"

"If it makes you feel better, I'll do it."

"No," she said with a shake of her head. "I should do it."

Tony grabbed both of her hands while they were still on the hangers. He stood close. So close that she noted the golden flecks in his dark eyes. "Okay but not today. It can wait. Agreed?"

She nodded, breathing in his subtle, musky scent. A lump formed in her throat thinking of his stirring kiss before. She didn't want to be attracted to Tony. She'd gotten over him a long time ago, yet when he touched her or looked deep into her eyes or kissed her, emotions rolled around inside. And made her nervous. "I'll make dinner."

"Thank you."

She strode out of the room, confused by what she was feeling and angry for feeling anything at all.

Rena stirred the spaghetti sauce, watching as little bubbles broke on the surface sending a pungent, garlic scent into the air.

"Smells great." Tony came up behind her, his body close again, surprising her in how quietly he appeared in her kitchen. He reached for the wooden spoon. "May I?"

She handed it to him. "I hope you don't mind pasta tonight."

"Are you kidding? I'm Italian. You know I love pasta." He stirred the sauce, then lifted the spoon to his mouth, tasting it.

"What do you think?"

"Needs a little salt," he said, then grabbed the salt shaker and added a few shakes. "There."

"You like to cook, don't you?"

He shrugged. "I get by. When a bachelor wants to eat, he's got to know more than how to boil water."

"I didn't think you'd ever have to cook a meal for yourself."

Tony continued stirring the sauce. "When my gourmet chef was off, I had three other servants waiting on me hand and foot." He turned to her and grinned.

"You're teasing."

"Yeah, I'm teasing." Then he set the wooden spoon down and stared at her. "I'm not going to apologize for how I live. I've earned it. Racing has afforded me a good life. But there were sixteen-hour work days, long lonely times on the road. Times when I had to cook for myself when I longed for a home cooked meal. Eating out is overrated."

"There must have been plenty of women happy to cook for you. Never mind," Rena said, catching herself. She didn't really want to know. "Forget I said that."

Tony's expression changed, and he gave her a quick shake of the head. "Your image of me is way off."

Rena pursed her lips. "It really doesn't matter."

Tony grabbed her arms gently as steam rose up from the sauce and bathed them in heat. "Yes, it does matter. I'm your husband. I care what you think of me."

Rena stared into his eyes, unable to answer. She had mixed emotions when it came to Tony Carlino, but for the most part, she didn't want to see any good in him. She wanted to keep him a safe distance away in her mind and heart.

When he realized she wouldn't respond, he let her go and she went about filling a big pot of water for the pasta noodles.

Tony watched her work at the stove for a long while before he spoke again. "What can I do to help?"

Grateful to give him something to do, she barked orders. "Take out the romaine and tomatoes from the refrigerator. I think there's a cucumber in there, too— and anything else you can find for a salad."

She heard him going to work, and much to her surprise, he fixed a delicious salad, and, adding black olives and herbs, he made his own olive oil-based dressing.

When she walked over to taste it, she cast him a nod of approval. "Yummy."

"My mother's. One of a few recipes I learned from her before she died."

Tony's mother died when he was fifteen. Rena hadn't known her, but she'd heard she was a saint among women. She'd have to be in order to be married to Santo Carlino. Rumor had it she'd kept him in line. When she died, Santo poured himself into building his business taking no prisoners along the way.

"And you remembered it," Rena said. "It's funny the things we remember about the ones we love."

"What do you remember about your mother?" he asked.

Rena smiled wide, recalling her mother's favorite pastime. "That's easy. She had a morning and nightly ritual of walking three miles. No matter how tired she was, no matter the weather. She'd get into her walking clothes, put on these beat-up old shoes and go for a walk. She said it cleared the mind, cleansed the soul and kept the weight off." Rena grinned, confessing. "My mama liked to eat."

Tony chuckled. "That's a good way to remember her. Walking, I mean. Not eating."

"Hmm, yeah." Rena blinked herself back to reality. Even with all her exercise, her mother still contracted a deadly disease. She'd lingered for years, missing her daily walks and everything else that required a bit of effort. It was a brutal reminder of the unfairness in life.

Once the meal was ready, they sat down to eat at her country oak kitchen table. She wondered what Tony thought about this rustic house. To her it was home, and she wasn't ashamed of it. Through the years, she'd put personal touches throughout, cheerful curtains, comfy sofas with throw pillows she'd sewn, refinished tables, armoires and cabinets. When she looked around her home, she saw bits and pieces of her parents' life here as well as her life with David.

Facing Tony at her kitchen table reminded her once again how it had all changed so quickly.

Tony ate up heartily. There would be no salad-only dinners for him. He was a well-built man who enjoyed a good meal. He was halfway through a large dish of pasta when he lifted his head. "I want to see your accounts tomorrow. I hope to get through them by the end of the week. Then I'll know better how we can get your winery back on track."

Grateful that he'd taken the first step, Rena discussed with him her conversation she had with the banker. Tony hadn't even blinked when she told him her financial situation and how much money she owed.

"I'll take care of it," he said, without pause. "You'll make your payroll, and any other debts you have will be dealt with."

"Thank you." Humbled by his generosity, she put her head down.

"Rena?" She looked up into his dark eyes. "We're in this together from now on. You don't have to worry about the winery."

"I know. I appreciate everything, really. I just can't help feeling like a failure. I tried. David tried. We had some bad luck, equipment that needed replacing, problems with distributors and well, the bigger wineries tried to shove us out."

Tony covered her hand, and the instant spark jolted her. "Carlino Wines being one of them. That's not going to happen anymore."

She tried to ignore sensations rippling through her. "The Fairfields have always taken pride in their livelihood. *I* have a lot of pride. I feel like I let my parents down. I had to remarry to save the business."

Tony stroked her hand, his fingers caressing hers. It felt good—too good—to pull her hand away. Lord help her, she needed to feel his touch.

"I won't take offense to that," he said. "I know I'm the last person on earth you'd want as a husband."

She watched as his fingers slid over her knuckles so gently. "At one time, I wanted nothing more."

"And now?"

She gazed deeply into his eyes and lifted a shoulder in confusion. "Now, I don't know, Tony. I really don't know. I'm just so tired."

Tony rose from the table with concern in his eyes. "Go. I'll take care of this." He took up their plates and headed toward the dishwasher. "You need to rest. It's been a long day."

Rena got up, ready to argue, but Tony had already rinsed their dishes and began loading them into the dishwasher. With his back to her, she noted his broad shoulders tapering down along his back and slim waistline. His slacks fit perfectly over his buttocks, and she recalled the quick flash of excitement she felt when he'd stepped out of the shower yesterday, buck naked. She'd only caught a glimpse, but oh, that image wouldn't leave her anytime soon.

"I, uh, thanks. I'll take a quick shower and go to bed. What will you—"

He turned sharply and met her gaze. "I'll come to bed later, Rena."

She gave him a clipped nod, turned around and strode

out of the room. Her exhaustion catching up with her, she was too tired to think of the implications of sleeping with her new, extremely sexy secret husband.

Seven

Rena snuggled deeper into her bed, rebelling against thin rays of dawn creeping into the room. She closed her eyes tighter, rolling away from the light and into familiar warmth. Cocooned in the heat now, she relaxed and let out a stress-relieving sigh.

Her eyelids blessedly shut, she breathed in a pleasing musky scent and smiled. A warm breath brushed her cheek, then another and another. She popped her eyes open. Tony was there, inches from her face, his eyes dark and dusky. He lay stretched out on his side, apparently watching her sleep. "Morning, beautiful."

Alarm bells rang out in her head. She couldn't believe she was in bed with Tony. And enjoying it. His warmth surrounded her. She focused on the firm set of his sculpted jaw, then opened her mouth to speak, but

Tony placed his finger to her lips, stopping her words. "Shh. Don't overthink this, Rena." He wrapped his arms around her waist and drew her closer.

She remembered putting on her most unappealing nightshirt last night, a soft, brushed cotton garment with tiny cap sleeves just in case Tony held true to his word to sleep with her. But Rena liked to feel feminine in bed, so the least suggestive nightgown she owned was still a far cry from head-to-toe flannel.

"Don't overthink what?"

"This," he said, moving closer and touching his lips to hers. The heat of his mouth and the intimate contact should have caused her to panic. Yet, she didn't resist, her body and mind not fully operational at the moment. He pulled away long enough to search her eyes and must have been satisfied with what he saw in them.

Tony knew how to kiss a woman, and he held nothing back with the next kiss. He drew her in with expert finesse, coaxing a reaction from her. His hand on her waist, she felt his strength through the thin cotton fabric of the nightgown. He squeezed her gently, and immediate tingles coursed through her body. She sighed aloud, a throaty little sound that emanated from deep within. Tony moved his hand up, stroking her side slowly up and down, his fingers brushing the underside of her breast.

Oh God, it felt good to have him caress her, teasing her breast until she ached for his touch.

Rena loved the physical act of making love. She loved the intimacy, the joy of having her body succumb to infinite pleasure. Tony had taught her that. He'd taken her virginity and taught her to enjoy sexual intercourse. Of course, back then they'd been so much in love that holding back wasn't an option. She'd given herself fully to him, surrendering her heart and her body. She'd only been with two men in her life, and each in their own way had taught her about loving a man. Where David had been sweet, patient and dependable, Tony had been irresistible, hot-blooded and sexy.

Tony's passionate kisses unnerved her. His touch drew her like a magnet. She moved closer, arching toward him, her breaths heavier now. He nibbled on her lips, whispering how beautiful she was, how much he wanted to touch her.

She gave him permission with a sigh.

His hand came up and cupped her breast over the fabric of her cotton nightie. He flicked a finger over the tip, rubbing back and forth, sending shock waves through her body. Intense heat swamped her, and she longed for more.

She knew the instant Tony's body went taut. His breaths deepened, and his kisses became more demanding as he parted her lips. His tongue beckoned hers, and she met him halfway. They sparred in an endless search for satisfaction.

While her body craved the physical release, her heart and mind screamed no. Torn by indecision, she stilled, forcing herself to think this through.

"You're overthinking again, Rena," Tony said in a low rasp. He continued to stroke her breast, unraveling her mind.

She mustered her willpower and covered his hand with hers, stopping him. "One of us has to."

"I told you I don't plan on being celibate in this marriage," he said quietly. "If I thought you weren't ready, I'd back off. But the woman I was just kissing wasn't protesting at all. You were enjoying having my hands on you. In another second I would have taken off your nightgown, and we would have been skin to skin. I want that, and I know you want that, too."

Rena's heart pumped hard. He was right, but she had to voice her innermost thoughts. "Wanting and having are two different things."

"Rena's rules, not mine."

Rena drew oxygen in. "I can't forget who you are. I can't ignore what you did to me. My heart is empty where you're concerned."

"So you've said." Tony flopped onto his back and looked at the ceiling. "What's done is done, Rena. I can't change that."

"I know. And I can't change how I feel. I may want you physically, but you'll never really have me. I can't love you again. I won't. You'll never own my heart."

"As long as you're faithful to me, that's all I'll ask for now."

Stunned by the statement, Rena lifted her head off the pillow. "You know me, Tony. I'd never even consider—"

He turned onto his side again to face her. "What you don't know about me is that I'd never consider it, either. But I'm a man with physical needs, and since we're married and compatible in bed, there's no reason not to make love."

"You mean, *have sex?* Because without love, it's just sex," Rena pointed out.

He lifted a strand of her hair, eyeing it as he let it fall from his fingers. "Just sex?" Tony cocked her a playful grin. "Even better."

Rena shook her head in bewilderment.

"C'mon, Rena. We've cleared the air. I get it. You don't love me, but you crave my body."

"I never said that!"

"Oh, no?" he said innocently. He was such a tease. He crushed his mouth to hers and kissed her passionately. She'd hardly come up for air when he grabbed her hand and set it on his chest. "Touch me."

Crisp scattered hairs filled her palm and underneath muscles rippled. She wove her hand up along his sculpted shoulders then down to tease his flattened nipple. His intake of air let her know he enjoyed her flicking her finger over him, the way he had to her.

Laying her hand against his torso, she inched her way down, tempted by a perfect body and powered by the sounds of Tony's quick jagged breaths. Okay, so maybe she did crave his body. She had memories that wouldn't go away. Sexual flashes that entered her mind at the most inopportune times. She'd remembered how he'd made her feel, how potent his lovemaking was, how satisfied she'd been afterward. If anything, Tony had matured into a stunning male specimen. He knew how to give pleasure, and he knew how to take it. He'd always made Rena feel special and cherished, no matter what act they performed.

She slid her hand farther down, slipping below Tony's waistline. When she reached the elastic band of his boxers, she hesitated, tentative in her approach. Myriad thoughts flitted through her mind one right after the other, but Tony interrupted that train of thought. "Just let go, Rena," he whispered. "We both need this."

Rena touched him then, her hand gliding over silken skin. His arousal shocked her, though she didn't know why it should. He was a virile man, and they were in bed together, ready to consummate their marriage.

"I want you." Tony's low tone held no room for doubt. He cupped her chin and brought her lips to his. There was a sense of urgency to his kiss, yet he remained gentle and patient, waiting for her to respond. She stroked him with trebling fingers, bringing him to a fuller state of arousal.

"This is not—" Rena began, but Tony kissed her again, his mouth generous and giving, coaxing her to fulfill their destiny. Torn by indecision, she shoved all thoughts of the past years aside and tried to focus on the future.

"We'll have a life together, Rena." Tony's words mirrored her own. Her life included him now, whether planned or not, whether she liked it or not. She had no other option now.

"I know," she said, finally resigning to her fate.

Tony removed his boxers then placed her hand back on him, skin to skin, and her insides turned to jelly. There was life to Tony, a vitality she'd missed during these past months. He filled the void, the hollowness that beseeched her since she'd become a widow. She had her precious child, yes, but this intimacy fulfilled her need to feel alive again.

She stroked him until his pleasure heightened. Instincts, or perhaps recollection, told her that he'd reached his limit. He flipped her onto her back, and in one quick sweep, he removed her nightgown, pulling it up and over her head. His kisses burned her through and through, and his hands roamed over her, touching, tormenting, caressing and teasing every inch of her skin. His voice was low and consumed with passion. "You're as beautiful as I remember."

He brought his mouth down to suckle her breast, his tongue wetting her with long swipes. After laving each nipple, he blew on them, and every ounce of her body prickled with need. Her pulse raced with exquisite excitement. Unmindful of any repercussions, she relished the thrill of the moment.

Tony praised her body with quiet expletives and cherished every limb before moving on to touch her at the apex of her legs. His palm covered her, and she arched up.

"You're ready for me, sweetheart," he acknowledged. Without hesitation, he rose over her. She gazed up at him, and images of their past, of doing this very thing with nothing but love in their hearts, played out in her mind. She'd relished their joining, eager to show the man she loved how much he meant to her. It had been perfect. Blissful. Exciting.

Tony stared into her eyes in the dawn light, and she

witnessed that same spark. The memories had come back to him, as well. His lips lifted and his eyelids lowered. Then he gripped her hips and she squeezed her eyes shut, ready for him to take her.

"Look at me," he commanded.

"Tony," she murmured, popping her eyes open. It was clear what he wanted. No memories of any other man. No memories of David.

He nodded when their eyes met, apparently satisfied, then he moved inside her with extreme care. Rena adjusted to his size and accommodated him with her body. It wasn't long before his thrusts magnified, their bodies sizzled hot and the burn she'd remembered from long ago returned fiercely.

Infinitely careful and recklessly wild, Tony made love to her, seeing to her needs, giving as much as taking, gentle at times and feral at others. He was the perfect lover—that much hadn't changed. And all the while, Rena gave up her body to him but held firmly onto her emotions.

It was *just sex*.

And as Tony brought her to the peak of enjoyment, her skin damp, her body throbbing for the release that would complete her, she wrapped her arms around his neck and arched up, her bones melting but her heart firmly intact.

Tony wrapped Rena in his arms. They lay quietly together on the bed after making love, each deep in thought. It had been months since he'd had sex, and his release had come with powerful force. Rena had responded to him as she always had, with wild abandon. At least her body had reacted as he'd hoped. He knew what she liked and how to please her. She'd been his first love, too, and a man doesn't easily forget how to please the woman he loves.

They'd been so young back then, full of dreams and plans for the future. But Tony had been a rebel. He'd hated being under his father's thumb. He hadn't wanted any part of the family business, not when racing cars meant so much to him. He'd never planned on leaving Rena behind. It just happened. While his professional life had been great, his personal life had suffered.

Once he'd become a champion, he had women knocking at his door at all hours of the night. They followed him from race to race. They'd called him, showed up when he least expected it. Beautiful, sexy, outrageous women. He'd never fallen in love with any of them. He'd had flings and a few casual relationships that never lasted more than a couple of months.

He'd held hope for Rena in the early years, but he hadn't blamed her for giving up on him. He hadn't known what the future held for him other than racing cars. He was on the road a great deal of time, thrilled by his success but heartbroken about Rena.

His gaze fell to Rena's face, her expression glum, her eyes filled with regret. Hardly the loving wife in the aftermath of lovemaking.

Hell, he felt like crap himself, guilt eating at him. He wanted to do right by David, but he couldn't forget that a few months ago, his friend was alive and well and living with the woman he loved. He was to become a father, something that David always wanted.

Tony had suspected David had feelings for Rena early on. They had been good friends in school, yet all three understood in an unspoken agreement that Rena and Tony were meant for each other. When Tony left town, David stayed behind to pick up the pieces of Rena's shattered heart. He'd loved her that much to forego a chance to enter the racing circuit with Tony. To Rena's way of thinking, David was her white knight coming to her rescue, where Tony was the villain who'd abandoned her.

Now they'd consummated a loveless marriage.

Her remorse irritated him more than it should. Was it ego on his part? They'd just made incredible love, and now Rena looked so darn miserable.

Damn it, what did she expect? She was his wife. He would raise her child as his own. They'd both agreed to honor David's last wishes. That meant living as man and wife and sleeping together. He blinked away anger and guilt then rose abruptly, mindless of his state of undress. "I'll grab a shower, then I want to go over your accounts."

Rena glanced at him for an instant, bit down on her lip then focused her attention out the window. "I'll make breakfast."

"I'm not hungry," he said. "Coffee will do. Meet me in the office once you're dressed."

Rena nodded without looking at him.

Tony showered quickly and dressed with clothes he'd taken from his bag. He put on a pair of faded jeans and a black T-shirt then shoved his feet into a pair of seasoned white Nike shoes.

He heard kitchen sounds as he walked down the hallway, the aroma of hot coffee brewing, whetting his taste buds. But instead of greeting his new wife in the kitchen, he strode outside and closed the door. The northern California air was crisp and fresh, the brilliant sky laced with white puffy clouds.

He filled his lungs several times, breathing in and out slowly, enjoying the pristine air. The vineyards were far removed from the city, elevated to some degree, the vistas spread out before him, glorious. Funny, as a young boy, he'd had no appreciation for the land or its beauty and solitude. He'd never seen this country as his father had seen it.

Now he'd make a life here. The irony that his father was getting what he wanted in death, rather than in life, was never far from his mind.

Tony entered the office adjacent to the gift shop with the key Rena had left for him on her dresser. He glanced around, noting two tall file cabinets, an outdated computer, a desk that had seen better days and shelves displaying certificates, wine awards and pictures of Rena and David. He walked over and picked one up that was encased in a walnut frame. He looked at the image of the couple standing among the vines ripe with cabernet grapes.

"It was a good year for cabernet. Our fifth anniversary." Rena walked into the office with a cup of coffee and set it down on the desk.

Tony stared at the photo. "You look happy."

"David made me dinner that night. He set up twinkling lights out on the patio. We danced in the moonlight."

Tony put the frame back, deciding not to comment. What could he say to that? "Thanks for the coffee."

She shrugged. "Well, this is the office. Our accounts for the past ten years are in those file cabinets."

Tony picked up the coffee cup and sipped. The liquid went down hot and delicious, just what he needed. "I'll start with the past year and work my way backward."

"Okay, I'll get those for you."

"Are they all paper files? Do you have anything loaded into the computer?"

Rena glanced at the machine. "We have our inventory computerized now. And David had started to enter the paper files. But he didn't get very far, I'm afraid."

Tony sat down at the desk and signed on. "Want to show me where everything is?"

Rena came close, her hair still slightly damp from her shower. She bent over the computer, clicking keys. Her clean scent wafted in the air. "What is that?" he asked.

She looked at him in question. "What?"

"You smell great."

She smiled softly. "It's citrus shampoo."

Tony met her eyes, then took her hand gently. "Rena... listen, about this morning."

She squeezed her eyes shut and shook her head. "Don't, Tony. I can't help how I feel."

"How *do* you feel?"

She hesitated for a moment, but Tony fixed his gaze

on her and wouldn't back down. She sighed quietly. "Like I sold my soul."

"To the devil?"

Her lips tightened as if holding back a comment.

Tony leaned in his chair, releasing her hand. "Physically, are you okay?"

"Yes," she said. "I'm fine. I see the doctor next week, but I'm healthy."

She continued clicking on keys, showing him where the files were kept and how to access them. Then she came upon a document and lingered, her gaze drawn to the words on the screen: *Vine by Vine.* "Don't worry about this," she said, her finger on the delete button.

"Wait." Tony stopped her. "What is it?"

"It's nothing." Rena said, but he wouldn't let it go. Something in her eyes told him, whatever it was, it was important to her.

"I need to see everything, Rena. If I'm going to help you."

"It's got nothing to do with the accounts, Tony. Trust me."

"So why won't you let me see it?" Determined, he pressed her.

"Oh, for heaven's sake!" Rena straightened, her eyes sparkling like blue diamonds. "It's just a story I was writing."

"A *story?*" That sparked his curiosity. "What's it about?"

"It's about a girl growing up in the wine country."

"It's about you?"

"No, it's a novel. It's fiction, but yes, I guess some

of it is about what I know and how I feel about living here. It's sort of a wine guide but told from a different perspective. It's an analogy of how a girl grows to womanhood—"

"And you relate that to how a vine grows? Sort of like, how you need to be cared for and loved and nourished."

"Yeah," she said, her expression softening. "Something like that."

"You're not finished with it?"

She made a self-deprecating sound. "No, I'd forgotten about it. There's too much to do around here." She shrugged it off. "I never found the time."

"Maybe someday you'll have time to finish it."

Rena stared deeply into his eyes. "Right now, I'm more interested in saving my winery."

Tony glanced at the computer screen, satisfied that she'd removed her finger from the delete button. "Agreed. That's the first order of business. We have to find a way to keep Purple Fields afloat."

Rena walked into the gift shop through a door adjacent to the office, leaving Tony to work his magic on their books. She'd given him all the files, answered his questions and left once he was neck-deep in the accounts, unaware of her presence any longer.

Her small little haven of trinkets and boutique items always perked up her spirits. She loved setting up the displays, making each unique object stand out and look desirable to the customer. They made very little profit on the shop, but it complimented the wine-tasting room and made the whole area look appealing.

Rena sighed with relief rather than anguish this time. For so long she'd had the burden of saving Purple Fields on her shoulders, and the weight had become unbearably heavy. Now she knew that with Tony's assets backing her up she had salvaged the future of Purple Fields, thus insuring her baby's future as well. She could only feel good about that.

But saving the winery had come at a high price. If it weren't for the promise she made to David, she wondered if she'd be standing here right now. She'd been set to sell Purple Fields and move away, making a fresh start with her child. Now she was tied to Tony Carlino, and the notion prickled her nerves.

She didn't want to enjoy being in his arms this morning. She didn't want to admit that having sex with him made her world spin upside down. She *hated* that she'd liked it. That she'd responded to him the way she always had. Tony wasn't a man easily forgotten, but she'd managed it for twelve years. Now he was back in her life and planned to stay.

Solena entered the gift shop, thankfully interrupting her thoughts. "Hey, you're up and out early this morning."

Rena smiled at her friend, happy to see her. "It's just another workday."

Solena eyed her carefully. "Is it? I thought you got married two days ago."

"Seems longer," Rena said, lifting her lips at her little joke.

"That bad?"

Rena glanced at the door leading to the office. "I shouldn't complain. He's in there right now, going over all our files and accounts. He's owning up to his end of the bargain."

Solena walked behind the counter and spoke with concern and sympathy. "Are you doing the same, my friend?"

Rena lowered her lashes. "I'm trying. I'm really trying. I never thought we'd live together like this. We, uh—" Heat reached her cheeks, and she realized she'd blushed, something she rarely did.

Solena spoke with understanding. "Tony's a very handsome, appealing man, Rena."

"So was David." Tears welled in her eyes.

Solena leaned over the counter to take her hands. Rena absorbed some of her strength through the solid contact. "David is the past, Rena. As hard as that is to hear, it's true. You have to look forward, not back."

"But I feel so...guilty."

Solena held firm. "Remind yourself that David wanted this."

"There are times when I really hate Tony," she whispered. "And I'm ashamed that I'm not too thrilled with David for making me do this."

"But we both know why he did."

Rena tilted her head to one side. "There's more. I should have told you sooner."

"What?" Solena's dark eyes narrowed with concern.

Rena hesitated, staring at her friend. Finally she blurted, "I'm pregnant."

Solena drew in a big breath then let it go in relief. "Oh! You had me scared for a second there, imagining the worst." Quickly, she walked around the counter to give Rena a hug. "This is good news…really good news."

"Yes, it is. I know." A tear dropped down her cheek. She'd already fallen in love with her baby. "I'm happy about the baby, but now do you see why I'm so, so—"

"You're torn up inside. I can see that. But you have hope and a new life to bring into this world. Oh Rena, my dear friend, I couldn't be happier for you."

She glanced at the office door and lowered her voice, speaking from the heart. "David should raise his child, not Tony."

Solena's eyes softened with understanding. "But that can't be. Your feeling bad isn't going to change that. It takes a remarkable man to raise another man's child. Tony knows?"

"He knows."

"You resent him."

"Yes, I do. I resent him for so many reasons. I'm so afraid."

"Afraid?" Solena met her gaze directly. "You're afraid of Tony?"

She shook her head. "No, not of him. Of me. I'm afraid I'll forgive him. I don't want to forget the hurt and pain he caused me. I don't want to ever forgive him."

Tony spent the morning loading the Purple Fields files into a new database program. His first order of business was to update the computer. He wasn't a genius at business like his brother Joe, but he knew the value of state-of-the-art equipment. Rena needed a new computer, but for now he'd do what he could and download everything to a flash drive.

Rena walked into the office holding a plate of food. "It's after one, and you haven't eaten lunch."

Tony glanced at his watch, then leaned back in his seat. "I didn't realize the time."

She set the plate down onto the desk. "Ham and cheese. I have chicken salad made if you'd prefer that instead?"

Tony grabbed the sandwich and took a bite. "This is fine," he said, his stomach acknowledging the late hour. "Did you eat?"

"Solena and I had a bite earlier. Since David's death, she's been babysitting me. She thinks I don't know it, but it's sweet. We usually have lunch together."

"What about Ray?"

"He eats a huge breakfast at home and skips lunch."

"Do you have time to sit down?" he asked. "I could use the company."

He rose from his chair, offering it to her. He waited until she took the seat before he sat on the edge of the desk, stretching his legs out. He wasn't used to poring over a computer screen for hours. He wasn't used to being holed up behind a desk in a small office either.

He gobbled his sandwich and began working on the apple she'd cut into wedges. "How's your day going?"

"Good," she said. "I gave a wine tour at eleven, and we sold a few cases today. Want something to drink?"

"I'll have a beer later. I'll need it."

She tilted her head, her pretty blue eyes marked with question. "Too many numbers?"

"Yeah. I'm inputting files. Setting up a database. My eyes are crossing."

She laughed. "I know what you mean."

Tony liked the sound of her laughter. He stared at a smile that lit the room. "You do?"

"All those numbers can make you crazy."

He grinned. "I think I'm there now." He gobbled up the apple wedges. "Thanks for lunch."

Rena watched him carefully. "You're welcome."

"You need a new computer and some stuff for the office. This thing is outdated. We'll work out a time to do that."

Rena's eyes widened. "A new computer? I, uh, we never could afford—"

"I know," Tony said softly. "But now we can."

"And you need me for that?"

"Yes, I need your input. Look, we can drive into the next town if you'd feel more comfortable, but—"

"I would." She offered without hesitation.

Tony's ego took a nosedive. He'd promised her a secret marriage and he'd stick to it, but he wasn't accustomed to women not wanting to be seen with him. Usually, it was just the opposite—women enjoyed being seen around town with him.

Irritated now, he agreed. "Fine."

"So what are your plans?" She stood and picked up his empty plate.

"I loaded the info to a flash drive. I'm going to have Joe take a look at everything. Though I have my suspicions, I need his opinion."

"You're going home tonight?"

Her hope-filled voice only irritated him some more. With legs spread, he reached out and pulled her between them, the plate separating their bodies. "Yeah, but I'll be back." He kissed her soundly on the lips reminding her of the steamy way they'd made love early this morning. He nuzzled her neck, and the devil in him added with a low rasp, "I have more inputting to do."

Rena's eyes snapped up to his.

He smiled and then released her.

He'd told her no more tiptoeing around and he'd meant it.

Eight

Tony entered the Carlino offices, a two-story building set in the heart of Napa Valley. The older outer structure gave way to a modern, innovative inner office filled with leather and marble. The mortar and stone building had been classified as a ghost winery, once owned by an aging retired sea captain who had run the place in the 1890s until Prohibition put him out of business, along with nearly seven hundred other wineries in the area. While some wineries had been turned into estates and restaurants, some held true to their original destiny, haunted not by ghostly spirits but by the passage of time and ruin.

The place had lain dormant and in a state of wreckage until Santo Carlino purchased the property then renovated it into their office space.

Tony walked into the reception area and was greeted by a stunningly gorgeous redhead. "Hi, you must be Tony Carlino." The woman—her cleavage nearly spilling out of her top—lifted up from her desk to shake his hand. "Joe said you'd be stopping by. I'm Alicia Pendrake, but you can call me Ali."

"Hi, Ali." He grasped her hand and shook.

"I'm Joe's new personal assistant. Today's my second day on the job."

"Nice to meet you," Tony said, curious why Joe didn't mention hiring anyone new when they spoke, especially one who looked like an overly buxom supermodel, with rich auburn curls draping over her shoulders, wearing a sleek outfit and knee-high boots.

She pointed to the main office door. "He's inside, crunching numbers, what else?"

Tony chuckled. The woman was a spitfire. "Okay, thanks."

"Nice meeting you, Mr. Carlino."

"It's Tony."

"Okay, Tony." She granted him a pleased smile that sent his male antenna up.

He found Joe seated behind his desk, staring at the computer screen. He made sure to close the door behind him. "Whoa…where did you find her?"

"Find who?" Joe said, his attention focused on the computer.

"Alicia…Ali. Your new PA."

Joe's brows furrowed and he took off his glasses, rubbing his eyes. "I met her in New York last year. She's efficient and capable."

"I bet. What happened to Maggie?"

"I had to let her go. She wasn't doing her job. This place was in chaos when I got here. I remembered Ali, and I called her. Offered to pay her way out here, gave her an advance on her salary to get set up. I didn't think she'd take the job."

"But she did. Just like that?"

"Yeah, I got lucky."

"*You got lucky?* Joe, the woman is beyond gorgeous. Haven't you noticed?"

Joe rubbed his jaw. "She's attractive, I suppose."

"You suppose? Maybe you need better glasses."

"My glasses are fine. I'm not interested, Tone. You know that I've sworn off women. After what happened with Sheila, I'm basically immune to beautiful women... to all women actually. Ali is smart. She's dedicated, and she does her work without complaint. She's very organized. You know how I am about organization."

Tony's lips twitched. "Okay, if you say so."

"So, what's up? You said you needed a favor?"

Tony tossed the flash drive onto the desk. "I need you to compare these accounts from Purple Fields with ours, for the same dates. I've been going over Rena's books. I just need your expert opinion."

"How soon?"

"Today?"

"I can do that." Joe inserted the flash drive into his computer. "I'll upload the files and let you know what I find out."

"Great, oh and can you burn them to a CD for me? There's something else I want to check on."

"Sure thing. I'll do that first."

While Joe burned the information to a disk, Tony walked around the office, noting the subtle changes Joe had made to Santo Carlino's office. Joe had secured even more high tech equipment than his father had used and updated the phone system. He was determined to make the company paperless, sooner rather than later.

It would seem that the only thing left from the older generation of the winery were the vast acres of vineyards—six hundred in all—the grapes that couldn't be digitalized into growing faster and the wine itself.

After a few minutes, Joe handed him a CD of Rena's accounts. "Here you go."

Tony tapped the CD against his palm. "Thanks."

"So how's married life?"

Tony shrugged, wishing he knew the answer to that question. "Too soon to tell. I'll be back later. You don't have plans tonight, do you?"

Joe shook his head. "Just work."

"Okay, I'll see you around six."

Tony walked out of the office after bidding farewell to Ali, who was as intent on her computer screen as Joe had been. He drove out of town and up the hills to the Carlino estate, waving a quick hello to Nick as he drove off the property with a pretty woman in his car. Tony only shook his head at his happy-go-lucky brother, thinking "been there, done that."

Tony entered the house and grabbed a beer out of the refrigerator. Taking a big swig from the bottle, he walked upstairs to his quadrant of the house, entered his private office and sat down at his desk. He logged onto his computer and inserted the CD into the slot.

He stopped for one moment, contemplating what he was about to do. Taking another gulp of beer, he sighed with indecision, but his curiosity got the better of him. He searched the files and finally found what he'd been looking for. The screen popped up with the title *Vine by Vine* by Rena Fairfield Montgomery.

Tony began reading the first chapter.

Roots.

In order to make great wine, you need good terroir, meaning the soil, climate and topography of a region that uniquely influence the grapes. A wine with a certain terroir cannot be reproduced in close resemblance of another, because the terroir is not exactly the same. Much like the DNA of a person each wine has a one-of-a-kind profile.

I guess I came from good terroir. That is to say, my parents were solid grounded people, rich, not by monetary standards but by life and vitality and a grand love of winemaking. My roots run deep and strong. I come from healthy stock. I've always been thankful for that. I've had the love of the best two people on earth. A child can't ask for more than that.

My parents, like the trellis system of a vine, show you the way yet cannot dictate the path you will ultimately choose. As I grew I felt their protection, but as I look back I also see the strength they instilled in me. After all, a new vine needs to weather a vicious storm now and again. It needs to withstand blasting winds, bending by its might but not breaking.

I remember a time when I was in grammar school...

Tony read the chapter, smiling often as Rena portrayed anecdotes from her childhood, relating them to the ever-growing vines, taking shape, readying for the fruit it would bear.

He skimmed the next few chapters until he came upon a chapter called "Crush and Maceration."

The crush in vintner's terminology is when the grapes are harvested, broken from the vine by gentle hands. The crush happens each year between August and October, depending on the kind of grapes that are growing in your vineyard. For me, the crush happened only once. It's that time in your life when you break off from the ones that graciously and lovingly nourished you to become your own person. I was sixteen when that happened. I grew from an adolescent girl to womanhood the autumn of my sophomore year. The day I met my first love, Rod Barrington.

I had a big crush on Rod from the moment I laid eyes on him. He was new to our school, but his family was well known in the area. Everyone knew of the wealthy Barringtons, they owned more property in our valley than anyone else.

While my friendship with Rod grew, I fell more and more in love with him. For a young girl, the pain of being his friend nearly brought me to my knees. I couldn't bear seeing him tease and joke with other girls, but I kept my innermost feelings hidden, hoping one day he'd realize that his good friend, Joanie Adams might just be the girl for him.

Tony read a few more passages, skimming the words on the page quickly, absorbing each instance that Rena relayed in the story, vaguely recalling the circumstances much like Rena had written. It was clearly obvious that though Rena had changed the names, Rena had written about his relationship with her, reminding him of the love they once shared. As he read on, the smile disappeared from his face, Rena's emotions so bold and honest on the page. He knew he'd hurt her but just how much he hadn't known until this very moment.

In winemaking once the grapes are gently crushed from the skins, seeds and stems, allowing the juices to flow, maceration occurs. The clear juice deepens in color the longer it's allowed to steep with its counterparts, being in direct contact with stems and seeds and skins. Time blends the wine and determines the hue and flavor, intensifying its effect.

And that's how I felt about Rod. The longer I was with him, the more direct contact I had with him, the more I loved him. He colored my every thought and desire. I knew I'd met the man of my dreams. We blended in every way.

Tony skimmed more pages, his stomach taut with regret and pain. He stopped when he came to a chapter titled "Corked."

He knew what that meant. He forced himself to read on.

Wine that is "corked" has been contaminated by its cork stopper, causing a distinctly unpleasant aroma. The wine is ruined for life. It's spoiled and will never be the same. Fortunately for wine lovers, only seven percent of all wine is considered corked or tainted. A sad fact if you'd invested time and energy with that bottle.

Wine shouldn't let you down. And neither should someone you love.

Tony ran his hands down his face, unable to read any more. But a voice inside told him he had to know the extent of Rena's feelings. He had to find out what happened to her after he'd left her. He continued to read, sitting stiffly in the chair, woodenly reading words that would haunt him.

"Rod called today, after his first big sale. It killed me to talk to him, I felt selfish for wishing he'd flop in his high-powered position in New York. I was dealing with my mother's terminal cancer, needing him so badly."

After reading Rena's story, which ended abruptly when Rena's mother died, Tony slumped in the seat.

Drained, hollowed out by what he'd learned, he simply sat there, reliving the scenarios in his mind.

Eventually Tony logged off of his computer, leaving the disk behind, but Rena's emotions and her silent suffering while he was winning races and pursuing his dreams would stay with him forever.

He met Joe at the office at six o'clock as planned, his disposition in the dumps. "Did you find anything unusual?" he asked his brother.

"No, not unusual. Dad did screw a lot of people over, but I've never seen it so clearly as now."

Tony groaned, his mood going from gray to black in a heartbeat. "I was hoping I was wrong."

"No, you're not wrong. Your instincts are dead-on." Joe shuffled papers around, comparing notes he'd written.

"Looked to me like Dad deliberately undersold cabernet and merlot to the retailers to drive Purple Fields out of business. We make five kinds of wine, but he chose the two Purple Fields are famous for to undercut them. From what I've found, he sold for a slight loss for at least ten years. He knew he could sustain those losses without a problem, while Purple Fields couldn't compete."

Tony winced, hearing the truth aloud. "I'd asked Dad to leave Purple Fields alone. To let them make a living. But I'm betting he did it to spite me."

Joe's brows rose. "You think he singled them out because you chose a different career?"

"He'd never approved of my choices. He didn't want me to succeed. He wanted to dictate the course of my life, and it pissed him off that I wouldn't listen to him. I chose racing over him."

"Yeah, Dad was angry when you took off. He wanted to hand down his business to his firstborn son. Hell, he wasn't too fond of me not sticking around either. I've got a head for business, not grape growing."

Tony's lips curved halfway up. "You're a computer geek, Joe."

"And proud of it," Joe added, then focused his attention back on the subject at hand. "Dad was an all-around brute. I bet he used the same tactics on half a dozen other small wineries to drive them out of business."

"Doesn't make it right. Hell, he made millions. He didn't need to shut down his competition."

"Apparently, he didn't see it that way."

Tony let go a frustrated sigh. "At least there's something I can do about it. I'm going to renegotiate those contracts. We'll sell our wine at a fair price, but we won't undercut anyone, especially Purple Fields."

Joe nodded and leaned back in his chair. "That should make Rena happy."

"Yeah, but it won't make up for all the past pain this family put her through."

"You're not just talking about Dad now, are you?"

Tony took a steadying breath and shook his head. "No. But I plan to make it up to Rena. Whether she likes it or not."

"Those sound like fighting words, Tone."

Tony rose from his seat. "They are."

"Oh, before I forget, someone called for you today."

Joe shifted through a pile of notes, coming up with one. "Something about your racing contracts. They've been calling the house and couldn't reach you."

He handed Tony the note, and when he glanced at the name, he cursed under his breath. He didn't need this right now. "Okay," he said, stuffing the note in his pocket. "Thanks. I'll take care of it."

Now he had three things to deal with, the note he tucked away being the least of his worries. At least he knew now how to save Purple Fields, but after reading *Vine by Vine,* Tony wasn't sure how he could repair the damage he'd done to Rena.

The promise he made to David far from his mind, Tony wanted to save his hasty marriage for more selfish reasons. He couldn't deny that reliving the past in these last few hours made him realize how much Rena had once meant to him.

He got in his car and drove off, speeding out of town, needing the rush of adrenaline to ward off his emotions and plaguing thoughts that he was falling in love with Rena again.

Tony entered the house, and a pleasing aroma led him straight to the kitchen. He found Rena standing at the stove top stirring the meal, her hair beautifully messy and her face pink from puffs of steam rising up. She didn't acknowledge his presence initially until he wrapped his arms around her waist and drew her against him. He kissed her throat, breathing in her citrus scent. "Looking good."

"It's just stew."

"I meant you," Tony said, stealing another quick kiss. Coming home to this domestic scene, something grabbed his insides and twisted when he saw her. "You're beautiful behind the stove. I want to come home to you every night."

She frowned and moved slightly away. "Don't say those things."

"Why?" he asked softly. "Because I've said them before and now you don't believe me?"

Rena kept stirring the stew. "You're astute."

"And you're being stubborn."

She shrugged, moving away from the stove to grab two plates from the cabinet. Tony took out cutlery from a drawer and set two glasses on the table.

So now they were resorting to name-calling? This certainly wasn't the scene Tony pictured in his mind when he first entered the house.

"Did you find out anything from Joe?" Rena asked.

"Yeah, I did. But let's eat first."

"Whenever someone says that to me, I know the news is not good."

"There's bad news and there's good news. I think we should eat first before discussing it."

Rena brought the dishes to the stove top and filled their plates, adding two biscuits to Tony's plate. She served him and sat down to eat. Her long hair fell forward as she nibbled on her food. She wore jeans and a soft baby-blue knit blouse that brought out the vivid color of her eyes. She hardly looked pregnant, except for a hint of added roundness to her belly.

Sweeping emotions stirred in his gut. He wanted to protect Rena. He wanted to possess her. He wanted to make love to her until all the pain and anger disappeared from her life. So much had happened to her in her short thirty-one years from losing her mother and father, to losing David, but it had all started with him. And Tony determined it would all end with him as well.

After the meal, Rena started cleaning up. Tony rose and then took her hand. "Leave this. We'll take care of it later. We need to talk."

She nodded and followed him into the living room. Oak beams, a stone fireplace stacked with logs and two comfortable sofas lent to the warmth of the room. Tony waited for her to sit, then took a place next to her.

They sat in silence for a minute, then Tony began. "What I have to say isn't easy. Joe and I went through the records and have proof now of how my father manipulated sales in the region."

"You mean, my father was right? Santo set out to destroy us?"

Tony winced and drew a breath. "I can't sugarcoat it, Rena. My father undercut Purple Fields, even at a loss to his own company to drive you out of business. Joe's guess is that it wasn't personal. He'd been doing the same to other small businesses for years."

Rena closed her eyes, absorbing the information. "My father knew. He didn't have proof. His customers wouldn't talk about it, except to say that they'd found better deals elsewhere. They'd praised our wine over and over but wouldn't buy it."

"My father probably strong-armed them into silence," Tony said.

Rena opened her eyes and stared at him. He couldn't tell what was going on in her head, but he suspected it wasn't good.

She rose from her seat and paced the floor. "My mother was worried and anxious all the time. She loved Purple Fields. She and my father poured everything they had into the winery. They worked hard to make ends meet. She held most of it in, putting up a brave front, but I could tell she wasn't the same. My father noticed it, too. He'd stare at her with concern in his eyes. And that all started around the time when we broke up and you left town."

Tony stood to face her. He owed Rena the full truth or at least the truth as he saw it. His voice broke when he made the confession, "I think he targeted Purple Fields after I left."

She stiffened and her mouth twisted. "My God," she whispered, closing her eyes in agony. "Don't you see? The stress might have triggered my mother's illness."

Tony approached her. "Rena, no."

She began nodding her head. "Oh, yes. Yes. My mother was healthy. There was no history of that disease in our family. Mom was fine. Fine, until the winery started going downhill. She worried herself sick. The doctors even suggested that stress could be a factor."

Rena's face reddened as her pain turned to anger. She announced with a rasp in her voice, "I need some air."

Tony watched her walk out of the house, slamming

the door behind her. He ran a hand through his hair, his frustration rising. "Damn it. Damn it."

He'd never hated being a Carlino more than now. He could see it in Rena's eyes—the blame, the hatred and the injury. When she'd looked at him that way, he understood all of her resentment. He knew she'd react to the truth with some degree of anger, but he'd never considered that she'd blame his family for her mother's illness.

Could it be true?

Tony couldn't change the past. All he could do now was to convince her he'd make things right. He gave her a few minutes of solitude before exiting the house. He had to find his wife and comfort her.

Even though in her eyes, he was the enemy.

Nine

Rena ran into the fields. The setting sun cast golden hues onto the vines, helping to light her way. She ran until her heart raced too fast and her breaths surged too heavy. Yet she couldn't outrace the burning ache in her belly or the plaguing thoughts in her mind. She stopped abruptly in the middle of the cabernet vines, fully winded, unable to run another step. Putting her head in her hands, tears spilled down her cheeks. Grief struck her anew. It was as if she was losing her mother all over again. Pretty, vivacious Belinda Fairfield had died before her time. Her sweet, brave mother hadn't deserved to suffer so. She hadn't deserved to relinquish her life in small increments until she was too weak to get out of bed.

Rena's sobs were absorbed in the vines, her cries

swallowed up by the solitude surrounding her. Her body shook, the release of anguish exhausting her.

Two strong arms wrapped around her, supporting her sagging body. "Shh, Rena," Tony said gently. "Don't cry, sweetheart. Let me make it right. I'll make it all right."

"You…can't," she whispered between sobs. Yet Tony's strength gave her immeasurable comfort.

"I can. I will. We'll do it together."

Before Rena could formulate a response, Tony lifted her up, one arm bracing her legs and the other supporting her shoulders. "Hold on to me," he said softly, "and try to calm down."

Rena circled one arm around his neck and closed her eyes, stifling her sobs, every ounce of her strength spent.

Tony walked through the vineyard, holding her carefully. In the still of the night all that she heard was the occasional crunch of shriveled leaves under Tony's feet as he moved along.

When he pushed through the door to her house, her eyes snapped open. He strode with purpose to the bedroom and lay her down with care, then came down next to her, cradling her into his arms once again. "I'm going to stay with you until you fall asleep."

Rena stared into his eyes and whispered softly, "I hate you, Tony."

He brushed strands of hair from her forehead with tenderness then kissed her brow. "I know."

The sweetness of his kiss sliced through her, denting her well-honed defenses.

He took off her shoes and then his own. Next he undressed her, removing her knit top over her head and unzipping her jeans. She helped pull them off with a little tug, ready to give up her mind and body to sleep.

Tony covered them both with a quilted throw and tucked her in close. She reveled in his warmth and breathed in his musky scent despite herself. "Just for the record, sweetheart," he began, "I'm not here just because of the promise I made to David. It goes much deeper than that. And I think you know it."

Rena flinched inwardly, confusion marring her good judgment. She should pull away from Tony, refusing his warmth and comfort. She couldn't deal with his pronouncement. She couldn't wrap her mind around what he'd just implied. Yet at the same time, she needed his arms around her. She needed to be held and cradled and reassured.

Was she that weak?

Or just human?

"Good night, Rena." Tony kissed her lips lightly, putting finality to the night. "Sleep well."

Rena slept soundly for the better part of the night but roused at 3:00 a.m. to find Tony gone from bed. Curious, she slipped on her robe and padded down the hallway. She found him sprawled out on the living room sofa with his eyes closed. He made an enticing sight, his chest bare, his long lean, incredible body and handsome face more than any woman could ever hope to have in a mate.

Rena shivered from the coolness in the room. She

grabbed an afghan from the chair and gently covered Tony, making sure not to wake him. She lingered for just one moment then turned to leave.

"Don't go," he whispered.

Surprised, Rena spun around to meet Tony's penetrating gaze. "I thought you were asleep."

"I was—on and off." Tony sat up, planting his feet on the ground and leaning forward to spread his fingers through his hair.

"Sorry if I disturbed your sleep."

Tony chuckled without humor. "You did. You do."

Stunned by his blunt honesty, Rena blinked.

"Sleeping next to you isn't easy, Rena." Tony shook his head as if shaking out cobwebs. "Sorry, I wish I could be more honorable, but you're a handful of temptation."

Rena's mouth formed an "oh."

Tony stared at her. "You shouldn't find it shocking that I want to sleep with you. You remember how we were together."

Rena's spine stiffened. "Maybe you should sleep in another room."

"I have a better idea." He took her wrist and tugged her down. She landed on his lap. Immediately, he stretched out on the sofa, taking her with him. "Maybe I should make love to my wife."

A gasp escaped from her due to his sudden move. "Oh."

He untied the belt on her robe, his tone dead serious. "I want you."

His hands came up to push the robe off her shoulders,

revealing the bra and panties she'd slept in. His appreciative gaze heated the blood in her veins. "You can't blame me for that."

"No. But for so many other things," she said quietly.

"I get it, sweetheart. I understand." Tony pulled the robe free, exposing her fully.

Positioned provocatively, feeling his hard length pressing against her, excitement zipped through her system. Her breathing rough, she barely managed to utter the question. "Do you?"

"Yes, I do. And I want to make it up to you. Let me do that," Tony said, cupping his hand around her head and bringing her mouth to his. He kissed her softly. "Let me wipe away the pain." Again his lips met hers. "Let me help you heal, sweet Rena. You've been through so much."

His sincerity, his tone, the breathtaking way he looked at her softened the hardness around her heart. She wanted to heal, to release her defenses, to feel whole again.

"Tony," she breathed out, unsure of her next move.

"It's your call, sweetheart," he said, stroking her back in a loving way that created tingles along her spine. Another notch of her defenses fell.

Images flashed of the good times she'd had with Tony. The fun, the laughter and the earth-shattering lovemaking they'd shared. As much as she wanted to forget, the good memories came back every time he touched her. "I want the pain to go away," she whispered with honesty. Even if it was only for a short time tonight.

"Then let me take you there."

She closed her eyes, nodding in relief, surrendering herself to the moment. "Yes."

Rena touched his chest, her fingers probing, searching, tantalizing and teasing. He felt incredibly good. Strong. Powerful. She itched to touch him all over.

Bringing her head down to his, she claimed his mouth in a lingering kiss. She took it slow, pushing aside her misgivings. His body seemed in tune with hers. Every little action she took brought his sexy reaction. Every moan she uttered, he answered with a groan. She liked being in control. It was the first time she'd ever taken the reins so fully, and Tony seemed to understand what she needed. He encouraged her with a gleam in his eyes and a willing body.

"I'm all yours," he whispered.

Her breath caught. She knew he meant it sexually, but Rena seized on the reality of that statement. He was all hers. But what she didn't know was, could she ever be *all his?*

"You're thinking again," Tony scolded with a smile.

"Guilty as charged." Rena reached around to unhook her bra, freeing her breasts. Letting her bra drop, she freed her mind as well, pushing all thoughts away but the immediate here and now.

Tony reached for her then, his touch an exquisite caress of tenderness and caring. He kissed her lovingly, cherishing every morsel of her body with his lips and hands until his unexpected compassion seeped into her soul.

Their lovemaking was sedate and measured, careful and unflappable one moment, then crazy and wild, fierce and fiery the next. They moved in ups and downs, from highs to lows, they learned and taught, giving joy and pleasure to one another. The night knew no bounds. And when it came time to release their pent-up tension, Rena rose above Tony, straddling his legs. He held on to her hips and guided her. Taking him in felt natural, familiar and so right. She enjoyed every ounce of pleasure derived from their joining. She moved with restless yearning, her body flaming, all rational thought discarded.

Tony watched her, his eyes never wavering, his body meeting her every demand. He was the man she'd always wanted, the man she'd been destined to love. He'd pushed his way back into her life, but Rena couldn't trust in him, not fully, not yet. But each time they came together, her resolve slipped just a little, and her heartache slowly ebbed.

When she couldn't hold on any longer, her skin prickling, her flesh tingling and her body at its absolute limit, she moaned in ecstasy.

"Let go, sweetheart," Tony encouraged.

And she shuddered, her orgasm strong. She cried out his name when her final release came. Tony tightened his hold on her and joined her in a climax, taking them both to heaven.

Rena lowered down, spent. Tony wrapped her into his arms and kissed her forehead. "Do you still hate me?" he asked.

"Yes," she replied without hesitation. "But not as much as before."

Tony squeezed her tighter and chuckled almost inaudibly. "Guess, I'm going to have to work on that."

During the next week, Tony left Rena during the day to work on saving her winery. He made calls out of his Napa office, meeting with customers personally to explain the new pricing structures. Tony liked winning but not at the expense of others trying to eke out a living. If there was a contract he could renegotiate, Tony was on top of it.

He made sure that their company held their own in the marketplace, but with Joe's help they'd come up with a pricing plan that would realize profits and still allow the smaller wineries to compete.

Unlike his father, Tony didn't need to crush his opponents. The company's profits would go up on certain types of wine while the other local wineries of comparable quality would also make a profit on their specialties. It was a win-win situation in his opinion.

Satisfied with what he'd accomplished today, he called it quits, gathering up the papers on his desk. He was anxious to get home to Rena. Little by little, she was coming around, softening to him, smiling more and looking less and less guilty about their circumstances.

As he got ready to leave, he pondered how at night he'd join her in bed, and more times than not, they'd make love. Slow and sweet one time then wild and hot another time. Tony never knew what the night would bring. Some nights, when both were exhausted, they'd just fall asleep in each other's arms.

Tony enjoyed waking up next to Rena in the mornings. With her hair messy and her eyes hazy with sleep, she'd look at him and smile softly for a second or two before her memories returned and a haunted look would enter her eyes.

He clung to those few seconds in his mind, telling himself that one day that troubled look would be gone forever and she'd accept him completely as her husband and the father of her baby.

Tony smiled at the thought. Rena's stomach showed signs of the baby now. He was amazed at how quickly her body had transformed, her belly growing rounder each day.

"Excuse me, Tony," Ali said, stepping into his office.

Tony glanced at her, and as usual, the same thought flitted in his mind. He couldn't believe Joe wasn't interested in this vital, gorgeous, very capable woman.

"There's a call for you. From your agent. A mister Ben Harper? He says it's important. Line one."

Tony's smile faded. "Okay, thanks." He glanced at the flashing red light. He couldn't ignore Harper anymore. "I'll get it in here."

He waited until Ali walked away before picking up the phone. "Hello, Ben."

His agent read him the riot act for not returning his calls. Tony slammed his eyes shut, listening to his tirade.

"You know damn well you're under contract. My ass is on the line, too."

"It's not a good time right now," Tony said.

"You told me that two months ago. They gave you an extension because of your father's death, and you were recovering from your injuries, but I can't put them off much longer. They're threatening a lawsuit, for heaven's sake. You need to give me something. *Now,* Tony."

Tony sighed into the receiver, caving in to these last few contractual commitments. He still had an endorsement deal with EverStrong Tires and was expected to do interviews for a few of the races. "How long will it take?"

"Filming could take up to a week for the commercial."

"When?"

"Yesterday."

"Make it for next week, Ben. I'll do my best."

"You better be there, Tony. You've pushed them too far as it is. And don't forget, you're expected at Dover International Speedway for the first interview."

"I'll be there."

"I'll call you with the details."

"I'm holding my breath," he mumbled and hung up. He paced the office, shaking his head. Things were just getting better with Rena, and he didn't want that to end.

Rena hated anything to do with racing. Understandably so, but Tony had no choice in the matter. The last thing he needed was a lawsuit. And, if he were truly honest with himself, he missed the racing scene. Tony had recognized that it was time to leave it behind. Exit while still on top, they say. He'd accomplished what he'd set out to do, but a man doesn't lose his passion that easily. His blood still stirred with excitement when he stepped foot on the raceway.

The difference was that now Rena and the baby took precedence over racing. He was committed to his marriage and determined to get that same commitment from her.

Tony left the office and drove to Purple Fields, eager to see Rena. He entered the house and found her finishing a conversation on the phone in the kitchen. He came up behind her and wrapped his arms around her waist, his hands spreading across her stomach. He caressed her tiny round belly and nibbled on her throat. It had only been a few days that she'd allowed him this intimacy, and Tony couldn't get enough. "Who was that?" he asked, setting his chin on her shoulder.

"The doctor's office. I have an appointment tomorrow."

"What time are we going?"

"We?" Rena turned in his arms. "You can't go with me, Tony."

He blinked. "Why not?"

Rena stared at him. "You know why."

Tony's brows furrowed. "No, I don't. You tell me."

She moved out of his arms and shrugged. "This is David's baby."

Tony rolled his eyes. "I'm aware of that." She reminded him every chance she could. "So?"

"No one knows we're married. How would it look if I showed up with you?"

Tony summoned his patience and spoke slowly. "It would look like a good friend is supporting you at your doctor's appointment."

"No," she said adamantly. "I can't. Solena is taking me."

"No, *I'm* taking you."

Rena's eyes closed as if the prospect disturbed her sanity. Tony's ire rose, and he calmed down by taking a few breaths. "Maybe it's time to expose our marriage. Then you'd have a legitimate reason to have me there."

She shook her head. "I'm not ready for that."

"Why, Rena? Why not stop this ruse? We're living together. *We're married.* Don't worry about what people think. It's no one's business. This is about us, our lives and our family."

"It's not that," she rushed out, giving him her uplifted chin.

Tony stared at her. Then it dawned on him. "Oh, I see. You're not ready to accept me as your husband. As long as no one knows, you can pretend it isn't so. You can stay in your own world and not face reality."

Rena didn't deny it. She put her head down, refusing to let him see the truth in her eyes.

"Tell Solena I'm taking you tomorrow. I promised David and I won't break that promise."

But Tony's truth was that he wanted to be beside Rena during her appointment. He wanted to provide for her and protect her. He wanted to lend her support. And

more and more, he found his desire had nothing to do
with the vow he made to his best friend.

"Everything looks great, Rena. You're in good health.
The baby has a strong heartbeat," Dr, Westerville said,
smiling her way.

"Thank you, Doctor." Sitting upright in a green-and-
white checkered gown on the exam table, Rena sighed
in relief. Though she felt fine, hearing it from the doctor
relieved her mind.

After he'd finished the checkup he'd reminded her of
the do's and don't's regarding her pregnancy. Eat smaller
meals, more times a day. Keep on a healthy diet. Stay
active, but don't overdo anything.

Rena had been doing all those things since even before
her first appointment with the doctor. The second she
realized she was having a baby, she'd read everything
she could about pregnancy and gestation.

"I'll let your friend in now," the doctor said.

She gave him a small smile.

The doctor opened the exam room door and let
Tony inside. She'd relented in letting him take her to
the appointment, but absolutely refused to have him in
the room during the examination.

Tony walked a few steps into the room with his
concerned gaze pinned on her. Before she made in-
troductions, she answered his silent questions. "I'm fine
and the baby is healthy. Dr. Westerville, this is David's
good friend, Tony Carlino."

"Of course." The doctor put out his hand. "Nice

to meet you Mr. Carlino. I've been a fan of yours for years."

Tony nodded and shook the doctor's hand. "I appreciate that."

"All of us locals have rooted for you since day one."

Tony accepted his compliment with grace. "I've had a lot of support from this area. It means a lot. But now I'm retired and home to stay." He turned to Rena and she shot him a warning look. "Rena's a family friend. I plan to help her as much as possible."

"That's good. She's doing fine. She's very healthy and I don't foresee any problems. With all you've been through these past few months," the doctor said, focusing back on her, "it's very good to have a friend go through this with you. I recommend childbirth classes in a month or two, but for now, just follow the list of instructions I gave you."

"I'll do my best."

"Still running the winery?" he asked.

She nodded. "I promised David I'd keep Purple Fields going. Not that I want anything different myself."

"Okay, good. But in your later months, you may have to back off a little. Delegate duties more and—"

"I'll see to it," Tony chimed in. "I'll make sure she takes it easy."

The doctor glanced at Tony, then at Rena. He smiled warmly. Heat crawled up her neck, and at the same time, she wanted to sock Tony into the next county.

Dr. Westerville patted her shoulder. "I'll see you next month, Rena. I know your husband would be proud of you and glad you're going to have the support you need." He turned and shook Tony's hand once again. "David was a good man and it seems that he picked his friends wisely."

When he left the room, Rena glared at Tony. "I need to get dressed."

"I'll help." He grinned.

She shot him another warning look.

"Come on, Rena. Lighten up. The baby is healthy and so are you. That's good news."

Rena sighed and admitted joy at her baby news, but it struck her anew that she'd be going through all of this with Tony. "Can't you see that this is hard for me?"

"I know, Rena. You remind me every half an hour."

Rena twisted her lips. "No, I don't."

"Seems like it," Tony muttered. "I'll wait for you outside."

She stepped down from the table and walked into the small dressing area, untying her gown and throwing on her clothes. Had she been too hard on Tony? At times, she felt like a shrew, but it was only because every time she softened to him, she felt like she was losing another piece of David. Little by little, David's memory was fading. And that wasn't fair to him or to her. A woman needed time to grieve and recover. But Tony had bounded into her life, hell-bent on keeping the vow he'd made to David.

Her feelings were jumbled up inside and half the time she didn't know which emotions were honest and true. She'd never been in a situation remotely like this. She chuckled at the absurdity—she was a secretly married, pregnant widow.

Not too many women could say that.

After Rena's doctor's appointment, Tony took her to lunch at her favorite little café in town. Thinking about the new life growing inside her, she couldn't deny her happiness. Seeing Dr. Westerville made it all seem real, and knowing that the baby was healthy and hearing the due date for the birth lightened her heart. The joy and love she held inside couldn't be duplicated.

After they ate their meal, they stopped at an electronics store where she and Tony ordered a top-of-the-line computer with all the bells and whistles. To overcome her resistance to such a complex-looking computer, Tony had promised to set it up when it arrived and get her acquainted with it. Whatever they couldn't figure out, his brother Joe would certainly be glad to explain to them.

Tony made other purchases as well—new phones for the house and office and a four-in-one fax machine he insisted they needed at Purple Fields. She certainly couldn't fault her husband his generosity. Where she and David had pinched pennies to make a go of the winery, Tony had no trouble spending money for the cause. Of course, he was a millionaire in his own right, famous in the world of racing, and he could afford these things.

They strolled down the street past a baby store, the window displaying a white crib and matching tallboy dresser, strollers and car seats. Rena lingered for a moment, aching with yearning.

"Rena, any time you're ready," Tony said.

Her emotions kept her from taking the next step. Something held her back. "Maybe soon. First I have to clean out the room and paint it. I thought we'd use the room across from ours to be closer to the baby."

Tony surprised her with a kiss. "It's a great idea."

Her gaze lifted to his noting the pleased gleam in his eyes. She'd *surprised* both of them with her comment, but more and more she was learning how to trust him again. So far, he hadn't given her any reason not to. He'd made good on his promise to fix Purple Fields. He'd spoken with customers and renegotiated contracts all in order to save her from ruin. He'd been patient with her. He'd been kind. He'd been a magnificent lover and a good friend.

He'd set out to prove that he wasn't like his ruthless father, and so far, he'd succeeded. If she could put the past behind her, they stood a chance. For her baby's sake, if not her own, she wanted to take that chance.

"I'll help you with the room. I'm pretty good with a paintbrush. What color?"

Rena grinned, letting go a little bit more of the pain trapped inside. "Sage-green or chiffon-yellow."

"What, not pink or blue?"

Rena tilted her head and sighed. "We don't know the baby's sex yet." She glanced inside the store again, then placed her hand over her belly and admitted, "I don't want to wait until we find out."

"Me, either," Tony said, taking her hand. "Let's go find us some sage and chiffon paint. There's a hardware store up ahead."

By the time they returned home, Rena was in the best mood she could remember. They'd picked out paint colors together—unable to decide, they'd bought gallons of each shade—paintbrushes, rollers and drop cloths.

"Do you really want to help me paint the bedroom?" Rena asked after dinner as they retired to the living room. The day had exhausted her physically. Tony sat beside her on the sofa, and he brought her into the circle of his arms. She rested her head on his chest.

"You doubt me after I badgered that salesman with questions about baby-safe paint for half an hour?"

A wave of excitement stirred as she envisioned her baby's room all fresh and clean, filled with furniture, just waiting for his or her arrival. And Tony had been there every step of the way. She'd resisted giving him anything more than her body, but Tony wasn't a man she could easily put out of her mind. Ever so slowly he was making inroads to her heart. "I'm anxious to start."

"I'll clear my calendar, and we can start tomorrow," Tony said. "We'll have it done by the weekend."

"Oh, I can't. I have a vendor coming for an appointment tomorrow. We have three wine tours booked this week, and I can't leave Solena to do it all. Can we start on it first thing next week? Monday?"

Tony looked into her eyes, hesitating. Then he rose to stand before the large double window facing the front yard, his hands on his hips. "I can't do it next week, Rena."

His tone alarmed her. "Why not?"

He scrubbed his jaw a few times, as if searching for the right words. "I was going to tell you tomorrow." He paced the room, walking slowly as he spoke. "I'm up against a wall. I have commitments I made a long time ago, and my agent can't find any wiggle room. I'm going out of town on Sunday. I'll be gone at least a week."

"A week?" Rena's heart plummeted. A serious case of déjà vu set in.

I won't be gone long, Rena. I'll come back as soon as I can. Or you can come meet me. We'll be together somehow, I promise.

"What are you going to do?" she asked.

"Some interviews and a commercial. It's one of the last endorsements I'm contracted to do."

Rena felt numb. "Okay," she said once she'd gathered her wits. She kept her voice light, her tone noncommittal. "You don't need my permission." She rose from the sofa. "I have some work to do to prepare for my meeting tomorrow."

"I'll help you," Tony said, gauging her reaction.

Rena could only manage a curt reply. "No. I can do it myself."

Tony approached her. "Rena?"

She halted him with a widespread hand. "It's okay, Tony. Really. I understand."

"Damn it! You don't understand." Frustration carried in his deep voice. His olive complexion colored with heat. "I've put this off for as long as I can. They'll sue me if I don't show up, and that's not what either of us needs right now."

"You don't have to explain to me." She hoisted her chin and straightened her shoulders. "I never wanted any of this to begin with."

Tony strode to face her. Taking her into his arms, he yanked her close and narrowed his eyes. "This isn't twelve years ago. The situation is different. You think I won't come back?"

"Darn right, it's different. I'm not that love-smitten young girl anymore. Whether you come back or not, I know I'll survive. I did it once and I can do it again."

Tony released her arms and then barked off a dozen curses, each one fouler than the next.

"As far as I'm concerned, you owned up to your obligation to David. You married me. Purple Fields is on its way to becoming solvent again. I won't fool myself into thinking we have anything more. You did your duty, Tony. Congratulations."

"Anything else?" Tony asked, clearly fuming.

"Yes," she said, unmindful of his state of anger. She was plenty angry, too. To think he'd nearly had her fooled that they might have something to build on. But somehow, racing had always come between them. David was gone to her. But Tony? She'd never really had him to begin with, and this was a brutal reminder that she would always come in second place. "Thanks for ruining the best day I've had since my husband died."

Ten

Nick and Joe were relaxing outside on the patio overlooking the Carlino vineyards when Tony strode in. The stone fire pit provided light and heat on this cool spring night. The weather was always cooler atop their hillside than in the valley below, and tonight, Tony welcomed the brisk air.

His brothers welcomed him with curious stares. "Want a beer?" Nick asked.

Tony shook his head. "I need a real drink." He strode over to the outside bar and poured himself two fingers of whiskey. Without pause, he gulped down one finger's worth of the golden liquid before returning to sit on a patio chair facing the flames. He slouched in his seat, stretched out his long legs and crossed one ankle over the other, deep in thought.

After several moments of awkward silence, Nick asked, "What's up, Tony?"

Tony sipped his whiskey. "What? Can't a guy come home to spend some time with his brothers?"

Joe and Nick chuckled at the same time.

"Seriously, why are you here?" Joe asked.

The fire crackled, and Tony watched the low-lying flames dance. "I had to tell Rena I still have racing obligations. I'm leaving on Sunday for a week. She didn't take the news well."

"She's mad?" Nick asked.

Tony shook his head. "Worse. She's indifferent. She's not sure I'll come back and pretty much told me she doesn't care."

"She's recalling past history, Tone. She's protecting herself," Joe said.

"I know. But the hell of it is that we were working out our problems, getting closer, until this came up. What am I supposed to do? My agent's butt is on the line. Ben's been with me since the beginning, and he's been a loyal friend. I owe him. If I get sued for breach of contract, it reflects on him, too."

"It's not like you can tell anyone you have a pregnant wife at home," Nick added. "Ben doesn't know?"

"No, he doesn't. There's no need to tell him." Tony finished his whiskey, not revealing his opinion about the subject. He'd tell the world about their marriage, if Rena would agree. "The problem is that we were getting closer. I took her to the doctor today. We'd planned on fixing up the nursery together. It's the first time she's let me in. And it felt good. Damn good. If I had any choice at all, I'd stay here and paint the baby's room instead of flying off to do a commercial."

"Wow," Nick said, catching his gaze. "I didn't realize you were in love with Rena."

Tony couldn't deny it. He set his glass down and stared into the flames. "I don't think I ever stopped loving her."

"You two are a perfectly matched set," Nick offered, his statement hitting home.

Joe sighed. "I'm the last one to give advice on romance, Tony. But it seems to me from a logical standpoint that you need a gesture of some sort. Some way to show her how much she means to you."

"You mean like blowing off this deal?"

"No, by asking her to go with you."

"She won't go. She hates anything to do with racing. It would just remind her of all the bad things that have happened in her life."

"Then I suppose you'll just have to make it up to her when you get back."

Tony agreed. He'd have a lot of making up to do. "Listen, will you two check on her next week while I'm gone?"

"Sure." Joe nodded.

Nick added, "No problem. I like Rena. She's family now, and I don't have much on my nightly agenda at the moment."

"Which means you're not dating three women at the same time," Joe said, with a teasing grin.

"Never three." Nick leaned back in his chair and

sipped his beer. Thoughtful, he added, "I only date one lady at a time. I like to keep things simple."

"You're not off to Monte Carlo anytime soon, then?" Tony asked.

"No. I'm here for a while. The contractors have the renovations at my house under control and it'll be ready soon enough. At least dad's timing was good in that respect."

Tony exchanged a glance at Joe. Of the three, Nick held the deepest grudge against Santo Carlino. With good reason, but the damage was done and they all had to move on with their lives.

"Besides," Nick added, "I told you I'd help out with the company for as long as it takes. Once we figure out which of you two will be running the company, I'm moving back there."

"What makes you think it'll be me or Tony?" Joe asked.

"Because it sure as hell won't be me. You know how I feel about this place."

Tony raised his brows. "It's just us now, Nick. Santo is gone."

Nick ignored him. "You're both invited. You've never seen my place in Monte Carlo. I want you to come as soon as you can."

Tony rose from his seat, ready to get back home to Rena. Talking with his brothers had helped. He'd gotten his dilemma off his chest, but he wasn't at all sure that they'd come up with a solution. "I'll feel better leaving knowing you both will call Rena and stop by Purple Fields for a visit."

"We have your back," Joe said.

"Thanks. I appreciate it."

"You leaving already?" Nick asked.

"Yep, I'm going home to my wife." He needed to see her. He had to sort out their differences and try to make his marriage work.

Rena's last parting comment had stung him.

Thanks for ruining the best day I've had since my husband died.

He was her husband now.

It was time Rena realized that.

The next three nights Rena claimed exhaustion, turning in early and falling asleep long before Tony came to bed. In the morning, she'd find herself tangled up in his arms. He hadn't pressed her for more. In fact, she admired the patience and consideration he'd shown her. He'd kiss her hello in the morning, then rise from bed early.

They lived life like a married couple. He'd shave in front of her, and she'd catch glimpses of him showering, the vision often lingering in her mind long after he'd toweled off and dressed. She cooked for him and cleaned his clothes, and he thanked her politely.

Often, he'd take a cup of coffee and buttered toast into the office and not come out until well past noon. He spent a great deal of time working on her books, but once in a while she'd spot him out in the vineyards speaking with Raymond or checking the vines.

She found him today amid the merlot grapes. "The

computer just arrived. And all the other things you ordered."

"Great," he said, squinting into the bright sunshine. "I'll be right there. With any luck, I'll get it up and running before I leave tomorrow."

"Okay," she said, not in any hurry to return to the office. Her mind was in a jumble. On the one hand, she didn't know if she could trust Tony's intentions, but on the other hand she hoped she wasn't making a big mistake by misjudging him.

She'd spoken with Solena about Tony leaving for a week to keep his contractual obligations. Rena had been honest about her feelings and concerns, and while Solena had always been supportive, this time she hadn't seen it Rena's way.

"Are you sure you're being fair to him?" she'd asked. "Doesn't seem like he has much choice in the matter. Or maybe there's more to your anger than that?"

"Like what?" Rena had asked.

Her friend had given her a knowing, yet sympathetic, look. "Like maybe you want to keep friction between the two of you because you're falling in love with him again."

Tony broke into her thoughts, staring at her over her obvious reluctance to leave. He cast her a big smile. "Is there anything else?"

Her heart lit up. "No, nothing else. I'll be giving a wine tour in a few minutes. I'd better go."

"Yeah, me too. I'll walk with you."

He put his hand to her lower back, and together they left the fields.

"Tony?" she began, as they headed for the house.

He looked up. "Hmm?"

She stopped at the very edge of the vineyard and peered into his eyes. Sunlight cast a glow over his dark hair and deepened his olive skin. He was gorgeous-times-ten, and that never hurt his cause. But she had loved the man *inside* that hunky body, the one who'd slay dragons for her. Or so she'd believed.

"I may have overreacted the other day."

His brows rose.

"I'm not saying I did, but just that there's the possibil—"

"Shut up, Rena." The softness of his tone belied his harsh words.

He grabbed her waist and yanked her against him, taking her in a crushing, all-consuming kiss. When the kiss ended, she opened her eyes and swayed in his arms, feeling quite dizzy.

"How long before your tour group shows up?" he asked in a rasp, nuzzling her throat.

"Ten minutes."

Tony groaned. Then he kissed her once more, bringing her body up against his again, fitting them perfectly together. "Tonight, after dinner."

Rena's breath caught in her throat. She couldn't pretend she didn't know what he meant. She wouldn't protest. Sleeping next to him and waking up wrapped in his arms, pretending indifference hadn't been easy on her. She was a mass of contradictions when it came to Tony. But she wouldn't deny him. She wanted him. Not that her sexy husband would take no for an answer.

Judging by the hot gleam in his eyes or the way he'd just kissed her senseless, Rena knew they were in for a memorable night.

Dinner seemed to take forever. Rena fumbled with the meal, undercooking the potatoes and forgetting the garlic toast in the oven. They ate raw potatoes and burnt bread, and all the while Tony's gaze never wavered as he watched her stumble her way around the kitchen. She apologized a half dozen times, but Tony continued to eat her nearly inedible meal. "I'm not complaining, sweetheart."

Once they finished, he helped clear the dishes, moving about the kitchen and touching her whenever he could, a casual graze here, an accidental bump of the shoulders there. Rena's nerves stood on end. This was foreplay, Carlino style. And it was working! His dark, enticing eyes made her wish she was tumbling in the sheets with him rather than doing dishes by the sink.

Tony came up behind her, pressed his hips to her rear end and wrapped his arms around her, his hands just teasing the underside of her breasts. His warm breath teased her throat. If anyone could make her feel desirable wearing an old apron with her hands in soapy dishwater it was Tony.

"I know what I want for dessert," he whispered, nibbling on her neck.

The glass she'd been rinsing slipped from her hand and shattered in the sink. "Oh, no!"

Tony chuckled and turned her around to face him, his body pressed to hers. "Calm down, Rena. It's not as if you broke your parents' prized antique goblet. Like when you were a kid."

Rena's brows furrowed. "What?"

"You know, your great-grandmother's goblet that you broke when you were trying to surprise your mother by washing the whole set."

"I know what I did, Tony." Rena chewed on her lip, her mind reeling. She'd never told anyone about that incident. She'd replaced all the glasses in the curio praying her mother wouldn't notice that one of the eight were gone. "But how did you know? I never told a soul about that."

Tony blinked. A guilty expression crossed his features.

Rena shoved at his chest and moved away from him. Anger bubbled up. "You read my story, didn't you?"

Tony hesitated for a moment then nodded, not bothering to lie. "I did."

"How could you do that, Tony?" Rena's voice rose to a furious pitch. "That wasn't meant for anyone to read. I can't believe you'd invade my privacy like that!"

"Sorry, but I had to know."

"Know what?" she shouted. "That losing you had devastated my life? That when my mother was sick I cried for her every night, needing you so badly? That after she died, I was at my wit's end and David, poor David, came along and picked up my shattered life and made me whole again." Rena paced the kitchen floor, her temper flaring. "I needed to write that for myself, Tony. Don't you see? Those were my innermost, heartfelt thoughts. Those were mine and mine alone!"

Rena whipped her apron off and tossed it aside, her body trembling. Regret and remorse set in. "Damn it, Tony. You were never meant to read that."

"Maybe I needed to read it, Rena. Maybe it made me see what a big mistake I made back then."

"No," Rena said, shaking her head. She didn't want to hear any of this. Not now. It was far too late. "Save it, Tony. For someone who cares." She directed her gaze right at him. "I thought that maybe this marriage could work, but now I see it never will. You abused my trust one too many times. I want you to go, Tony."

Tony shook his head. "I'm not going anywhere."

"You did what you set out to do. You saved my winery. I'll make it on my own from here on out. I'm not afraid of hard work. You've repaid your debt to David."

"This isn't about David anymore, Rena. You know it and I know it."

Rena faced him dead-on, her bravado slowly dissipating. Tears threatened and she held them back yet her voice cracked with anguish. "I know nothing of the kind. Now I'm asking you to please leave my home. You were leaving me anyway tomorrow. What's one more night?"

"You're my wife, damn it. I'm not leaving you tonight."

"Fine, do whatever you want. That seems to be what you do best. Just leave me alone."

Rena walked out of the room with her head held high. She slammed the bedroom door and fell onto the bed, tears spilling down her cheeks.

Tony's vivid curses from the living room reached her

ears. She curled her pillow around her head, blocking the sound of her husband's frustrated tirade.

At least she knew that tomorrow morning he would be gone.

Eleven

Stubbornly, Tony refused to leave Rena's house. He'd made himself comfortable on the sofa, listening for her. Once he was sure she'd shed all of her tears and had fallen asleep, he opened the bedroom door to check on her.

She looked peaceful tucked in her bed, her face scrubbed of makeup, her thick, dark hair falling freely onto her pillow. She made an enticing picture, one gorgeous leg extending out of the tousled sheets, her body glistening in the slight moonlight streaming in.

Tony's heart lurched seeing her alone in that bed. Certainly the night hadn't ended on the happy note he'd planned. He wouldn't join her tonight. She'd made it clear what she thought of him. She'd made it even clearer that she didn't want him near her.

As complex as their situation was, Tony believed that they belonged together. He hoped that the time they'd spend away from each other would help her see that. He wouldn't even consider the possibility of not having Rena in his life.

Right now, she was angry with him. She had a temper. And so did he. They were both passionate people, and that's one of the things he loved most about Rena—her zest for life. She wasn't a wilting flower. Not by a long shot.

She'd been hurt many times by him and by his family, but she refused to let him make it up to her. It was as if she'd relished the rift they'd had so she wouldn't have to face facts. She wouldn't have to realize that she had strong feelings for him.

Tony closed the door quietly and took up a place on the sofa with a bottle of Purple Fields' award-winning merlot. He poured a glass and knew he wouldn't be sleeping any time soon. The wine would lull his senses somewhat, but Tony couldn't shake a bad feeling that had wedged its way into his gut.

Before sunrise, Tony rose from the sofa. He stretched out the kinks in his shoulders, slanting his head from side to side and shaking out the rest of his body. With stealth, he moved through the house to peek in on Rena again.

She slept.

Tony cast her one long look before turning back around. He showered in the bathroom down the hall, and once he was dressed in the same clothes he'd worn the night before, he made himself a cup of coffee and walked outside. Sipping the steamy brew, he glanced toward the winery, glad to see Raymond's car parked in front.

He found him checking on the crusher. "Morning," he said.

Raymond glanced at him. "It's a beautiful one."

Tony nodded, his mood not so bright. "Listen, I have a favor to ask. I have to go out of town for a while. Can I depend on you to check on Rena for me?"

"Sure, you can count on me. And Solena will be around all week, too. Those women are like two peas in a pod."

"Yeah, Solena's a good friend. Both of you are."

Raymond removed his latex gloves. "Is there any reason you're asking? Is Rena feeling poorly?"

"No, she's fine. It's just that," Tony began, scratching the back of his head, hating to admit this, "I doubt she'll take my calls when I'm gone. We had a disagreement, and she's being stubborn."

Raymond laughed. "I hear you. I'll keep an eye on her. You can call me anytime."

Relieved, Tony slapped him on the back. "Thanks. I appreciate it. Well, I'd better get going. I've got a plane to catch."

Tony drove to the Carlino estate and packed his clothes in a suitcase, hoping to find his brothers there. No one was around but the housekeeper and gardening crew. He'd been on his own, traveling from city to city for the better part of twelve years but had never felt the sense of desolation he felt now.

Tony knew it was a short trip and that he'd be back,

but leaving with Rena angry at him didn't sit right. He was sure no amount of persuading would change her mind. He conceded that they needed time away from each other, yet as his driver dropped him off at the airport and he boarded the plane heading for his first on-screen interview in Charlotte, North Carolina, as the retired champion, a sense of foreboding clutched him.

And as the plane landed and Tony was picked up by ESPN's limo driver, he couldn't shake the strange feeling in his gut.

Rena deliberately waited until she heard Tony's car pull away before she rose from bed and showered. Her anger had turned to sadness in the light of day, and her heart ached at the sense of loss she felt.

She'd tried trusting Tony, and he'd once again disappointed her. The situation was so darn tangled up in her mind, the past and present mingling into a giant miserable heartache. She had every reason to feel the way she did. Tony would always put *his* career and *his* life ahead of hers. He looked out for *numero uno*.

Even if she were able to put the past behind her, how could she trust him to raise her child? She couldn't bear the thought of him disappointing her child again and again. Scenarios played out in her head, and she envisioned Tony simply not being available when they needed him.

Rena dressed in a pair of stretch jeans that accommodated her growing belly and a loose tank top. She pulled her hair up in a ponytail and secured it with a rubberband.

She didn't have to give any wine tours today, which she deemed a good thing. Her heart just wasn't in it. She'd cried so hard last night that even now her breathing was less than even.

Digging deep in her soul, she'd have to admit that the house seemed empty without Tony here. He had a presence about him. Life wasn't dull when he was around. But Rena would have to get used to that. She'd be alone again. She'd come to the realization that maybe she wasn't meant to have anyone in her life.

She'd endured so many losses, and if it weren't for the new life she nurtured, she wouldn't know how to go on.

But the baby above all else gave her hope.

When a knock resounded at her door, her nerves jumped, and images of Tony returning home to her flashed instantly in her head.

She opened the door wide and faced Raymond. Disappointment registered, surprising her. She'd analyze that feeling later. "Oh, Ray. I didn't think you'd come to work today."

"I wanted to check in. Uh, I was checking the crusher and destemmer yesterday, and I didn't like the way they sounded."

"Is there a problem?"

"No, not really. They're just old. Don't work like they once did. I fiddled with the crusher a bit. We sure could use a new one."

"Well, maybe we'll be able to get one soon." Rena hoped so. They'd be making a profit again, thanks to

Tony. Purple Fields was due for some refurbishing. "There's a few things I'd like to change around here."

"Sure would be nice."

"Want to come in? I was just going to have some orange juice and toast. You're invited if you have time."

"No thanks, Rena. Solena fed me a big breakfast already." He patted his flat stomach.

She chuckled, shaking her head at the dark-haired man who'd become such a good friend. "I don't know where you put it." Raymond could eat like a truck driver, yet he remained lean and fit.

"One day it will catch up with me," he said, with a certain nod. "Well, I just wanted to say hello. Everything okay here?"

"Just fine. I plan to have a quiet day. Maybe do some reading."

"We're home today if you need anything."

"I won't. But thank you. I'll see you both tomorrow."

Rena bid farewell to Raymond and finished her breakfast. She sat down on her sofa and read five chapters of her book on what to expect as a new parent, did a load of laundry and as she walked down the hallway to put the folded linens away, she passed the empty nursery filled with paint cans. Excitement stirred in her stomach. Distraction kept her loneliness at bay, and she'd run out of things she'd wanted to do. Except for one.

"Why not?" she asked herself. "I have all the supplies I need."

You were going to paint the room with Tony.

"Can't wait around for something that might not happen," she grumbled, answering aloud her innermost thoughts.

Rena put on one of David's old shirts, grabbed a ladder from the supply room behind the winery and set out the drop cloths on the floor of her baby's room.

Sunshine beamed into the undressed windows, and warmth flowed into the room. She imagined a few months ahead, when her baby cooed with happiness in his crib, surrounded by all his things, the room a very light shade of sage-green.

"That's it," Rena said with a smile. "Not yellow, but green."

She grabbed her father's old boom box from the hall closet, dusted it off and plugged it in. She sang along with the pop music blaring from the radio, humming when she didn't know the words. She opened the paint can with a screwdriver and stirred the lead-free paint feeling assured that the fumes wouldn't hurt the baby.

When the phone rang, Rena turned the radio down and listened to the voice speaking into her answering machine.

"It's Tony. Just wanted you to know that I'm here in North Carolina. Rena, we need to talk when I get back. I know you won't believe me, but I miss you."

Rena squeezed her eyes shut. She nibbled on her lip, putting the paint roller down, wishing Tony wouldn't say those things. Though he sounded sincere, his words always contradicted his actions.

"Well, I guess you're not going to pick up the phone. I'll call you tomorrow. Goodbye, Rena."

Rena sunk down to the floor and sat there for a long time, rehashing everything in her mind. But the bottom line, whether she deemed it rational thinking or not, was that Tony had once again left her. He hadn't put her needs first.

Rena's mood shifted then. She'd been enjoying painting the baby's room until Tony ruined it—like he seemed to ruin everything else in her life. She had a good mind to tell him not to call again, but that would warrant her picking up the phone and speaking to him. She couldn't do that for fear of what she might say.

In truth, she didn't know how she'd react with him saying nice things to her from miles away.

She had no faith in him.

And yet she was deeply in love with him.

Yes, she finally admitted that she'd fallen in love with him when she'd been a lovestruck teen, and those feelings just wouldn't go away. Having him back in her life had rekindled that love, as much as she had fought it. As much as she didn't want it to be true. As much as she thought herself a fool for allowing him back into her heart.

"Why is it so complicated with you, Tony?" she whispered. "Why do you constantly torture me?"

On a deep sigh, Rena stood and decided to fight those feelings. She wouldn't allow Tony's phone call to mar the joy she'd felt just moments ago. She picked up the paint roller and continued on until she'd finished painting two walls. After an hour, she stopped and stepped back to view her work.

"Not bad," she said, her mood lightening. The sage paint on the wall dried to the prettiest hue of green.

She took a quick water break and peeled an orange she'd picked from her kitchen fruit basket. Sitting down at the table, she gobbled up orange wedges and rested for a while, flipping through a baby magazine, getting decorating ideas.

Eager to finish, she headed back into the nursery and turned the radio volume up. Frank Sinatra crooned, "Our Love Is Here to Stay," the disc jockey deeming the song ageless. Rena saw irony in the song's lyrics as she hummed the melody.

She positioned the ladder against the third wall where an opened window faced out toward acres of vineyards. Late afternoon air blew through the screen and cooled the room. "This is the best room for you," she said, laying a loving hand over her tiny round belly. It gladdened her heart that her child would see Purple Fields at its finest, when the leaves grew strong and tiny beads of grapes flourished to plumpness.

Rena filled the tray of paint atop the ladder and began rolling the uppermost part of the wall. When the news broadcast came on the radio, Rena tuned it out, too enthralled in baby thoughts to focus on anything the broadcaster had to say until she heard Tony's name mentioned. She stopped to listen.

"And in sports news, retired race car champion Tony Carlino is back on the scene. In an interview today in Charlotte, North Carolina, amid thousands of fans, Carlino admitted that he'd been contemplating a return to racing...."

beautiful young blond woman taking a seat beside him. "You're Tony Carlino, the racecar driver, aren't you?"

"That would be me." He sipped his drink.

"Would you like to buy me a drink?"

Tony stared at her and saw the bold, provocative look in her eyes. She made no bones about what she wanted; she had "groupie" written all over her meticulously salon-tanned body. At one time, he might have indulged her and welcomed the fringe benefits that would've come afterward. Now, his thoughts were of his pregnant wife and the miles between them.

He finished off his drink and set a fifty on the bar. "Sure, have whatever you want on me. I'm going home to my wife."

And hours later, Tony put the key in the lock and turned the doorknob to Rena's house. The three-hour time difference from the East Coast put him back in Napa in the late afternoon, and he was grateful for regaining those hours. He'd spent more time in the air today than he'd spent on the ground in North Carolina. Wondering about Rena's reaction when she saw him, Tony opened the door slowly.

"I'm the last one to give advice on romance, Tony. But it seems to me from a logical standpoint, you need a gesture of some sort. Some way to show her how much she means to you."

Joe's words had stayed with him, and grand gesture or not, Tony knew in his gut that he had to return home to Rena tonight—it had to be tonight.

There were things he had to say. He needed to

clear the air between them. Especially after what had happened in North Carolina earlier today.

"Rena?" he called out, noting how quiet the house seemed. Again, he called her name and was met with silence. He hadn't seen her in the fields when he'd driven up, but then he wasn't really on the lookout at that time. He strode down the hallway and heard static coming from a radio. "Rena, are you here?"

He followed the sound to the room across from their bedroom. One look inside made his skin crawl. "Oh my God." A pool of green paint oozed from an overturned paint tray, the drop cloth doing its best to contain the puddle. Near the radio on the floor, Tony spotted something red. Initially, he froze and prayed that it wasn't what he'd thought. He moved quickly and bent to touch the crimson liquid and bring it to his nose. It wasn't wine or paint.

It was blood.

"Rena's blood," he breathed out. Plaguing thoughts of her being injured and bloody raced through his mind. "No," he said, shaking his head. "Please, God."

His cell phone rang.

Tony answered it immediately. "Tony? It's Solena. I've got some news—"

"Where's Rena?" he bellowed into the phone.

"We just arrived at Napa Hospital. I'm in the ambulance. She took a fall—"

"I'm coming. I'll be there in ten minutes."

"Ten minutes? Where are you and how—"

"I'll explain later." Tony shut off the phone and ran out of the house. His main concern was to see Rena.

He climbed into his car and hit the road, driving twenty miles an hour above the speed limit. Luckily, the roads were nearly empty, but even if they hadn't been, it wouldn't deter him. Nothing was going to stop him from getting to Rena.

He arrived at the hospital in eight minutes and strode with purpose to the emergency room desk. The clerk questioned his relationship to Rena Montgomery. "Damn it, she's my wife." He clenched his fists.

"There's no paperwork to support that," the woman said, glancing once more at her files, then slanted a look at the security guard standing in the corner. Sometimes his fame made his life a living hell. Everyone thought they knew everything about him. "Her name is Rena *Carlino* now. We just got married."

The clerk blinked. "Oh, uh. Well, then Mr. Carlino, I'll let you right through."

She buzzed him in. "Third door to your left."

Tony was there in seconds. He found Rena on the hospital triage bed, her eyes closed, her head wrapped in a white bandage. Solena stood by her side and smiled when she saw him. "How did you get here so fast?" she whispered as she strolled over to him. She gave him a hug then guided him just outside the door. "We all thought you were in North Carolina."

Tony glanced back at Rena. It pained him to see her looking so frail and weak. "I was already home when you called. I found the room a wreck and panicked. What the heck happened?"

"I don't know, other than she fell off the ladder. I

stopped by with dinner for her. When she didn't answer the door, I got worried and used my key to get inside.

"Apparently, she hit her head on the radio when she fell. She was unconscious when I found her."

"How long ago?"

"You missed us by fifteen minutes."

Tony's heart ached. He was to blame for this. He knew it in his gut. "Has she woken up?"

"Yes, in the ambulance. We've been speaking on and off. She's a little woozy. The doctor wants her to rest while they are preparing for the CT scan."

"What did she say?"

"She was worried about the baby."

Tony closed his eyes and nodded. Immense fear coursed through his body and he sent up silent prayers. "Me, too."

That baby, that beautiful new life growing inside Rena was Tony's responsibility, too. But it was so much more. It was to be his first child. He already knew he loved that baby. Rena had been through too much pain in her life to endure another tragedy. Tony wouldn't allow it. As irrational as that sounded, he would make sure that Rena never knew another bad day.

"The doctor was optimistic. She has a concussion and a little bump on her head, but they don't think the fall affected the baby."

"That's good," Tony said with relief. He'd never forgive himself if something happened to the baby. Rena would be inconsolable, and he wouldn't blame her.

"I'm going in now. I'll stay with her," Tony said.

"Do you want me to stay, too?" Solena asked.

Tony shook his head. "No, I have to speak to her. There are things I really need to say."

Solena smiled. "I understand."

"It's a good thing you found her when you did. I can't thank you enough."

"You were only minutes behind," she said. Then she cast him a curious stare. "Why *are* you here? I thought you'd be gone a week or more?"

Tony drew oxygen into his lungs. "That's why I have to speak with Rena. I'm here, and I'm not leaving her again."

Rena lay with her eyes closed in the hospital bed feeling slight relief, the throbbing in her head much less painful now. She remembered the reason she was here. Solena had called for emergency help and had traveled with her in the ambulance. The events of the past day came to mind at a snail's pace—but with surprising clarity.

A gentle touch to her hand brought her eyes open. She knew that touch. It was the person she'd dreamed about. The one person she'd wanted to have by her side.

"Hi, sweetheart," Tony said. "You're going to be okay."

"Am I?" she whispered on a breath.

Tony nodded, his dark eyes soft and glistening. Had he teared up? "Your CT scan is perfect. Dr. Westerville said the baby is fine. You can go home later this morning if you feel up to it."

With a slight nod of her head, she choked out, "That's good news. I'm so relieved about the baby. If something happened…" She couldn't even manage the words. She couldn't go there, couldn't think of the possibility of another loss in her life. This one would crush her.

Tony took her hand and squeezed. "It didn't, honey. You both are going to be fine."

Rena sat up a little straighter in the bed, grateful the movement didn't cause her pain. "What time is it?"

"Five o'clock in the morning."

"Have you been here all night?"

"Right here," he assured her. "All night."

"But how? You were in North Carolina last I remember."

"Yeah, well. I shouldn't have gone in the first place. The minute I landed there I knew I'd made a mistake. I knew where my place was. And that place was with you."

"Tony?" Rena couldn't believe her ears. "What do you mean?"

"I did that interview, the whole time wishing I was with you."

Rena looked away then, unable to meet his eyes. She removed her hand from his. She remembered the reason for her fall now. She remembered the pain and shock she felt, hearing that news report on the radio. His presence here confused her. Why had he come back? None of it made sense.

"Rena? What is it?" His question was marked with concern.

She stared out the hospital window, looking at the new dawn breaking through. Birds chirped and tree branches swayed in the breeze. It was a glorious day to be alive, yet Rena's stomach knotted with heartbreaking anguish. "I was so hurt when you left. I guess I never got over you leaving me. And I thought it was happening all over again. I didn't know what to do with myself, so I started to paint the baby's room." She turned her head slightly to gaze into his eyes. Might as well give him the whole truth. "I figured I was on my own again. I wasn't meant to be with anyone. It would just be the baby and me from now on. I didn't want to rely on you or anyone else."

Tony clenched his teeth. Pain entered his eyes, but she continued. "The radio was on when I climbed the ladder, and I heard a news report about you. They said you were contemplating a racing comeback. When I heard that I felt faint. It was like my world was spinning in ten different directions. I couldn't get a grip. My worst fears had come true. That's when I fell."

Tony's eyes rounded. Shock stole over his face. He let go a vivid curse then took her chin in his hands and ever so gently lifted her face to his. "I'm so sorry, Rena. Sorry for everything. But you have to believe me. What you heard is not true. None of it is. My words were misconstrued. The press never gets anything right. That's why I had an argument with the newscaster. We almost came to blows, Rena. I called him every four-letter name in the book and then some.

"I swear to you that after the incident I took the next flight home. I didn't want you to hear that news report. It was a flat out falsity. But I didn't know if I could convince you how much I care about you from thousands of miles away."

"What about your obligations? You signed contracts."

He shrugged, his eyes hard. "Let them sue me. I can afford it. Losing a lawsuit is a million times better than losing you." He cast her a warm, sincere look. "I love you, Rena. I love you with all my heart."

He removed the sheet covering her and bent his head, laying the sweetest, most gentle kiss on her belly. "I love this baby, too. I love you both. I'll spend the rest of my life trying to convince you. But I'm asking for another chance. Give me a chance, sweetheart."

Tears entered her eyes. The loving gesture broke down all her defenses. Every wall she'd constructed against Tony fell to ruin, and her heart swelled. "Tony, is it true? Really true?"

"Yes, it's true. I love you. I want a life with you. A *real* life and not because of David's dying wish but because I have genuine love in my heart for you. I've always loved you, Rena."

He kissed her then, and it was the most tender brushing of their lips.

"I love you, too, Tony. I always have. Through everything, all the wrongs your family imposed on mine and all the hurt we've shared, I've never really stopped loving you. I think—" she began, admitting this truth to herself as well as to Tony "—I think David knew that. I think he knew that what we had couldn't be matched. And yet, I did love him. He was a good man."

"Yes, I know. He was the best. And I think he really wanted this for us. His child—*our* child—will have two parents who love each other as much as we love him or her."

Rena stroked Tony's dark hair, staring into his eyes, loving this strong powerful man with all that she had inside. "We can have a beautiful life."

"We will. I promise you. You and the baby will always come first."

"I believe you, Tony." She laughed as joy entered her heart. "I never thought I'd say that, but I really do believe in the strength of our love."

"And can you forgive me for everything in the past?"

Rena drew in a breath. "I think so. I think I already have."

"You won't be sorry, sweetheart. I will love and protect you the rest of my life. It's my solemn vow."

"Then I'm ready, Tony," she said decidedly.

"I am, too," he agreed, then shot her a puzzled look. "For *what*, exactly?"

"To shop for baby furniture. I want to fill our house with every baby thing imaginable."

Tony chuckled and drew her into his arms. "Now, I *know* you really love me."

"I do. I really, really do."

* * * * *

2 in
GREA
VALU

THE MILLIONAIRE MEETS HIS MATCH by Kate Carlisle

Adam Duke's mother plans to marry him off. And when his desirable assistant, Trish James, hints she wants more than just a business relationship, alarm bells go off…

DANTE'S TEMPORARY FIANCÉE by Day Leclaire

Rafe Dante's family paraded women in front of him. Until Rafe hired sweet Larkin Thatcher to be his fake fiancée…

HIS CONVENIENT VIRGIN BRIDE by Barbara Dunlop

Just weeks after their roll in the hay, virgin Stephanie Ryder was expecting his baby. Now millionaire Alec Creighton's proposing..

SEDUCTION ON THE CEO'S TERMS by Charlene Sands

Frustrated that her boss was judging her by her looks, Ali had a reverse makeover. Ironically, as a plain-Jane, she *really* caught the wealthy bachelor's eye.

VIRGIN PRINCESS, TYCOON'S TEMPTATION by Michelle Celme

Garrett Sutherland wanted his biggest claim to fame to be the seduction of Princess Louisa—the infamous virgin princess.

THE SECRET CHILD & THE COWBOY CEO by Janice Maynard

Trent Sinclair had never forgiven Bryn Matthews and her lies. But Bryn had returned…with a child he could not deny was pure Sinclair.

On sale from 17th June 2011
Don't miss out!

*Available at WHSmith, Tesco, ASDA, Eason
and all good bookshops*

www.millsandboon.co.uk

06

are proud to present

June 2011
Ordinary Girl in a Tiara
by Jessica Hart

from Mills & Boon® Riva™

Caro Cartwright's had enough of romance – she's after a quiet life. Until an old school friend begs her to stage a gossip-worthy royal diversion! Reluctantly, Caro prepares to masquerade as a European prince's latest squeeze…

Available 3rd June 2011

July 2011
Lady Drusilla's Road to Ruin
by Christine Merrill

from Mills & Boon® Historical

Considered a spinster, Lady Drusilla Rudney has only one role in life: to chaperon her sister. So when her flighty sibling elopes, Dru employs the help of a fellow travelling companion, ex-army captain John Hendricks, who looks harmless enough…

Available 1st July 2011

Tell us what you think!

millsandboon.co.uk/community
facebook.com/romancehq
twitter.com/millsandboonuk

BAD BLOOD

A POWERFUL DYNASTY, WHERE SECRETS AND SCANDAL NEVER SLEEP!

VOLUME 1 – 15th April 2011
TORTURED RAKE
by Sarah Morgan

VOLUME 2 – 6th May 2011
SHAMELESS PLAYBOY
by Caitlin Crews

VOLUME 3 – 20th May 2011
RESTLESS BILLIONAIRE
by Abby Green

VOLUME 4 – 3rd June 2011
FEARLESS MAVERICK
by Robyn Grady

8 VOLUMES IN ALL TO COLLECT!

MILLS & BOON

www.millsandboon.co.uk

BAD BLOOD

A POWERFUL DYNASTY, WHERE SECRETS AND SCANDAL NEVER SLEEP!

VOLUME 5 – 17th June 2011
HEARTLESS REBEL
by Lynn Raye Harris

VOLUME 6 – 1st July 2011
ILLEGITIMATE TYCOON
by Janette Kenny

VOLUME 7 – 15th July 2011
FORGOTTEN DAUGHTER
by Jennie Lucas

VOLUME 8 – 5th August 2011
LONE WOLFE
by Kate Hewitt

8 VOLUMES IN ALL TO COLLECT!

MODERN™

THE MARRIAGE BETRAYAL
by Lynne Graham

Sander Volakis has no intention of marrying—until he sees Tally Spencer. He can't resist her…little knowing that one night with the innocent Tally could end his playboy existence…

Doukakis's Apprentice
by Sarah Morgan

Wanted: willing apprentice to handle incorrigible, womanising (but incredibly sexy) tycoon! Polly Prince is determined to make a lasting success of the position, but soon learns that her workaholic boss *can* put pleasure before business!

Heart of the Desert
by Carol Marinelli

One kiss is all it takes for Georgie to know Sheikh Ibrahim is trouble, Trapped in the swirling sands, she surrenders to the rebel Prince—yet the law of his land decrees that she can never really be his…

Her Impossible Boss
by Cathy Williams

Successful New Yorker Matt Strickland's sexiness is off the scale, but new employee, feisty nanny Tess Kelly, thinks his capacity for fun definitely shows room for improvement! Although he's *determined* to keep things professional…

On sale from 17th June 2011
Don't miss out!

Available at WHSmith, Tesco, ASDA, Eason
and all good bookshops
www.millsandboon.co.uk

THE ICE PRINCE
by Sandra Marton

No opponent can penetrate Prince Draco Valenti's icy exterior…except high-flying, straight-talking lawyer Anna Orsini! They're at odds in business, but in the bedroom Draco's desire for Anna has the power to melt *all* his defences!

SURRENDER TO THE PAST
by Carole Mortimer

Mia Burton thinks she's seen the last of Ethan Black—the man who haunts her heart. But Ethan's returned in all his very real glory, and it's clear he'll do *whatever* it takes to win her back!

RECKLESS NIGHT IN RIO
by Jennie Lucas

Gabriel Santos offers Laura Parker a million dollars to pretend she loves him. But they've already shared one unforgettable night in Rio, and Gabriel's not aware he's the father of Laura's baby…

THE REPLACEMENT WIFE
by Caitlin Crews

Theo Markou Garcia needs a wife—or someone who looks like his infamous fiancée—so offers disowned Becca Whitney a deal: masquerade as the Whitney heiress in exchange for her own true fortune…but don't fall for her husband!

On sale from 1st July 2011
Don't miss out!

Available at WHSmith, Tesco, ASDA, Eason and all good bookshops

www.millsandboon.co.uk

Dating and Other Dangers
by Natalie Anderson

After being trashed on Nadia Keenan's dating website, Ethan Rush faces three dates with her! *He's* determined to clear his name. *She's* determined to prove him for the cad he is…

The S Before Ex
by Mira Lyn Kelly

World famous celebrity Ryan Brady's secret wife is filing for divorce! Unfortunately for Claire Brady, her soon-to-be-ex is *still* the only man her body wants…

Girl in a Vintage Dress
by Nicola Marsh

Lola Lombard, 1950s style siren, is petrified: she's got to organise a terrifyingly glam hen do! Worse still, the bride's gorgeous brother seems interested in the shy woman behind the red lipstick…

Rapunzel in New York
by Nikki Logan

When a knight in pinstripe rushed to the aid of this damsel, she declared she didn't want saving, even by a billionaire! *Yet sometimes even modern Maidens secretly need rescuing…*

On sale from 1st July 2011
Don't miss out!

Available at WHSmith, Tesco, ASDA, Eason and all good bookshops

www.millsandboon.co.uk

Polo, players & passion

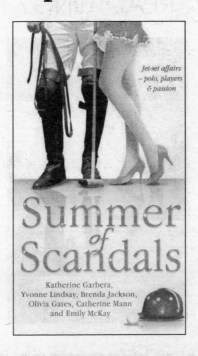

The polo season—the rich mingle,
passions run hot and
scandals surface…

Available 1st July 2011

www.millsandboon.co.uk

1/25/MB345

SIZZLING HOLIDAY FLING...OR THE REAL THING?

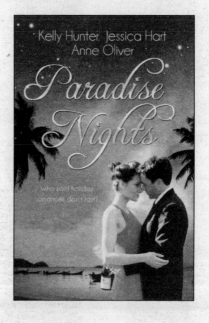

Who said holiday romances didn't last?
As the sun sets the seduction begins...
Who can resist the baddest of boys?

Royal Affairs – luxurious and bound by duty yet still captive to desire!

Royal Affairs: Desert Princes & Defiant Virgins

Available 3rd June 2011

Royal Affairs: Princesses & Protectors

Available 1st July 2011

Royal Affairs: Mistresses & Marriages

Available 5th August 2011

Royal Affairs: Revenge Secrets & Seduction

Available 2nd September 2011

Intense passion and glamour from our bestselling stars of international romance

Available 20th May 2011

Available 17th June 2011

Available 15th July 2011

Available 19th August 2011

FREE BOOK
AND A SURPRISE GIFT

We would like to take this opportunity to thank you for reading this Mills & Boon® book by offering you the chance to take a specially selected book from the Desire™ 2-in-1 series absolutely FREE! We're also making this offer to introduce you to the benefits of the Mills & Boon® Book Club™—

- **FREE home delivery**
- **FREE gifts and competitions**
- **FREE monthly Newsletter**
- **Exclusive Mills & Boon Book Club offers**
- **Books available before they're in the shops**

Accepting this FREE book and gift places you under no obligation to buy, you may cancel at any time, even after receiving your free book. Simply complete your details below and return the entire page to the address below. You don't even need a stamp!

YES Please send me a free Desire 2-in-1 book and a surprise gift. I understand that unless you hear from me, I will receive 2 superb new 2-in-1 books every month for just £5.30 each, postage and packing free. I am under no obligation to purchase any books and may cancel my subscription at any time. The free book and gift will be mine to keep in any case.

Ms/Mrs/Miss/Mr _____ Initials _____

Surname _____

Address _____

_____

_____ Postcode _____

E-mail_____

Send this whole page to: Mills & Boon Book Club, Free Book Offer, FREEPOST NAT 10298, Richmond, TW9 1BR